ISBN-13: 978-1514?
ISBN-10: 151434

Copyright © Thomas M D Brooke 2015

All rights reserved. No part of this publication may be reproduced, stored in a retrieval system or transmitted, in any form or by any means, electronic, mechanical, or otherwise, without the prior written permission of the author, nor be circulated in any form of cover or binding other than that in which it is published and without a similar condition being imposed on the purchaser.

Cover by 'Design for Writers'
Image of Kalkriese mask courtesy of Creative Commons Corporation (US)

Roman Mask

Thomas M D Brooke

For Fergus.

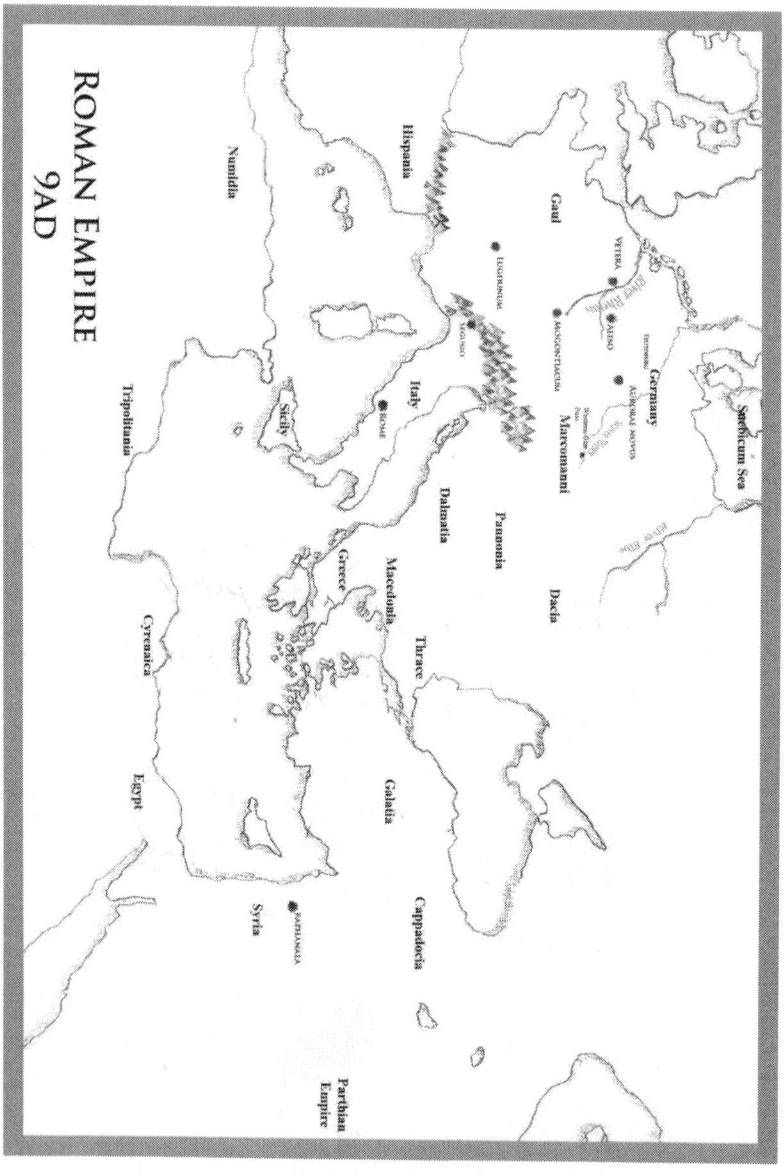
ROMAN EMPIRE
9AD
Hispania
Numidia
Gaul
Germany
Suebicum Sea
Marcomanni
Italy
Sicily
Tripolitania
Dalmatia
Pannonia
Dacia
Greece
Macedonia
Thrace
Cyrenaica
Galatia
Egypt
Syria
Cappadocia
Parthian Empire

Prologue

Dawn was finally touching the sky to the east, turning it a bright scarlet, which was fitting considering how much blood had been spilt this night. My men were exhausted, lips blackened with dehydration, eyes creased with fatigue, their armour and weapons streaked with blood from a thousand vanquished tribesmen, who lay sprawled upon the improvised turf stockade we'd hastily erected upon the pass; it hadn't proved much of a barrier for the men to defend, but it'd been enough, and we'd cut the tribesmen down in their hundreds as they'd tried to crawl and hack their way over it.

All around me I could see death; heaps of giant warriors lay broken all around our position, but we knew there were still many more, too many to count, far too many to kill. I knew my men couldn't fend off another attack; we were all too exhausted after fighting throughout the night. Only three hundred of us remained able to hold a blade, surely not enough to repulse another wave of screaming warriors.

I walked along the line of men, assessing their condition, and passed a legionary binding his shield directly to his arm; his shield hand had been crushed into a bloody ruin in the last attack, which prevented him holding the three-ply oak and birch shield conventionally. I nodded my head in approval as he hefted the shield up, testing its weight – everyone was needed to push back the barbarian hoard, I couldn't afford to excuse any but the most severely injured from the line. 'Good as new, sir.' He tried to give a grin of bravado, but the pain etched in his face made this look more like a grimace.

I gave him as reassuring a smile as I could muster. 'You'll do fine, Legionary,' and continued down the line, stopping as I saw that the enemy tribesmen were mustering for another attack, just visible through the dim light of dawn. They were bellowing and screaming insults at us as they mustered the courage to make another assault and advance up the high ground to our position in the pass barring their path. It was difficult to assess their numbers, as some were sure to be their women, who followed them to battle and spurred them on from behind with wild screams and shrieks of hatred aimed at their foes. Even so, it was clear that my small pitiful force would be heavily outnumbered once again and we no longer had the cover of darkness to conceal how few of us remained standing.

A legionary nearby started to beseech any Roman god that cared to listen, tears streaming down his face, asking to be saved from this seething swarm of inhuman hatred as he watched the assembling tribesmen from the turf palisade.

I walked up behind him, resting my hand on his shoulder. 'Steady, soldier. No god is needed to get us out of this; we'll stop them ourselves, just like we have each time before.'

He looked round at me in surprise, wiping the tears from his face. 'Yes, sir, of course. I'm … I'm sorry.'

I shook my head. 'No need to apologise, Legionary. We're all scared, there's no shame in that. Just remember, they may look mean, but they haven't been a match for our steel as yet. We'll push them back. Just make sure you keep the line tight.'

He stood up straighter. 'Yes, sir. You can rely on me, sir, I won't let you down.'

I nodded in approval, then continued on my way, stopping to briefly tell a centurion to keep an eye on that legionary. If just one man started to panic, it could spread like wildfire through the entire body of men.

I couldn't blame the legionary for doubting our survival as I shared his fear. As I saw the great mass of Germanic warriors fan out from the base of the hill, screaming, shouting, waving their spears above their heads as they advanced, it was hard to believe that anything could stop such a display of malice and strength.

Optio Tetricus called over a warning, his voice now little more than a hoarse croak after a night of shouting orders. 'Look, sir, men to the west of us!'

My heart sunk further. 'What? How have they got behind us?' If they came at us from both sides we were finished. I couldn't afford to split my tiny force. I shouted at the *optio,* keeping my voice level to mask my rising panic. 'How many tribesmen are there?'

Tetricus' voice rose in excitement. 'They're not tribesmen, sir! They're ours!'

I shook my head in disbelief, looked over to the west to confirm it with my own eyes, not daring to believe what he was saying. Sure enough, the rigid lines of a marching column could be seen in the distance, too orderly to be anything except Roman. Cheers of jubilation swept around my small unit of men.

Tetricus was weeping. 'You were right, sir. You said the relief would come. You've saved us all. We all owe you our lives.'

I shook my head. 'We still need to repulse this attack. It'll do us no good if the relief force finds only corpses manning the palisade.'

Someone else shouted out, I was too confused now to tell who. 'No need, sir! Look, the tribesmen have seen them too. They're breaking off the attack.'

I stared over the palisade, watching the German tribesmen stream away from our position, giving up on their final assault which may well have been our end. I turned to the *optio*. 'It looks like we'll be living through this after all, Tetricus.'

He nodded his head and banged his shield with his bloodied *gladius*, getting the attention of the rest of the legionaries. 'Cassius, Cassius, Cassius!'

The rest of the men took up the chant, shouting my name, and banging their shields in time. I looked around stunned.

Tetricus came up to me, as the legionaries continued the chant. 'You're a hero, sir. There's no denying it now.'

Chapter One

I awoke in my bed, feeling the softness of the finest quality linen cool against my bare skin. I half-opened my eyes to the late March sunshine that bathed my room in light. Instantly I shut them again at the sharp pain in my head. I tried to swallow the unpleasant taste in my mouth, but it was dry and parched, my throat raw. I turned away from the sunlight and tried to will myself back to sleep – surely it couldn't be morning already? I hugged a small cushion to my stomach that was fighting for an equal consideration in my morning misery: it growled angrily and I groaned in discomfort. Oh by Hades, a hangover.

Slowly my senses returned to me and I remembered something very important: last night I hadn't slept alone. I gently stretched my arm behind me to see if there is a warm body still lying next to me. I sighed in disappointment as I found nothing – just the faintest impression of a female form pressed into the surface of the mattress. Tita had already left but, by the feel of it, not early enough to avoid notice. A moment's apprehension of the trouble this could cause was quickly replaced by the euphoria of finally managing to woo the senator's daughter to my bed. I grinned broadly despite my thumping headache and sour stomach. My elation almost overshadowed the fast-returning memories of the previous night's passion – almost but not quite. Her body was exquisite, her soft skin was as beautifully pale as a fine delicate marble figurine, and I remember my fingers tingling as I caressed her supple naked thighs. Thoughts of Tita brought arousal; I groaned in pleasure as I remembered her commenting on my athleticism and muscular form as she ran her long nails down my back.

'Look at him, Patrellis! The sun high in the sky and Gaius is still abed!' announced a sharp female voice that I knew only too well.

All sexual arousal was instantly shattered; my eyes popping open at once. 'Who let you in? Haven't you got anything better to do than snoop around my home?' I snapped angrily, the last person I wanted to see right now was my infernal sister.

'It isn't your home, Gaius. It's the property of our father, and as you've no income of your own, it's liable to remain that way,' quipped my younger sister by three years, Antonia.

'She insisted on seeing you at once, my lord. She wouldn't be dissuaded,' announced my trusted body slave Patrellis, a tall man with an honest hard-working face, his hair turning to grey from its original red. His Celtic roots showed in his bearing: powerful broad shoulders lay concealed under his simple but well-made slave's tunic, and he towered over the slight petite form of my sister in a light dress of silk. However, it was clear who dominated the doorway to my room and it wasn't the hulking Celt.

'Would you like to eat in the *tablino* or would you prefer the garden veranda?' demanded my sister, tapping her foot impatiently and making it perfectly clear that remaining in bed was no longer an option.

I grabbed a cushion and threw it at her. 'In the garden. I need some fresh air.' The cushion missed Antonia and instead knocked over and smashed a vase our mother had given me. 'In order to brighten the place up.' I fell out of bed whilst making the throw and landed heavily on the cold tiled floor with a great 'ompf!' Athletic grace? Was that how Tita had described me?

'Now look what you've made me do!' I shouted at my stern-faced sister as I lay sprawled on the cold floor. I glanced around the bedroom of bright red and black wall panels and conceded that my mother might have a point. Despite the obvious sumptuous wealth and rich furnishings, the choice of colours was a bit dour. Perhaps it was time to have it repainted, this time in a colour scheme of my choosing.

Patrellis jumped at the excuse to run off and find a brush to clear up the mess whilst my sister told me she would await me in the garden and, 'If you think I am telling mother about the vase, you should think again.'

I slowly picked myself off the ground, shaking my head to clear it. Only now did I realise that I was completely naked. I didn't mind Patrellis seeing me unclothed – he had seen me naked more times than anyone – but I did begrudge my sister having a good eyeful.

I staggered over to the large bowl of fresh water Patrellis had left out for me and started to splash water onto my face to wake myself up. I soon realised this wasn't having any effect so I submerged my entire head in the bowl Patrellis had carefully decorated with dried rose petals. 'Blurruuuuurrah,' I blurted underwater before bringing my head upwards and shaking off the excess water with a soft cloth. I walked over to a polished silver hand mirror, left on the side, and admired my reflection. Despite the bloodshot eyes, there was no hiding my classic Roman profile, dark colouring and handsome face. My bare shoulders showed well-defined muscles – due to extensive work with the *gladius*. The very picture of a Roman hero, I thought to myself, inwardly laughing at the notion.

I grabbed a light tunic – one conveniently left out by Patrellis – which I donned on the way to the garden, passing through the Ionian colonnade and a large *atrium* with its statue of Apollo standing grandly in the centre. Antonia often told me that this was far too large a house for me to live in alone, with a small group of slaves to keep me in comfort. It wasn't technically mine as Antonia had earlier pointed out. It was owned by my father, just as all the furnishings were, the statue of Apollo, and even Patrellis, his wife Prisca and the other household slaves. Well, if Antonia thought she could move me out so that she and her husband, the insipid lawyer Aulus, could move in, she had another thing coming.

Antonia awaited me in the garden, where a young dark Arabian slave named Badriyah served me a simple meal of dates and dried figs, accompanied by fresh bread and olive oil, on a small trestle table with a stool. Badriyah slammed the bowl of fruit down with a huff and gave me a fierce stare, which didn't suit her open and pretty face, but could wither the hide off a wild animal. She turned and stormed off to the kitchen without making her customary bow. I winced as she slammed the door to the kitchen – it looked as if Badriyah wasn't pleased that someone else had shared my bed last night. I nervously looked over at my sister, but she ignored the exchange. My sister already knew – and disapproved – of the fact that the boundaries between master and slave were more blurred in my household than respectability required, but this morning my sister had other concerns. She sat primly on another stool, legs crossed in a modest fashion, her face bearing only the slightest saffron to accentuate her fawn-like features. She could have been considered beautiful if she didn't have the habit of perpetually wearing a disapproving scowl, one that furrowed her forehead and creased her eyes to narrow slits. Her bare arms showed goose pimples but she made no complaint. It was too early in the year to be eating outside; despite the bright sunshine there was still a cool nip to the fresh breeze brushing across the large garden of vines, marble fountains, and a perfectly trimmed selection of bright flowers. I liked the breeze, however; it helped cool the unnatural warm flush to my face and was an invigorating balm to my sore head. I started to eat my meal whilst Antonia looked on with her customary face of disapproval.

'I noticed a litter leaving when I arrived this morning. Apparently attendants waited all night to escort a lady home.'

Hades! She had seen Tita leaving; this could prove difficult. 'Oh yes, that was good of them,' I said, feigning nonchalance between mouthfuls. I had forgotten about the slaves used to carry her litter. No doubt Tita had as well. Oh well, that will give the neighbours something to talk about. Not that they were short of things to talk about when it concerned me.

'I asked one of my slaves to catch the litter up and find out who travelled within,' my sister revealed. 'I found out it was the Lady Tita, daughter of Titus Cinna. Quite a beauty I seem to remember,' my sister added in a mild tone of voice.

'I didn't realise you'd ever met her?' This was dangerous territory.

'Of course I have. I was with you,' Antonia answered whilst clearing some leaves off the table which had blown there in the breeze. 'When I attended you at the theatre last summer, do you remember?'

'No,' I replied, although now I did.

'You must do. She was there with her husband.'

I dropped the bread I held and slapped the table with the palm of my hand. 'Alright, Antonia, if you have something to say, just come out and say it. Let's not hide behind this charade of politeness.' I grimaced as I swallowed a date; the prospect of moral guidance from my sister wasn't improving my appetite. 'Tita's husband is nearly three times her age and by the sounds of it, prefers young boys to women. Of course she is going to find diversion elsewhere!'

'You know I only have your best interests at heart, Gaius. I don't want you embroiled in another scandal the likes of last time.'

'That was over ten years ago! I was little more than a boy then!' I exclaimed; would I never be able to forget that regrettable episode?

'Yes, but your behaviour lately looks to be leading you down that same path. Don't you think you should practice a little more discretion?' answered Antonia in her most disapproving tone.

'Alright, that is enough! I don't have to listen to this, even from you, Antonia. Now leave me alone to eat my figs in peace!' I flapped my arms around in irritation, spilling the olive oil to the ground.

My sister stalked off with an exasperated cry: 'When will you grow up, Gaius?'

I knew Antonia was right. I needed to be more discreet or I'd end up in the same situation which had led me to join the army – a year earlier than my father had mapped out for me – eleven years ago. I had been lucky to survive that particular scandal with my life – some hadn't, and even the *princeps'* daughter ended up exiled.

The situation with Tita was completely different, I told myself. I'd had my eye on her for months now. I met her briefly with my sister the summer before, at the theatre, but I had not been formally introduced until I saw her at one of my friend Seneca's lavish dinner parties. Anyone invited to a banquet with Seneca could be relied upon to be just the wrong side of respectable. Seneca despised anyone he deemed dull, so everyone invited normally had some secret to tell. Tita was at the party, her husband was not; that alone said something. She arrived in a long silk gap-sleeved tunic with a shamefully plunging neckline – there was no matronly all-encompassing *stola* for Tita – and surveyed the room with a wicked glint of mischief in her light brown eyes. Her unbound hair was richly black and tightly curled, and her mischievous smile revealed even teeth under a small button nose which wrinkled prettily when she laughed at a remark another guest whispered in her ear. Her eyes met mine, and again I noticed the glint in her eyes as she sized me up. She handed her light cape to a house slave and stood there boldly, erect nipples protruding through her thin tunic – by the gods, she knew how to make an entrance.

I was a regular attendant at fashionable parties, and had been ever since I returned from Germany. It was over four years since the terrifying night at Western-Gate Pass, which resulted in my status being elevated in to one of the great heroes of Rome; a man known by reputation throughout the Roman world and possibly beyond. I was lauded as a war hero, and it reflected well on Seneca to have a genuine soldier at his party. It was, after all, a society which idealised the Roman fighting man above all others. I knew my reputation was in reality a sham but that didn't stop me from profiting from it shamelessly. I knew exactly how to play my part: I would play down my prowess with false modesty and claim that it was the men who had fought under my charge who were the real heroes. A leader is only as good as the men he leads, I'd tell them, with a serious note to my voice, as if it was a terrible burden being praised by others. They lapped it up in droves, admiring my supposed bravery and stating that I was a credit to the Republic.

Tita turned out to be no different; after being introduced to me, she listened avidly to my tales of the rigours of the march, the wild dress of the fearsome Germans, the cold harsh winters in foreign climes. Some of it was true, some of it was made up; I was no longer sure even I knew the difference. It never seemed to matter, people always took me at my word, and providing I always gave a consistent account, they believed anything I told them. I knew the reason why – it was because they wanted it to be true; they wanted to believe in Roman demigod heroes pushing further the realms of civilisation. Only a man who had faced combat knew the realities of war, the fear and the horror of it. But nobody wanted to hear that – tales of heroes were much more fun!

I began to notice that mine and Tita's paths would cross more and more often. The social scene in Rome was full of lavish banquets, and what started as mild flirting, such as the odd hand left on a leg, sly grins over a crowded room, became more serious as our feelings towards one another became clear. The more wine we consumed, the more daring we would become. A stolen embrace one night, a passionate kiss the next, culminating in us sharing her litter back from a party last night.

As we approached my home, in the gently rocking covered litter, I whispered in her ear, 'I fear you have captivated me completely, Tita.' I was more than a little drunk and my passions were running wild. In Seneca's parties it wasn't unheard of him to crush the iridescent green insect – the infamous Spanish fly which was a powerful aphrodisiac – and add it to the wine in order to liven up proceedings.

She gave a slight smile. 'But surely the mighty Cassius doesn't fear anything?' She ran her fingers along my biceps.

My pulse raced. 'With a sword in my hand I fear nothing, but you have broken through my defences with a single glance.'

She laughed at my pomposity. 'The only sword I am interested is this one.' She moved her hand up under my toga and caressed me there.

I swept the curtains aside and lifted her out of the litter. Her laughter pealed through the night as I carried her to my house, banged on the door, and barged past a sleep-befuddled Patrellis, who opened the door with a small oil lamp in his hand. We were ripping each other's clothes off before we reached my bed, and I kissed her passionately before moving my mouth to her breasts, whereupon she moaned in pleasure. I pulled the remains of her clothing off and looked down at her naked body and felt my breath catch in my throat. Never before had I seen such a beauty. With a thrill of excitement I opened her legs and entered her. As we made love she ran her fingers down my back, almost painfully, and bit my shoulder in a passionate release of pleasure. I was oblivious to the pain, as I was intoxicated by her, the taste of her hot mouth on mine as our two bodies wrestled with one another. The smell of her musk and cinnamon perfume filled my senses as I pushed harder into her, relishing her screams of passion as I finally erupted into her, my eyes stinging with hot tears of desire.

A cold gust of wind brought me back to my table outside with my half-eaten meal. What would happen now? I didn't know. Could we continue this adulterous affair?

Tita told me that her husband barely paid her any attention at all and cared nothing for whatever wild life she chose to lead. However, Tita's father was Titus Cinna, the very rich, very powerful friend of my own father. Bringing shame on to that family could even test my father's patience and my self-indulgent lifestyle could come to an abrupt end if my father's money wasn't forthcoming. Is Tita worth risking all this for? I pondered as I looked around the grand garden and chewed a fig.

I left the remains of my meal and walked back into the house, asking Patrellis to attend me whilst I got ready to leave; I hoped that my sister had left the house in a temper, leaving me alone to clothe myself in peace, but no such luck. She scowled at me from the doorway as I washed and shaved and donned my toga with the help of Patrellis.

'You cannot carry on like this you know?' she snapped.

'Carry on in what way?'

'You do nothing but exercise in the daytime, followed by the occasional wild party in the evening. You may have managed to maintain your soldier's build in such fashion but I am not fooled. You're no better than that reprobate friend of yours, Seneca!'

'Seneca is a perfectly respectable citizen,' I lied as I felt the smooth side of my freshly shaved face. 'Besides, you seem to forget the invaluable work I do helping train the Praetorian Guard.'

'Pah! You have no commission to train anyone. It is only your friend, Horatius, that allows you to take the odd drill. And how often is that? Once a month at the most!' she replied, exasperated.

This was all too true; my friend from the gymnasium, Horatius Rufa, was a leading tribune to one of the praefects of the Praetorians and occasionally let me take the men out on a training session or on a forced march. He claimed it was out of respect for my military record and that it gave his troops a chance to work alongside a genuine Roman hero, but in reality it suited him as much as me. He could spend more time with one of his many women in the city, whilst I took his men out and put them through their paces. It suited me because I could claim to my father and frustrated family that I was still actively working within the army – and thereby ensuring that my father's generosity never dried up – even if the reality was that it wasn't much more than a jaunt in the countryside once a month.

I wanted to change the subject away from my lack of employment so I took up the last fold of my toga and swung myself around with a flourish. 'There, how do I look?'

My sister's voice softened as she said sadly, 'Like a young Hercules, as ever, Gaius.' Her change in tone reminded me of the younger sister who had once looked up to me with adoration as we had grown up. That was long gone now.

'Yes, it is rather fine.' I once again blessed Augustus Caesar's decision to allow all members of a senator's family to wear the purple band on their togas rather than just the senator alone. My father was not just a senator, he was also governor of the province of Sicily. I could wear the toga with the band that marked me far higher than any other of equestrian rank, despite holding no office of my own. I then reminded myself that Augustus had also outlawed adultery; maybe not all the first citizen's laws were to my advantage after all.

'Yes, you look wonderful, Gaius. But why don't you ever wish for more in your life? When will you start a career of your own? You have served in the legions with distinction and now you could use that advantage to start a life in politics. It was what father always intended for you, and you always claimed to hold such ambition. You are twenty-eight years old now. It's high time you entered the political scene.'

Poor Antonia, she would never understand. I had once held ambitions to serve in the Senate and burn a triumphant path to high office, but no more. I'd long since given up on such lofty ambitions; besides I now despised politicians and all they represented. I wanted nothing more than to live my life in peace and enjoy the charms of Rome. I couldn't very well tell her that, so I came out with a complete fabrication, 'It is hard to put away dreams of returning to the battleground. I am a military man through and through.' The reality was that the only thing I would avoid more readily than becoming a politician was to return to the war and misery of Germany or anywhere else that required soldiers to actually fight rather than march around and look grand on parade.

I swept past my sister in the doorway and called for the young boy Silo to attend me. At the sound of his name the small boy came running. 'I am here, Cassius Aprilis!' As was proper, Silo addressed me by my *nomen* and *cognomen*.

I laughed as the skinny boy with scruffy blonde hair appeared. 'Good! Then I can be off.' I gave my sister a small kiss on the cheek. 'I trust you will be fine returning to your home alone, Antonia? Else I can always ask Patrellis to find someone to accompany you?'

'You will do no such thing. I'm not one of your loose wanton women, in need of a hasty exit from the neighbourhood. Besides, I have my own slaves to escort me home.' Her eyes narrowed into her familiar scowl. 'Now think on what I have said. It is time to put your wild years behind you and move on in life. You know the only reason I badger you so is because I know you could be so much more.'

'Yes, yes, of course I will, I must be gone now.' I wanted to leave my disapproving sister behind and get to the gymnasium.

As I walked away from my father's grand house on the Caelian Hill I gave her a last wave and left on foot with my young slave Silo running on ahead of me. I didn't own a litter or the slaves to carry one, despite my father's immense wealth. I enjoyed walking around Rome and liked to be seen by the people face to face. We strolled down the broad avenues of the Caelian Hill where all the wealthy houses, owned by the best families, were built. I was on my way to an exclusive gymnasium close to the Campus Martius, the great open grass fields that most ordinary Romans used to exercise on. It was a long walk but the advantage of this particular gymnasium was that many of the higher ranked officers of Augustus' newly formed Praetorian Guards exercised there, and I liked being associated with the military, even if my army career was finished: it helped perpetuate the myth of me being a hero to the Republic.

Augustus stationed the main headquarters of his guards outside Rome, so the people didn't see the armed presence of soldiers on the streets of Rome as a regular occurrence – the crafty fox knew that that would stir up old arguments about the death of the Republic – something Augustus claimed to have restored. But, not surprisingly, many of the officers preferred the comfort of Rome to the camp outside the city walls, and could regularly be found where I was heading.

As I reached the centre of Rome the crowds increased and Silo got to work running in front and announcing me, 'Make way for Cassius Aprilis! Everybody make way!' Most people moved aside readily enough; the people of Rome were used to being pushed out of the way by those of higher rank. Some senators' families used large men to beat a path for them if necessary, but that was not my way – I liked to remain popular with all the ranks of Rome – and therefore just had Silo announce my coming.

I wandered through the great marble Forum, where crowds of people gathered. Some were simply admiring the magnificence of Rome's central hub, whilst others came to meet friends or enjoy the impromptu shows put on by players or jugglers. I passed the great bronze doors of the Senate house, where as a young man I had been given the privilege to stand outside, alongside the other sons of the senatorial class, to eavesdrop on the debates of the learned men inside. Today however, the gates stood open, as no session was in progress; it was the festival of *Quinquatria*, and the Senate never sat at this time unless in an emergency.

As I left the grandeur of the Forum behind, I found a spring in my step as I made my way down the *Via Flaminia*, one of the busy thoroughfares through the city. Here the streets were still crowded and Silo had his work cut out moving people out of my path. I smiled at the earnest face of the round-nosed young boy, no older than eight, who took his role very seriously.

Silo had been purchased for me by my father, to make it easier, he said, for me to stay in touch with my mother. He thought that if I had a young boy to run messages for me, I would be more likely to keep her up to date with my whereabouts. My mother lived in a large villa close to Rome, and complained to my father, who lived in the province of Sicily where he served, that I neglected her. Each week, Silo would have to make the long trek to my mother's villa in order to give her a letter, composed by me, listing my goings-on. Most weeks the letter was a complete fabrication, but it kept her happy, and having Silo proved useful in other ways. Patrellis and his wife Prisca remained childless despite their thirty years of marriage and the young boy was just what the two of them needed. Silo's fair hair and blue eyes gave away his Germanic origin: one of the many slaves being sold in Rome these days as a result of the campaigning in the north. I wasn't initially pleased to have any reminder of Germany in my home, but the boy's natural cheerful nature soon won me over and I was very happy to use him as an attendant when I was about in Rome.

As we walked along the road, surrounded by the cheap overcrowded tenement buildings that made up so much of the city, I waved or smiled at the odd greeting called out to me along the way by the more prosperous *plebs* who owned workshops or stalls in the ground floors of the buildings.

I was a popular man in this area; I made this walk every day and normally would stop and admire some of their goods or stop to have a brief discussion on the goings-on of Rome. I loved to hear their views on Rome and its burgeoning provinces. I discussed how they felt towards Augustus – which was nearly always good – or who was hot or not on the stage or in the chariot racing. But not today, I rose late so I better get to the gymnasium before all my friends left for the day.

I instructed Silo to lead the way through the *Via Siren* – which was a short cut to the gymnasium but also held many of the city's brothels. Most respectable citizens avoided the place but I actually liked the seedier areas of Rome. On occasions I liked to go about Rome with no obvious sign of my rank. I would dress in a simple tunic and cape and frequent the taverns and back streets of Rome's poorer districts. I wasn't alone in doing this, even Augustus Caesar would travel incognito in the city on occasion – it was said he particularly enjoyed watching a street fight between local toughs!

As we made our way down the street, women came to doorways or windows and tried their best to entice me in. 'Handsome man, surely you can spare us some of your time today?' said a grinning set of twins in unison from their balcony. They both had striking blonde wigs and long sumptuous legs poking out of their gowns, which they revealed to good effect. 'Surely you want to see where these lead?'

I laughed at their fake smiles and continued on my way as they crowed with regret before losing interest in me and tried to entice the next man to walk down the street.

Finally we turned a corner, crossed a square with a temple that was dedicated to Diana, and the view opened up to the six hundred acres of the *Campus Martius*. Crowds of people were engaged in all forms of exercising: wrestling, running, lifting weights or honing their equestrian skill – strings of chariots raced around the field. The *Campus Martius* was situated just outside Rome's official boundary, so the rule against carts entering the city during the day didn't apply here.

On one side of the large field was situated the extensive *Gymnasium of the Horse*: an exclusive club for former high-ranking soldiers, young aspiring athletes, officers of the Praetorian Guard, and the odd senators' son, namely me.

Chapter Two

On arriving at the gymnasium, I asked the slave at the door to find Silo something to eat, whilst I carried on through their grand *atrium* and into the large training ground behind it. On my way, various members hailed a greeting to me or slapped me on the back.

'Cassius, you're a bit late today? Did you get waylaid coming through the *Via Siren*?' joked the grizzled veteran Grappus, a survivor from the civil wars. 'We can't have you worn out before you've started,' he said, referring to the female temptations to be found in that street.

'I was busy running errands this morning,' I lied.

'Well, whatever your reason, I don't think you'll have it your own way in the training yard for once. There is a young man in the yard who seems to be quite the athlete.'

I grinned modestly. 'All I can do is try my best, Grappus.' I was a popular man in the gymnasium and most knew my reputation as a soldier and respected it. I had built up a persona in Rome as a man of action, a war hero, a man of true steel and real grit. I knew it to be a lie myself, but my reputation as a soldier was not a complete fabrication. I spent six years in the legions and at one time was a promising young officer, a leading tribune, whose future beckoned command. It was impossible to deceive old soldiers in any other way; they knew a man who had spent time in the legions almost by instinct. The way a man walked, how he held himself, a certain hardness of eye: all were signs that men served.

I walked through to the changing room and stripped down to my loincloth. I walked out to the training field, which was basking in the warm afternoon spring sunshine. All around me, men of various ages exercised with different implements: some lifted weights, others ran, jumped, or threw a discus. The *Gymnasium of the Horse* was a large building with a courtyard nearly five hundred paces across, walled colonnades surrounding it, so there was plenty of room to exercise. I started off with some simple stretching exercises. It was a struggle to begin with, the wine hadn't yet given up its grip on my body and it made me slow and sluggish.

'You look to be making hard work of that, Cassius?' remarked a humorous voice.

I turned and smiled back at my friend Spento, whom I knew from our time together in the legions. He was a tall man, in rude health, with a plain but pleasant face. He was well-muscled, but at the end of one arm was a missing hand – a souvenir from the legions and the reason he left.

I groaned, 'I'm afraid I was up late last night. I won't be at my best today.'

'Another of Seneca's wild parties?' Spento scratched the stump at the end of his arm, a habit of his. 'I don't know how you do it, keeping so fit *and* attending such parties.'

'Oh, it isn't that often. Last night was a special occasion, celebrating *Quinquatria.*' I bent down and picked up two large weights, heavy lead bars, and started exercising my upper body. I wasn't a fool, I knew the damage wine did to my body; I needed to work hard today to offset its effects.

Spento picked up a large weight, stumbling with difficulty with his good hand and the stump of his other, and managed to clutch it to his chest. His infirmity made some exercises difficult, but you never heard him complain. With the weight held against his chest he bent his knees down into a squatting position and then raised himself up again. 'You'll never catch me at one of his parties. He's bad news, Cassius. You should steer clear of him.'

I chuckled to myself between deep breaths, as I lifted the hand weights. Spento never drank to excess and never let wild abandon take him. He was the sort of character Seneca never allowed anywhere near his parties, lest his moral abstinence frightened off the other guests. Besides, Seneca found Spento's stump ugly – he despised anyone with unsightly afflictions. 'You needn't worry, Spento. I won't ever invite him to dinner when you're there.'

'At least that's something.' He smiled at me. We socialised in completely different circles, but we got on well together each time we met in the gymnasium or he came round to dinner. Seneca might find Spento boring but I liked his kind heart, and besides, I owed Spento a debt of gratitude that went much further than friendship – from when I returned to Rome four years ago.

We continued to exercise together in silence, to concentrate better on what we were doing, and my attention was grabbed by four young men who were running laps around the courtyard of the gymnasium, throwing a large heavy leather ball between one another. The exercise took stamina and co-ordination and one of them really stood out from the rest: he was a strapping young lad, with brawny arms and an athlete's running gait. He was obviously the leader of this small group: the other young men jostled to be the next to receive the ball but always deferred to him. Was this the young athlete Grappus had mentioned earlier, I wondered? 'Do you know who that man is, Spento?' I asked my friend, discarding the hand weights and dropping to the ground to do some floor exercises.

'No, but I have been watching him all morning, beating all the regulars in various tests of skill or stamina.' Spento smiled at this – no doubt those beaten didn't take kindly to losing to this outsider.

I guessed his age to be nineteen or twenty, with sandy brown hair and a constantly smiling face. I watched him joke and goad his fellow companions, as they chucked the leather ball between one another. He was obviously running within himself, whilst the others desperately tried to keep up.

'Why don't you go over and join them? You'd make a better opponent than those young boys. I would join in myself, but this …' Spento held up his missing hand, '… makes that game particularly hard for me.'

I laughed. 'I doubt even I could keep up with him. He is younger, fitter, and more than likely only drinks well-watered wine and finds his bed at a sensible time.'

Spento chuckled. 'So should you, if only you could ever tear yourself away from Seneca's parties! He is due to fight in the *gladius* practice later; will you be taking part?'

The *Gymnasium of the Horse* was frequented by so many soldiers, both serving and retired, that it was unsurprising that contests with the blade were popular. I had always been good with a *gladius* and was considered an expert amongst my peers in the gymnasium, which was high praise, considering most, like me, had spent years working with the weapon daily in the legions. However, today was not the day to be fencing with blades – even a wooden training *gladius* – after last night's excess of wine. 'Not today, Spento. Today I will watch from the sidelines and enjoy the show.'

Spento strained to make his last lift and said through clenched teeth, 'That's a shame. I'm sure you could put him to shame.' Spento completed the lift and dropped his heavy weight. Bending over with his one good hand resting on his knee, he regained his breath.

'We'll never know now,' I replied, moving on to the next exercise. I was tempted to take part, but I knew I wasn't at my best and didn't want to embarrass myself.

We continued exercising for a long time, using a variety of training techniques to build strength and stamina, before finally deciding we'd done enough for the day and retiring to relax by the side of the training yard. A slave rubbed our bodies with oil and then worked the oil, together with the accumulated dirt, out of the pores of our skin with a *strigil*. My body relished the invigorating sensation and my muscles relaxed under the careful hands of the gymnasium's trained slave, an old Syrian with an expert touch.

Spento and I were joined there by Horatius, my friend from the Praetorians. Horatius was a heavy-set man, with a great barrel chest and a coarse black beard – unusual in the legions and even rarer in the Praetorians. If Spento was never invited to parties held by Seneca, Horatius was welcomed with open arms. He was a renowned womaniser and his legendary strength was only superseded by the even greater quantities of wine he was known to imbibe. He held a high office in the Praetorians – lead tribune to the third cohort of the guard – and was well thought of by his men, despite his reputation as a scoundrel. He was my type of soldier.

Horatius grinned. 'Cassius, I saw you watching our young hero, Marcus Scaeva, earlier?' he greeted me, lying down on one of the wooden benches so a slave could rub oil into his shoulders.

'Oh, is that his name? Is he one of your lads – does he serve with the Praetorians?' He could only be talking about the young athlete who had caught my eye in the training yard.

'No, he's not in the legions yet, although he plans to rectify that soon enough,' replied Horatius.

I should have known; Marcus Scaeva looked too young to serve with the Praetorians, who were made up of veterans.

Horatius grunted as the slave worked out a particularly hard muscle knot. 'He is the son of Tribune Appius, well known in our camp and a real prospect for the future. He's to join the legions in Germany to get some battle experience.'

'Leaving for Germany is he?' enquired Spento. 'He will learn there's more to soldiering than running around on a field with a leather ball.'

I remembered the young men's faces who died at Western-Gate Pass, so similar to that of Marcus Scaeva's. 'How many other young heroes will end up dead on the end of a barbarian's spear?' I inadvertently said aloud.

'End up dead in Germany? Marcus? I think you do him an injustice. He's not just a fine runner, he's even better with a blade – watch him when the contests start.' Many of the young men of the gymnasium were limbering up with training swords, the young athlete Marcus Scaeva amongst them.

'My friend, Justinius, was a fine swordsmen. It didn't stop him from being killed in his first skirmish in Germany,' added Spento. All three of our attentions were now on the young competitors, sizing each of them up as to their worth.

'Germany is not what it was, it's virtually another Roman province now. The fight has gone out of the tribes. Mark my words, by this time next year the Roman frontier will be pushed back as far as the River Elbe. Then the German people can be civilised properly and brought in fully to the empire,' boasted Horatius. It was a view held by most Romans now. The fighting in the previous four years since my return to Rome was said to have been one victory followed by another. Soon Augustus' ambition of extending the Roman world to the banks of the River Elbe, in the far north of Germany, was to be realised.

Spento was less sure. 'Hah, I think there may be more fight left in the Germans than you give them credit.' He brandished his stump to emphasise the point.

I wanted to steer the conversation away from Germany and waved my hand in irritation. 'Let's not talk politics now, my friends. Let's enjoy the swordplay.'

The contestants paired off, and Marcus Scaeva showed himself to be every bit as good as Horatius claimed. He fought with lightning speed and agility that appeared to give him so much time to make his parries or time his thrusts. He was without doubt a natural swordsman, and before long he beat his first opponent: a solid veteran from the legions.

I inclined my head at Horatius' raised eyebrow. 'Impressive,' I conceded.

Next up he was paired with a young man I had contested against myself, just the week before. I remembered him having a good sword technique but someone who lacked positional expertise; I had beaten him by gradually manoeuvring him into a bad position and then attacking swiftly. Marcus Scaeva didn't waste time in such a drawn-out process – he simply attacked with all-out ferocity and beat him within a half-dozen swift exchanges, neatly disarming him, then laying his wooden *gladius* against his opponent's throat.

'There – what did I tell you! He's a wonder!' exclaimed Horatius. 'A faster blade you'll never meet outside the arena!'

I agreed. He certainly was something special. I thoroughly enjoyed these contests in the *Gymnasium of the Horse*. Most Romans enjoyed live combat in the arena where gladiators fought to the death for the pleasure of the baying crowd. I, however, no longer enjoyed the games, and preferred to watch my contests in the security of the gymnasium, where no one was ever hurt and I could take part myself if I felt like doing so. I clapped alongside the other spectators as Marcus Scaeva basked in the praise – a great smile cracking his face, ear to ear.

Spento, clearly excited by the contest, took a different view. 'I'll bet you a hundred silver denarius that he loses his next bout – his overconfidence will be his downfall.' Spento seemed unconvinced by the young man's cockiness. 'Cassius, why don't you put him in his place? You can beat any man here.'

I wasn't quite so sure after seeing how good he was. 'Not today, Spento. There are plenty of others eager to match swords with him. Let's see for ourselves how good he is – it looks as if he plans to match himself against three of our comrades!' I laughed at the temerity of the young man: practising against more than one foe was never easy, and as all three were soldiers in the Praetorians, he would have little or no chance, no matter how good he was.

Spento laughed. 'I admire his optimism. But really – *three opponents?*'

Even Horatius' unshakeable faith in the young man looked dented; a deep frown covered his forehead, and he declined to take Spento's bet of one hundred denarius.

On an impulse, I said, 'I'll take the bet, Spento.' I felt there might be something to the young arrogant Marcus Scaeva, possibly because he reminded me of myself at a similar age: before Germany had taken my courage and crushed my aspirations. It was probably money thrown away, but it was my father's money in any case; plenty more where that came from.

The three of us looked on eagerly as the contest prepared to take place, revelling in the tense atmosphere descending over the gymnasium. Marcus Scaeva was matched against Hirtius, Amandus and Crescentius. All three were accomplished swordsman and they were confident of beating the young prodigy. As soon as the contest started they attacked in unison, charging in and trying to bewilder the young man by attacking from three opposing angles. Marcus Scaeva expected this and rolled out of the way, emerging behind Amandus and striking him on the back with his wooden blade, taking him out of the contest.

I clapped in approval, cheering the audacious move alongside the other spectators as Amandus left the combat area with a rueful grin on his face.

If Marcus Scaeva thought it would be easy from now on, he was soon to be disappointed. Both Hirtius and Crescentius knew what they were about and now approached more carefully, a new determination furrowing their brows. Each time Marcus Scaeva tried to force one back, the other would attack from the other side, making Marcus Scaeva leap out of the way, lest he leave one side open. The two Praetorians began to read Marcus Scaeva's attacks and were anticipating his moves with increasing regularity.

Marcus Scaeva, who had appeared so tireless earlier, started to show the first signs of fatigue. The day's contests, which included running, wrestling, and many more, started to catch up with him and no man has limitless energy. The wooden training blades were actually heavier than a normal *gladius*, in order to build strength in the wielder's sword arm, and Scaeva's arm must now feel like a lead weight. I frowned, it wouldn't be long until I was handing over one hundred denarius to Spento – I always was a fool with money. Hirtius and Crescentius sensed this too and signalled to one another that this was the time to finish the contest. They both attacked in tandem – wooden blades whirling with speed and new purpose. Back and back they forced Marcus Scaeva, who defended manfully but was right up against it now. He slipped and Crescentius took the opening, slashing down at the exposed boy. Marcus Scaeva somehow managed to avoid the blow, rolled out of the way, then danced himself back to his feet, quickly catching Crescentius' attacking blade with his own – swiftly countering and forcing his sword into Crescentius' belly, who grunted as the heavy blade doubled him over. Marcus moved onto Hirtius, reacting faster than the final Praetorian, breaking through Hirtius' defence and slapping him on the side of his chest, winning the contest to rapturous applause.

'Well, well! That was better entertainment than I saw in the Circus Maximus yesterday! Who needs gladiators when you can see Marcus Scaeva in the *Gymnasium of the Horse*!' crowed Horatius.

The Circus Maximus was originally built to house the chariot racing but now Augustus Caesar also held public spectacles of gladiatorial combat there: it was the only structure large enough to house the hugely popular sport on festival days, and they were halfway through the festival of *Quinquatria*: a particularly good, or bad – depending on your point of view – time for gladiators.

'Here, Marcus, come here and meet my friends!' Horatius shouted over at the young man, who was being congratulated by other contestants and spectators alike.

Marcus Scaeva walked over to them, grey eyes under his sandy brown hair. Many a young lady would be lured by those soft eyes and that good-looking face, I thought to myself.

He smiled brightly. 'Tribune Horatius, I didn't realise you were here. Did you see me fight?' he said eagerly, obviously delighted with his performance in the competition.

Horatius grinned. 'You did well, my boy! You cost my friend Spento one hundred denarius!'

Spento ruefully told me, 'I'll have to give you the money next time I see you Cassius. Unfortunately I don't carry that much coin to the gymnasium. It has turned out to be quite an expensive afternoon.' He chuckled and turned to the young athlete. 'I'll admit you surprised me at the end there. I thought you were lost.'

The youth's voice was very earnest. 'I was taught never to give up, no matter how hopeless the situation. Only the gods can predict the outcome of combat.'

Spento looked up from his bench and appraised the young swordsman. 'That is very true, but fighting in the training yard is one thing. What about when you meet a real opponent, one intent on killing you?'

Marcus went bright red. 'It's true. I've never faced genuine combat. But that will soon be put right. I leave for Germany in only a few days.' His voice was flushed with excitement.

'You sound eager to go.' Spento sounded as uneasy as I was.

The youth did not notice the inflection in Spento's voice. 'Of course I am. I want to test myself in true warfare. I want to honour our glorious dead, do justice to their memories on the battlefield, help further the limits of our great Republic's empire. Only through war can we find out what we are truly capable of.' He struck his clenched fist to his chest.

Oh by the gods, save us from stupid young heroes! I wouldn't want to be within one hundred miles of this man when he met the enemy; I'd met his sort in my past. He would march off to Germany, be given command, and thereby the trust, of several young men, and lead them all to their deaths in one great charge; all in the vain hope of achieving glory, which any true soldier knew didn't exist. If his commander had any sense, he would pair him with a wise centurion, one who could temper his exuberance. If he couldn't, this man was as good as dead already, along with many others who would have the misfortune of fighting by his side. I snorted in contempt.

Young Scaeva looked baffled by my cynicism. 'Have I said something wrong? Surely you believe in the ideals of the Republic?'

I smiled crookedly and considered telling him where he could stick his pompous ideals, but Horatius interjected. 'Marcus, meet Gaius Cassius Aprilis.' He then leaned over from his wooden bench and laid a hand on my shoulder, reminding me of my manners. 'He's a veteran of the wars, and has therefore earned his occasional bad temper.'

The youth's tone changed to one of excitement. 'Cassius Aprilis! I apologise. I have heard of you and your great deeds.' The boy then knelt! 'You held the barbarians at bay at Western-Gate Pass. I bow to your greatness.' With this he lowered his head.

Well, how do you answer that? I was used to people treating me with respect, but this was ridiculous. I had never had a grown man, if that is what you could call this innocent youth, kneel at my feet before. Even Tita had not been that gullible! I was literally lost for words and looked down blankly at the young fool.

'Get up, boy!' snapped Horatius, 'You're embarrassing yourself! Try and conduct yourself as a soldier, not a moonstruck simpleton!'

Marcus stumbled to his feet, the effortless grace displayed on the training yard now gone, replaced by the gangly awkwardness of adolescence. 'My apologies, sir, Cassius … Cassius Aprilis … I did not wish to embarrass you. I have admired your bravery in the field for many a year now, ever since I heard of your story, and I hope one day to emulate your deeds.'

So the most terrifying night of my life, one I would have done anything to avoid, was inspiring another generation of young idiots to follow in my footsteps and get themselves killed. What hope did the Republic have? I recovered my poise and addressed Marcus for the first time. 'You would do better to find your own path in life, young Scaeva. Don't follow a story to an early grave.'

He stood straighter. 'If I die in the service of the Republic, I will be proud to have died doing my duty.' There really was no saving him. 'But if I may, Cassius Aprilis, allow me to cross swords with you in training. I have heard you are a master swordsman, and it would do me the greatest honour to match my strength against yours – however inadequate mine may prove to be.'

He was so awestruck by me, I may well be able to beat him. But I wasn't about to put that to the test – I had just seen him defeat three capable swordsmen with my own eyes. 'No, no. It is too late in the day to be training with the *gladius*.' I got up from my wooden bench and clapped the young man on the shoulder. 'I wish you luck in Germany.' And with that I left him, his eyes wide with wonder as Spento, Horatius, and I retired to the *Baths of Agrippa*, which was only a short walk from the gymnasium.

We dipped in the *Tepidarium* before luxuriating in the hot waters of the *Calidarium,* laughing at the earnest young man's innocence and placing bets as to how long it would last in Germany and the realities of life on campaign. We had a freezing plunge into the *Frigidarium* before clothing and decided to eat at the fine bathhouse named after Augustus' greatest general; the man who secured the empire for the young nephew of the divine Julius Caesar in the civil wars. The best baths in Rome also provided its higher ranking guests, which we all were, with high quality food, cooked by the finest slaves; after my afternoon of exercise I had a huge appetite.

We tucked into a meal of sea bream, cooked with a sweet Spanish wine, and covered in peppercorns and dried onion. It was garnished with sea urchins and we ate heartily. The fish was followed by a hot lamb stew flavoured with coriander and cumin, which burnt my tongue as I wolfed it down too quickly.

'You look to be enjoying your food today, Cassius,' commented Spento with a wry smile.

'You cannot beat the fare served here. Even my slave, Prisca, cannot serve a better meal.' I salved my burnt tongue with the honeyed wine served with the food.

A commotion broke out as Silo came bursting through the double doors to our eating chamber. 'Cassius, Cassius! We have a message from the *imperator*!'

I held my hand up to stop the boy and tried to elicit what he was talking about. 'What do you mean a message from the *imperator*? What would Augustus want with me?' My mind was whirling with the implications.

'It's true, a Praetorian in uniform came to deliver the message. You're to join *Princeps* Augustus immediately at the Circus Maximus.' Silo's eyes were wide with excitement – this was almost certainly the most important message he'd ever delivered.

The wine suddenly tasted like vinegar in my mouth. What did the most important man in the world want with me?

Chapter Three

'Perhaps this is good news, Cassius. Maybe your father's to be given a new honour, or you're to be given an official role,' said Horatius, the concern in his voice telling me how likely he thought that really was.

'So you know nothing of this?' I demanded of him.

He opened his arms wide in a gesture of innocence. 'Nothing at all, the Praetorian who delivered the message must be from another cohort, I swear it.' I believed him; Horatius genuinely liked me, and would have warned me of any trouble with Augustus.

'What will you do, Cassius?' asked Spento.

'Well, what do you think I will do? I will join him at the Circus Maximus as he requested. What else can I do?' By all the gods, I hated the games, why did I have to meet him there of all places.

'Can I go with you, Cassius? Can I see the great Augustus?' squeaked Silo excitedly, oblivious to the unease the summons produced.

'Certainly not, Silo. I want you to return home and inform Patrellis what has happened. He will look after you.' If this summons had anything to do with Tita, it couldn't be anything good and I didn't want Silo caught up in it. Had my scandalous behaviour been brought to Augustus' attention? Was I going to the games as a spectator, or would I end up as the spectacle? I hadn't heard of Augustus executing any of his guests at the games, but then I hadn't been to the games for quite some time! Why, by Hades, did he want to speak to me? I should be far beneath the notice of Augustus. It must be Tita; what else could it be? Could her husband have made a complaint directly to the *imperator*?

I sent a sulky Silo off home and composed myself before starting my journey to the Circus Maximus. To their credit, both Spento and Horatius offered to accompany me, but I declined their offer; neither could help me with the wrath of Augustus and it was pointless to take them down with me. How, by the gods, did Augustus know where to send his messenger? Did the messenger visit my home first? Or did one of Augustus' spies keep an eye on me? If so, they were sure to have seen Tita's slaves waiting outside my home last night.

My mind was awhirl with terror as I walked through Rome's crowded streets, bumping into people along the way due to my preoccupation, thinking up ever more terrible consequences to my adulterous affair with Tita. It was only one night, I told myself over and again. Surely Augustus couldn't hold one night against me? Maybe there was another explanation to my summons? But what? What else could it be? I tripped on my purple striped toga, muddying it in the process. I brushed off what dirt I could; with all my troubles, I didn't want to compound them by appearing before Caesar dressed slovenly. There, not so bad I thought, and took a deep breath and hurried towards the stadium.

This was not the first time I had been embroiled in a sex scandal in Rome. It was eleven years before, and my best friend Julius had already left to join the legions, leaving me to become involved with the wrong crowd of people. I was an innocent, much like the young Marcus Scaeva was now; I was brought up in the closeted confines of the Augustan school, set within Rome, but sheltered from outside malign influences. My background gave me an excellent education in poetry, art, music, history, riding, and weapons training but nothing of the true wider world. I returned home to my father's villa outside of Rome, where I worked on the estate for a year. Then my father told me he wanted me to return to Rome for one year to work in public service as a minor magistrate, the job any aspiring young senator's son should fulfil if he held future political aspirations. I was to be quartered in Rome, to make my face known in the Forum, then after a year I could be sent off to the army properly educated in the workings of the city. In this year, he wished me to ingratiate myself with the noble families who resided in Rome and, under the tutelage of Augustus, ruled it.

Instead I was attracted to the growing clique that surrounded Augustus' daughter, Julia. I met her at a dinner party organised by her to welcome the new sons of noble families to Rome, of which I was one. She was thirty-eight years old, but still beautiful, and I was instantly transfixed by her. Others spoke of her graceful slender neck or her long eyelashes, but for me it was her husky sultry voice which spoke with such eloquence that captured my heart. My sheltered background never involved women of such sophistication and the fashionably glamorous entourage that surrounded the *imperator's* daughter was far more attractive than the stuffy toadies who grovelled around Augustus. Julia's coterie were different. They were cultivated, debated intelligently and with wit, spoke their minds when an unpopular edict came down from the Senate. To a young seventeen-year-old idealist like me, they were everything I imagined free-thinking citizens should be. Unfortunately, the free-spirited Julia and her friends were also trouble.

Julia's relationship with her father was uneasy at best. Although he was said to admire her intelligence, he railed against her wilful nature. He insisted that she marry his sensible stepson Tiberius, a man poles apart from the free-thinking, independent Julia. Tiberius didn't like his intractable new wife much and, after a couple of years, withdrew himself from public life and retired to the island of Rhodes to contemplate poetry or some other nonsense. This left Julia alone in Rome to take on any lover she desired. At this time it was Iullus Antonius, son of the great Mark Anthony, who had been the bitter rival of Julia's own father, Augustus. A more ill-fated partnership never existed, but I was too young, stupid, and naive to see it.

Iullus was a similar age to Julia, but kept himself in impeccable shape. He looked the very model of the heroic republican and he would bemoan the lost freedoms that the Republic had been afforded up until Augustus' uncle, Julius Caesar, seized power.

There were other leading lights within this group, such as Sempronius Gracchus and Cornelius Scipio, well-known young political agitators whose behaviour was only tolerated due to their association with the *imperator's* daughter. It amused them to bring me in to their fold: an impressionable senators' son; one more young man to be turned against Julia's father. I accompanied them in their debates, which they held regularly at public gatherings, speaking out against Julia's father's strict new laws concerning personal freedoms. I was never much more than a very minor player, but gradually they began to trust me more, and I was introduced into their wild social scene of parties and heavy drinking. At first I was shocked by their behaviour, but a seventeen-year-old is so easily swayed, and before long I found the pleasures of strong wine taking hold of my life.

Party would follow party. Open fornication and seditious talk were commonplace, as Julia and Iullus Antonius held sway over Rome's respectable families' sons and daughters. Julia revelled in her reputation as a maverick, and cared nothing for the damage it was doing to her father's reputation; on the contrary – it was this that spurred her on.

I watched from the sidelines as Julia and Iullus Antonius led us all down the path of moral ruin, whilst I enjoyed every minute of it. Until, one night, we pushed our luck too far.

Around twenty of us, both men and women, were returning from a late-night party through the deserted Forum, and as usual, drunk to the eyeballs. As we staggered through the deserted streets, Julia stopped and looked around the Forum, the centre of Rome, which had been transformed since Augustus had taken power. New public buildings made of the finest marble and crafted by Rome's finest stonemasons surrounded the great square; but in the centre, by a small pool, a statue of Marsyas, playing a flute and holding a wineskin over one shoulder, still stood. The satyr Marsyas traditionally represented Rome's liberty and was erected back in the days of the old Republic. Julia looked at the statue of the satyr with a thoughtful expression, her eyes unfocused from the wine, and said softly, 'Poor Marsyas, you have seen the freedom of your people taken away. Just as the vine trees which used to surround you were replaced by suffocating marble, so it is with us – imperial glory has replaced the dignified ideals of the Republic and has left us poorer, despite all our apparent riches.'

Julia took the wreath from her brow and placed it on the statue of Marsyas, a small tear creeping down her cheek. She lay down under the statue, and took Iullus by the hand. 'Come, join me Iullus. Make love to me here, under poor Marsyas – so he can witness that some still believe in the old ways, when people were free to act as they will, and not constrained by the shackles of my father.'

Iullus never needed much encouragement and before long started thrusting away in front of us. Then we were all at it, ripping each others' clothes off, right on the steps of Rome's governmental seat. I coupled with a plump young girl from Alba who had taken a shine to me. She had full breasts and eyes that shone with desire. I remember little more than that, not even her name. It didn't seem all that important at the time.

When we were done, our passion spent, the two of us laughed out loud as we left the steps of the Forum, following our two heroes, Julia and Iullus and their ragtag followers of free thinkers, libertarians, and spoilt aristocratic youth, sure of our invulnerability – as only the young can be.

However, the Forum had not been as deserted as we all thought. Before long, news of our impromptu stage show reached the ears of Augustus, who finally decided enough was enough. He expelled Julia to the island of Pandateria, after hastily decreeing a divorce between herself and Tiberius. Iullus Antonius was first tortured and then persuaded to take his own life. The other young aristocratic men and women in attendance were all rounded up and exiled from Rome, one by one, as the names were extracted under torture from Iullus.

I thought myself finished and returned to the family home outside Rome and confessed all to my father. He was furious and told me that he could not protect me from Augustus and that I had brought it all on myself. Each night, I would tremble in my bed, a cold sweat covering my entire body, sure that soldiers would be knocking on the door to take me away. But each night, nothing. Days passed, then weeks, and still the soldiers never came. My father said it was not his doing and I believed him: even my father could not have protected me from the scandal that had rocked the foundations of Rome itself. I was not foolish enough to think that Iullus would have tried to hide my name from the torturers; he would have sold me out in a blink of the eye. The only conclusion I could come up with was that I was such an insignificant member of Julia's group of rebels: he simply hadn't noticed that I was there! Such luck!

After the death of Iullus and the expulsion of Julia, my father told me that the gods had spared me for a reason and it was high time I repaid that favour. I was despatched to the army, a year earlier than planned, to join my boyhood friend Julius in the legions in Syria, where I learned to be a soldier and put my wild drinking days behind me – at least for a few years.

I heard the crowd long before I reached the great gates to the Circus Maximus. They cheered loudly after a collective 'Ooooh!' went round the stadium; perhaps a particularly nasty wound had been inflicted, or maybe someone had just had something chopped off. The gates were surrounded by the usual hawkers for tickets – tipsters and bookmakers – who would take bets on the contests to be fought today and later tonight. It was now late afternoon, and the more popular gladiatorial ties would begin to take place. The walls of the building were covered with murals depicting who would be fighting that day, with listings of their previous wins. This was the third day of the festival of *Quinquatria*, so the best gladiators available would be taking part. The first day of *Quinquatria* was actually a solemn religious day, when no bloodshed must be taken. To make up for this lack, the next four days of the festival were a positive carnival of bloodletting: gladiatorial contests were billed every day and played out in front of thousands of spectators at the Circus Maximus – whilst the benevolent Augustus was in attendance, overseeing his fellow citizens as they enjoyed their blood-lust.

I could hear the trumpets and water organ, being played in the arena to the tempo of the fight, as I made my way through the gates and up the stairs to the imperial box of Augustus and his family. The tempo was fast paced and dramatic now, which probably signified the current contest reaching its climax. I emerged into the sunshine and took in the sight of the Circus Maximus thronged with people in good voice as crowds shouted their encouragement to the gladiators below on the arena sand. Even I could not fail to be moved by the excited buzz rippling through the thousands of spectators. The Circus Maximus was designed for chariot racing, a great oblong ring with a central plinth to race around. Unfortunately, this was not the ideal shape for a gladiatorial contest, so all the spectators were gathered along one side, so they could see the two combatants. Even so, the seats this side of the stadium were all taken and it looked to be a good turnout to the games today – hopefully that would put Augustus in a good mood.

I looked at the fight below as I made my way through the final rows to Augustus' box. A lightly armed *thraex,* with a small shield and helmet, was desperately trying to fend off an aggressive heavily armoured *murmillo*, who advanced relentlessly, beating away his opponent's attacks with his sword and large rectangular shield. The *thraex* was bleeding from several wounds to his largely unarmoured body, and as he weakened, his attacks became more ragged and wild. It reminded me why I avoided the games these days. It wasn't that I objected to what befell any of the slaves; after all, it was none of my business what their owners did with them. It was because I knew what it was like to be in the position of that *thraex*, fighting for one's life in desperation and panic. Anything that brought back such uncomfortable memories, I avoided, even if I was one of the only men in Rome who didn't enjoy the games.

I approached the guard outside Augustus' box and told him that I was expected. The man conferred with a superior, armoured resplendently in burnished breastplate and plumed helmet, who let me through but told me to wait at the edge of the box until the current contest was concluded so I could be announced to Augustus properly. I entered and did what I was told, trying to hold myself in as dignified a pose as I could muster, waiting in trepidation to be called. Even from the back of the box there was an excellent view of the proceedings, and I saw the *thraex* finally collapse and raise his finger in a signal of submission. The crowd then roared their opinions as to whether the man should be spared or not; a great cacophony of noise reverberating around the stadium. Their sentiment was mixed. Some were annoyed that the *murmillo* had won so easily, whilst others admired the *thraex's* courage in holding out for so long after it was obvious he was beaten. Drums replaced the water organ in an ominous drum roll whilst Augustus, who I could just make out at the front of the box, deliberated. The ruler of the Roman state sat on a large chair surrounded by his closest family, who were gathered for the day's entertainment; the elder members looked on bored whilst the younger nephews and grandsons fidgeted excitedly.

As I expected, Augustus raised his fist with the thumb safely inside, the symbol that the loser would live. Fights to the death were actually quite rare; the cost of training a gladiator was so much that their lives could not be tossed away frivolously. The Praetorian officer then whispered in Augustus Caesar's ear and I was beckoned over.

I walked through the box, eyes straight forward, and saluted in the military fashion to the seated Augustus. I thought it advisable that I remind him that I had once fought for Rome and was hopefully worthy of leniency. 'Caesar, this is a great honour,' I proclaimed in my best parade ground voice.

Augustus was never an imposing figure; he had always been slight of build and now, in his later years, his hair was white and balding and his back slightly stooped. However, his eyes radiated power, and when they turned to face me, my heart skipped a beat and I held my breath. He held me like that for several seconds, his eyes boring into mine, sizing me up. 'Cassius Aprilis, isn't it?' he said at last.

'Yes, sir.' I was pleased I managed to keep my voice so level.

A glint in his eyes showed amusement as he said, 'The hero at Western-Gate Pass, no less. You have made quite a name for yourself.'

'Thank you, sir,' I was not sure whether the glint in his eye signified he knew how unwarranted my reputation really was or not; either way, I could hardly acknowledge it. 'I was told you wished to speak to me. I came as soon as I received the summons, *Imperator*.'

A look of irritation passed across his face. 'Please address me as *Princeps*, not *Imperator*.' I inwardly cursed my stupidity; it was well known in Rome that its ruler preferred to be known only as her 'first citizen' and not as the dictator that in reality he was.

I stumbled an apology, 'Of course, *Princeps*, I meant no offence.'

The '*princeps*' paused, looking me up and down before telling me, 'I know your father well. I wonder whether you have his mettle?'

'He always speaks well of you, *Princeps*,'

Augustus chuckled. 'Of that I doubt.' It was true: my father served Augustus loyally, but in private bemoaned his often abrasive demeanour. Augustus' tone turned more serious, 'My wife wishes to speak to you. You may leave me.'

As quickly as that, I was dismissed; he turned his gaze back to the stadium and for a moment I was completely at a loss as to what I should do next.

The Praetorian officer came to my assistance, nudged my arm and inclined his head towards the back of the box where Augustus' wife Livia sat. I made my way over and approached the regal Livia, garbed in a matronly *stola*, whose stern face held eyes that radiated the same power as her husband's. 'Cassius

Aprilis, how good of you to join us.' She smiled as I came over; although that smile did nothing to lessen her severe demeanour, accentuated by her tightly bound hairstyle that left her skin drawn tight against her high cheekboned skull. 'Please sit down and join me.'

Someone once told me that her hairstyle was copied by many women throughout Rome; for the life of me I couldn't see why – it certainly wasn't flattering. 'It is an honour to be invited,' I told her and bowed my head before taking the empty seat next to her.

'Please forgive my husband, he really can be quite rude when he is watching the games – it doesn't do for the populace to see him at the games not paying attention – his uncle would do that and they never liked it.' His uncle, the now almost mythical Julius Caesar, had used the popularity of the games to serve his own ends; his nephew Augustus learnt that lesson well. Livia continued, 'He has instructed me to speak to you on his behalf. It is but a trifling matter.'

I sat more easily in my seat, a semblance of calm returning to me; perhaps this was nothing to do with Tita after all. 'I am always at your family's service, you know that.'

'Yes, of course we do. You remind me so much of your father, always such a true friend to Augustus,' she assured me, although it was not strictly the truth. During the civil war, between Augustus and Mark Anthony, my father had chosen the wrong side. My father switched sides soon enough when Augustus' victory looked certain, but Augustus remained deeply suspicious of him, which was why I had found myself at the Augustan school at a young age – having his first born son held close to Augustus' reach was surety of my father's continued loyalty. My father eventually earned the trust of Augustus and was awarded the governorship of Sicily as reward, but it had been a different story in the early days.

'I will pass on your warm words to my father when I next see him,' which was not likely to be anytime soon, as he had not returned from Sicily for the last two years. 'It is very good of you to extend your hospitality to me.'

She smiled as she glanced over at me, although that smile did not reach her eyes. 'I seem to remember that you went to the school set up by my husband? Isn't that correct?' she asked.

I was baffled by the question. She would know full well that I went to that school. We were all awarded a first-rate education, even though we were little more than bargaining counters in a far larger political game; could this mean my loyalty was being questioned? I'd have to be careful. 'They were some of the happiest days of my life. I owe your husband a lot.'

'No doubt you do. Do you remember a fellow student named Arminius?'

Before I could answer, the trumpets peeled to announce the next two gladiators to fight.

'Ah good! I've been looking forward to this one,' declared Livia, completely changing the subject and leaving me wondering about her question. Of course I knew Arminius, he was my best friend in my youth: Julius Arminius, a foreign German prince kept hostage in Rome to ensure the loyalty of the Cherusci tribe and to be educated in the Roman fashion. He had grown up to be a good soldier and left Rome to fight in the legions as an auxiliary cavalry commander.

'Yes, I served with him in Syria. Has he come to some harm?' I would be genuinely upset if anything befell Julius. I still thought of him as my closest friend – even if I hadn't seen him in nearly six years.

'Oh no, nothing like that. Oh! Don't both fighters look fine!' she said, drawing my attention to the two combatants who were striding out into the arena to the warm applause of the spectators. One was conventionally armoured with sword, shield and helmet, whilst the other held no shield but was armed with two swords – a *Dimacheri*.

Livia had seemingly lost interest in our conversation so I looked at the small wooden card left by the side of my chair which listed the fighters today and tried to discern who these two gladiators were. I saw the name which brought such a stir to the crowd: Atius Longus, a well-known *auctoratii*, one of the poor deluded fools who actually volunteered to fight in the arena for the supposed fame. What made Atius Longus unusual was that he was from the equestrian class, from a very privileged background. 'I know of Atius Longus,' I asked Livia, 'but who is the man he is fighting – the one with two swords? – I've never heard of him?' The carte simply listed him as 'Buteo'.

'My husband shipped him in from the school at Capua. We've been looking forward to this contest all day. I asked for it to commence when you joined us – you're very privileged.'

The contest was in my honour? This day was getting stranger by the moment; why would they go to the effort of playing out the day's most important tie when I arrived? 'I am honoured, my lady. I had no idea you were going to such effort on my behalf.'

'It's no trouble. Now you say you remember Arminius?' She fixed her eyes on mine, like a hawk when its eyes are fixed on a field mouse.

The abrupt change of topic was unnerving; was she deliberately trying to keep me off balance? 'Yes, I served with him in Syria. He was a close friend.' I saw no reason to hide this.

'Then you will be delighted to hear that he has come of age, returned to his people, and taken up his rightful place at their head.' Again the sly smile that never reached her eyes.

Julius, returning to Germany? I couldn't fathom the idea. He was more Roman than the Romans after his upbringing; imagining him back in the backwards poverty of Germany? – he would hate it. 'What do you mean by his rightful place at their head?' I queried.

'I mean he now leads the Cherusci tribe. His uncle died last winter. There were other claimants to the crown, but with the aid of Rome, Arminius has overcome them and been declared King of the Cherusci nation.'

I completely forgot myself and blurted, 'What, Julius? King? That's preposterous – did he want to return to be their king?'

'I really wouldn't know.' Her gaze returned to the two fighters in the arena who were now circling each other and making the first feints towards one another.

I watched them distractedly, still reeling at the news of my friend Julius. It did not take me long to realise that it was not so crazy after all – who better for Rome to lead one of the troublesome German tribes than one of their own. Rome had been setting up client puppet kings for generations. Julius had the birthright. He was the perfect choice, whether he liked it or not. An ugly thought occurred to me: what did any of this have to do with me?

Chapter Four

'Actius Longus always was such a fine athlete. He looks in fine shape, don't you think?' Livia remarked on the famous gladiator.

The two gladiators circled one another, then Longus came in for a blistering attack. His sword was as fast as a serpent's tongue, darting in and away. The two blades of Buteo successfully parried each strike but he was forced to back away from the onrushing Longus. They broke apart and they went back to circling each other again, now showing each other the utmost respect. Both were master swordsmen; there would be no easy victory here.

'Er ... yes, a fine swordsmen.' I wasn't interested in the infernal fight, but couldn't say as much. 'I'm glad everything has worked out well for Julius. I'm sure he'll serve Rome with credit in Germany.' Now to distance myself from him. 'It's been so many years since I've seen him, he's probably forgotten me altogether – I'm sure there are others in Rome that knew him better than I.' Unlikely – but I was now desperate.

Livia shifted her eyes over to me. 'You do yourself a disservice. Surely he'd have heard of your exploits at Western-Gate Pass? I'm sure it made him proud to hear how his friend helped suppress an uprising in his home country?'

That damn story was getting me into trouble; couldn't anyone in this city look past it? 'I was a small part in the wars. I have left that part of my life behind me now. I'm sure I no longer warrant notice in the German legions.'

'The campaigns in Germany are drawing to a close. Germany will soon be a province like any other. However the commander of our legions in the region says the situation is still not entirely stable. Do you know Commander Varus?'

'No, my lady.' They couldn't pin that on me at least. The new commander in Germany was previously a governor in Syria, but from before my time there. I'd heard of him, of course. The older veterans in my unit said he was a fair ruler but could be ruthless when tested, brutally suppressing a revolt in Judea.

All in all, a typical henchman of Augustus: my father and he would have a lot in common.

'He's a competent fellow, but diplomacy was never his strong point. What we need is someone who can help smooth relations between the German tribes and the Roman presence in Germany. The Germanic tribes have all heard of your valour in the field, therefore you should command their respect. You're also good friends with our greatest ally in the region. Who better than you to fulfil this role?'

There, it was out in the open now; this is what the invitation to the games was all about. I saw the logic behind it; Julius may now rule the Cherusci, but his position must be precarious, and he would need Roman advisors to help him. Why not send a boyhood friend to ensure that Rome's interests were being observed? I wanted nothing to do with it. Even if the Cherusci stayed loyal to Julius, they were just one of many tribes. I wanted no part of a war of supremacy between the Germanic nations.

I pretended to be engrossed in the fight being staged on the arena sand – in order to give me time to think of a way out of this. The two fighters were fully committed now, hacking, slashing and parrying each other's blows in a blistering display of skill. The double-bladed Buteo was genuinely ambidextrous, wielding each sword with strength and skill. It was beginning to trouble Longus, who had probably never faced such a rare and talented opponent. I composed myself. 'I am very flattered that you would think of me for such a role, but in all honesty, I am probably the wrong man. I know nothing of diplomacy and politics – ask anyone who knows me.' This at least was true. 'I would be sure to misrepresent Rome's interests.'

'Oh don't worry about that. We wouldn't expect you to oversee any treaties or such things. We have other specially trained men to fulfil that task.' It seemed even they weren't stupid enough to give me a job that involved genuine tact. 'We just need you to help advise Governor Varus on the Germanic tribes. He can be mule-headed sometimes and an experienced veteran who knows the tribes well could prove invaluable. Your friendship with Arminius is simply a bonus. It would only be for this summer, until Varus can find his feet.'

The crowd's voice roared as one as Buteo opened a cut along Longus' bare chest. The blood was a bright red and poured freely down the champion gladiator's body, spurring him on to attack again.

It was time I changed tack. 'Much as I would love to serve Rome in this venture, I have other concerns in Rome. I fulfil a vital role in helping to train the Praetorian Guards, whose responsibility it is to guard both you and your husband.'

I only saw them once a month, granted, but I was sure I could persuade Horatius to say it was more.

'Oh yes, the Praetorians. My husband plans to increase the number of cohorts from nine to twelve in the next year. We'll need officers to lead them. You were once a tribune in the legions, maybe you'd be interested? We'll need veterans from the wars. The Praetorians cannot be led by any but the best.'

So this will be my reward: a commission in the Praetorian Guard. Oh, it was tempting. I was jealous of Horatius' position in the guard and always had been. It gave him genuine power within Rome, and respect. If I were given such a command, my father could no longer look on me with disdain and it would quieten my sisters nagging once and for all. The Praetorians were more than just an honour guard: they were the backbone of Augustus' power. They ensured the Senate always voted as the *princeps* wished and the people of Rome were kept in order. What is more, they were based in Rome and far away from the horrors of war; I could continue my life of parties and heavy drinking and be respected to boot. It was perfect except for one matter: I would have to go to Germany first, a land I'd sworn never to return to.

I cleared my throat to make my response as clear as possible. There was nothing for it – I'll just have to tell her I'll not go.

'My lady ...' I started but was halted by her raising a hand and silencing me. The gladiatorial contest was reaching its conclusion and she didn't want to miss any of it. She peered down at the two combatants, a light in her eyes showing a flutter of excitement, as the tempo of the water organ increased. Longus was now in serious trouble: he was bleeding from multiple wounds and the speed of his sword was no longer the blurring blade we had witnessed earlier; now it was slow and cumbersome. Buteo parried the last blow aimed at his throat whilst simultaneously using his other blade to strike at Longus' legs. Longus tried to deflect the blow with his small shield but he was too late and with a cry collapsed to the sand, a deep wound open in his thigh. Buteo kicked his assailant's sword away from him and placed his sword to Longus' throat as he lay in submission. The crowd started bellowing their verdict as Augustus deliberated to the sound of the rolling drums. Some of the crowd always bellowed for the loser to be despatched but most shouted for him to be reprieved; he was a crowd favourite and had fought well – he had just come up against someone better in Buteo.

Livia sat herself straighter in her chair. 'They say Longus was once a good friend of my husband's daughter Julia, such a shame.' The mention of Julia's name shocked me to silence. What was happening here?

Augustus turned in his chair and looked directly at his wife. It was very subtle; I would never have noticed if I had not been looking directly at her, but I saw Livia's eyes narrow and harden ever so slightly. That was enough for Augustus – he turned back to the arena and raised his fist. This time the thumb was shown sticking out of the side and he turned his thumb towards himself to signal that Buteo should end it. The gladiator struck his sword down through the throat of his stricken opponent, producing a sudden gout of blood.

A shocked silence went around the stadium, before erupting into wild applause. Longus had fought well, but if Augustus decreed that he should die, they weren't going to argue with it. I swallowed hard and thought about what I'd just witnessed. Was all this the design of Livia? Livia said this contest was in my honour; was Buteo brought up from Capua simply to demonstrate Augustus' power over all his citizens, including me? Longus must have thought himself safe, even after he submitted, due to his good name and family. It had afforded him no protection and the casual mention of his friendship with Julia was not missed by me either – perhaps Livia knew more of my involvement with her disgraced stepdaughter than I realised. The ghosts of my past were catching up with me this day and my heart sank as I realised I had no choice in the matter: if Augustus wanted me to go to Germany, I would have to go, willing or not.

I looked at her then, the austere face of the woman who held my life in her cruel grasp, and was reminded that this was the same woman who had discarded her first devoted husband to further her own ends and be with Augustus; she always got what she wanted and she was every bit as ruthless as her husband. I swallowed hard and took the only option left to me. 'Livia, it will be an honour for me to represent Rome in Germany once more. When do you wish me to leave?'

I wasn't even awarded a smile of triumph: my compliance had never really been in doubt as far as she was concerned. 'There's no need to leave straight away, stay until the end of *Quinquatria.* I wouldn't want you missing the end of the festival.' She waved her hand as if she was granting me a great favour. 'Then you can be on your way – so you don't miss the start of the summer's campaigning.'

She wished me to leave in three days time. Three days until I leave my comfortable life and probably go to my grave; the gods alone knew how perilous such a journey was this early in the year, 'I will make all haste, my lady, although the snows will have barely melted along the Alps, it will be a difficult journey.'

Her composure remained cool and composed. 'You'll find the roads much improved since you last travelled them. My husband has improved all routes immeasurably.'

When I had last travelled them I'd been half-mad with starvation and despair, but it wouldn't help to explain that to her now. 'Very well, my lady, the weeks of solitude will help focus my mind on the task ahead.'

She looked at me in surprise. 'Oh, there is no need for you to travel alone. Your rank of tribune will be reinstated – therefore you need an aide to accompany you. I will give this some thought and send someone to your home before you leave.'

No doubt she already knew the identity of this 'aide' she spoke of – spy would be a better term – to ensure that I carried out my mission and didn't abscond to a small villa hidden away in the countryside. I should be affronted by how little she trusted me, but I wasn't. If I thought hiding could get me out of this, I'd certainly consider it. 'I look forward to meeting him. I hope he proves good company.'

She looked me up and down appraisingly. 'You'll do very well, Cassius Aprilis. We'll be sure to write a letter to your father, telling him of this great service you do us.' I supposed that would at least cheer up the old goat. 'Now, of course you are welcome to stay to see the end of the games tonight.'

I wanted to be as far away from this harridan as I could get but appearances wouldn't allow me to leave straight away. I sat through a large melee of *equites*, battling away on horseback, until only one remained mounted and was declared the victor, whilst I inwardly fretted about my impending journey back to Germany. This was followed by a *retiarii*, armed with net and trident, who successfully hooked and snared a heavily armed *murmillo*. These contests were always popular and put the crowd in a joyful carnival mood; I deemed it the most opportune time to make my excuses and leave. 'I would love to enjoy your company for longer, my lady, but I really should be on my way,' I told Livia. 'I have to tie up all my affairs before I leave.' There was little for me to tie up, but at least it would get me away from her and her husband's blood-letting spectacle.

'Well, I do hope you enjoy the rest of your evening.' As ever she was polite and gracious, and gave no outward sign that she had just turned my life upside down.

I paid my respects to Augustus upon leaving, thanking him for his hospitality, and feigning enthusiasm for the task set me by his wife, and left his box. I made my way through the throngs of spectators, who were eagerly awaiting the next contest, whilst I furiously tried to think of a way out of this. There was none. I was hooked just as effectively as a *murmillo* in Livia's net whilst Augustus held the trident to my throat. This morning I had awoken to memories of a blissful night in the arms of Tita and without a care in the world. Now I was on my way back to Germany, and a return to the terror, cold nights on campaign, and the prospect of an early death.

By the gods! Tita! How could I tell her? She'd be heartbroken for sure. I avowed to spend as much as time possible, in the three days left to me, in bed with her, and to Hades with the scandal. Now I was a tribune on a special mission for Augustus himself, any indiscretion would be overlooked.

I started to visualise how I would tell her; I would once again come across as the brave soldier, risking his all to serve Rome on a dangerous mission. Rome needed its brave hero to fulfil a task they dare not give anyone else. She would cry tears of remorse but wouldn't be able to hide the mixture of awe and admiration she felt for me. I got caught up in the daydream of a willing and pliant Tita coming to my bed willingly once more, infatuated with her selfless warrior.

I made my way out of the Circus Maximus by a side door, to avoid the press of the crowd, and walked along its outer perimeter, listening to the crowd within bellow and chant. It was early evening now, and a beautiful sunset lit the outside cloisters of the stadium. I was not alone in these streets; gates here led to the gladiator's quarters, and more than a few well-respected ladies came here to meet their favourites who would fight the next day. The gladiators were all officially slaves, even those who entered service voluntarily like Atius Longus – the gods be merciful to his shade – but they were treated to luxury and much comfort, and were afforded a lot of freedom. The night before combat, the gladiators were thrown a great feast, and it was here that respectable ladies could meet their gladiatorial lovers. I gave a little laugh as I glimpsed someone in brightly coloured cloth leave a covered litter and slip inside a small doorway. It reminded me of the poet Ovid's treatise on the art of love when he said: '*The Circus brings assistance to new love, and the scattered sand of the gladiator's ring.*'

I loved the hypocrisy of Rome. Inside the stadium sat a man who was a dictator in all but name, whose power was total, and who decreed many edicts forbidding adultery or wanton behaviour, whilst outside, not one hundred paces from where he sat, respectable married women were having illicit affairs with base-born slaves and nobody raised a whiff of concern.

My mood was dour, but I started to think through my situation. Maybe it wouldn't be so bad. Yes, it's true I didn't want to return to Germany, but by all accounts the place had changed. Everyone said so; they said it was now a peaceful province just like any other in the empire. The resistance of the tribes was broken, the populace were beginning to see the benefits of civilisation, and peace and prosperity beckoned for the region. Livia said I only need stay until Governor Varus finds his feet: one summer's campaigning followed by a winter's confinement in the Roman military base. Yes, it would be cold, boring, and miserable, but I would have the finest soldiers in the world to protect me. Who better to keep me from harm? I was not re-entering the service for active duty. I was simply an advisor to the governor, someone to help smooth relations between the army and my friend Julius.

Julius leading the Cherusci. I still couldn't reconcile that. As children we used to joke and tease him for being a German prince, which he hated. I once received a black eye from him, as an enraged eight-year-old, for teasing him on the subject – I still remember the blow. I knew of his origins, but I never thought he was to be used as anything other than a minor bargaining tool. He had joined the legions, been promoted to lead his own cavalry unit, and given equestrian status as a reward. A life ensconced in Roman civilisation beckoned, only for him to be sent back to his people – who, let's be honest, were rather crude and uneducated – to be set up as a figurehead ruler. If my situation was bad, it was nowhere near as bad as it was for poor Julius; I could just imagine him, turning his nose up at their awful ale, despising their ribald humour and poor diet.

My musing was stopped short when I saw the next woman in the street leave her covered litter. She wore a light dress with a plunging neckline; her face was veiled but I recognised the eyes – they held the same mischief in them that I found so attractive – and my worst fears were confirmed as the veil dropped. It was Tita, and she was slipping in one of the side doors to visit a gladiator.

Chapter Five

I shouldn't have been so surprised; it was all so clear now. Seneca's sly remarks that she liked, 'real warriors with fire in their loins,' suddenly gained clarity. I thought he was referring to me, but this was what he meant. He must have known all along and laughed watching me try and ingratiate myself with her: the gladiators were the men she craved. I was just a pale imitation of one, someone with a muscular frame, who resembled one in the dark. I should have remembered the next line in Ovid's poem: *'Venus' boy often fights in that sand,'* and realised that a woman so addicted to danger would be drawn to the virile muscular warriors. These men risked their lives every time they entered the arena but were adored by the masses in return; such a mix of danger and fame would prove an irresistible erotic temptation.

My stomach felt like it had been hit by a charging bull and I leant against one of the fig trees lining the avenue and closed my eyes in despair. I was such a fool.

It was no wonder she was unconcerned that her husband might find out about me; I was the least of her indiscretions – compared to coupling with slaves, our affair was relatively respectable! That Seneca knew was certain, his smirking remarks confirmed it, but how many others? Maybe everyone I met at Seneca's parties knew of Tita's nature and revelled in watching me make a complete fool of myself. I started to look at my reputation as a hero of Rome in a different light; maybe the reason Seneca and others invited me to their parties was not because they honoured my military record but the opposite: they hated my reputation and wanted to see me brought down low, down to their level. Well, they could all have a laugh at my expense now.

As I walked past Tita's litter I looked at her slaves and wondered if they recognised me. If they did, they made no sign, they just stood there impassively, staring straight ahead, ready to escort their lady home once she had finished bedding her latest fancy. I noticed that they were all big, strong, muscular men; how many of these had Tita slept with? I thought about leaving a message with them to deliver to their mistress on her return, a damning put-down to fill her with shame and remorse at her behaviour. But I didn't bother; what would be the point? I was suddenly tired with Rome and all her corrupted citizens. I was no better; the last four years of my life incorporated enough vice to shame a Syrian brothel owner. Rome would always be like this: a seething mass of humanity, whose worst flaws and baser instincts were kept hidden from view by false reputations, lies, and deceit. The grander the marble façade, the cruder the masonry hidden behind it.

I stumbled my way home, in a daze, too shaken to take in my surroundings. Maybe I was better off out of Rome. I could leave this corrupted city for a return to the rugged military life of routine and discipline. I had prospered in the army once. Before Germany I served in Syria; those years were structured, and, in the main, I was content. I found myself longing for that simpler time: when I knew with a certainty where my life was going and what was expected of me.

I stopped at a taverna on the way back to my home and purchased a small amphora of crude wine. The innkeeper's eyes goggled at seeing someone with a toga marked with a broad purple band enter his stinking and dirty watering hole, but I was beyond caring. I gulped the unwatered wine down deeply, despite its sour, almost rancid quality. The other patrons huddled around its edges, whispering to one another, guessing at what brought me to their small establishment.

I examined my cracked drinking vessel, which was engraved with a crude depiction of Janus – the god of gateways. It was quite apt, I thought, as I took in how quickly this particular capricious god could change a man's fortunes. I'd lost Tita for sure, that much was obvious; I could never overlook her infidelity with the gladiators, even if her husband could. Also, the easy comfort of Rome was soon to be exchanged for the cold bogs and rain of Germany. What did I ever do to offend Janus? I laughed bitterly to myself. Was there ever such a cruel reversal of fortune? Returning to Germany would mean once more serving alongside the men of the XVIII: one of my former legions. I still thought of myself as a proud veteran of the X. The men 'of the sea straits', with whom I'd served in Syria. But I also served one year of my life with the XVIII in Germany. They were good men in the main, but I didn't relish the reunion – I'd have to meet fellow survivors of Western-Gate Pass – that wasn't an enticing prospect. I downed the cup of wine then refilled it – damn you Janus, at least you can help me get drunk.

I stayed in the taverna until it was dark outside and my head was swimming. As I left, I inclined my head to the innkeeper and stumbled out, knocking over a couple of stools in the process.

The night was cool and I reached the Caelian Hill and saw the grand litters of the noble families escorting their masters and mistresses to lavish parties, much like the ones I attended. The sight sickened me and I felt no desire to join them and be greeted by the smirking smiles and sharp whispers that would accompany me. My legs felt heavy and my mind was in pieces. In the space of a day my entire world had been turned on its head.

I knocked on my door and Patrellis opened it. He must have seen the anguish in my eyes. 'My lord … are you alright? … Is something amiss?'

I sighed heavily. 'I'm fine, Patrellis. Please prepare me some food. I wish to eat.' It felt good to hear the gentle concern of Patrellis.

'Is that Gaius? About time!' questioned my sister in her shrill voice.

As if my day hadn't been bad enough. 'What are you still doing here? You've got your own home, Antonia. Why spend so much time in mine?' The last thing I needed right now was my interfering sister.

'Are you drunk?' she asked walking sharply up to me.

'What if I am? It's no business of yours.' I was no longer concerned what she thought of me.

She folded her arms and pinned me with a fierce stare. 'If you're rejoining the army, you'll need to sharpen up your attitude. Your drinking days are over!'

'If I'm to rejoin the army? How in Hades do you know about that?' Not even the infamous Rome gossip could travel that quickly. I had only just heard myself!

Patrellis cleared his throat and gestured towards my bedroom. 'After you left for the gymnasium, a courier from Augustus delivered this.'

I followed where Patrellis was leading and saw what he was talking about. Displayed on a stuffed bust stood a breastplate, tunic, helmet, and arms of a tribune. The tunic and stiff overlapping leather strips that protected the wearer's upper legs were a vibrant red, whilst the breastplate was bronze, polished to shine brilliantly. The helmet was steel and crested with a red plume, whilst a *gladius* with a silver plated handle and scabbard lay on a neatly folded scarlet cloak. Augustus and that evil harpy Livia hadn't even bothered to wait until I accepted the mission before delivering the uniform I was to wear, so sure were they of my compliance. I stood there transfixed by the armour and sank to my knees, my eyes never leaving it. The reality of returning to Germany suddenly hit me: there was no easy campaign in that land. I was returning to Germany, where the natives learnt to fight before they could run, where every field, forest, and hillside was steeped in Roman blood. This was Germany I was returning to: may the gods have mercy on me.

'It's not the same as entering politics, but, I grant you, it's worthy. Why did you not tell me you were rejoining the army? Father will be so pleased.' The approval in Antonia's voice was unmistakable; finally I was doing something she could not criticise. 'Will you be joining the Praetorian Guard? The armour is very becoming. You'll look so handsome with it on. Why don't you try it on now?'

'You just don't get it, do you?' Did she really have no idea what this armour signified?

'What do you mean? Don't get what?'

'This is what I will die in. You look on at how I will be dressed when my body is cold and lifeless.'

Antonia was shocked. 'But isn't this the armour of the Praetorians? What do you mean?'

I didn't turn to address her; my eyes remained focused on the armour. 'I'm not joining the Praetorians. I'm to leave for Germany in three days' time.'

Antonia gasped: she remembered the wrecked man who returned from that demon-spawned land. I was half-mad then. I wasn't certain that I wasn't going to return that way, just contemplating returning there. 'Oh Gaius, I'm so sorry.'

To give her credit, she knew that I wouldn't voluntarily opt to return there. Antonia was wise enough to know that sometimes people were given no choice. 'Leave me,' was all I uttered at Antonia and Patrellis.

I stayed there for quite some time, simply staring at the armour and contemplating the trials laid before me. Oh, by the gods, why did it have to be Germany?

The next day, I slept late. My sleep, unsurprisingly, was fitful and full of nightmares. I dreamt I was back in Western-Gate Pass again, but this time the big, bearded, blonde warriors trying to kill me were urged on by a stern-faced Livia and a laughing Tita. I desperately hacked and chopped to keep myself clear of the impending tide of men, but eventually they overpowered me and the last I remember of the dream was Livia standing over me and saying, 'Such a shame, he once held such promise.'

'Oh, don't worry about him,' replied Tita scornfully, 'he was never worthy of Rome's respect.'

I awoke with a thumping headache as Patrellis gently shook me. 'My lord, you have a visitor.'

My eyes were still glued together with sleep. Had I cried myself to sleep? 'Well tell whoever it is to go away! I'm in no mood for entertaining.' Why couldn't the world just leave me alone for a while, I thought, groaning as I tried to rouse myself.

'I am afraid the Lady Antonia has already admitted him,' he said, an edge of caution tingeing his words.

Patrellis knew I was not much of a morning person at the best of times, and today was no exception. My temper flared. 'Antonia! What's she still doing here? Has she moved herself in before I've even left the country?' Antonia always liked this house and claimed it was wasted on me; that insipid husband of hers was probably here too!

'The Lady Antonia returned early this morning. She said you'll be needing her help as you prepare for your travels.' Patrellis' voice was calm and soothing – how you'd talk to a wilful child.

If anything, this worsened my mood. 'Well, who is it anyway?' I snapped.

'Prisca met him at the door, so I didn't catch the name but he is in military attire, and claims you're his commanding officer.'

'Nonsense. I was only readmitted to the army yesterday, how can …' I trailed off as realisation slowly came to me. This would be my spy, the man Livia was sending with me to keep me honest. I collected myself and told Patrellis, 'Tell him I will be there shortly.'

Patrellis left and I rose and pulled a tunic over my head. At least if he described me as his commanding officer, he didn't outrank me. He can spy and report back to Livia as much as he pleases, but he won't be bossing me around and issuing orders. I splashed some water on my face and dampened my hair down a bit to try and give it some order; I didn't want to appear as if I had just risen from my bed at this late hour. I laced some sandals on and walked through the *atrium* to the *tablino* where I could hear my sister laughing. As I entered the grand dining area, I was shocked by what I saw: reclined on a divan, dressed in identical armour to my own, was Marcus Scaeva. He was smiling ear to ear; my sister reclined on her divan, and looked at him with open admiration.

Her attention was drawn by me as I entered, and she proclaimed, 'Oh here he is, the man in question! I have just been telling Marcus how proud of you we all are.'

Antonia had spent the last four years telling me almost daily what an embarrassment I was to the family, but I wasn't interested in her ludicrous statement. 'What in Hades' name are you doing here?' I demanded of Marcus Scaeva.

He stood up from his divan and saluted me bristly. 'I am reporting for duty, sir. I have just been given my orders – I'm to accompany you to Germany and guard your back. It's an absolute honour, sir. I couldn't believe my luck when I was told. Why didn't you tell me yesterday that you were to rejoin the army?'

Because I didn't even know myself, I could have said, but I didn't, I just stood there dumbstruck as this latest shock sunk in. If this didn't top it all! Not only was I expected to negotiate my way through the most hostile lands known to Rome, I was to do it with a raving lunatic at my side, one itching for a fight, and so green and naive I would be better off with an untrained lion from the arena. I eventually muttered, 'Disaster,' and sat down heavily on a divan.

'Gaius!' Antonia snapped, 'You're being rude! At least compliment Marcus on his uniform – doesn't he look the model hero.'

I was momentarily distracted by my sister's behaviour. She was fluttering her eyelids at young Marcus Scaeva, and beaming a great smile in his direction; where was the customary scowl and acid tongue? I had thought that Scaeva's muscular frame and comely face would prove a hit with the ladies, but I hadn't expected one of them to be my own sister! She was a married woman – scandalous! What would her poor husband say?

I turned my attention back to the young man and took in his young eager face. I sighed and asked him wearily, 'So you have been ordered to accompany me to Germany have you? What else do you know of our mission?'

'Very little, sir. I've just been told to offer you any assistance that may arise. It's a real honour for me to serve by your side.'

I stood and started pacing the room, my mind on the journey ahead. 'I take it you haven't journeyed out of Italy before?'

'No, but I won't let you down. I'll prove myself to you.' His voice was very sincere.

Antonia jumped in, 'Of course you won't let him down! Gaius realises that, don't you?'

I gave her a firm stare, letting her know not to interrupt again, this was a serious business, not a quick jaunt up the *Via Cassia* to pick up some local souvenirs. I addressed Scaeva, 'Do you have a horse?'

He stood also. 'I can take the pick of my father's horses.'

I wasn't sure about any of his father's horses: they would be show mounts, not the rugged sort suitable for a long arduous journey to Germany. 'That won't do. Meet me tomorrow morning at the horse dealers near the Temple of

Minerva, close to the western wall on the other side of the Tiber. Do you know it?' This particular horse dealer was owned by Lycoris the Greek – the best, if most expensive horse dealer in the city.

Marcus stuttered a reply, his natural good temper disrupted by my strict manner. 'Yes ... I think so ... if you think that will be best.'

'I do. Now, if you please, I have a lot to prepare. We leave the day after tomorrow. We must be ready.' I put my arm on his back and led him to the door – after he briefly inclined his head to my sister, who blushed prettily.

'Until tomorrow then,' I said, slamming the door as soon as he walked through it. I returned to the *tablino* to find my sister had found her customary scowl: this was the Antonia I knew and loved.

She folded her arms under her breasts in annoyance. 'You didn't have to be so rude to him! He's from a good family and of respectable character.'

I laughed at her. 'Just because you took a fancy to him, don't expect me to pander to him. He's a young boy and in need of seasoning. If we're going to survive this mission, he'll need to grow up quickly.'

Antonia went bright scarlet. 'Take a fancy to him! Nonsense!'

'You were like a moonstruck milk maid. I'm surprised you didn't offer to accompany him home.'

'How dare you! I am a respectable married woman, and unlike the women you consort with, I take my vows of fidelity seriously.'

I never really thought anything else, but it was fun to rile her. I thought better of pushing my luck too far though; her temper was not to be trifled with. I kissed her on the forehead which placated her for the time being at least.

'What's your mission anyway?' she asked, still obviously peeved but prepared to move on.

'Do you remember my friend Julius?'

'Yes, of course I do, have you heard from him?' Antonia knew Julius from our childhood and had been quite fond of him at one point.

'Well, believe it or not, Augustus has set him up as a puppet king of the Cherusci tribe in Germany.' That still sounded odd.

'You're not serious – Julius, a king!' her eyes popped out of her head.

'Ridiculous, I know, but he was a good soldier. Who knows, maybe he will make an equally good king.' I laid down on one of the divans and folded my arms behind my head, 'There's a new commander in Germany, a man named Varus. Augustus and his wife think I might be useful in advising him, due to my close ties to Julius.'

'That sounds an important job, you should be pleased,' she reclined on the other divan and looked at me with concern.

I grunted a half-formed laugh. 'Nothing in Germany pleases me, Antonia. You don't know what the place is like. It's beyond brutal.'

'Well at least Marcus Scaeva looks as if he can handle himself in a fight.'

'That's the problem. Men like him attract trouble. I want to avoid fighting, not go asking for it. I'll have to rein young Marcus in, if either of us are to live through this.'

'By the gods, now that's a horse,' exclaimed Marcus Scaeva at a great black stallion which was rearing and trying to pull away from its two terrified handlers, who were desperately pulling on the horse's reins.

'I see you have an eye for a horse,' said Demetrios, a cousin of the horse owner Lycoris, and whose eyes lit up with greed at Marcus' admiration of the fiery black monster.

'I like a horse with spirit!' Marcus clapped his hands together in eagerness.

'Don't be a complete idiot,' I told him, effectively dousing Marcus' enthusiasm, and pointing out to Demetrios which one of us was in charge here.

'But, Cassius, surely you can see power and speed in those long legs of his?' Marcus wasn't ready to give up on the prize mount yet.

'Used as a horse to pull a chariot at the Circus Maximus maybe, but for a battle steed – never.' I wasn't used to being up at this early hour, which made me irritable and I really wasn't in the mood to explain the blatantly obvious.

Marcus wouldn't let it go. 'But why? Surely a stallion such as this was born for battle.'

Like most Romans, Marcus was proving his complete ignorance of anything equestrian. I explained to him, 'In battle you want a horse with a placid temperament and one easily biddable. On that horse, your attention will be on controlling him, not your weapons. Any distraction can cost you your life in the field.' I turned to our attendant, Demetrios. 'Take us away from these show ponies. I want to see your Libyan stock.' He bowed his head and led the way.

I wasn't surprised at Marcus' lack of knowledge. As Romans, our strength was always our legions, the greatest infantry in the world, who marched to battle on foot and destroyed anything that got in our path. Our cavalry as a result was neglected, and was never renowned. Julius Caesar was the first to realise this lack, and found a simple solution to the problem: take the best cavalry from other nations and put them in our army. Rome's armies were currently supplemented by crack horse units from Germany, Spain and Gaul and even further afar. They were taught Roman discipline and adapted to use our armour and weapons; together this made a formidable force. My friend Julius, who was at the heart of my new mission, had led such a cohort in Syria. They were German irregulars who had taken employment from Rome, and, with Roman leadership, were a fine unit. Rome's power was still her legions but the army was more adaptable now it had an effective cavalry as well. Marcus must have been given the typical Roman military upbringing, focusing on the *gladius* and fighting on foot. I was different; I had the experience of years of friendship with Julius to set me in good store.

'Here you are, my lord, the finest Libyan horseflesh you will find this side of the Internal Sea.' Demetrios waved his arm at the fenced paddock, which held Libyan horses. The Libyan horses were slightly larger than the slender-limbed Celtic varieties and were swift, but more importantly knew nothing of fatigue. I was set on trying my hardest to avoid any conflict in Germany, but if the worse happened, and a fight couldn't be avoided, I was going to be sure I had the right horse under me.

'Wow, I like the look of these ones too! Which one will be mine?' exclaimed Marcus, sounding like an overexcited young child being taken to market for the first time. He ran over to the fence of the corral and made a whooping noise which sent the horses scattering around their paddock.

'Your friend takes great enjoyment from his life, I think,' remarked a smirking Demetrios, amused by Marcus' antics.

'So does a pet dog, but at least they are easier to train,' I grumbled, looking at the horses run around the paddock. I spotted two I liked the look of and asked Demetrios to bring them over to me.

'These look well enough, but I still fancy the black stallion,' said Marcus, grin stretching across his face as usual, as the two geldings were brought over to us.

They were both around fifteen hands high at the withers, sturdy, and had the look of speed about them. I ran my hand down their light dun coats and checked their teeth. Both were sound, and I looked in their eyes, which were bright and alert – a good sign.

'Surely these two horses will not be taking us the entire journey to Germany?' questioned Marcus.

'Whyever not? They are both of good stock.' I answered.

'They are fine mounts, but surely we will change our horses regularly along the way?' Marcus was referring to the fact that as we were under the direct orders of Augustus, we were entitled to change our horses at each way station along the road, just as the official messengers did, in order to prevent them running their horses to death.

'As long as we don't overexert them, they will be fine.' I had no intention of reaching Germany any earlier than I had to. I certainly wasn't going to race there, changing horses at every opportunity; I intended to take the journey at a measured pace. If, however, there was ever the need to make a break for it, these horses fitted the bill nicely.

'But ... surely ... why ...' Marcus looked crestfallen we would not be breaking all records to reach our destination. I held up my hand to silence him, and started the laborious process of haggling the price for the two horses with Demetrios. He robbed me blind, of course, but I wasn't that interested in getting the price down in any case. It was only my father's money.

Before we left I asked Demetrios, 'Do you also have any Gallic saddles?'

Demetrios look confused but answered, 'We could probably find you two if you really want?'

'Do so and I will throw in another ten denarius.' The Gallic saddle was used by some of the Celtic tribes from Gaul and consisted of four horns which protruded from the saddle and gripped the rider's thighs. Though not common, some Roman auxiliary units were starting to adopt them, including Julius'.

'How well do you ride?' I asked Marcus.

'Well enough,' he answered with a wink of bravado.

I grunted. 'I hope you're right, we've a long path ahead of us.' I told Demetrios that we would pick the horses and the saddles up the next day – just before we left Rome.

Chapter Six

The next day, I was ready to leave. Everything was packed into my saddlebags and I was fitted out in my new armour. It fitted perfectly, and despite my misgivings about being clothed in armour again, I had to admit I looked exceedingly good. Antonia fussed around me as I made the last checks to my kit. I slung the saddlebag over my shoulder. I could have one of my slaves carry it to the horse dealers by the city gates, but it was time I started doing things for myself – I'd have no slaves to carry my things in Germany.

'You will write, won't you?' Antonia brushed away a tear running down her cheek.

'Of course I will.' I was never much of a correspondent but it would do no good to remind her of that.

'To mother as well, not just me?'

A pang of guilt hit me: I hadn't made time to visit my mother before I left; I imagined the floods of tears this act would engender. I decided to change the subject. 'Have you written to father and told him of my mission?'

'Yes, I wrote to him yesterday. He will be so proud of you, Gaius.' She stroked the side of my face with her hand, which I pushed aside in embarrassment; I was not a young child.

'You'll look after the house, Patrellis?' I asked my retainer, who stood by the gateway to my home, one arm around an openly tearful Prisca, the other on the shoulder of a crestfallen Silo, who stared firmly at his feet, too sad to raise his head. Badriyah had been too upset to see me off, preferring to cry herself to sleep in her own room. My household held me in genuine affection, I realised, despite my errant lifestyle.

'It will be waiting for you when you return,' he replied with a steady voice, maintaining his stoic demeanour.

I kissed my sister on the cheek and turned to leave. 'Goodbye, Antonia.'

Antonia started crying, 'You will take care, won't you. Don't be brave and get yourself hurt. You don't need to prove yourself to anyone.'

The last thing I intended to do was be brave, but it was nice that my sister still thought me capable of such a thing. 'I'll be back in no time. You look after that husband of yours.'

She nodded her head in between sobs. 'He's not half the man you are, Gaius,' she blubbered.

As gratifying as it was to hear her finally acknowledge this, a drawn-out goodbye was achieving little. It was time I left. I walked away from the house, saddlebag over my shoulder and helmet under my arm, dressed head to toe in burnished armour – at least I still looked like a model soldier.

'And make sure you behave yourself. You know you cannot be trusted with unwatered wine,' my sister shouted at my retreating back – scornful tone returning – as she wiped away her tears. I raised my hand in a final farewell and walked from the house of my father, swallowing hard, and blinking back tears of my own.

I'd received a visit from Spento and Horatius the night before. They spent most of the evening making bad jokes and reassuring me that once I returned to Rome I'd be the talk of the city again. A career in the Praetorian Guards beckoned, which in turn would lead to all the ladies of Rome playing court to me. I went along with them and tried to sound enthusiastic, but at the back of my mind I kept on thinking of Tita. I received no word from her or Seneca. It was as if I was already dead in their eyes – I was to leave Rome, therefore I no longer counted. It annoyed me that their opinion still mattered to me, and despite all that she had done, thoughts of Tita still clouded my mind. I kept on expecting her to appear from around a corner, and explain that everything was all a big mistake – I was her true love, and the gladiators were just a passing fancy.

As I walked through the Forum, on my way to the western side of the city, I looked for her litter, or a flash of her hair in a huddle of Roman ladies, but there was nothing; she never did make a last appearance to bid me farewell. It wasn't really that I expected anything different – it was rare for her ever to be up and about at this early hour – but still my heart felt heavy.

I stopped whilst crossing the *Pons Sublicius*, Rome's oldest bridge, and looked over at the River Tiber flowing underneath with small boats busily moving back and forth, full of rowdy boatmen shouting out insults to those that got in their path. The bright spring day made a nice backdrop and the water glistened pleasingly. On any other day, the site would lift my mood, but not today: I was leaving Rome; soon all this will be lost to me.

I met Marcus Scaeva at the horse dealer's as planned. He clapped me on the back as I greeted him, and we picked up our horses. They had found us two Gallic saddles, which were old and worn but well made, and the leather was still sound, so it would suffice for the journey. No Roman was allowed to ride in the city without first being awarded a triumph – the highest accolade granted to its finest Generals – so we waited until we left the city gates before mounting up, and then circling around to the north. We rode together, with me taking the slight lead, and I initially set a fast pace, so as to leave Rome far behind as quickly as possible. Even so, I found it impossible not to have one last look back at the great city, once we were on the *Via Aurelia* heading north. We were alongside some old tombs which lined all the roads from Rome, some five miles from the city gates, and we had a superb view of the city and its great aqueducts crisscrossing the countryside leading to her. The city's seven hills were still visible in the clear blue sky and she stretched away as far as the eye could see, a great blanket of marble and white plaster, with statues, monuments and fountains in every square. It took the breath away to think that men could build anything so magnificent, and I imagined the hundreds of thousands of people going about their lives in that great sprawling city and felt envy that I was leaving it and may never see it again.

'That has to be the greatest sight in the entire world,' I said to Marcus.

Marcus removed his helmet and smiled at the view. 'Maybe one day we can return at the head of a triumph. Now that would be a sight.'

It was the dream of every aspiring young officer of Rome to one day march through Rome at the head of a column of men, celebrating a great victory. I chuckled at his excitement. Had I ever been so young and innocent? I was certainly beyond it now. I turned my horse away and set us on our way again.

Before leaving, I gave a lot of thought to our route. Although I didn't wish to reach Germany any earlier than necessary, I needed to reach there before the summer's campaigning started for real. Anything less would look like open defiance to Livia, something I dare not do. The most direct route was to take the *Via Cassia* up to Bononia and then over the Alps. However, at this time of year, the eastern mountain passes were treacherous and instead I decided to take the *Via Aurelia* along the coast, which Augustus recently extended. We would then cross the Alps at the pass at Sugusio and once in Gaul we could take the major routes north; it meant for a longer journey but good roads should cover most of the journey and I estimated we could reach Germany by mid to late May. Early enough to comply with my orders and a relaxed enough pace to mean we needn't overexert ourselves on the journey.

In next few days we made good time along the coastal road, finding inns to stop each night on the well-populated road from the city. I envisioned it being a miserable journey with little cheer and me longing for home. However, I was wrong. I was stiff and sore each evening from the day's riding but my body felt invigorated to be back in the travelling routine. My head was clear now that I was free from Seneca's parties and the temptations of unwatered wine. I found my spirits rising despite our destination. Germany was still a long way off; right now I was enjoying the Italian countryside in the spring sunshine as we made steady progress north.

I was also becoming used to the company of Marcus Scaeva. When we left Rome I was distrustful of him, thinking him a spy for Livia, someone to keep an eye on me and to make sure I fulfilled my mission. But the more I got to know Marcus, the more apparent it became that he was wholly unsuited to this task, being far too open and honest to be using any subterfuge.

'Do you think Commander Varus will let me command any men when we reach him?' Marcus asked me when we were mounting up after a particularly good meal in a small inn just north of the town of Pisae.

This sort of question was common from him; he was brought up on stories of leading men into battle and thought that his senatorial class meant it was something he was born to. Our meal of baked trout put me in a good mood so I decided to answer him this time, 'Would you trust a young man, with no battle experience, with the lives of any other men?'

He frowned at this. 'I guess I wouldn't. But how can I ever prove myself if I am not given the opportunity.'

I laughed at this. 'Oh, don't fret, Marcus. There will be plenty of opportunities for you to bloody your sword in your career, don't worry about that. Just make sure you listen to the centurions around you.'

'Listen to the centurions! But I outrank them!' He sounded outraged as we brought our horses back onto the main road and continued north.

It was another warm day, and I enjoyed the sun on my face. 'So what? Just because you outrank them doesn't mean you know what you're doing. The centurions are veterans. Listen to them and they might just save your life.'

He thought about this for a while. 'Won't they lose respect for me? If I take my lead from them?'

Marcus was not stupid, just naive and inexperienced; he needed to learn some truths. 'Not if it means staying alive. When you're in battle very little else matters. When you're being assailed from all sides, you want to listen to people who have been in that situation before – chain of command be damned.'

'Your orders at Western-Gate Pass. Did your centurions agree with you then?'

'Not all of them, but that was an exceptional situation. Pray to the gods you never find yourself in a similar one.' Throughout our journey, Marcus' faith in my ability remained unshakeable. I wished I shared his confidence in myself. I didn't want to talk of Western-Gate Pass; it was spoiling my good mood. 'We're not going to Germany to lead men into battle, in any case. I am to be an aide to Governor Varus and you are to help where we deem suitable.'

'Do you know Varus?'

'No, I only know of his reputation. He was said to be a strong and capable governor in Syria – firm but honest, they say, although it was before my time there. But I do know Julius Arminius. He is the client king of the Cherusci tribe and our best chance of having a peaceful settlement in the region.'

'How do you know him?'

I thought of my childhood friend with his unruly blonde mop of hair, ready grin, and sharp wit. 'We grew up together and I served with him in Syria. He was an auxiliary commander, an excellent soldier. You'll like him.'

'What makes you so sure?' the sun was high in the sky and Marcus shaded his eyes with his hand as he looked at me.

'Because he was eager to lead men at an early age, just like you. When he was only seventeen, a large patrol he was on was ambushed by a vastly superior force, and his commander was killed. He took command and led his men out safely, cutting their way through the enemy lines.'

As a reward Julius was granted equestrian status and given permanent command of the auxiliary unit – a rare honour for one so young. It happened before I joined him in Syria, whilst I was drunkenly following Augustus' daughter Julia around. When I arrived there and heard how successful Julius was, I was pleased for him, but also secretly seethed with jealousy.

'He was well respected then?' I could tell that Marcus liked the sound of Julius. I wasn't surprised. Marcus was always dreaming of being a hero. Julius really was one.

'Oh yes, his unit was made up of horsemen from his home country and Julius turned them into a real fighting force. They had quite a reputation in the region. No mean achievement in a land beset by raids from the Parthians – who command some of the greatest cavalry in the world.'

Invasions into Parthia had been the downfall of many a famous general, Crassus and Mark Anthony to name but two, and so Augustus, rather than risk further setbacks and despite many senators calling for an all-out war, brokered an uneasy peace with Parthia in return for the legionary standards that had been lost

Roman Mask

to them. This meant for a long and hostile frontier with the eastern empire, and confrontations and conflicts were common.

'Did you ever fight alongside him?' Marcus was warming to the subject.

'Sometimes. I was lead tribune to the Tenth legion based near the river Euphrates, as a permanent guard against Parthian incursions.' I still felt a blossom of pride when I spoke of my former legion – we were a crack unit and were rightly feared by the Parthians. 'We were involved in several large skirmishes and repulsed many raids across the border. Julius' fast-travelling cavalry fought alongside us and proved to be particularly useful in the borderlands, tracking down raiders and maintaining the peace. Julius and I both managed to forge reputations as good soldiers respected by our men.'

I thought back to that time when my whole existence was consumed by training and leading my men well; it felt another lifetime now. I explained to Marcus, 'When my military posting came to an end after four years, I was expected to return to Rome and start a life in politics – now I was proven in the field. But I sent my father a letter, begging him to let me remain in the army and take another military posting immediately. He wasn't happy, saying that I wasn't taking my political career seriously enough, but he couldn't begrudge me one more posting. Tales of my valour in the field were filtering back to Rome, and all agreed I was a good soldier. The military deployment I was given was to Germany.'

'You must have been pleased when you heard the news?' Marcus said brightly.

'For once you're right, Marcus. I was delighted when I heard I was going to Germany.' The more fool me, I now know, but I was unaware back then. 'I celebrated with Julius until late into the night. He was remaining in Syria guarding the frontier with Parthia, but was full of envy that I was to go and fight in his homeland without him. We drank many wine amphorae dry that night.'

'And you went on to prove yourself as great a hero as he ever was!' declared my greatest supporter, Marcus, 'Holding the tribes back at Western-Gate Pass!'

Mention of Western-Gate Pass brought back the cold reality of what happened next. My tone changed to one far cooler. 'You really give me too much credit, Marcus. Enough talk of the past, let's see if we can put some distance between us and Pisae today.' I kicked my horse into a canter and left him behind me. He was left bemused by my abrupt change of mood but soon shrugged and spurred his mount after me.

I circled around my opponent, keeping my breathing even, my *gladius* high, and my eyes focused on his every move. He was stripped to the waist, a light loincloth all that was left protecting his modesty, as his muscles rippled in the cool breeze off the foothills of the mountains.

He struck, faster than a mountain cat, striking for my groin, which I parried, then another strike towards my thigh, one to my stomach, then back to my thigh. Each time I countered, our blades clashing loudly in the quiet woodland clearing. His attacks were concentrating on this lower part of my body, I noticed. Was there a weakness in my defence he has noticed, I wondered? Careful, Gaius, don't let your mind become preoccupied. I needed all my wits, and my reflexes to be fully focused – his speed was such that only my best will keep him at bay.

We circled again. Brambles surrounded the ground we'd chosen. Careful with my footwork, a slip near the edges would finish me. It was time to mount an attack of my own – I struck, my blade in perfect balance with my body, an extension of my arm. I aimed for his torso, and he parried my blade. I struck again and again, and each time he parried, but moved further back. I needed to take advantage of my ascendancy. I struck harder, making my blade more difficult to deflect – I smiled in grim determination to finish him this time, but he took me by surprise, swaying back with surprising agility in a man so large, leaving me striking at thin air. He swung his blade at me, and I desperately raised mine to stop it striking my head. Our blades locked together, but I was now unbalanced – he had the advantage.

'Are you strong enough to hold me, Cassius?' he grunted through gritted teeth, a smile showing on his face. From my position I wasn't, and he knew it. I was sent sprawling to the ground.

I lay prone on the floor, but acted quickly, picking up some dirt from the campsite floor and throwing it in his face as he attempted to lay his sword to my throat. 'Whaaa!' he bellowed, backing off to rub the dirt from his eyes.

I didn't miss my opportunity. I lunged my wooden *gladius* into his belly, scoring a rare victory against him. Laughing, I said, 'That's one for me!'

'Pah! You cheated. I had you.' He spat the remains of the dirt from his mouth, his face breaking into a rueful grin.

'You cannot always expect your opponent to follow the rules of fair play, Marcus. We are not practising in the gymnasium now.' I signalled to him that we should stop. He helped me up from the floor and we returned to our campfire. 'Besides, I have to win sometimes, Marcus. You have been getting it your own way far too much lately.' Marcus won two or three bouts for every victory I managed. He was faster and more evenly balanced than I was; as hard as it was for me to accept – he was the better swordsman.

'You still have a few tricks you can teach me.' He smiled as he sat down heavily beside me at the small fire we'd built by the roadside. 'Not many have ever beaten me, Cassius. And none as many times as you.' Despite being the better swordsmen, he still looked up to me.

I stretched my arm, loosening the knots in my muscles. 'It's good for me to match *gladius* with you. I think my sword work is improving. It takes being matched against someone better to raise my level.'

Marcus blushed at the praise, but I knew he relished the compliment. He tried to hide his pleasure by changing the subject. 'How long until we reach Sugusio?' he asked.

We were already in the southern foothills of the Alps, deep within the Romanised province of Cisalpine Gaul, and the weather was noticeably chill. 'We'll reach it tomorrow,' the last road marking said it was less than twenty miles, 'then we can sleep in a proper bed. We'll find the best inn in the city.'

'Do you think the journey through the Alps will be difficult?' he asked, and he lay down by the fire, his head pillowed on his cloak.

'It shouldn't be too hard going by this route. Crossing through the western passes is not deemed a difficult crossing these days. It's one of the reasons I chose this path to Germany.' I had even been tempted to bypass the Alps altogether and take the route along the sea towards the Greek city of Massilia, but decided that would be testing Livia's patience too far – that would require us to travel an extra hundred and fifty miles at least.

'Have you ever travelled over the eastern passes of the Alps?' he said in a distracted tone as he lay staring at the stars overhead. He was probably reliving our last sword bout – correcting any perceived errors in his mind, in order to come back stronger next time.

I answered quietly, 'Yes, and I never wish to relive that experience again.' Marcus was no longer listening. A chill ran down my spine, and I threw another small branch on the fire, shaking my head to try and clear it of the past and bad memories; as always, I failed.

The eastern passes had only been made passable in recent years by the almost complete extermination of the Alpine tribes by Augustus' armies. Even so, it was never a comfortable journey, and I was desperate when I last travelled them. I looked over at the good-natured Marcus and thought to myself, 'Does the same path lay in store for him? Will he leave Rome a hero, only to return a broken man?'

The following day we arrived in the city of Sugusio which was flourishing from the trade with Gaul and the rest of the empire. Wealthy merchants swaggered around town with round full bellies and stout women sat by the doors to their homes, with ruddy cheeks from the Alpine air, and chatted to one another in a dialect of Latin that held the strong regional burr of Cisalpine Gaul.

We stopped to admire the magnificent triumphal arch, erected by the local praefect twenty years before in Augustus' honour. It was a strange mix of Gallic and Roman traditions and showed the prosperity the town now enjoyed since Augustus had improved the trade routes between the two nations.

We took a room in a friendly and well-kept inn, near the centre of town, and enjoyed a fine meal of mountain hare, stuffed with pine kernels and mixed nuts, and a peppery sauce. Marcus and I both ate with gusto and I raised a toast in honour of our imminent crossing of the Alps. 'May we return soon, in equally good health!'

Marcus lifted his cup of well-watered wine. 'With my thanks to my intrepid commander!'

I acknowledged his thanks with a broad smile and clashed my cup against his. 'If you are lucky, maybe we can find you a nice Celtic girl, once we make it through the Alps.'

Marcus flushed a bright red but tried to pass off the remark with false bravado. 'Yes, just what I was thinking,' he stammered, but I wasn't fooled; I noticed that he never met my eye when answering.

To judge by how my sister reacted to him, and also the various serving wenches we had encountered on our journey, he was not short of female admirers. But he was clumsy when speaking to them, and looked more the young boy than the powerful athlete when confronted by a young woman. Could it be that Marcus was innocent in matters of the flesh as well as being a virgin to the battlefield? His behaviour certainly suggested so; possibly this journey would make a man of him in more ways than one.

I pretended not to notice his uneasiness and finished my wine before making my way up to my room. I realised then that I hadn't drunken to excess since I left Rome; it was strange how little I missed it. Maybe this journey was good for me as well as Marcus.

Once I reached my room, I lay on my bed and thought on this. Since starting our travels my mind had quickly cleared of thoughts of Tita, Seneca, and the other vultures of Rome whom I once described as my friends. Each night, the exhaustion of the journey, and the many sword bouts with Marcus, took me to my bed early, and my body was responding well. In Rome, I had thought of myself as fit, but only now was I really reaching my peak physically. Maybe I wasn't so far removed from the soldier I once was. It was a good thought, and soon I drifted off into a dreamless sleep.

The next morning we replenished our supplies and set out on the well-paved road which passed through the Alps, with towering snow-capped mountains on each side making a spectacular backdrop to our journey. Marcus remarked on their beauty, but each time I looked up at their lofty heights, I had to suppress a shudder of apprehension: the sooner we were through them the better.

We were not the only travellers. Overburdened carts, pulled by straining oxen, passed us by, carrying grain, onions, turnips, and a whole host of other goods grown in the great agricultural fields of southern Gaul and destined for the markets of Roman cities, grown rich and fat from the flourishing trade. There had always been trade along the Alps, but since the conquering brilliance of Julius Caesar, who brought Gaul into the empire, the potential of the two nations had been realised – and what we witnessed here along the Alps was nothing compared to the shipping trade, great sailing behemoths with high prows and sterns, that sailed between Pisae, Cosa, Ostia, and the Gallic ports of Narbo and Massilia. It was no wonder that Rome was so eager to find yet more provinces to tame; after Germany what next? The frontiers were being pushed further back.

We camped by the side of the road each night and sometimes shared our fire with other travellers, exchanging stories and information as we went. By the third day a cold drizzle settled over us, soaking us to the skin and dampening our spirits. Even Marcus' customary good mood was affected and we rode on in silence, water dripping from our cloaks, hands clinging on to our reins tightly to prevent them from shaking from the cold. The sombre conditions and the surroundings turned my mind to the events which led me to crossing the Alps the last time, when I last returned from Germany.

Chapter Seven

After Western-Gate Pass, I tried to resume my military career. The commander of the legions in Germany back then was the dour Tiberius, the same man who'd married Julia years earlier before retiring from public life. After his divorce from Julia, Augustus persuaded him to return to serve once more and used him as his highest ranking commander, with full imperium status, of the Roman forces. The straightforward approach of Tiberius was just what Germany needed, and he was the most capable general I ever met. If he ever knew anything about my earlier connection with his estranged wife, Julia, he never gave any indication. After Western-Gate Pass he clapped me on the shoulder, told me I was a credit to my family and that he was to send a despatch back to Rome, acknowledging my role in the recent battle. Everything was perfect. My commander respected me, the soldiers treated me as a hero, my fellow tribunes envied me; I got everything I wanted, except for one thing: I could no longer do my job.

Even the simplest of patrols or guard duties sent me into a panic. A cold sweat covered my back whenever I left the security of the Roman camp. The forest around the camp started to take on menacing proportions. I imagined wild tribesmen waiting there in their thousands, with spear and dagger and bloodstreaked faces. Just beyond the trees they were hiding; ready to give me the death I escaped at Western-Gate Pass. Worse was to follow. My dreams were plagued by the dead faces of soldiers who died at my side at the pass. They raised accusing fingers at me, and their cold dead eyes haunted me, reminding me that their deaths were my doing. I thought I was losing my mind, but what could I do? My nerve was broken but I couldn't admit this to anyone. Overwhelming fear of anyone discovering my new-found weakness increased my anxiety. Each panic-stricken day was followed by another, with only a fitful night's sleep, full of nightmares and the accusing dead, separating them. I knew it was just a question of time until someone noticed my erratic behaviour and then I was finished. I wasn't the first senior officer to lose my nerve and I wouldn't be the last. The options for such men were strictly limited. If I ran from combat, I would be given two options: either to voluntarily fall on my sword or face execution. Cowards were always treated with contempt.

After one particularly bad day, whilst overseeing a work party being used to clear an area of the forest, I almost completely shamed myself in front of the men. A tree was mistakenly felled just behind where I and a few of my senior centurions were located in a command tent. It fell with a great crash – the terrible wrenching sound of the trunk splitting followed by the sharp bangs of great tree limbs snapping was a cacophony of noise that took us all by complete surprise. The centurions instantly ran out to berate the poor *optio* who was overseeing the tree felling. Good for me they all left the tent – if not they would have seen me break down in tears. The noise, the shock, the sudden fright to my nerves had all been too much, and floods of tears streamed down my face. Before they returned, I managed to clean my face and calm myself down, but it had been too close a call. I knew this couldn't go on.

That night I tried to kill myself. I knelt alone with sword drawn, in my private tent, next to my small camp bed and the few meagre possessions I owned, and thought about my family back home. I thought of my younger sister Antonia, who looked up to me so much, my sombre but proud father, and my ever emotional mother. I thought of my best friend Julius, so much stronger than I ever was. They would all be hurt by this but it was far better this way, I told myself. Being found dead, after taking my own life, would tarnish my reputation somewhat – after all, why had I done it? I must be hiding something? – but it wouldn't completely destroy my family's honour. I'd soon be forgotten, just another casualty in the war with the German tribes – with death all around, one more wouldn't cause much of a stir. I knelt there and with shaking hands I willed myself to push my *gladius* home. I burst into bitter tears of self-hatred when I realised I couldn't do it. Not even the threat of shaming my entire family was enough to let me take my own life. At Western-Gate Pass I'd seen the closeness of death, the reality of my mortality, and found the fear of it stronger than any notion of honour I still might possess. There would be no escape for me by this route. By the gods, I hated myself.

The next day I knew I must leave Germany and soon. I needed to get away from these damn forests and the ghosts of the fallen and I needed to do this quickly, before I was discovered as a coward.

As luck would have it, Tiberius was concerned with other matters. He had just learnt that the Pannonian province was in open rebellion and he was required to join the Roman forces there to quell this uprising. I thought of asking to accompany him, that at least meant leaving Germany, but I wasn't sure whether my nerve could endure that war any better than it could this one. I couldn't take the risk so I outright lied. I went to him and told him, 'Legate, I have just received a letter from my father.'

Tiberius was busy shuffling papers around on his desk, trying to get his things in order before leaving. He was an unattractive man, with bad skin and a perpetual dour expression – it was no wonder Julia had found him distasteful. This was the army, however, and his reputation was respected by all the officers and the men, me included. 'Well, what is it man, why does this concern me?'

I took a deep breath. 'My father says the crops have failed on our estate near Rome, and he cannot deal with the situation as he is required to take up his position as Governor of Sicily. He asks whether I can return and take over the running of things.'

Tiberius looked up at me then. The thick black brows that overhung his dark brooding eyes locked onto mine. 'Leave the army? Now? I need all the good officers I can get – to look after things whilst I'm gone – and you're one of my best. Surely he cannot expect you to leave the legions at such a time?'

I stared straight ahead as I answered, 'The timing is unfortunate, but the pestilence that has ruined all our crops is very severe. Some action must be taken.'

If Tiberius was ever to check any of my story I was finished, I knew that, but I needed to take the risk. Fortunately for me, Tiberius trusted me completely. Why shouldn't he? I was a model officer up until this point and held an unblemished six year record in the legions. He dropped the papers he was holding and said, 'Well, a family's livelihood is often dependent on their eldest son. If you wish to go, I won't prevent it. It is a shame, and you're giving up a lot. Command of your own legion is surely not far away with a new war now assailing us.'

Command of my own legion – something I always dreamt of. 'I understand this, sir, and maybe I can resume my military career at a later date, when my family's immediate crisis has passed.'

Tiberius went back to sorting his papers. 'Then go with my blessing. I'm afraid I cannot speak further on this. I have a lot I need to do before I leave.'

I walked out of his tent and out of the army. I rode out of the camp and galloped my horse almost to death in haste to leave Germany behind me.

As soon as I was away from the frontier I discarded my armour and donned civilian attire. I was a disgrace to the Roman army and let both my commander and legion down at a time when they needed me most.

I remembered conversations with Julius, before I left Syria, when I spoke of the need for the army to take a hard line with cowards and weaklings.

'The legions are only kept strong by sifting out the chaff!' I remembered arguing with him, when we disagreed over the lenient treatment he dished out to a young recruit who struggled from a fear of water and took fright when falling from a pontoon in a bridge-building exercise.

Julius had informed me, in his firm confident manner, that the soldier in question was, 'always calm in combat. I'll just never put him anywhere near water again. Besides, it is nothing to do with you. He is under my command.'

I remember gnashing my teeth in frustration but reluctantly agreeing to his argument; the trooper in question was directly under Julius' command and army decorum allowed that he should be the one who rewarded or punished as he deemed fit. How foolish I looked now. I was the weakling, the one who lost his nerve when tested at the highest level. I wasn't strong enough for the legions.

The next question had been where to go to next. I thought of the shame and the disappointment to my family that a return to Rome would bring. Could I face them and tell them the truth? Would my father disown me? I certainly deserved no better. I rode to the town of Mogontiacum in Gaul and took stock of my position. For the moment, money was not an issue – although it would become so in time, unless I thought of a way to obtain more. In a run-down inn near the outskirts of the city – to avoid notice – I started to drown my sorrows in wine. During my years in the legions I always drank my wine well-watered. The year I spent drinking at wild parties with Julia and Iullus were now a distant memory; that run-down inn in Mogontiacum was where I first started to return down the old path. I stayed at that inn for several days, simply drinking each day, taking very little notice of my surroundings and wondering where life was taking me next. The unwatered wine initially helped dull the pain and despair in my heart but it was no answer to my problems – I was cut adrift from all I knew in the world: family, legion, elevated position.

I ended up drifting through the new Roman settlements of Gaul; wine was ever my companion. After two months the money ran short. With no way of receiving more from my father, I took work from a local merchant in a small town. I was still a large and imposing man who was skilled in the use of weapons; he took me on as a guard for his warehouse. The pay was not much, but he never asked questions as to why such a well-spoken man needed work as a guard when my background was obviously one of privilege. Besides, my needs weren't much, wine was cheap and I cared for nothing else. I lost that job after I was found drunk and asleep by him one morning. I found other work quite quickly but then lost that job in similar circumstances. No one else in the town was prepared to hire a known drunk so I travelled to the larger city of Lugdunum, where it was possible to lose oneself in the large mass of humanity.

I started to become bitter, and blamed all my troubles on others. I got drunk in inns and started ranting to any who cared to listen. I blamed politicians, the craven senators who sent soldiers to die in order to protect their position in life; I blamed Augustus for turning the Republic into a dictatorship; I blamed the officer class in the army, the men who came from privileged rank and did nothing to earn their commissions; I blamed anything and anyone that reminded me of my former life and the position I came from; all these were the true enemies of Rome, I argued when deep into my cups. Others argued with me and fights were common. By this stage my sanity was seriously in jeopardy and respectable citizens gave me a wide birth.

After of few months of this, my seditious talk and endless brawls brought me to the attention of the city watch who deposited me outside their gates and told me to leave and never to return. I travelled east, sometimes working, sometimes begging for enough coin to buy enough wine to keep me warm through the cold winter nights. I arrived at a small town near the base of the Alps and after being ejected from there, resolved to return to Italy. Anything had to be better than this miserable life in the Roman provinces; and besides, I missed my home. Maybe I could get to see Rome one more time. I decided to try and make the hazardous journey through the eastern passes.

The passes through the Alps had only become passable in recent memory. Tiberius and his brother Drusus, under the orders of Augustus, waged many brutal campaigns through the region twenty years previously, destroying the Alpine clans and forcing the survivors from their traditional homeland. This left the region largely unpopulated and meant being waylaid by bandits was now unlikely. However, little aid was ever to be found for travellers caught in bad weather and I was hopelessly underprepared for such a hazardous journey. My luck held for the first few days. The weather was cold, but the skies were clear and bright, and I became hopeful that I could get quickly through the pass.

On the sixth day, disaster struck. A blizzard came in from the north-east, carrying mountains of snow on the back of a cold biting wind. My threadbare cloak and inadequate clothing offered me little protection from the bitter cold as I struggled through the thick snowdrifts which were filling the pass. I should have died there; I welcomed it – anything to get me away from the cold howling wind. But then, the god Janus smiled on me and showed me another path. I noticed a

Roman Mask

small shepherd's stone hut, far up on one of the passes' hillsides. It was almost obscured by the deepening snow and travelling up to it was risky; night was coming, and if this stone hut didn't afford me shelter, death was sure to follow. I took a chance and climbed up to it, cutting my frozen hands on the sharp jagged rocks that lined the route up the hillside. On arrival, I was gladdened to see that the hut's roof was still sound; a thick thatch covered the hut, and I pushed open the door and found my salvation. Not only was the hut dry and sheltered from the wind, a previous traveller had even laid the base of a fire – tinder, and dry wood – in its small hearth. My hands shook so much, it was a struggle to light the wood with the flint and tinder, but eventually I got a fire burning and I blessed the goddess Vesta for this safe haven, and blessed the traveller who left this small refuge so well equipped. I noticed a further pile of dry wood in a corner of the hut. I swore to make a sacrifice in his honour on my return to Rome, and have often wondered at the identity of my saviour that day.

I stayed in the hut for a further three days as the blizzard raged outside. When it finally broke, my supplies were all finished and I left it hungry but dry. To my shame, I did not have the time to replenish the hut's stocks of wood, but I did leave the hearth with enough tinder and wood to light at least one small fire. It wasn't much, but it was all my malnourished body could achieve under the circumstances.

A further long, hungry ten days travelling was needed until I finally made it through the eastern pass. I was emaciated, my clothes little more than rags, and a beard covered a face of bloodshot eyes, which glowed with the unhealthy tint of madness, when the bedraggled version of me finally reached Italy. Only nine months had passed since I'd left the army a well-respected senior tribune. My fall from grace was sharp and spectacular. With nowhere else to turn, I returned to Rome, no longer caring what my family thought of me.

I didn't go to the family estate outside the city; I walked through Rome and took in the great wondrous city which I hadn't seen for seven long years. Her magnificence brought tears to my eyes, and upon reaching the Forum, I fell to my knees and knelt there staring at the marble colonnades and statues and swore that I would never leave her again. It wasn't long until a member of Augustus' Praetorian Guards moved me on, thinking me a beggar and a nuisance. There was no fight left in me. I didn't resist and moved away from the centre of Rome to areas where a man of my appearance didn't warrant a second glance. It was here that a chance encounter did much to turn my life around. I was walking through Rome's backstreets when a man in civilian attire, but the military gait of a soldier, was walking briskly in the opposite direction. He looked at me quizzically as he passed, and I flinched, turning my face away, not wanting to bring any attention to myself. I shuffled on but he stopped. 'You there! Wait … do I know you?'

It had been years since I was last in Rome and my appearance was nothing like when I was last here, so I thought it unlikely; either way, there was no one I wished to see so I continued on my way. He ran up behind me and grabbed my arm; I spun round ready to strike him, but then noticed the hand on his other arm was missing. I looked up into his face for the first time and recognised the face of Spento, a junior tribune who served alongside me in Germany before losing his hand in a brief skirmish at the start of the summer's campaign.

'By all the gods, it is you! Cassius Aprilis, here in Rome! By the gods, you look a sight!' His eyes were full of compassion; Spento always held a soft heart.

Never before or since have I ever been as ashamed of my appearance as that moment in time. I cowered from his gaze as tears welled up. 'Please, Spento. I am not the man you think I am. That man is dead.'

He put his arm around me and softly said, 'No, Cassius, you're not dead. You may wish it now, but that time will pass, I assure you. Come with me now. My home is not far.'

I let him lead me, my face huddled against his breast, and he took me into his home on the Quirinal Hill. His house was well constructed and a full household of slaves awaited him. He instructed them to prepare food for us both. I was ravenous and ate, but still tears rolled down my cheeks from shame and self-disgust. He ate also, but in silence, never once asking me questions of why I was there, or what brought me to such a pitiful state – for which I was hopelessly grateful.

After eating he gave me the opportunity to bathe and wash the accumulated grime from my body. A razor was left out for me to shave but my hands shook too much and I had to instruct a slave to do it for me; another indignity which I have never forgotten, and I have never let a slave shave me since. Afterwards I was given clean clothes to wear and only then did Spento come and speak to me.

I awaited him in a small bedroom which was given me; it had a single bed, with immaculately clean linen sheets and a small table and stool; compared to the accommodation I was now used to, it was a palace. I sat on the bed staring at the floor and he pulled up the stool and spoke to me. 'I heard about Western-Gate Pass. I guess it was pretty bad.'

I nodded but said nothing.

He scratched the stump of his arm, where his hand used to be. 'You know what I think?'

I was terrified by what he must think of me and looked up at him.

His eyes met mine, but they still held compassion. 'I think some injuries leave no marks but hurt as much as any blow to the body. I lost my hand in Germany, but what hurt me the most was feeling I let the legion down when I had to leave them.'

'But you were discharged with honour. You were given no choice but to leave.'

'Even so, the feeling remained.' He stood up and walked to the doorway. 'I think you received a blow that hurt you as much as losing a hand but you never knew it.'

'How so?' my voice croaked with emotion.

'The man I knew in Germany was the best soldier I ever met. He would never let his body reach the state yours is now in. Something happened to you in Germany and you blame yourself. It is not your fault, Cassius. War brings out the worst in people.'

I stared down at my feet. 'Many would think differently from you.'

'They were not there. I was. I know.' He let out a breath, as if saying something he did not wish to. 'You can stay here for as long as you wish, but do the army seek you?'

He was asking whether I deserted. I shook my head. 'Tiberius gave me leave to go.'

'That is good. I will see you tomorrow.' He left and I slept in a clean bed with a full stomach. It felt good, and for the first time since Western-Gate Pass, I felt the anxiety around me lessen ever so slightly.

After resting for a couple of days at the house of Spento, I deemed I was ready to face my family again. Spento lent me a horse and I rode out to the family estate with a knot of trepidation in my stomach. I knew my father would not be present, thank the gods. He was now the Governor of Sicily and ruled that province to the south. I knew my mother never accompanied him there, however. Their relationship was always strained and over the last few years, according to letters I received from Antonia, their marriage had broken down completely. He lived in the governor's residence on Sicily alone, taking no new mistress, his rigid morals preventing him betraying his marriage vows, even if he no longer lived with his wife. So I was expecting to see my mother still at the estate; that alone was a daunting prospect. There was no way to disguise my emaciated frame, which I'd gained from nine months of poor living and near starvation, but I looked respectable in the clean clothes Spento furnished me with and my neatly trimmed hair and shaved face.

I rode my horse through the gates and dismounted and handed the reins to a young slave I didn't recognise; after seven years it was unsurprising some of the slaves were different. Then the familiar face of Patrellis came out into the courtyard, who greeted me with a great bear hug, before sending another slave to give word to my mother that her son was back.

As soon as I saw my mother, a small petite woman with long grey hair and a similar elfin face to that of Antonia, she rushed into my arms in floods of tears, telling me how she'd missed me and how she loved me.

'Mother, get hold of yourself, please, stop crying.' I tried to assure her as best I could, but she was always very emotional: it was why my stoic father found living with her so hard.

'But I have my hero son back at last. Your father is so proud of you,' she said, still clinging onto me with racking sobs. Antonia warned me that she still didn't accept that her marriage was over and often referred to him as still being around.

'Hero? What do you mean, Mother?' I was genuinely surprised.

A smiling Patrellis filled me in. 'We received word from Rome. Tiberius sent a despatch back to the Senate, praising your bravery in person. Everyone in Rome knows the story of your exploits at Western-Gate Pass.'

I'd forgotten of Tiberius' pledge to write to Rome: said to me before the both of us left Germany. I presumed he meant a brief side-note in his official reports on the war. But no, he'd sent a despatch naming me in person, read in the Senate itself, eulogising my bravery. I was to find out that the Pannonian revolt that Tiberius left to put down was turning out to be more serious than first thought. He would be tied up in that conflict for at least another two to three years, by which time my untimely exit from the army would be well forgotten. The bad news in Pannonia meant that Rome needed something to celebrate, and my action at Western-Gate Pass fitted the bill perfectly: a hopeless cause, victory achieved against all the odds, and a true hero in the middle of it – me. It was a complete distortion of the truth, but in the following days I learnt that it was no good explaining this to anyone; they thought I was just being too modest. I began to enjoy the praise I received from strangers who wished to meet the great hero of Western-Gate Pass. After months of hating myself, it felt so good to be well thought of again.

I didn't fool everyone. Antonia, for one, noticed how anxious I was in those early days and how I flinched at loud noises or broke into a cold sweat when voices were raised in a room. She realised that my experience in Germany was worse than I was letting on, but she didn't probe further, for which I was grateful, and in time all outward signs of my nerves disappeared.

Well-wishers flocked to me, from Rome and the surrounding countryside. All were agreed that I was a hero and deserved great credit. If any asked why I was back, I simply told them that there were affairs I needed to attend to in Rome and Tiberius had given me leave to go. It was close enough to the truth to not arouse suspicion, and soon I almost started believing it myself. I still dreaded my mother, or worse, my father via letter, asking why I returned, but they never did; maybe they were so pleased to have me back alive and well they didn't want to question it further.

Before long I returned to Rome, to stay in my father's house on the Caelian Hill, and took Patrellis and Prisca along with me. I started to attend the *Gymnasium of the Horse*, and built my body back up to its previous strength. I got to know all the major socialites of Rome and was invited to all the best parties, and the distractions of Rome soon started to entice me in.

Germany was far behind me; I could now enjoy Rome and receive the rewards of a hero.

Except, here I was, heading back to Germany. Back to the land which took my courage and shredded my nerves. Back to the land of hulking great blonde muscular warriors and damp, mist-shrouded forests. Oh gods, save me from this fate.

Chapter Eight

Finally the cold and wet drizzle relented as we emerged from the Alpine passes and made our way through the foothills into Gaul. Despite our uneventful journey through the Alps, I was still pleased to leave them behind; something about the looming presence of the towering mountains was always intimidating, despite their beauty. From southern Gaul we took the main military road and headed to Lugdunum, passing through flat arable land in bright sunshine, and both our spirits rose. All around us, fields were being tilled and seeds sown by prosperous Gallic farmers; by summer all these fields would team with barley and wheat. Rich villas owned by Roman settlers or Romanised Gauls dotted the landscape and the impression was one of wealth and abundance. It was hard to envisage that, less than seventy years before, Patrellis' grandparent's generation were roaming these lands, with great broadswords, in fearsome warrior clans.

We were leading our horses as we walked; it was one of the many breaks we gave them from carrying our weight. The horses were bearing up well on the long journey, due to our good care of them.

Marcus strolled next to me on the well-paved road and gestured around him. 'You see the majesty of Rome. These people have never seen such wealth. Surely they've never been so happy.'

I smiled and nodded in agreement, but said, 'You don't think they'd prefer to go back to their warrior past then?'

Marcus looked at me incredulously. 'Why would they? Look at all they have gained.'

I grinned. 'Yes, but don't you think their previous lifestyle was more exciting? What would you rather be: a farmer or a warrior?'

Marcus laughed. 'You have me there. Who'd want to spend their days tilling fields – give me a *gladius* rather than scythe and plough. The poor old Gauls, we did them a disservice.'

'You can't halt civilisation. One day you will realise the benefits of a quieter life, just as the Gauls did.' I thought of my home in Rome, and the simple pleasures of relaxing in my garden on a bright spring day.

'Me? Never. I was born to be a soldier,' Marcus proclaimed with all the certainty of youth.

'How old are you Marcus?' I asked him.

He looked cagey and replied, 'I turned eighteen last summer.'

Only eighteen, even younger than I first thought. His large muscular frame made him appear older. 'You're only eighteen and yet you think you know what life has in store for you. I think when you meet the other soldiers in our camp in Germany you'll see a less noble side of soldiering.' I thought of the crude humour of the men, the farting and belching. A military Roman camp was the cleanest and most sanitary in the world, yet when you put several thousand men together in close proximity, you couldn't get away from the smell. 'The men take great pleasure in breaking in new tribunes.'

'Oh, don't worry about the men. I've lived most of my life in a Roman camp. They hold no fears.'

I was astonished. I never thought of his past. 'Really? How? You're so young.'

'My mother died when I was eight years old, shortly after my father returned from campaigning in Germany. He was appointed a tribune in the Praetorian Guards, a great honour. When my mother died he didn't know what to do with me, so I joined him in the military camp. I have lived there ever since.'

Brought up in a military camp? A less suitable upbringing was hard to imagine for a young boy. No wonder he was so desperate for military glory. The Praetorians were all veterans from the wars: he must have been listening to stories of their heroics – some true, others embellished – before he grew the first hairs on his balls. What was his father thinking, bringing him into such an environment? 'An unorthodox upbringing,' was all I said.

Marcus ran his hand through his short brown hair. 'Yes, it was, I grant you. I took the death of my mother badly, and my father didn't want to leave me in the care of a house slave. I am grateful for all he did for me.'

I was touched by his honesty; finally the military bravado was absent. 'How did your mother die?'

'She died giving birth to my younger sister, who also perished.' His tone changed to one of reverence. 'I am told she fought until the end, never once giving up hope. She was a true Matron of the Republic.'

It was no wonder he was so awkward around women. He cannot have met many women in the military camp he was brought up in: only a very slack legate ever let women in an encampment – they always caused trouble with the men – so it was probable that Marcus' only knowledge of women was the relationship he once held with his long-dead mother: someone he plainly now idealised. What a mixed up young man, I thought, as I gave his shoulder an affectionate clasp. He looked to give himself a mental shake, and the cheerful boyish enthusiasm returned. 'Enough of this, let's look forward to the *gladius* training tonight. I'm sure I've perfected that new sweeping move you taught me. You will see it this evening when we practise.'

I laughed. 'It's customary not to warn your opponent beforehand.'

'Ha! Little good it will do you. I'm improving every day.'

We both were. I felt my physical fitness was as good as it had ever been, whilst Marcus' swordsmanship was now so good that it was becoming harder and harder for me to score even the odd victory against him. He was probably right: even giving me prior warning of what he planned wouldn't prevent him from him soundly thrashing me once again. I let him continue his good-natured boasting, whilst I drifted away and started to daydream about my own past.

I supposed mine and Julius' upbringing in Augustus' Palatine school was also unusual, but unlike Marcus, at least we got to know girls. I was just fifteen when Julius and I lost our virginity together to two young sisters who visited the school each day with their father, the school's baker, who delivered his freshly baked bread.

Julius spotted them as they waited by their cart, whilst their father was embroiled with one of the school's keepers, regarding payment. The eldest was at least a year older than us, the younger maybe a year less, and they both had thick raven-black hair, thin supple waists, dark olive skin, and winning smiles. 'Gaius, let's go and have some fun with those girls,' he said excitedly.

'Don't be ridiculous. What do you want to speak to the likes of them for? We'll get into trouble.' The two girls were far below our class. To be caught conversing with them would mean a severe reprimand from our teachers. Besides, I was a young pompous prig at that age. 'What will the others say if they see us speaking to them?' I imagined the scornful ridicule of the other students, who seized any opportunity to tease anyone who didn't conform to the rigid social structures of Rome.

Julius was completely unconcerned by my worries. He was different from the other boys – he liked to challenge conventions. 'Stop worrying. It's only a bit of fun.'

Julius sauntered over to them with a cocky swagger, with me lagging reluctantly behind. 'Good morning, fine ladies. What a lovely day to be out and about, don't you think?' he asked.

The two girls giggled and huddled together. 'My, he's a pretty young thing,' remarked the eldest daughter to her sister.

'Do you think he has that golden thatch anywhere else on his body,' giggled the younger. They both spoke with the rough Latin dialect of the cheap tenement buildings of the Subura district: a notorious slum area, which housed many of the Roman poor.

The ever confident Julius was not the least perturbed by their coarseness. 'Sweet ladies, allow me to introduce myself. I am Julius Arminius, and this is my colleague, Cassius Aprilis. Both of us have the honour of studying in this fine establishment.'

They both let out a long whistle together, amused at his flowery tone. The younger giggled. 'The blonde barbarian speaks better than us, Amata. Do you think he bathes like a Roman as well.'

Normally, questioning Julius' heritage, or perceived lack of civilisation, was a sure precursor to violence, but this time Julius simply bowed with an elaborate flourish, and gave them both a roguish wink.

The eldest, Amata, responded. 'He looks clean enough to me, Sulia.' More giggling. 'What about the other one?' She turned to me. 'Haven't they taught you to speak yet?'

I wasn't as confident as Julius, but managed, 'A pleasure to meet you,' in my pitch perfect Latin.

They both laughed, and the younger, Sulia, said, 'You look like a proper Roman?'

'Cassius is from one of the finest families in Rome, a true patrician,' declared Julius grandly.

If Julius thought he was going to come across deference from the two young girls, he was soon put right by the eldest. 'Is that supposed to impress us? Anyway, what's he doing hanging around with the likes of you?'

Julius bristled at the insult, but managed to keep a smile on his face. 'Cassius and I have been friends since childhood. We're closer than brothers,'

'In that case, you better bring him tonight.' Amata spotted her father returning and started to shoo us away.

I glanced anxiously towards their father and tried to pull Julius away, who said before leaving, 'Then we will see you again?'

Amata said hurriedly, 'Meet us when the moon is high in the sky, down by the old temple off the *Via Valeria* on the Esquiline Hill. Now go!'

I wanted to tell them that we weren't allowed out of the school after dark, but received a healthy whack from Julius. 'We'll be there,' he said as we backed away quickly.

Just before we were out of earshot, Sulia loudly whispered, 'And bring wine!'

I wasn't sure whether the baker heard, but he scowled as he spotted us running up the school's steps, our hearts beating.

'You can't be serious, Julius. We can't meet them out of the school grounds!' I was horrified by the risk, but excited as well.

'Why not, it'll be fun!'

That night we both absconded over the school's wall, each clutching a wineskin of the finest *Casinum* red, which we stole from the school's stores. Amata and Sulia met us where we arranged, outside the gates of the temple of Juno, an old temple near the foot of the Esquiline in the east of the city, which had seen better days and was now barely used. Most of the temples of Rome had been restored by Augustus and made from fine marble, but this one was still constructed from ancient mud and wattle walls: he probably thought one in such a poor area wasn't worth the effort.

'You've the wine?' was Amata's first question.

'Yes,' Julius and I chorused together in unison.

Sulia laughed. 'They sound eager, Amata,'

'Don't they just!' Amata gave us a great big smile, and whispered to us, 'But we need to sneak into the temple grounds first. There's a hole in the wall around the side.'

'We can't, that'll dishonour Juno!' I was never the most devout religious student, but even I knew that such an act was sacrilegious.

Both the girls laughed at me, and Amata came and grabbed the wine from my hands. She said scornfully, 'Well, you can always go back to your patrician's school if you prefer. But me and Sulia are going in. She turned to Julius and asked, 'Are you coming, barbarian?'

Julius never could resist a challenge, and said, 'I'm with you,' and the three of them ran off, laughing, to find the hole in the wall.

I was left alone and for the briefest moment considered returning to the school, but I soon followed, located the hole in the wall, which showed evidence of regular use, and crawled through into the temple grounds. The temple garden was overgrown and wild; the temple overseer was obviously slovenly and didn't

Roman Mask

take proper care of it. I located Julius and the two girls by the sound of their laughter; I only hoped that the temple was empty at night-times, they were hardly being discreet. The three of them sat in a circle outside an empty groundskeeper's hut, already taking swigs of the strong unwatered wine.

Sulia looked pleased to see me when I appeared. 'You decided that we were worth the risk then, rich-boy?'

I said nothing, just sat down next to Julius and grabbed the wineskin from him. I took a large gulp. Julius clapped me on the shoulder, and the four of us set about devouring the wine.

The two girls weren't much for conversation; they spent most of the time giggling – when they weren't guzzling our wine – but Amata asked Julius, 'So what type of barbarian are you?'

Julius' eye's flashed anger, but he controlled himself and replied, 'My blood was originally Germanic, but I am now a true Roman.'

The two girls laughed and Sulia said, 'You can't become Roman, silly. You're either Roman or you're not.'

Julius gritted his teeth. 'I am now a Roman citizen, just like you two!' He must be furious, I thought. Julius was a royal prince who'd been awarded Roman citizenship as a reward for his father's co-operation with Rome, yet here were two baker's daughters from the poorest region of Rome, uncultured and uncouth, who plainly thought they were superior to him simply because they were born Roman.

Amata placed her hand on her younger sister's arm: the two girls looked frightened by Julius' fierce tone. 'Shush! Sulia, don't upset him. He brought the wine remember.'

An uncomfortable silence spread out between us all until the anger left Julius' eyes and a smile returned to his face. 'I apologise. I didn't mean to scare you.'

Amata seemed reassured by his smile and tried to placate him further. 'Don't worry, I like your blonde locks and fearsome blue eyes – it leaves a touch of the animal in you.'

I winced at the remark but Julius took it well, laughed, took a large pull on the wine, and the tension dissipated. After a while he started to joke with the two girls, teasing them about their uncultured accents and course dialect. They roared with laughter when he mimicked their voices and Amata playfully tousled his hair and pinched his large biceps. 'Such a strong young man,' she teased.

The wine helped my nerves a little, but I was still awkward around the two girls. They were hardly the brightest girls you could meet. I certainly shouldn't have been intimidated by them, but I still found conversation difficult.

Why was it so hard? They're not the first girls I've met, I told myself. On visits back to my father's estate, Julius and I played often enough with Numeria – daughter of the neighbouring estate and, if my father got his way, my future betrothed – but I'd known her since birth, and talking to her felt little different than talking to Julius. There was a strange barrier between myself and the girls that left me tongue-tied and inhibited.

Luckily, sparkling conversation was not what they'd come for, and once they'd drank their fill of wine, they made it clear they had other intentions for us. Amata led Julius inside the groundskeeper's hut with a big smile. This left me outside with Sulia and an awkward silence ensued. I'd barely spoken to Sulia all night, directing most of my questions at the elder girl, Amata. The silence stretched on into eternity – I couldn't think of anything to say – it was agonising.

Eventually Sulia let out a breath of exasperation and demanded of me, 'Aren't you even going to kiss me?'

I was shocked by her forwardness but was still excited as I nervously moved over to her and gingerly kissed her brow, then her cheek.

'Not like that, you fool!' she guffawed, then stuck her tongue in my mouth and grabbed my hand, placing it squarely on her right breast.

Gods! She tasted of wine and smelt of baker's flour, but her enthusiastic wild body writhing up against mine was sending me into raptures of desire. Better still, the soft yielding plump breast under my hand now worked itself free of her light tunic and her erect nipple was now exposed. I placed my mouth over it, and as I suckled, she moaned with pleasure. I was unsure what to do next, but she wasn't. She hitched her tunic up over her hips and exposed the dark mound of thick black hair between her legs. I fumbled with shaking hands at my groin, pulling up my tunic, and tried to guide myself into her – as I had heard the other boys in the school boast it was done – but my clumsiness and inexperience meant I was making a terrible job of it. She giggled again at my ineptitude and took hold of me, in her cool hands, and put it in herself. The warm sensation was all-consuming and I quickly pumped away in excitement. It didn't take long before I completed ten thrusts, and I discharged into her with a wild scream of pleasure. I collapsed on top of her, delighted with my performance and inordinately happy with myself.

She was less convinced and complained that she preferred it, 'when it goes on for longer', and that, 'that's what you get when you play with young boys who don't know what the gods gave them their cock for.' She pushed me off her and pulled her tunic back down over her hips and searched around for the depleted wine skin.

Roman Mask

I didn't care about her disappointment. I was now a man in my own eyes, and when I walked back to the school with Julius, high up on the Palatine Hill, we regaled each other with tales of our sexual prowess.

Julius and I saw them several more times after that. We took care that none of the other boys found out, and sneaked out of the school at night for clandestine meetings.

The brief affair was abruptly cut short by their father, who married them both off to two merchant sons from Pompeii. They never even got the chance to say goodbye; we only found out when their father came to deliver the bread one day without them. I never felt anything other than carnal lust for Sulia, but I was slightly crestfallen when she first left Rome. I admitted as much to Julius, but he told me not to worry about her. He said that he'd had her himself, and she wasn't anything to fret about. I was furious with him, and struck him hard in the face, felling him to the ground – the first time I ever achieved this in a fight – but he just looked up from the floor in bemusement and shouted, 'Why do you care? They are too far below your rank to be anything more than a bit of fun. Stop taking it so seriously!'

I realised he was right. They were baker's daughters; I was a senator's son from a noble patrician family. My temper cooled, and I apologised for hitting him as I helped him off the floor. He smiled and rubbed his jaw. 'By the gods, Gaius, if you fuck as well as you hit, she won't be forgetting you in a hurry.' We laughed together and before long forgot about the two girls and moved on to other conquests.

It was funny remembering Amata and Sulia. I wonder what they are doing now, I thought. I hope their husbands proved to be better lovers than me, I laughed to myself.

'Why are you laughing?' asked Marcus, snapping me out of my reverie. 'Surely you don't still think you're the better blade?'

I looked over at my young companion. 'My dear Marcus, you'll learn there is more to the measure of a man than the speed of his sword.' I resolved to find Marcus a woman as soon as we reached Lugdunum.

The weather stayed pleasant in the few days it took to ride up to the large town of Lugdunum, a major trading centre of Gaul, home to both Celts and Roman settlers – rich, prosperous, and the personification of Roman Gaul. The same town I'd almost drunk myself to death in four years previously. Thatched cottages lay nestled against grander Roman buildings with tiled roofs and glassed windows. More of the town was paved than I remembered, and a new monument in the town square had been erected in Augustus' honour. Smoke from the cottage's chimneys mixed with that from the many forges and tanneries to give the unmistakable smell of a major settlement.

I felt a little trepidation at revisiting an area so full of painful memories, but I held my head high as I rode through the newly cobbled streets of the town, Marcus beside me, both looking resplendent in our tribunes armour; even if it was by now a little travel stained.

'We could stay in the army camp. Why do you want to stay in the town?' asked Marcus.

Lugdunum was home to two Roman legions, the centre of Rome's military presence in Gaul. Politeness would demand that I at least paid my respects to the military commander before we left, but I had no intention of sleeping in the military camp – I'd never find Marcus a woman there. 'We will be spending the entire summer in a Roman camp. Let's enjoy the last vestiges of civilisation whilst we can.'

I trotted my horse over the stone bridge which spanned the river that ran through the town, and noticed one of the broken-down inns I'd frequented in my last stay here. I recognised old Edan, sat slumped on a wooden table outside, as drunk as ever I remembered him. I was glad to see him still alive; he spent every day in a similar state of drunkenness – it was amazing how some old drunks could carry on going, when healthy fit soldiers can die from the mildest ailment. For sure, the god Bacchus, if he looked on you fondly, looked after his own. I wasn't planning on meeting any old acquaintances if I could help it, so I rode past him and the inn. I doubted that anyone would recognise me now, clean shaven and gleaming with health, but I wanted to take no chances. I took Marcus to an inn situated in the merchant's quarter at the top of a small hill – this inn was grander and more expensive than the others in the lower town, and I had therefore avoided it – here I could be anonymous.

We gave our horses to the young slave who worked as the inn's stable boy. I was telling the young boy how to care for the horses when the innkeeper, a fat Celt with a magnificent long moustache, came to greet us in person. 'Noble Roman officers, welcome! You do my establishment great honour. Please let us take your saddlebags.' He directed another young slave, with Germanic colouring and a slight limp, to take our saddlebags. 'Will you be staying the night or are you just after a hot meal before joining the military camp?'

'We'll be staying the night. Please furnish us with two rooms. Make sure they're clean and the rushes on the floor have been changed recently,' I told him whilst passing the bags over to the slave.

The innkeeper looked delighted, a great toothy smile partially obscured by his facial hair. 'Of course, only the finest for our Roman guests!' His cheerful manner was slightly spoilt by him pausing to flick the young slave around the head for some misdemeanour I couldn't fathom.

'Two rooms?' queried Marcus. In most of the inns along the journey we had shared the one with two beds.

'Why not,' I answered, 'we can afford it.' Along our journey we were entitled to stay in any inn or way station free of charge, as we held a warrant from the Senate, but in the inns I chose to pay my own way. Money was not an issue, and I liked to keep the innkeepers happy.

We walked into the busy common room, with a great roaring fire in the hearth, where merchants sat, drank, and ate the roast pork which was spitted across the fire. There was a spirited cheerfulness to the scene and I decided to have our evening meal here, once we had seen our rooms.

We took a table near the fire and ordered two helpings of the pork, alongside some roasted chestnuts and turnips. We ate this with some of the local wine, but I looked on in dismay as I saw how heavily Marcus always watered his wine from the clay jug of water on the table – I would never get him to approach a woman unless I manage to get him to relax a little. I called over a serving girl and ordered two Celtic ales, which most of the other merchants were happily drinking away. She returned promptly and laid them on our table with a shy smile at Marcus, who ignored her and asked me, 'What's this? This is what the locals drink?'

I sighed as the girl scurried off. 'Yes it is. You need to broaden your horizons. Try it, it's not that bad.' I took a long pull of the beer from my tin tankard.

Marcus followed my lead before spitting it out over rushes strewn across the floor. 'Ahhhh! It's disgusting! How can you drink such vile gruel?'

I laughed loudly. I'd forgotten how bad the ale was. 'You wait until you try the stuff the Germans drink, it's even worse! Come on, it's not so bad after the first few gulps.' I took another long pull. Yuk! How did they stomach it?

Marcus tried again. At least this time he knew what to expect and managed to drink it without spitting it out afterwards. His face was a comical display of disgust as he swallowed the foul-tasting beverage. 'Do I have to drink it all?' he asked.

'Of course, you'll insult their hospitality otherwise. Now look, two musicians are about to play.' An old man with a harp and a pretty young lady with a flute started up at the other side of the common room. They played light cheerful tunes that were a nice background to the loud buzz of people's voices. 'Don't you think the girl's pretty?' I asked him.

Marcus went bright red. 'Yes, but do you think she should be in here? On view, in front of all these men?'

I sighed loudly – why did he have to be such a prude? I realised I was going to have to get him to drink more than one ale tonight. I drained my tankard and asked the serving girl to fill both our tankards up again.

'Do I have to?' moaned Marcus looking mournfully at his refilled frothy brown tankard.

'Yes, you do. Now, do you want to hear any stories about my time in Syria or not?' Marcus always wanted to hear more about my time in the army, and although I avoided discussing it normally, I realised it was the only way I was going to get him to enjoy himself tonight.

'Yes, please!' he replied, eyes bright with excitement, taking a large swig of ale as encouragement.

I told him stories of border raids, hidden ambushes and the traps my unit and Julius' cavalry laid for the hostile Parthians, who regularly tried to sneak through our lines and rustle our farmer's livestock or cause other disruption to the area. The amount they took was never worth the risk – Julius always said that they only persisted to show us that they still, 'defied the might of Rome.'

Marcus listened avidly, eyes wide, whilst we supped away on our ales, which the helpful serving girl refilled regularly. Time passed as the warm fire roared in the hearth, music played, and even I started to warm to my recollections of Syria. I started to realise Marcus was getting a little drunk when his interjections to my tales gradually became more stupid. 'Were you never tempted to take your men directly into Parthia – finish that viper's nest once and for all?' was one ludicrous suggestion. 'Did you ever challenge their leaders to single combat?' was another.

I laughed at him and clapped him on the shoulder. 'I'm sure you'd have made a great Achilles, Marcus. Challenging the mighty Hector to a duel outside the gates of Troy! Unfortunately, real warfare is far less noble. The Parthian's would think nothing of shooting you full of arrows as you issued your challenge.'

His brow furrowed in seriousness. 'What filthy barbarians. Trust them not to know the conventions of war.' He drained his tankard and held it out for the girl to refill.

Roman Mask

I swallowed my beer and laughed. 'You think Julius or I would be any different? Trust me, if a great Parthian warrior came bearing down on me and I had a bow to hand, I'd shoot him myself.'

'I don't believe you, Cassius. You're the best swordsmen I've ever met – after myself that is – you're not a man to hide behind bows and arrows.' He never did believe anything bad about me. Marcus then stood up, slightly unsteadily, and declared loudly, 'I'm going for a piss!'

He weaved his way through the crowded bustle of people, who were now clapping and banging on the table tops to the sound of the merry musician's tunes, and the sound of the young lady's voice, who after discarding her flute, now sang a Celtic tune about an ancient hero of theirs who fought sea monsters and wrestled bears with his bare hands. Whilst he was gone, to the latrine pit dug outside the back door, I signalled over the wonderfully moustached landlord of the establishment. He dropped what he was doing immediately, and came over to me, the rich Roman tribune with money to spare. I beckoned him to bow down, to whisper in his ear, 'Would you be able to arrange some company for my companion tonight? We've been on the road a long time, and he is a young man after all?'

He smiled a great toothy grin. 'Of course, my lord. I will get one of my slaves to fetch someone from the main town. Would he prefer a young lady or a boy?'

'A young lady, to be sure. Make sure she is clean and comely – no old hags.' I didn't want Marcus to catch the pox on his first sexual encounter. I thought about asking her to wait for him in his room, but worried that in his drunken state he might mistake her for an intruder or a thief. 'Instruct her to wait outside our rooms. I wouldn't want her to come to any harm.'

The landlord licked his lips, no doubt at the prospect of the money he expected to extract from me. 'Of course, my lord, and how about yourself? Surely, I can find someone for you also?'

I was sorely tempted, the warm embrace of Tita was now a distant memory, and I have my own needs. But for me, the excitement of the hunt is always the game, and I wanted to try my luck on the young Celtic singer, who even now was invoking wild cheers from the boisterous crowd with her crystal clear voice – surely she could be swayed by the dashing Roman tribune with his patrician's profile? 'Not for me tonight. But I will make it worth your while if you can find someone who can teach my young friend the odd trick.'

He let out a great deep-chested laugh. 'I will see what I can do.'

He left to organise my request, before an excited Marcus returned.

Marcus sat down and took another long pull of ale. 'This place is such fun. I've just met the nicest people in the latrine. And you're right about the ale, it doesn't taste nearly so bad after three or four.'

'We'll make a man of you yet, Marcus,' I told him and clashed my tankard with his. We both laughed and took large swigs.

We drank our ale and joined in clapping along to the sound of the music with the other drinkers in the inn. Marcus was very enthusiastic with his acclaim, even attempting to dance to a few of the more lively tunes, to the great amusement of all watching him. At the end of each song everyone hollered for another, whilst I tried to catch the young female musician's eye. Her long tightly curled hair was a vibrant red, which she wore unbound and over her shoulders in a great wild mane. Her green eyes flashed in the firelight and I felt my desire growing as I watched her play her flute or sing in a high lilting voice. Judging by the eager cheers from the other customers, I wasn't her only admirer. But then again, none of the others were Roman tribunes, decked out in resplendent armour, and with rippling biceps – well, except for Marcus, but he was already taken care of.

After a number of songs, the musicians stopped to catch their breath, and the crowd started to shout out requests as to what to sing next. The crowd was overwhelmingly Gauls, but a few Roman traders requested common Latin songs that any street musician would know. The female singer whispered to her companion, and a quick heated exchange looked to take place between them. Evidently, she got her way, as her male companion, a man in his sixties if I was any judge, reluctantly nodded and started playing the notes to a slow lament on his harp.

The female singer joined in her native Celtic dialect, reaching each high note exquisitely. The room hushed, and furtive whispering started, wondering at this change in tone.

Marcus was transfixed by the sound. 'It sounds so beautiful, so perfect ... and yet so sad. Do you know what she sings of?' he asked me.

My command of Celtic tongues was never strong, but I understood enough. She was singing of the last time the tribes united together and fought as one nation against the Roman invader, and about the tragic defeat that ensued. It was no wonder her companion was reluctant to play this song. They were taking a great risk singing this song in front of a crowd which included Romans, not least two Roman tribunes. I could report them to the nearby legion, and in all likelihood the punishment would be harsh. 'She sings of an old lost love,' was all I told Marcus. I liked the song, and I didn't have any interest in getting the two singers in trouble, although I acknowledged that my chances of wooing her to my bed had just disappeared.

When she finished, the crowd clapped politely, but those seated nearest to us gave us sly looks, to see how we would react. Marcus, who was oblivious, clapped wildly and asked for her to sing it again. I smiled and clapped myself, much to the relief of those customers who realised the significance of the song. So much for me turning the lady's head with my nicely polished armour, I thought. I wondered whether it was too late to ask the landlord to find me someone else to warm my bed?

Marcus drained his tankard and turned to me. 'I'm going to find the serving girl – I want more ale. Shall I get you one?'

'I think we have had enough for tonight. It is time to retire.'

Marcus stood up from his chair. 'Nonsense! The night's just starting! Let's get another ... opps!' He knocked over his chair and stumbled into the person sitting behind him.

I chortled. 'I think you have had a little too much to drink, Marcus.'

'What me? Never. I never drink to excess. It is something my father always taught me.' He was trying to pick up the felled chair, with little success.

'Leave the chair, Marcus. Someone else can get that, whoa ... steady there!'

Marcus reeled backwards and fell flat on his backside, whereupon he let out a loud peal of laughter. 'But don't you see, Cassius. I never get drunk.' Marcus collapsed backwards and passed out.

I tried to rouse him by slapping his face, but soon realised it was hopeless. He was completely inebriated, and I knew I only had myself to blame. I had wanted him to relax a little, not get completely drunk! There was nothing for it now: I needed to get him up to his room. The serving girl came rushing over, offering to help me carry him upstairs.

'Don't worry,' I told her, 'this is undignified enough. I will manage on my own.'

I put my arm around him and lifted him up. I managed to partially wake him, enough to get him to walk with me, and I half dragged, half walked him, out of the common room. This was accompanied by loud cheers and the encouragement of other revellers. I smiled awkwardly and took one last look at the pretty musician, who looked over in amusement; no doubt this behaviour vindicated her view of Romans perfectly.

Once out of the common room, the real challenge started when I reached the stairs. It was only a small flight to the first floor but Marcus was a heavy large-boned man packed with muscle. I resolved to walk up the stairs backwards, with one arm under each armpit, dragging him up, one step at a time. By the gods, he was heavy!

'Excuse me, can I help you at all?' enquired a timid female voice from behind me.

I half turned my head and caught a glimpse of blonde hair and burst out laughing. I had forgotten about the prostitute! 'I'm afraid you won't get much action from him tonight.'

I heard her take a large intake of breath, as if in shock.

'Don't worry, I'll still pay you. Now help me get him up to his bed.'

'Cassius! It is you!' she exclaimed.

I dropped Marcus where he was and turned to see who she was. She was a little older, and the years hadn't been completely kind to her – a half-healed bruise still showed around one eye. But she was still pretty and her large blue eyes under her unruly mop of blonde hair were still bright, if a little sadder than when I last saw them in Lugdunum over four years ago. 'Hello Lentula, it has been a long time.'

'What are you doing in that armour? You must take it off before someone sees you! You will get into trouble.' She always was the caring sort, if not that bright.

'Don't be silly, Lentula. I'm a tribune now.' I took hold of Marcus under the armpits again and started heaving him up the stairs again. 'Give me a hand with my friend. I can explain.' Although she would never believe me.

She ran down and took hold of his legs, 'You can't be a tribune, Cassius. That rank is only for very rich Romans.'

'I am a very rich Roman. I was just going through a difficult time when I knew you.' That was an understatement: I was a broken-down drunk then; most people avoided me if they could help it. Lentula was the exception; she put up with my drunken behaviour, shared her bed with me, and was the closest thing that I could call a friend during that time.

We reached the door to Marcus' room and I kicked it open, and we shuffled him over to the bed.

Lentula, the effort of carrying Marcus making sweat bead on her forehead, asked, 'How can you be rich? You used to borrow money off me.'

'Money I still owe you, no doubt,' I chuckled. 'Look, you knew I'd once served in the legions?'

We laid Marcus on his bed and sat down on one corner of it. Lentula was still incredulous, 'Yes, but not as a tribune! By the gods, Cassius? Why didn't you ever tell me?'

I looked at her then, taking in the sad blue eyes that I now noticed were running with tears. I had left her here to a life of prostitution and poverty and had never given her a second thought. In those days I was so caught up in my own self-pity that I never stopped to consider how selfish I was. Poor Lentula, she never did have a bad bone in her body. I moved a blonde lock of her hair that was partially covering the eye with the half-healed bruise. 'Who did this to you?'

She flinched away from my touch and averted her eyes. 'No one of importance. Just a drunken fool who blamed me when he couldn't perform.'

Anger flared in me. 'Tell me who it was, and I will kill him for you.'

She started to sob. 'Once I would have believed you, Cassius. But do you really think killing one man will make any difference to my life now?'

I felt shame at my rash words. Most of the prostitutes who worked in the brothels were slaves of the brothel owner, but not Lentula. She was one of the girls who, although freeborn, were forced into prostitution on simple economic grounds – a dead husband and a starving babe had left her with few options. 'No, I suppose not.'

'I once loved you, Cassius. I knew you were a bit mixed up in the head. But you always touched me with tenderness and treated me with respect. Not like the other men. Even after you were thrown out of town by the watch, I thought you would find a way to come back to me. Find a way to come and take me and my boy away from this life. But you never did, and I was left with tears and bitterness as my only companions.'

I didn't know what to say. I knew she had once cared for me, but never really realised the depth of her affection. I tried the truth. 'During that time, Lentula, I hated myself so much. I could never have believed anyone could love me. I'm sorry I never came back to you.'

Marcus turned over loudly in his sleep. 'Too noisy,' he drunkenly slurred.

This brought a smile to Lentula's face, which still had the power to light up her face. 'Your friend has much in common with you it seems. When I first met you, you were in a similar state.'

I laughed gently but told her, 'That part of my life is over now, Lentula. I'll not return, not even for you. I'm sorry.'

She turned to me. 'I'm glad you're alive, Cassius. I wasn't always sure whether I wished you alive or dead, but now I see you, I'm happy that you are.'

There's not much you can say to that, so I just took her hand and led her out of Marcus' room. When we reached my own, she looked pitifully eager to join me in there, but I couldn't let her. Not now. She knew me when I was at my lowest, and the pain of that burnt inside me. 'I'm sorry I can't do more, but please take this.' I pulled the cord that I wore around my neck and pulled up the small bag I kept secreted behind my breastplate.

'You wish to give me coin?' She sounded hurt, but also agreeable.

I traced my finger down her soft cheek. 'Not just ordinary coin. Please take these.' I handed her the small pouch which held twenty gold *aureus*. I had taken it with me on my travels because I knew the effect gold had on barbarians that nothing else did – I thought I might need it to bribe myself out of any difficult situations I found myself in.

She inhaled a deep breath, 'Cassius, surely not!' Each gold *aureus* was worth twenty-five silver *denarius*. A fortune to a lowly prostitute in a provincial town and easily enough to start a new life.

'It is the least I owe you, Lentula. You cared for me when all others hated me, including myself.'

Chapter Nine

I slept uneasily that night. Returning to Lugdunum was disturbing unwanted memories. My fear of returning to Germany had left me blind to other difficult periods of my life; it was time to put some distance between me and my past. I rose early and went to wake Marcus.

As soon as I entered the room, I smelt the vomit. Marcus was on his bed, lying on his front, still fully clothed, and even still wearing his heavy bronze breastplate – maybe I should have removed that for him last night! A pile of sick lay strewn by the side of his bed.

I held my nose as I approached him. 'Ahh! It smells disgusting in here.'

Marcus groaned, and half-opened one eye. 'Leave me, I have been poisoned.'

I snorted. 'No, Marcus. You haven't been poisoned. You just have a hangover. Now get up. I want to make several miles today.'

Marcus' face was definitely a tinge of green. 'No, I'm dying. You must go on without me.'

I burst out laughing. 'You're not dying, Marcus. Like many a young man you indulged in a tankard of ale too many.' I shook his shoulder roughly. 'Come on, up!'

He started flailing his arms about to ward me off. 'Leave me alone. The Celts have poisoned me.'

'You were just drunk last night, nothing more than that.'

Marcus turned and sat up in his bed. He really did look awful, with bloodshot eyes, drool running down his unshaven chin, and his hair in disarray. 'Drunk?' He scratched his head in confusion. 'I can't have been. I never drink more than two cups of well-watered wine.'

'So you told me, but I'm afraid that wasn't the case last night.' I turned to leave, but paused at the doorway. 'Gather your things. I'll get the horses.'

Marcus looked at me in despair. 'By all the gods – the shame of it! Please, Cassius, how can you ever forgive me?'

I thought it prudent not to tell him that it was me who got him drunk in the first place, in a failed effort to get him laid. A little bit of guilt over his supposed lapse would do him good. 'You can make up for it at a later date. Be sharp now, I intend to set a hard pace today.'

I paid the innkeeper a little extra, due to the mess in Marcus' room, and before long we were back on the military road, travelling on to Germany. I kept to my word and set a fast pace, riding the horses hard, without pushing them too far and breaking them. Marcus was quiet for a few days after Lugdunum, still sheepish from his first encounter with Celtic ale. I didn't mind, I had worries of my own, running from my past.

The days were long and hard, but we made excellent time travelling through Gaul. We stayed in military way stations for the main as we progressed north. Marcus steadfastly refused to drink anything more than one cup of heavily watered wine at each meal. It was still early May, a few miles from the great city of Oppidum Ubiorum, the regional capital, when we reached the banks of the swiftly flowing river Rhenus – the natural border between Gaul and Germany. It was a grey and miserable day, and a light drizzle soaked our clothes and chilled our armour.

'I'd forgotten how cold and unwelcoming the water looked,' I remarked to Marcus as we stared at the impossibly wide river that lay in our path. Darkly silted water rushed underneath us, and a fallen branch from an overhanging tree floated past at alarming speed, bobbing and turning as it went, like a drowning man beseeching help from the rain swollen river.

'I've never seen a current so swift. Bridging it must have been quite something,'

'It is said that Julius Caesar's engineers built the bridge at Mogontiacum in ten days – that must have shocked the locals.' That was an understatement. Building a bridge in so short a time that still stood today – some sixty years later – beggared belief, even for the finest engineers of the empire.

'Really?' quizzed Marcus, 'I didn't realise Julius Caesar was ever interested in Germany?'

'He wasn't really. He only led a few punitive raids against the tribes to stop them interfering in his wars in Gaul – and to show them who was the real master of the battlefield.' I scanned the dark forested shore opposite, at the great trees that loomed over the water and concealed a dark and imposing interior. I shuddered at the thought of travelling through those dark pathways, and a cold sweat broke out and ran down my back. I hated Germany.

Marcus stared across the river and took his first sight of the German forests. 'I wonder why he stopped there.'

I laughed. 'Because he quickly realised there wasn't anything worth taking in Germany – nothing except forests, swamps, bogs, and very hostile locals. Nothing really to compare with taking control of Rome, wooing an Egyptian queen, and being declared dictator for life. Which would you have chosen?'

Marcus smiled. 'You're a cynical one, Cassius. Rome must have some uses for Germany – why else would she go to so much trouble to subjugate her?'

I turned my horse away from the banks and we started walking towards Oppidum Ubiorum. 'I suppose Rome derives some benefits from Germany: cattle, animal hides, an abundance of slaves, but precious little else.'

'You forgot about the amber. German amber is highly sought after,' said Marcus waving his finger.

'Hardly sort after enough to warrant a war.' I looked up into the skies to see if there was any prospect of the relentless drizzle letting up: there was none. I sighed. 'No, the real reason Augustus wishes to acquire Germany as a province is for tactical considerations.'

This baffled Marcus. 'What tactical benefit does Rome gain from ruling Germany?'

'Well, as formidable a barrier as the river Rhenus undoubtedly is, it does stop short of protecting the Roman lands lying directly south of Germany. This leads to an awkward frontier, one that extends at a right angle across nearly the entire northern limits of the empire. It would be much better for the empire's frontier to end at the River Elbe, four hundred miles further east – then our northern borders are secured by the northern Suebicum Sea.'

'I suppose that does make a certain amount of sense. But it does seem an extreme measure simply to make the border frontiers easier to secure?'

I smiled darkly at his remark. How many times had I stated the exact same sentiments, years ago, drinking my life away in Lugdunum? Times were different now; I could at least appreciate Augustus' thinking. 'Don't forget we have Maroboduus and his Marcomanni to consider.'

Marcus snapped his fingers. 'I've heard of him. Doesn't his tribe reside near the Danube?'

'I'm glad your geography is better than your history. Yes, the Marcomanni reside between the Danube and the Elbe. Whilst they are nominally allies of Rome, his seventy thousand warriors and large cavalry are far better equipped than the Germanic nations – hemming him in, and surrounding his nation with the legions will prevent him ever getting ideas above his station.'

'Is he really such a threat?' Marcus looked doubtful – to him, nothing could challenge the Roman legions militarily.

'Augustus has always thought so. Maroboduus is a canny warrior, and he has a full-time standing army – not the usual rabble of farmers and hunters you can expect from your average barbarian race.' A few years previously, Rome had thought of invading and finishing the threat of the Marcomanni once and for all. The Pannonian revolt put a stop to that, and a hasty peace treaty was signed with their King Maroboduus. '"Maroboduus is the greatest threat to Rome still in existence," stated Augustus a few years ago. I'm not inclined to disagree with him.'

'Pah! We'll deal with him in time. You wait, once we get Germany under control, Maroboduus will have his comeuppance!'

I laughed out loud. 'That's what I like about you, Marcus! Always the optimist! No sooner will we finish one war, you'd have us to running off to fight another!'

He didn't notice the heavy sarcasm in my tone. 'It's what Rome does best. Why stop at Germany!'

I sighed and shook my head. 'You'll learn that war isn't a game soon enough, Marcus. I think I've had enough talking politics for one day. Let's find a nice warm bed in Oppidum and get out of this damn rain.'

We rode the horses into Oppidum Ubiorum but didn't stay there longer than a day. Now we were so close to Germany, I didn't wish to dally too long: If I didn't cross over into the land of my nightmares soon, I worried that I would never be able to summon the courage to do so at all. We followed the road north and by early afternoon crossed the Rhenus at the bridge at Vetera, which had once been an imposing Roman fortress that guarded Gaul and one of Rome's traditional invasion paths into Germany, but now was little more than a glorified supply depot. Here I wished to join up with a military convoy, so Marcus and I would not have to travel into the German interior alone. I was told by the camp commander that one had just left, and that if Marcus and I travelled quickly, we could probably catch it up before nightfall. I prevaricated, not wishing to venture into Germany without at least a semblance of a military escort.

'Don't worry!' he assured me, with a great booming laugh and a reassuring clap on my shoulder. 'Germany isn't the lawless place it used to be. It will be quite safe for you to travel up to Aliso. The route is well marshalled and patrolled.'

What could I do? To delay further meant completely losing face in front of the commander and Marcus. I agreed to go, and Marcus and I rode over the wooden bridge … into Germany.

When I first alighted on the opposite bank, I felt a rush of relief. I have finally done it, I told myself – I have faced my fears and returned to Germany. I was standing on German soil and I hadn't lost my nerve. Maybe, I could do this.

'Come on, Marcus. Let's see if we can't track down that convoy.' We kicked our horses into a canter and took off down the military road which followed a fast-flowing river, a large tributary of the river Rhenus. The land was still heavily forested, but at least Roman engineers had cleared the woodland either side of the road to prevent the chance of ambush. It reassured me that it was difficult for anyone to come on us unawares.

It wasn't long before our luck turned for the worse. Within a few miles a heavy downpour erupted and made the road almost impassable. 'I knew we shouldn't have left by road – we should have sailed to Aliso by boat,' I shouted to Marcus through the heavy rain.

'That would have taken too long. Besides, it is too late now. We can't turn back,' Marcus shouted back, wiping the rivulets of rain pouring off his helmet from his eyes.

I conceded that he was right; the way back would prove just as difficult. Instead we sought shelter in an isolated farmstead that had been built a short distance from the road, in a small clearing in the woods. It was a rectangular timber-framed long house, with a thatched roof, that was so typical of Germany. The farmer, a gruff-looking man in his forties with a thick blonde beard that was turning to grey, beckoned us inside when he saw us coming. His wife, who was a stout matron with a heavily lined face and stern eyes, took our soaking wet cloaks and hung them by the large fireplace in the centre of the room to dry. Our horses were led to a stable by a large muscular young man, who I presumed was the farmer's son.

Conversation was limited with the German family, as none spoke Latin and I'd forgotten nearly all of the Germanic vocabulary I'd learnt in my last stay in Germany. The wife served us some warm broth that she heated over the fire, which we gratefully accepted as we huddled around the fire for warmth. The family watched us from the shadows of the long house, none of them speaking, just watching us with wary eyes, as if we were dangerous guests they dare not anger, but were unwelcome just the same. Their homespun woollen clothing was well enough made, but lacked the quality of the Celtic cloth we'd grown accustomed to travelling through Gaul. I imagined it scratchy and uncomfortable but none of our hosts showed any sign of discomfort.

The sound of the heavily pouring rain outside ensured we stayed with them that night, sleeping directly in front of the fire. Our elevated rank meant we could have insisted they give up their beds to us, but I didn't want to abuse the simple generosity of their hospitality and I was grateful for the warmth and shelter of their homestead.

Late the next morning, after the rain had finally cleared, we thanked the family and I offered the farmer some coin. He shook his head in refusal and I shrugged at Marcus's questioning look. The Germans had a strange sense of honour; taking money off travellers caught in a storm may well be against their principles regarding hospitality and guests.

We set out again, slowly and cautiously leading our horses along the deserted road, after waving them goodbye. Marcus said, 'They were a strange lot. They kept staring at us. You'd think they'd never seen a Roman before.'

I gave a gruff laugh. 'They're the friendly ones. Trust me, most aren't so welcoming.'

'At least the broth was nice, if a bit salty. What do you think was in it?'

'I'd rather not know – Germans will eat anything.'

Marcus chuckled, 'We have little chance catching the convoy if it pushed on through the rain.'

The thought had occurred to me as well, I considered pushing on quickly to Aliso, but was reluctant to quicken our pace in case we blundered into something unexpected. 'It is unlikely we will find such accommodating hosts again. You can expect to spend tonight camping outside.' The prospect filled me with dread.

'That suits me fine. A night under the stars doesn't bother me. We can continue our sword bouts,' said Marcus enthusiastically.

That night, sleeping by the side of the road, was difficult for me. Spending nights in the open was something I was becoming accustomed to after our long journey through Gaul, but this was different: this was Germany. I lay still as a stone by our small fire, eyes wide open, listening to the sound of the wind rustling through the trees and the small night creatures scurrying around on the forest floor. Next to me Marcus slept soundly, his even breathing testifying to a deep slumber. Each small noise sent a sharp panic through me, leaving me on edge throughout the night. Eventually, long after the fire burnt itself out, exhaustion took me, and I fell asleep, waking only when dawn lit the sky. The next day was easier. Several mounted patrols made up of Roman auxiliary units passed us, leaving me full of confidence that the commander at Vetera was right: this was now a subjugated land and Romans could travel with impunity. But more than this: I felt my nerve was returning.

I was becoming the soldier again, the man of action, a man ready for whatever Germany held in store. 'I have faced my fears,' I told myself, and proved I could be the professional soldier again who had once been respected by all the men who followed me. I was Gaius Cassius Aprilis, Tribune of Rome, once more.

My amazement at the transformation of Germany increased when we reached Aliso, nestled behind a great silver mountain alongside the river. The large military camp remained much the same as I remember it: a stone and timber palisade, well maintained and kept in strict order, but the civilian settlement that surrounded it was now changed beyond all recognition. It was now a proper Roman town, with a large forum, aqueducts providing fresh water, and Roman settlers living side by side with newly civilised Germans.

'It's as if we never left Gaul,' stated Marcus in wonder, as we passed a large ornamental fountain, constructed in a cobbled square en route to the Roman camp.

'It looks as if Varus has been busy.' I was no less amazed but could see the reasoning behind all the building work. 'Germany is seeing the benefits of empire already.'

Marcus looked slightly crestfallen. 'It looks as if all the wars with the tribes have been won. We've arrived in Germany too late.'

I laughed. 'I think you may be right. There's no turning back for Germany now.'

We rode our horses through the gates to the Roman fortress. The sentries admitted us and as I passed through I noticed by their insignia that they were from the XIX legion. The Nineteenth had served alongside my own legion, the XVIII Germanica, under Tiberius five years before, and it was good to be back with soldiers I knew and trusted. As we rode along the *Via Principalis* to the camp *praefecti's* residence we passed a centurion inspecting his century. As we passed, he stopped and must have recognised me, as he suddenly stiffened, saluted and cried out, 'Cassius Aprilis, the men of the Nineteenth stand ready to salute you!'

His line of eighty men all saluted me as I passed; filling me with pride that an old veteran of the wars, which this centurion clearly was, still remembered me with such fondness. I inclined my head as acknowledgement but gave no other sign of gratitude: I knew what the men respected: a no-nonsense professional, not someone whose head could be turned at the first sign of praise.

Marcus on the other hand could not mask his glee; he said to me after we passed, 'He knew you, Cassius! After all these years, he remembers the hero of Western-Gate Pass! One day, I hope to be as well respected as you, Cassius!'

'Try not to let it go to your head. There are less men here than I expected. It means Varus must have left for the summer's campaign already. We're already late.' The camp at Aliso was large, easily large enough to accommodate three or even four legions, but apart from the men we had just seen, the camp was now largely empty, only holding one cohort of men.

We dismounted at the camp's headquarters and handed our horses to a soldier to care for them. The camp's commander came out to speak to us, a *primus pilus*, commander of the first cohort and an experienced soldier named Caedicius. I remembered him vaguely, but had never been close to him. 'Well, well. New arrivals from Rome,' he said on greeting me. 'Aprilis, isn't it? It's been a few years since you've been in these parts.'

'Too many. It's good to be back,' I smiled at him.

'And it's good to have you here. Who's your young companion?' I introduced Marcus, who beamed with praise as I described him as, 'a young hero in the making!'

Caedicius was now in his early forties, with silver hair and a lined face, but lean and fit, and he appraised Marcus with the shrewd eye of someone used to assessing men's worth. 'If he ever emulates your deeds, he'll do fine. Tell me, what brings you two to Germany?'

I briefly outlined our mission, explaining my connection with Julius, and said we were to be aides to Governor Varus.

'Well, I'm afraid you have missed them both. Varus and Arminius left together. Back at the start of April, to the summer camp to the north-east.'

That was good. If they left at the beginning of April, there was no way I could have been expected to join them before they left – even if I had ridden our horses to death. 'Then we'll have to join them there.'

'I don't have many men, but I suppose I can lend you a few to act as a military escort. You're tribunes and shouldn't be travelling unguarded.'

Marcus jumped in. 'Oh, we don't need an escort. We have travelled this far alone. If you don't have men to spare, we can make our own way.'

My new-found bravery led me to say, 'I agree. We can take care of ourselves.'

Caedicius smiled and nodded his head in approval. 'If you're sure. Remember, there are no roads past Aliso. You will be making your way through country paths. Don't get lost.'

I assured him, 'Don't worry. I haven't been out of the field that long. I'm sure I can still follow the path of an army.' Varus would have taken three legions with him, twenty thousand men at least, only a month or so previously – it would leave a path a blind man could follow.

We rode out the next morning. I was full of vigour and enthusiastic to reach Varus' camp as quickly as possible. Caedicius had told me that Julius was in good health and had been of invaluable help to the Roman army. His canny battle tactics and the discipline he was instilling in the Cherusci warriors helped them become the foremost allies of Rome in the region.

We followed the path of the army, and, as I expected, it was easy to tell the direction they travelled by the work the army's engineers did along the way. They travelled in front of the main body of men, removing logs, cutting down trees, and fording streams, small rivers, and marches. It made our journey easy going and we travelled late into the evening each night, making sure we covered as much ground as possible.

'It won't be long now until we reach Varus. We are well into the interior of Germany now. A few more days at most,' I told Marcus as we set up camp for the night. It was late, and the sun was now dipping below the trees, long dark shadows stretching down from the towering tall pine and spruce.

'It will almost be a shame. I'm beginning to enjoy life in the wilderness. There is a peace and tranquillity here,' mused Marcus, and he lit a fire in the small clearing in the trees we decided to build our camp in.

I chuckled. 'You've become overly sentimental lately. You'll soon appreciate the comforts of the camp once we reach there. I'm getting tired of sleeping on the cold ground.' I looked up at the sky. 'It looks clear tonight. I don't think we need to erect the tent.' As there were no longer any way stations or inns for us to stay in, Caedicius had equipped us with a small leather tent, but we found it tiresome to erect and only used it when rain threatened.

'Fine by me. I enjoy looking at the stars at night.'

'There you go again: overly sentimental. It is no way for an officer of Rome to behave,' I cheerfully told him as I rubbed my horse down.

Marcus smiled at my teasing. 'Shall we forgo our sword bout tonight? It's too dark to see properly now.'

'Probably for the best. Although as you suggested it, I count it as a victory for me.' I finished with my horse and laid down next to the fire. My muscles were aching from the long day's riding, so I was secretly pleased to miss it for one night.

Marcus scoffed. 'Pah! I'll give it to you, but I'm still way ahead.'

We ate some of the bread and dried meat we had taken from the Roman camp and dozed peacefully next to the fire until the sun disappeared altogether and the stars started to light up the sky.

A large snap came from the surrounding forest – the sound of a stick being broken. Marcus was the first to react. 'Did you hear that noise?'

I half-opened my eyes. 'It's probably just an animal. Don't start getting jumpy.'

'You're probably right, but I better go and have a look.' Marcus picked up his *gladius,* unslung his small round shield from his horse's saddle, and went over to the tree line.

I sat up, and rubbed the sleep from my eyes. What was this nonsense?

'Quick, Cassius, we're under attack!' shouted Marcus in a panic-strained voice.

I leapt upwards, grabbed my sword and ran to see what was happening. Marcus was already engaged, ducking and twisting from men armed with spears and knives. It was hard to tell how many in the dark, but it was obvious he was heavily outnumbered.

I jumped on my horse in panic and scanned the camp: there was too many of them. It was like Western-Gate Pass all over again: the dark, the confusion. It was already too late for Marcus. I couldn't help him!

I spurred my horse away, in the other direction, desperate to get away from these unknown assailants. I ran my horse headlong into the trees and collided with another warrior – knocking him down. My horse took fright at the unexpected collision, rearing and whinnying in distress, before turning and bolting back the other way, back to Marcus and the danger! I hung on and saw, unbelievably, that Marcus was still alive, still ducking and spinning from his assailants, parrying with his shield, and thrusting with his *gladius*. My horse galloped through them, and I kicked one in the face and struck another with my *gladius*, which I had held on to throughout my panicked flight, and scored a deep cut along the man's unarmoured head. He screamed loudly, falling back, trying to stem the blood with his hands. My horse galloped on, but I pulled on the reins and got him under control, heaving his head around. I looked back. Marcus took advantage of the confusion my headlong flight caused and struck one of the beaded warriors through the throat, and a great gout of blood spewed from the man's neck.

I roared in defiance and ran my horse back at the enemy, screaming for all that I was worth. It was too much for our attackers – the two remaining able-bodied men broke and ran. I took one from behind, chopping down at him, killing him with a vicious cut to the back of his head. I felt the blow reverberate through my arm as the thundering blow struck and cracked his skull. I pulled my horse up and let the other man go, blowing hard with the rush of adrenaline and shock.

Roman Mask

Marcus ran up to me. 'Should we follow him?' he shouted.

'No. We don't know how many more are hiding in the woods.' And there was no way I was following him into there.

Marcus bent over and leant his hands on his knees, breathing heavily, regaining his breath. 'By the gods, that was a close-run thing.'

I managed to master myself and dismounted from my horse, my hands trembling wildly. 'Are the others dead?'

'The man you wounded ran off the other way. I doubt he'll be back. He looked to be losing a lot of blood from his scalp.'

'Are you hurt? You faced four men with spears. You should be dead.'

'I'm fine. I received a scratch here,' he showed me his scored shoulder, 'but otherwise got off lightly. You saved my life, Cassius.'

It hit me then. I had tried to run and leave him.

Marcus didn't notice my distress in the dark, and continued speaking quickly between large gasps of air. 'I learnt a lesson today. Like a fool I ran to engage them, rather than coolly assessing the situation like you did.'

I was still in shock. 'What you did was remarkable, Marcus. How did you evade all their spears?'

'They were slow and cumbersome, and they had no strength in their arms.' He wiped his blade on the ground and then sheathed it.

I went over to one of the dead men sprawled on the ground face down; the man I killed by striking him from behind, and rolled his body over and saw that he was emaciated, his beard ragged and covered in filth, his clothes little more than rags. 'They're outcasts. That explains a lot.'

Marcus looked over my shoulder. 'What do you mean they're outcasts?'

'You see this brand here?' I showed Marcus the burnt mark on his forehead. 'This marks him as an outcast. He has been thrown out of his tribe. Exile is considered no better than death. Most take their own lives, but some, like these here, try to eke out a living in the forests in robber bands. No farmstead or tribes will give them aid, and unless they are good hunters, they can easily starve to death. By the look of them, none were too adept at surviving on their own. You can thank the gods for that, otherwise you'd be dead.'

'I'd be dead anyway, if it wasn't for you. I thought I was finished. Then you came charging in to them on your horse.' Marcus' speech was still hurried; that was the adrenaline rushing through his system. Soon that would cool, then he could reflect on how close he came to death.

I looked over at the other dead man, killed by Marcus. He was in a similar emaciated state to the other outcast warrior. Marcus paused by the man.

'You'd think they would fare better in the forest. I thought all Germanic warriors were also huntsmen?'

'Self-hatred can do strange things to a man,' and I should know, I thought to myself bitterly.

He looked down at the dead man, and said sadly, 'In that case, I probably did him a favour. Who would want to live the life he led?'

I said nothing. Once the battle rage left you, I knew how it felt to realise you had killed a man for the first time. I remember seeing my first kill's face in my sleep for weeks after, years ago in Syria. It affected men differently; some pretended elation, others remorse, but either way, you were never the same again. Marcus' days of wide-eyed innocence were now over; he was a soldier in his own right now.

'We've been complacent. If these men hadn't alerted you in their approach, they would have attacked us as we slept. We must take turns to stand guard each night from now on.' My voice grew sterner. 'We are in Germany now. It is time we acted like we were. This is still a hostile land. I'd forgotten that, and that almost cost us both our lives. It won't happen again.'

Marcus nodded his head in agreement but still looked at the face of the man he had killed.

Whilst Marcus was distracted, I went to the other side of the clearing and looked to see if the warrior I'd accidentally collided with was still there. He wasn't. He must have regained his feet, seen the melee was going against his comrades and run off. If not for him, Marcus would now be dead.

I was in Germany, and at the first sign of battle, my nerve had failed me again. Marcus might still think me a hero, but I knew the truth – I was no better than these outcasts.

Chapter Ten

The next day was bright and warm, and by the afternoon the sun was shining brightly on the green spring leaves as the swallows swooped and dived above, catching their fill of small insects emerging in the hot spring sunshine. The improved weather did nothing, however, to lift the dark cloud that hovered perpetually over my thoughts. It was hard to come to terms with the knowledge of what I had done. Even in the darkest chapters of my past, I had never left a fellow comrade in combat. Even when I fled Germany five years before, it wasn't at a time when my comrades were in direct danger. Last night I had done exactly that. That my flight was thwarted, and I returned to help save Marcus' life was more reliant on chance and blind fortune than any heroics on my behalf.

Marcus was still blissfully unaware of my cowardice, and boasted just that morning that he'd, 'fought alongside one of Rome's greatest heroes!'

I snapped at him, 'Don't be a fool! This is not a game we're playing. This is life and death!'

Marcus seemed to put my foul temper down to a desire for us to be more on our guard, and didn't guess that, inside, my mind was in turmoil. What was wrong with me? Why couldn't I summon the courage necessary for combat? I was no raw recruit, facing danger for the first time. I'd fought countless times in Syria, tested my nerve against greater warriors than last night's scuffle with half-starved brigands. Why was I now incapable of doing it? Was my life so precious to me? Was I now unwilling to make the ultimate sacrifice and put my life in the hands of Mars? I didn't think that was it. I hated myself so much right now that death looked an almost enticing prospect. The only honourable course of action following my shame was to take my own life. Yet, just as I had five years before, I held no desire to fall on my sword. I will make sure Marcus makes it to Varus and the army first, I told myself, but hated myself all over again, as I knew I was lying to myself. I had no more intention of taking my own life than I had five years before. My miserable life of cowardice and deceit would have to continue.

'It's nice to be out of the forests, don't you think?' asked Marcus, chewing on a strip of dried beef whilst we rode along a shallow valley which was only thinly interspersed with trees and woodland. Hills bathed in sunshine surrounded us, and a pleasant warm breeze was filled with the scent of wild flowers and spring blossom.

'At least it makes the chance of ambush less likely,' I replied, scanning our surroundings for danger, almost hoping to find someone lurking behind a tree or bush, so I could put right last night's wrongs and prove that I was still a soldier.

Marcus looked thoughtful. 'I still think we should have buried those men.'

'They were outcasts and robbers. They don't deserve your pity or any reverence after death. They got what they deserved.' We left the two dead men where they had fallen as carrion for the animals of the forest.

Marcus was still evidently troubled by his first kill, and the decision to leave them there still sat uncomfortably with him. 'Just because they were our enemies in life, doesn't mean we should dishonour them in death.'

I turned round and said in exasperation, 'Do you think they would have treated us any more kindly? After killing us, they would have taken all we own, probably mutilating our bodies in the process, chopping our fingers off for our gold rings.'

'Yes, but they were all uncivilised. We can't expect anything better from the likes of them. We're different. We're Romans.'

'Did you really want to spend half the day digging graves? We'd need to dig the graves deep. Any less and the forest animals would dig them up.' I'd been eager to leave that place. It was bad enough having to stay there through the night, worrying that our attackers might return, but travelling in the dark was a sure way to break a horse's leg, and I'd reluctantly realised we had no choice.

Marcus sighed. 'I suppose not. But when we reach the army, I will make a sacrifice to Mars, to honour them.'

This was too much. 'To honour them!' I shouted, genuinely annoyed. 'They wanted to kill you!'

'And thanks to you they failed. There is no disgrace in that. At least they died as warriors.' There was firmness to his voice.

I shouted back, 'By all the gods! What kind of fool are you! Warriors? Honour? They were no more than filthy thieves! Why do you think their tribes cast them out?'

For the first time ever, Marcus lost his temper with me, annoyed that I wasn't prepared to play along with his game. 'So what if they were brigands? At least they died with weapons in their hands!'

Argh! How could he spout such nonsense! 'And you think that is the most important thing in the world? It doesn't matter how you live your life, as long as you die with a weapon in your hand?'

'Of course! How else should I die, as an old man in his bed?' He said this as if such a prospect was the worst calamity that could ever befall anyone.

I was speechless with rage, 'Why you young, stupid, idiotic—'

A firm female voice cut across our argument. 'Two grand officers of Rome squabbling like children, riding through the countryside without a care in the world, arrogantly making enough noise to shout their location to any who might care. How very Roman.'

Both Marcus and I were startled. We looked up the hillside to our right where a woman sat on a horse, draped in an enveloping cloak of Roman design with a deep hood that obscured her face. Where had she come from? So much for being more on our guard! 'My lady, you took us by surprise. What is a Roman woman doing in these parts?' I asked. Her Latin was pitch perfect; this was no Romanised German.

Her voice sounded amused but also scornful. 'An army of war elephants could have taken you two by surprise. Don't you pay any attention to your surroundings? Have you forgotten all you once learnt?'

The last question was directed at me. Who was she? I stood there dumbstruck as Marcus said to her, 'My lady, you shouldn't be travelling in these parts alone. Let us escort you to the camp of Governor Varus.' He cleared his throat and added lamely, 'Once we have located it.'

She laughed. 'Young brave Tribune, it is I who should be escorting you. Do you have no idea where you are? From that vantage you can see Varus' camp.' She pointed at a high hill which loomed above us. 'Shall we ride there?' she asked and turned her horse, a magnificent Gallic thoroughbred by the look of it, and spurred it towards the hillside.

Marcus was too surprised to react, but I spurred my horse after her and galloped up the hillside. Impossible as it was, I suspected who this mysterious woman was – her voice was tinged with familiarity. What she was doing in this barren wilderness, I couldn't begin to fathom.

She rode well, leaping her fast horse over small streams and fallen trees. Her cape blew backwards, revealing long flowing brown hair. My equally fine Libyan gelding was hard pushed to catch her. I gritted my teeth and spurred him ever faster, the frustration over my failings the night before making me determined not to reach the hilltop behind her. 'Come on boy,' I urged, 'faster!'

I jumped over the small stream that ran down the hill and prayed to the gods that my horse didn't trip; a fall on this rocky ground could prove my end, but my determination not to be beaten was spurring me on.

I pulled level just as we approached the brow of the hill, both of us in full gallop, the wind rushing past my face, filling me with adrenaline. An ancient dyke, made by some long-dead farmer, ran across the hill. It was too high to jump safely but it was interspersed with several gaps where the hillside's streams had washed it away. The nearest gap favoured her, being on her right side whilst I was on her left, and she directed her horse towards it. I cursed loudly, but refused to admit my inevitable defeat. I galloped my horse straight at the dyke, knowing that if he refused to jump, I'd be sent sprawling.

'Stop!' she shouted when she realised my intention.

I ignored her and rode my horse to the dyke. He leapt, and we sailed through the air, me holding my breath, as we jumped clean over the stone dyke. We landed heavily, and for a moment I thought I would fall from the saddle, but the four prongs of the Gallic saddle griped my legs and held me in place, and a great grin spread over my face. I'd made it! Ha ha!

I pulled my horse up on the top of the hill, relishing my victory, and spied in the distance the great Roman camp and our destination. A thousand small fires were making tendrils of smoke into the sky. There lay twenty thousand of the finest fighting men in the world and complete safety – what a beautiful sight!

'You could have easily broken that poor animal's leg making such a jump!' scolded the woman, trotting slowly up the hill, with Marcus trailing behind her. His horse was blowing hard too; he had obviously followed us on our wild race.

I laughed. 'You're just disappointed that you lost. Don't be such a bad loser.'

'I mentioned no race.'

'Pah! You don't ride a horse like yours if you want to arrive second at the top of the hill. You haven't changed a bit!'

'Yes, well. You always did have more courage than brains, Gaius.'

If only she knew, I thought. I could tell she was still peeved. Her brow was furrowed and her eyes flashed anger. It was a sight that years ago I'd become accustomed to.

Marcus broke in as the two of them joined me on the hilltop. 'You know each other? How's this possible?'

I laughed at his confusion, although I admitted that I never expected to run into her on the frontiers of the empire, in Germany of all places. 'Marcus Scaeva, let me introduce you to Numeria, daughter of Senator Numerius Scipio, eldest child of one of the finest families in Rome – oh! And my one-time betrothed.'

Chapter Eleven

'You have no right to make reference to our betrothal, Cassius Aprilis,' she snapped in anger, 'You gave up that right when you left Rome eleven years ago.'

Was it really eleven years since I'd last seen her? She was a young girl when I left her, the beautiful daughter from the neighbouring estate, a childhood companion and the main focus of my adolescent fantasies. Now she had grown into a striking mature woman, her light brown hair, flawless features, and bright eyes had lost none of their intensity; she was still a beauty, and now that her cape was blown backwards from her face, I could see that she still had a smattering of freckles under lightly sun-browned skin. Seeing her was worth travelling the thousand miles from Rome, although I was as sure as anything that I wasn't going to let her realise that. 'You can't still be angry over that? I was called away to serve. We are all servants of the Republic, after all.' My swift departure from Rome eleven years ago, to avoid further embroilment in the scandal that engulfed Augustus' daughter, ruined any plans of our marriage. Numeria's father never found out my full involvement in the scandal, but the dark shadow of suspicion that hung over me was enough to rule out marriage to the daughter he doted on.

She laughed out loud. 'Oh, don't flatter yourself, Gaius! Do you really think I still pine for the immature young fool who played court to me all those years ago? I met a real man, who I then took to be my husband. I soon forgot you!'

Ouch! That stung. Antonia had told me via letter, a couple of years after I left Rome, whilst I was serving in Syria, that Numeria was to marry: 'A man of respectable family, but one far below her rank.'

Her choice of husband was hardly surprising. Numeria was always one to challenge conventions and her father was always too open-handed with her. 'I'm sure he is a wonderful man. Will I get to meet him in the camp?' Some high-ranking officers did take their wives and families on campaign with them. It wasn't a practice I approved of; an army camp was no place for women and children as far as I was concerned, but I knew it happened from time to time.

Her tone changed, more serious. 'Otho is here – you'll find him to the north-east of the ramparts, on the knoll that commands the northern approach to the camp – but I'm sure you'll hear of him as soon as you reach the camp.'

So he was one of the popular officers was he? She sounded touchy about him, probably because he was below her social rank, and mine for that matter. I smiled politely but really wanted to gnash my teeth. 'I'll introduce myself to him as soon as I can.'

She shook her head as if to clear it. 'Enough talk, it is time you reported yourself to Varus. The gods know that he needs some sound counsel. I hear you once fancied yourself a good soldier, or was that only to impress the ladies? We certainly don't need another officer from Rome full of bravado but no action.' She turned her horse and started walking it briskly towards the Roman camp.

That was too close to the mark. I blasted in anger as I followed her, 'How dare you question my military record? I was awarded the oak leaf crown in Germany five years ago. No doubt you were safely at home in Rome, being pampered and spoilt.'

She turned her head around, and said scornfully, 'Pampered and spoilt? That sounds a good description of you. Your sister still writes to me, did you know that? I have heard all about your decadent life in Rome.'

Antonia still writes to her! She never told me that! Why didn't Antonia warn me that I could walk into Numeria here? Conniving women – they were all the same; even my own blood betrayed me. 'Antonia has no right to discuss my life, and neither do you,' I snapped.

She laughed out loud. 'You can't hide behind Roman pomposity with me, Gaius. It's time you remembered how to be a soldier again.' She spurred her horse into a quick trot and left me seething in anger.

I turned to Marcus, who sat his horse next to me, an amused smile on his face. 'Infernal woman,' I remarked.

Marcus watched Numeria skilfully manoeuvre her horse down the steep hillside. When she was out of earshot, Marcus whispered to me, 'You were once betrothed to her?'

'A very long time ago and it wasn't through choice. Our fathers proposed the match,' I said defensively.

'You should have never let her go,' he said thoughtfully.

I looked over at him, shocked, to see if he was serious. 'What? You see what a nightmare she is? She has the temperament of a feral cat.' I said, exasperated.

He looked over at me, laughed, and said, 'No, Cassius, not a feral cat: a lioness.'

'Pah! I bet her husband doesn't agree. The poor man, whoever he is, probably sleeps with a dagger under his bed for protection. A woman should be pliable and soft, not a bag of nettles and thorns.'

Marcus laughed. He seemed to be enjoying my irritation. 'You're forever telling me that I know nothing of women, but even I can tell that a soft and pliable woman would never satisfy you for long.'

'Shut up, Marcus.' Grumbling to myself, I followed her down the hillside. Marcus just chuckled and led his horse after mine.

It took a while for Marcus and I to catch her up, and we were nearing the Roman camp by the time we did. Straight away I noticed that this was no ordinary Roman military summer campaign camp. All Roman camps attracted a civilian settlement outside their gates; it stood to reason that such a source of power and wealth attracted followers. But normally these camps were ramshackle and poorly constructed. Here, the civilian town bore all the signs of a permanent settlement being built. The wooden long houses were well constructed and stone Roman-built municipal buildings were interspersed throughout the town: a stone bathhouse, a forum, a large temple, and even an aqueduct was being constructed by Roman engineers to provide the town with fresh water.

Curiosity dampened my annoyance with Numeria, and I asked her, 'Why is Varus wasting time with building work in this town? He will have to abandon it as soon as winter approaches.' The Roman army couldn't possibly winter here; there was no road connecting it with Aliso and the other military camps. Once the winter snows set in, the twenty thousand men needed supplies, so by autumn the full Roman occupational force would retire to its winter quarters in Aliso.

A small smile twisted on Numeria's face. 'Governor Varus claims that the Germanic people need to see the benefits of Roman rule. What better way of demonstrating that than by Roman building works? This new town of Aurorae Novus is to mark the new dawn in Germany.'

'Aurorae Novus? He's even named it! But won't the local population just ransack it once the camp is abandoned in autumn?' I even saw that a statue of Augustus had been erected in the centre of the town.

She laughed. 'You'd think so wouldn't you? But Varus has been assured by your friend, Julius, that he will safeguard the town in Varus' absence.'

'Julius? You've seen him?' I felt a leap of excitement. Numeria knew Julius almost as well as I did. Julius often visited my father's estate with me when I was given leave to go from Augustus' school, and the three of us had been close as children.

'Oh yes. Julius Arminius is well known in the Roman camp. As well as being the tribal leader of the Cherusci, he commands a contingent of Roman equipped auxiliaries – made up from the finest Cherusci cavalry.'

Ha! That is just like Julius. Instead of sitting back and letting Rome assure his position at the head of the Cherusci tribe, he would insist on taking an active military position supporting his allies. 'Same old Julius,' I said, 'always finding another way to make a name for himself.'

'Will I finally meet this Julius?' asked Marcus enthusiastically.

Numeria let out a small sigh, 'I really couldn't tell you. He comes and goes from the camp a lot. He might well be out on one of his long patrols. You will have to ask in the Roman camp for him. I am hardly briefed on military matters.' There was surprising bitterness in her last sentence.

'You sound critical?' I was curious as to why there was a brittle edge to her words whenever she discussed Varus, 'Don't you like the governor?'

Her eyes narrowed. 'Like or dislike has nothing to do with it. I simply disagree with some of the governor's actions.'

And I bet he likes you pointing them out about as much as an ice bath in winter. I was getting the feeling there was more to this story than she was prepared to let on, but I wasn't interested in pursuing it now. We were entering the outskirts of the town, and the familiar sounds and smells of a thriving settlement greeted us. 'When we get to the camp I could do with a nice hot meal.'

Numeria made a very unladylike snort. 'I am sure Governor Varus will be able to help you – he is known for his hospitality and lavish dinners.'

Definitely no love lost between those two. 'Let us hope so.'

We rode through the small town streets and I saw both German and Roman working side by side in the busy little community. Carpenters shaped wood, stone masons chiselled works, and smithies banged hammers as they shaped iron tools. All around, work was taking place, improving the town and its houses.

Marcus was pleased at the progress being made. 'This is the future of Germany. Look at all this industry. What a great sight!'

Numeria smiled at his enthusiasm but I wasn't so sure. Would Julius be able to protect all this without the support of the Roman legions come autumn? He was a braver man than me. I wouldn't want to be the one left guarding it.

Numeria noticed another Roman lady, dressed with a brightly coloured shawl covering her head, and called over to her, 'Julia, Julia, wait.'

The woman looked to try and walk off without acknowledging Numeria, until Numeria changed her tone. 'Julia. Stop. Don't you dare ignore me!'

The lady stopped, turned around and removed her shawl, which revealed a very pretty young girl of perhaps eighteen or nineteen, dark hair, olive skin, two large doe eyes with long eyelashes. 'Hello Numeria, how nice to see you,' she said, blushing red from being caught trying to avoid her.

Numeria dismounted from her horse and went over to the young lady. 'What do you think you're doing, walking around the town on your own? You know that isn't fitting behaviour,' she asked firmly – clearly her own solitary ride in the surrounding countryside had no bearing on this.

The young girl, Julia, hung her head, looking like a scolded child. 'I just needed some fresh air, staying indoors can be so tiresome.'

'Fresh air? Since when has the back of a tanner's yard constituted fresh air?' Numeria questioned angrily. The tanner's we were standing behind gave off its usual putrid stench of half-cured animal hides.

Julia motioned to reply, but Numeria held up her hand cutting her short. 'Not now, Julia. First meet our two guests,' she turned to us, 'these are two officers, who have come all the way from Rome. Excuse me, I don't know your full name?' she asked Marcus.

He stood straight in his saddle. 'Marcus … Marcus Scaeva. Here on attachment, to provide assistance to Governor Varus and the field army in any capacity I can,' he blurted.

'It's alright, Marcus. You're not reporting for duty,' I chided, amused, and the young girl giggled, turning Marcus bright red.

Numeria came to his rescue and waved her hand vaguely in my direction, 'And this is Gaius Cassius Aprilis, a soldier of mild renown.'

Mild renown? I gritted my teeth, curbing my temper. 'A pleasure to make your acquaintance.' I nodded formally.

The young girl lowered her eyes, as a proper Roman lady should, and replied, 'We are grateful that you have come to aid us in Germany. Your very presence assures our safety.'

Numeria nodded in approval at her polite greeting, but as she turned her attention back to us, I noticed the young girl shoot Marcus and I a saucy smile. What do we have here, I thought? There is more to this girl than it seems. Trouble – if I was any judge.

Numeria didn't notice. 'I need to speak to Julia alone. Please go onto the camp without me – you don't need me to escort you further do you?'

I bristled at the affront; of course we didn't need her to escort us! I still had a thousand questions for her, but I supposed there was plenty of time to seek Numeria out later. It wasn't that big a town, and I was sure I could find her again

Roman Mask

without too much trouble. 'Lady Julia, a pleasure meeting you, and Numeria, it has been good to see you again. I will see you both again soon hopefully?'

'No doubt you will, Gaius.' She bowed her head slightly in deference to me – a rare sight in Numeria – and gave Marcus a parting polite smile. I turned to Marcus and noticed his eyes were staring straight at the young girl, Julia. I laughed and clapped him on the shoulder. 'Come on young Tribune, plenty of time to go sightseeing later.'

We left the two Roman women and walked our horses up to the military camp.

'You didn't have to make me look such a fool in front of those two ladies!' Marcus sternly rebuked me.

'Oh, you didn't need my help in that, Marcus,' I chuckled, as we rode towards the gates of the main military camp, 'you can do that all on your own.'

Marcus looked crestfallen. 'I know, I'm such an idiot. I just didn't know what to say to that young girl.' He then looked up hopefully at me. 'She was so pretty. Do you think we'll see her again?'

'It's a small town. We're not in Rome now. You'll get to see her again.' I kept my reservations about her to myself; at least he was finally showing an interest in girls.

'Good,' he declared, 'I'll come across better next time.'

'Let's hope so. Now, get your mind back on where we're going. I don't want you making fools of us in front of Varus.' We were nearly at the gate, where two sentries stood stiffly to attention.

As we approached them, a centurion, with greying hair and stern disposition, came out to greet us. 'Hello young sirs, where do you come from?' he asked us.

'Tribunes Aprilis and Scaeva, we have travelled from Rome and wish to see Governor Varus,' I declared.

'Then pass, friend. You will find him in the headquarters.' He motioned his arm down the main *Via Principalis*, the main road that existed in all Roman camps, this one leading from east to west.

We rode past him and the sentries and made our way to the large headquarters. Either side of us stood stone and timber barracks, soundly built, row upon row of them, housing thousands of men.

'This isn't what I was expecting to see in the summer campaign camp,' said Marcus.

Neither was I. In campaign camps, the men were normally quartered in tents so they could move swiftly on to the next marching camp. Campaigns were mobile, and the army needed to keep one step ahead of the enemy. Having the soldiers quartered in permanent buildings was not how the Roman army fought wars. 'Maybe Varus has pacified all the German tribes? Possibly the wars are over in this part of the world?' I was hopeful, but Marcus looked concerned. I knew what he was thinking. Had he travelled all the way to Germany for battle experience only to find that the fighting was now all over?

Men sat outside the barracks and played dice or joked around a midday meal. The camp was full to bursting. By the looks of it, all three legions were in attendance. Some of the men eyed us as we passed, but most ignored us completely. 'Ah, camp life!' I said, 'Isn't it good to be back in the army.' I meant it. The feeling of security in an armed Roman camp was completely reassuring.

'My father keeps his camp in stricter order than this,' criticised Marcus, and he wrinkled his nose at the acrid smell coming from the nearest cooking pot.

'Come now, Marcus. You're not with the Praetorians now. These are real soldiers who fight in the field. They may look like scruffy villains, but they are all as unyielding as iron – real men.'

A woman's laugh peeled out from one of the barracks, ruining my ringing endorsement, and I spun my head around trying to locate where the sound issued from. A slovenly camp was one thing, men smuggling women into the camp, something else entirely – was discipline so slack here? Such a thing would have been unheard of in one of Tiberius' military camps. 'Did you hear that?' I asked Marcus.

'It sounded like a woman.' Marcus' disapproval matched my own and he looked intent on pursuing the culprit. 'Shall we search the nearest barracks?'

None of the other soldiers looked the slightest bit perturbed by the noise; how common an occurrence was this? 'We're not here to run the camp for them,' I told Marcus. If these were my men, I wouldn't appreciate officers unattached to my legion interfering with internal discipline. 'We'll report this incident to the camp praefect later and take it from there.'

Marcus looked disappointed but said, 'Very well, Cassius. You probably know best.'

We rode to the camp headquarters, a large timbered building surrounding a sizeable courtyard; it was another semi-permanent structure, I noted. We handed our horses to a groom and took our saddlebags with us as we walked over to a tribune, a young man with fair brown hair and a long chin, who sat reclining on a chair, legs stretched out in front of him balanced on a wooden balustrade, dozing, enjoying the late afternoon sunshine.

'We're here to see Governor Varus,' I announced in a firm parade ground

Roman Mask

voice, expecting the tribune to jump to attention, embarrassed at being caught napping.

The tribune half-opened one eye. 'Do you have an appointment?'

Marcus was as shocked as me. 'An appointment! We have come all the way from Rome. Of course we don't have an appointment!'

The tribune closed his eye again. 'Then you can't see the Governor. He is busy with his legates.'

Marcus looked furious, but I held up my hand to quieten him whilst I dealt with this rude officer. 'We've come a long way. Surely you can arrange for us to be billeted in the camp whilst we wait to see the governor?'

He let out an impatient sigh, opened his eyes, and looked at me for the first time. 'Most of the officers stay in the town now. I suggest you find accommodation there. The large inn near the new temple is passably good.' He settled back into his former position, closing his eyes and folding his hands over his belly, clearly thinking the matter was at a close.

That's it, enough was enough. I reached over, grabbed one of the chair legs he was balancing on, and pulled it from under him. The tribune went sprawling, landing in an unceremonial heap. I shouted at him, 'My name is Cassius Aprilis. I expect those I outrank to stand to attention when they address me!' Both Marcus and I held the broad stripe on our tunics marking us from the senatorial class, whilst this rude officer held the thinner stripe and was therefore only from the equestrian class.

The tribune blustered as he quickly tried to regain his feet. 'What ...? Who ...? By Hades, I'll report you!'

I walked up to him, looked him straight in the eye, and said in a measured tone, 'Go ahead. My orders come from Augustus himself. Do you think you can go to a higher authority?'

He looked at me and swallowed hard, finally realising that he had misjudged the situation. 'I'm sorry, sir. I apologise. I will see if Governor Varus can see you at once.'

'You do that.'

He scurried off, and Marcus clapped me on the back, chuckling. 'You know how to make an impression.'

I smiled wryly. 'If he was under my command, I'd have him digging latrines morning till night, speaking to us like that.'

We waited outside in the courtyard patiently whilst the staff officer told of our arrival. Eventually he returned, still flustered, sweat marking his brow. 'Commander Varus will see you at once. Please follow me.'

'That's better. You see, politeness isn't so hard is it?' I told him, pleased that he was now treating us with respect.

We followed him into the building and up to a set of large double doors being guarded by two sentries. Raised voices were coming from behind them.

A loud deep voice said, '... the men are becoming idle, we need to get them further out in the field.'

A weary, resigned tone responded, 'Not until I have heard the response back from the Angrivarii. Peace negotiations are at a delicate stage, I am not willing to jeopardise them so you can play at war.'

'They have been stalling for months. Shall we lose the entire campaigning season sitting here?' shouted the first man – his voice was vaguely familiar. Was this someone I knew?

On hearing the raised voices, our long-chinned tribune didn't know what to do, but I instructed him to knock on the door immediately. Better to be announced at a difficult time than be accused of eavesdropping.

Silence greeted the knock on the door, followed by the weary voice saying, 'Come.'

The tribune popped his head round the door and said, 'The two tribunes from Rome, sir. Can you see them now?'

'Yes, yes. Show them in.'

I felt a moment of apprehension before Marcus and I entered the room. I was about to meet the man who held complete authority in Germany. In this province, his word was law – and Varus was a man with a reputation for being ruthless when necessary: thousands had died by his word after one uprising in Syria. What would this man make of me – a broken soldier – sent here on the whim of an old harpy, who had just assaulted one of his staff officers – maybe that hadn't been such a good idea after all – and with a young boy in tow, who blushes on his first encounter with a pretty girl? Would Varus be impressed? I doubted it.

Chapter Twelve

We walked into the room and saw Governor Varus sat on a large chair, fully armoured, seemingly at ease but with a tired expression on his face. I recognised him from the descriptions I'd had of him. He was in his mid-fifties, his face now slightly portly, with large jowls and thinning silver-black hair. Next to him stood a dark imposing man, wearing the armour of a legate, with a crooked grin and dark hooded eyes. Also in the room was a man in the armour of the *praefecti castorum*, the camp commander, and another legate, the man with the deep voice, someone I recognised instantly: Gaius Numonius Vala. We had both served together as lead tribunes for our respective legions the last time I was in Germany. Now, by the looks of it, he was a legate of his own legion.

I cleared my voice and announced, 'Tribunes Cassius Aprilis and Marcus Scaeva, bring greetings from the Senate and Caesar.' We both saluted stiffly.

Varus stood from his chair, a sombre look on his face. 'So, the two birds from Rome have arrived. I had word of your coming in our last despatch. Two men I neither asked for nor require.'

In that case, let me go home and let me escape this dreadful land, I could have said, but I felt diplomacy was the better option, and let out a small breath. 'We have been told to be of whatever assistance we can offer.' I handed him the scroll, with Augustus' mark, that outlined our orders.

'Yes, yes, no need for all that now. The last man sent by our esteemed leader Augustus, when he wasn't questioning my orders, spent his time here complaining about the weather. What did he expect? The winters in Germany are cold.'

The legate with the hooded eyes chuckled. 'And a right sour man he was. The fever that took him this spring has done us all a favour if you ask me.'

I swallowed hard. So Augustus' last spy had perished. Was it really a fever, or had these men disposed of an annoying nuisance? I cleared my throat. 'I promise you, I have no intention of questioning your orders or complaining about the weather. I have been in Germany before. I know what to expect.'

This took the interest of Varus. 'Really? You've been here before? What did you say your name was? The despatch never gave this.'

'Cassius Aprilis'

He gave me another hard look. 'Any relation to Senator Antonius Aprilis.'

'He is my father, sir.'

Immediately Varus demeanour changed, and a smile broke his face. 'My dear boy.' He came over and embraced me. I was too shocked to say anything, as Varus explained, 'I know your father well. A fine man. It is an honour to meet his son finally.'

My father had never mentioned knowing Varus to me, but that was hardly surprising, considering how strained our relationship was. 'He speaks very well of you, Governor Varus,'

'You're too kind. A man of real integrity, your father. Any son of his is welcome here.' He was smiling now.

Well, this was a turn-up. Who would have thought that Varus was an old friend of my father's? I better not tell him that my father thought I was possibly the biggest disappointment of his life – no need to spoil Varus' cheerful mood!

'Welcome, welcome. I heard that Antonius' son was a renowned soldier. Your reputation serves you well.' I inclined my head at the compliment. 'How lucky we are to have you with us. And who are you?' Varus asked Marcus.

'Marcus Scaeva, sir, newly appointed tribune.' Marcus stood ramrod straight, and saluted again.

'Please, please. Relax. Please excuse my earlier frosty reception. These are difficult times, and the last thing I needed was new men sent by Augustus upsetting all my plans. I realise I have misread the situation. No son of Antonius would ever be the tool of the *imperator*.'

No not the *imperator*, his wife. Varus' tone encouraged me to be bolder. 'Does Augustus interfere with your rule here, Governor?'

'Where doesn't Augustus interfere?' he shook his head in dismay, 'Don't get me wrong, this isn't seditious talk from me. I firmly think Augustus is the best man to lead the empire, and we all owe our welfare to him. But sometimes a man in the field is in a better position to make decisions, not someone in faraway Rome. I wish he would just let me get on with the job at hand, and not send me impossible directives.'

The dark legate cleared his throat in discomfort. Clearly he thought Varus was being too candid with me, son of an old friend or not.

Varus took the hint. He changed the subject. 'So, Marcus Scaeva, are you happy to be in Germany?' he asked warmly.

Varus' friendly manner rubbed off on Marcus, who responded proudly. 'Yes, my lord. It is an honour to be here and to serve you.'

'Such eagerness. You see, gentlemen, with the finest crop of Roman youth here to aid us, we will soon make the province of Germany a jewel to rival any in the empire!'

Numonius Vala was less impressed. 'Yes, my lord. But could we get back to the discussion at hand. The men must be allowed to …'

Varus said exasperated, 'Not now, Numonius! We have guests who have travelled all the way from Rome.' He sounded irritated more than angry at Numonius Vala. 'You have served in Germany for years, you must know Cassius Aprilis? Don't you want to greet your former comrade?'

Numonius Vala was obviously still frustrated, but he turned to me and inclined his head, 'Of course, Cassius. It has been many years. It is good to see you again.'

Numonius Vala and I had never been close. I always thought he was jealous of the popularity I enjoyed with the men, whilst he felt my informality with the legionaries was unfitting for someone of my rank. However, there are worse men, I supposed, so I greeted him warmly. 'It is good to be back, Numonius. I see you are a legate now. It is richly deserved.'

Numonius Vala was in his early forties, and had spent much of his career in the military; he was a safe choice as a commander of a legion, if an uninspiring one. He looked as supremely fit as I remembered, with no excess fat on him, and iron-strong muscle cords linking his thin frame. He nodded rigidly in acknowledgement to my compliment, 'Yes, I now lead the Eighteenth.'

My heart sunk; that was my old legion.

Vala turned back to Varus. 'If we cannot discuss this matter now, I would like to be excused. I have tasks that need attending.'

'Very well,' responded Varus wearily, 'if you cannot be relied on to be civil to our new guests, you may as well leave. Good day to you.'

Numonius Vala saluted stiffly then walked briskly out of the room. As soon as he left, Varus let go an exasperated sigh. 'The gods damn that man. His rudeness gets worse daily. How am I ever going to put up with him once you are gone, Asprenas?'

The other legate laughed. 'You need to order him to spend a night in the town whorehouse. I've never met a man so in need of getting laid.'

Varus laughed also and turned to me. 'Sorry to speak so ill of your friend, Cassius. But his strict adherence to matters of military protocol makes him the most tiresome of men at times.'

How to be tactful to this one? I held my hands behind my back, leant forward and confided to Varus. 'When last I was in Germany, his nickname amongst the troops was 'the old mother', on account of his constant nagging. Maybe a night in a German whorehouse is not such a bad idea.'

Varus bellowed with laughter. '"The old mother"! Yes, that suits him perfectly!' Varus clapped his hands in order to alert an attendant, a young blonde slave-boy duly appeared. 'Fetch us some wine and set two extra places for dinner – we have guests.' He turned back to me and said, 'You must be exhausted after your long travels. I hope you don't mind joining us for our evening meal. I do so wish to hear the latest news from Rome.'

'It will be an honour, my lord,' I replied, and Marcus nodded his head in happy acceptance. Both of us were pleasantly surprised by Varus' friendly manner; could this really be the same man who had once crucified two thousand rebels after a revolt in Judea?

Varus introduced us to the other two men in the room. Firstly the camp praefect. 'This is Ceionius. A good man, but never play him at dice – he cheats!'

The camp commander, a man with thinning hair and an amenable smile chuckled and greeted me. 'Don't believe a word of it. Pleased to meet you.'

Varus then introduced me to the other legate, the large man with dark colouring, one thick eyebrow crossing his hooded eyes, 'And this is Asprenas, my nephew. Unfortunately he will be leaving us soon to take command of the two legions based in the west at Mogontiacum. I will sorely miss him.'

Asprenas gave me a crooked grin. 'I have heard of you. You were once based in Syria, isn't that right?'

'Before being posted to Germany, I was lead tribune to the tenth legion.' I said with a little pride.

'The men of the sea straits!' exclaimed Varus. 'I know them well. You must have been based in Raphanaea. A fine unit, and it's always good to have another man from the Syrian sands. What do you say, Asprenas?'

Asprenas sized me up. 'You're right, a fine unit, good to have you with us.' In all likelihood, Asprenas would have served in Syria as well, when his uncle served as governor there – nepotism was rife throughout Rome's army. The legate turned his attention to Marcus. 'And how about you?' he asked. 'Don't tell me that you've fought in Syria as well. You don't look older than my last bed companion, and she was barely old enough to know her trade.'

Varus reprimanded his nephew. 'Please, Asprenas. Don't be so coarse. You don't have to debase every conversation with your sordid night-time pleasures.'

'It is quite alright, my lord,' responded Marcus enthusiastically. 'It's true, Germany is my first posting. But I promise one and all that I won't let them down.'

Asprenas snorted a laugh. 'That's what they all say. Doesn't stop them freezing when they first face danger and pissing their britches.'

I suddenly felt protective over young Marcus and told Asprenas, 'Marcus has already faced danger. We were waylaid in the forest on the way here. A few outcast robbers. Marcus didn't freeze. He fought bravely and made his first kill. He is a boy no longer.'

Marcus beamed with pride.

Varus sounded genuinely concerned. 'You were waylaid in the forest. How awful, I'm so sorry. My province isn't the safest of lands as yet. Didn't you have a military escort?'

'We were offered one, but turned it down,' I told him, still not believing how stupid I was to decline one. 'No harm was done, we were both uninjured.' Which was true I supposed, although I learnt that I could no longer face combat, but I wasn't going to tell him that.

'Tell me all about it over dinner. Would you like to freshen up from your journey first?' asked Varus.

Marcus and I accepted his hospitality and stored our possessions in Varus' own house, built behind the military headquarters. We were given a room each with a small bed and a stuffed mattress. It wasn't exactly luxury, but it was a great step up from sleeping on the cold ground. Varus' home was extremely large and well provisioned. A small bathhouse had even been built into the back of the house, which I gladly used, soaking the accumulated dirt from my body, and relaxing in the pleasant hot water provided by Varus' own household slaves. Only the sound of a large group of horseman arriving into the courtyard outside pulled me out of my bath-time dozing, and I reluctantly left the bathhouse and got ready for dinner. Now I had cleaned away the grime of my travels, I shaved and dressed in a clean tunic that was left out for me, re-donning my armour, which had been cleaned by a slave and once again gleamed in immaculate brilliance. I met Marcus, given the room adjacent to my own, and we left together and walked out into the courtyard.

The courtyard was full of Germanic warriors; I presumed an escort for a tribal chieftain who more than likely was joining us for dinner. Their horses had been led away by slaves and the honour guard milled around the courtyard, staring arrogantly about, to all the world looking as if they were the masters here, and not in the centre of an occupying force's military camp. The sheer size and physicality of German warriors always surprised the uninitiated. Marcus grunted, taken aback at being confronted by these huge men with long limbs and great barrel chests, far heavier and more thickset than the Celtic warriors from Gaul or the poor emaciated outcasts we encountered in the forest the night before. Most were blonde, but some had red or brown hair, and all wore long trousers held up with a rawhide thong and cloaks of blackish or brown wool. Some also wore a belted tunic, but the majority left their chests bare so their rippling muscles could be viewed clearly. Their hair was left long –either plaited or tied into a topknot – over their bearded faces, which looked at us with barely concealed contempt.

They were armed with heavy spears and oval or rectangle shields, painted brightly in either blue, green, or red, with large shield bosses and bronze edges. Many wore the single-bladed *sax* long knife from the belts, so useful for slashing and cutting into opposing warrior's flesh. A shiver ran down my spine as I stood facing them in that courtyard, remembering the thousands of similar warriors I'd faced at Western-Gate Pass.

Marcus cleared his throat. 'Please make way. We have business in the main residence.'

The Germans said nothing, just stared at him, and an uncomfortable silence ensued as Marcus turned red through anger and embarrassment. He took a deep breath, ready to try again, when the first of the warriors – a particularly ugly heavy-set brute with rotten teeth and bulging eyes – finally inclined his head, and the warriors shuffled aside to make a narrow pass through which we could walk.

We walked through them, trying to keep as much dignity as possible, our eyes straight ahead, as the burly warriors glared at us menacingly from either side. When we reached the other end, I shuddered in relief as I walked through the double doors into Varus' *atrium*. Slaves greeted us and shut the doors on the large group of warriors outside.

Marcus grumbled. 'Such rudeness! I have a mind to tell the governor about those men,' he complained.

I chuckled. 'That's them being polite. Remember, for a German warrior to give any ground is a great compliment.' I clapped him on the back and led him into the next room where Varus was expecting us for dinner. He had changed into a resplendent toga, in gleaming bright white, which carried his ample frame far better than the Roman armour he had been wearing earlier. As well as Asprenas and Ceionius being there, we were joined by another legate, a bull of a man called

Roman Mask

Avitus, and two lead tribunes of the army, both of senatorial rank, like Marcus and I. Besides the Romans at the dinner, the two German tribal chieftains I was expecting were there. One, a surprisingly slightly built young German with large blue eyes, wore a simple Roman tunic and sported a long blonde moustache, whilst the other, a giant with axe-handle shoulders and a fiery red beard, looked faintly ridiculous, dressed in a full Roman toga similar to Varus' own, only without the broad purple stripe Varus' carried at its rim. The two Germans were both seated on couches one side of Varus, whilst Marcus and I, as guests of honour, I supposed, were seated on the other, an honour normally reserved for the legates. We reclined on couches as we were served several courses of the finest foods, prepared by highly skilled slaves. The first course consisted of a highly seasoned fish I didn't recognise, but was told it could be caught in the local rivers. It was delicious and both Marcus and I ate greedily as Varus entertained his dinner guests and spoke at length about his plans for Germany.

'This town of Aurorae Novus is just the start. Once the population sees the benefit of Roman civilisation, they will soon fall into line. Already, we see Roman settlers and local tribesmen working side by side in the town.' Varus clapped his hands to instruct the slaves to remove our first course and bring on the main.

The large German in the toga, who I discovered was a chieftain from the Cherusci named Segestes, took a great swallow of wine and said in heavily accented Latin, 'It is the first of many great ventures between our two peoples.'

I licked the fishy sauce off my fingers. 'But isn't the town vulnerable without a road to Aliso?'

Varus smiled knowingly. 'Yes, of course it is. I am not a fool, Cassius. My plan was originally to build a road between here and Aliso before I started this project. Then we could winter here, instead of abandoning it come the autumn storms.'

'Then what stopped you?'

'The cost! What else?' Varus laughed. 'You've seen the land between here and Aliso. Nearly all of it is covered by forest or marsh. Do you have any idea how many men and resources are needed to build a road through such terrain? It will require a good portion of my army working on little else.' He shook his head in dismay. 'That is why I have had to delay the road building until next summer. By then I will have the extra engineers I need and the funds necessary to start such a large enterprise. All money needs to be extracted from the province itself. I have no imperial treasury to fall back upon – that's not how it works. I need to raise taxes from the province itself.'

It looked an expensive way to run a country to me. 'Why are you so eager to establish a Roman colony here?'

'Because this is the heart of Cherusci territory. Of all the German tribes, they are our closest allies.' He raised his goblet over to his two German guests who smiled broadly. 'Building a town here and enriching the Cherusci tribe over all of their rivals will show the benefits of the German tribes co-operating with us.'

The slightly built German, who turned out to be Segestes son-in-law, explained further in clear Latin. 'There are some amongst our people, even amongst the Cherusci, who still need convincing that the old ways should be put behind us. We have been hunters and warriors for so long, it is hard for some to accept that partnership with Rome will enrich and benefit both peoples.'

Segestes grunted and nodded his agreement and took another large swallow of wine from his goblet.

A troop of slaves came in the dining room with an enormous roasted pig and set about carving large slices off it for us all to enjoy. They brought food over to us and I relished the succulent taste of fresh meat served in a sweet wine and fig sauce. 'The Cherusci tribe is the main reason I have been sent here to assist you.'

The two Germans turned to me, and Varus raised an eyebrow. 'How do you mean?'

I explained my connection with Julius Arminius, how we had been close as children and fought together in Syria. I told him that Augustus felt my close connection with Julius could prove useful and help smooth relations between Rome and the Cherusci king. Varus listened with interest but when I had finished explaining said, 'But I am afraid your visit has therefore been in vain.'

I was shocked; had something befallen Julius? 'Why do you say that?'

'Because relations between Rome and the Cherusci couldn't be better.' He laughed and the two German chieftains joined him. 'Julius is not only a staunch ally. I value him as a good friend. Normally you can expect him to dine with us each evening. You're unlucky to miss him. He just happens to be away with his cavalry unit at the moment, fulfilling a task I set him. He is my eyes and ears in this region. Julius doesn't need any persuasion in co-operating with Rome. He joins my vision for the glorious future of Roman Germany.'

So that evil harpy Livia sent me all the way to Germany, thousand of miles – some of it hostile – for no reason whatsoever! That was just marvellous. I should be back in Rome, enjoying my wonderfully decadent life of drinking and fornicating, not be stuck out here in the armpit of the empire. 'So you don't need me?'

'Not really, no. Don't get me wrong. It is a pleasure to have the son of

Antonius Aprilis with me, a renowned soldier and pleasant dinner guest, but as far as being an intermediary between me and Arminius, what would be the point?'

The pork tasted like ashes in my mouth. All this way for nothing.

Marcus was less put off. 'I am sure we can be of use in other ways. Maybe we can take up another role, a more military one? We are both soldiers, after all.'

Varus slapped Marcus on the back heartily. 'Yes, that's the spirit! There are plenty of military assignments I can give you. Not all of the tribes are as friendly as the Cherusci. I'm sure your help will be invaluable. You two don't want to be stuck in the camp acting as aides. You can be out there using your martial prowess to tame the wilds.'

This just got better and better.

Marcus raised his hand at a passing slave, to receive more pork. 'Great! I can't wait to get started. I was worried I wouldn't get to see any action in Germany.'

Varus laughed. 'Don't worry, my boy. There is still plenty of work for warriors in my fledgling province. I fear it will be many years until Rome can lay down her sword arm in this land.'

Dinner stretched well into the evening, as more courses were laid out in front of us by Varus' slaves, most of whom were healthy young German boys yet to reach full manhood. I turned down the walnut cakes and the cheese served with honey and contented myself with a few poppy seed biscuits. Numeria wasn't wrong about Varus' reputation for generous hospitality. The number of courses and the sheer variety of foods on offer was impressive in a colony so far removed from the rest of the empire. Many a Roman host would be proud to produce such a lavish dinner, even one from the great city itself. The other officers all ate well and drank heavily, which fortunately helped distract me from my predicament. It was easier not to try and contemplate the months ahead, instead I tried to relax and enjoy the evening, which, apart from missing a few scantily clad women, and the presence of two barbarians, was not too different from the parties held by Seneca back in Rome – although I doubted Varus was in the habit of spicing his wine with the strong aphrodisiac 'Spanish fly'.

Marcus spoke politely to Varus and the camp praefect, Ceionius, although I noticed he was still drinking sparingly – that drunken incident in Lugdunum was still playing on his mind, no doubt. I turned my attention to Varus' nephew. 'So Asprenas, you leave the camp tomorrow?'

'That's right. Finally, the old man is letting me take my own command. Not before time. He's been holding me back here for one reason or another since the spring. He says he needs me, but I'm sure it's because he doesn't want to be left with Numonius' bellyaching.' He let out a loud laugh.

I offered my cup to a passing slave, who refilled it. 'Does Vala ever join you here for dinner?'

He laughed again. 'Not likely. He doesn't enjoy our company much and is always disapproving of any dinner more lavish than dried fruit and hard bread. I swear that man has ice in his veins.'

Same old Numonius then; he never was my sort. 'You won't miss him?'

'Not likely. I'll miss the old man, though, and a few of the others. Ceionius is alright, and so is your friend Julius. They can be relied upon to join me down in the town on the odd night.'

I was confused, and looked at him quizzically. 'Down in the town, what for?'

He turned and gave me an appraising look. 'Uncle's dinner parties are all very well, but it's best to go into the town to find some real entertainment in the evening. Why do you think most of the officers now stay there? Varus draws the line at allowing women in his own headquarters – it is a military camp after all. But boys never did do it for me.' He paused to slap a passing ginger-haired boy carrying a plate of honey cakes on the behind. 'Women are much more to my taste. Why don't you join me afterwards?'

I chuckled to myself. Asprenas was the sort of man I understood. Give me an honest rogue over a sanctimonious boor like Vala any day. 'I'm pretty tired after my journey. I don't think I'm up to the sort of entertainment you have in mind.'

Asprenas shrugged indifferently. 'Up to you, but at least join me in town for a drink in the taverns? You need to see the place.'

I supposed he was right. Besides, turning down an invitation from a man more senior in rank wouldn't look good. 'A drink or two won't hurt.'

'That's the spirit. Do you think your man Marcus will join us?'

I laughed. 'I can ask, but I doubt it. Marcus had an unfortunate incident with Celtic ale on our journey here, and he hasn't been fond of anything stronger than heavily watered wine ever since.'

Varus interrupted us by clapping his hands. 'Friends, please indulge me in a moment's notice.'

We all turned our attention to the governor, who was helped to his feet by two young slaves. 'Much as I have enjoyed your company tonight, it is time for me to retire.' Mock groans of disappointment greeted this. 'But, I will leave you with this thought: if the German tribes are ever to flourish as a province, it will be through the realisation that our culture can offer them so much, not by the bent of our swords alone. The work we do here is an example of how the tribes can profit from Rome and give them a better way of life: law and order, stone towns replacing wooden villages, agriculture, irrigation and organised religion. All are vital to show to the German warrior it is time for him to lay down his spear and shield and embrace Rome and her envoys.'

The officers in the room cheered loudly, and the two German chieftains looked delighted, but Asprenas whispered quietly to me, 'Sounds like uncle's been overindulging in the wine again. He always goes red as a beetroot, and then starts talking in pious platitudes.'

I stifled a laugh but bowed my head respectfully as the Governor Varus left us, after which I went over to Marcus to extend Asprenas' invitation to join him in the town. Sure enough, Marcus found an excuse not to join us. 'I would love to, Cassius, I really would, but I wish to write a letter to my father. The troop of men travelling to Mogontiacum with Legate Asprenas will be able to deliver it to the army messengers at Aliso. It may be my last chance for a while.'

Not likely, I thought. Messengers would regularly be travelling between the two camps, but I didn't argue with him. 'Farewell then, Marcus, I will see you in the morning. Remember to wake me if I don't rise by first muster. I might be back late and may be in need of the odd shake.'

Marcus laughed and retired to his room, and as I joined Asprenas, we ran into the two German chieftains who were waiting in the main courtyard for their horses to be brought to them. To my relief the German warriors who had greeted us earlier where engaged in mounting their horses and paid me and Asprenas no mind.

The giant Segestes clapped me on the shoulder. 'It has been a pleasure to meet the friend of Arminius. When he returns to us, you must join us in the halls of the Cherusci. We will show you a real banquet!'

I couldn't think of anything more ghastly but politely said, 'I look forward to that immensely. When do you think he will return?'

'Who knows with Arminius?' He laughed. 'He is probably chasing some young woman who caught his eye. He'll be back soon enough.'

Their two horses arrived and the younger one held the horse for Segestes to mount. Someone had clearly not informed Segestes that a toga is not the best outfit to wear for riding – without being held at all times it had a habit of coming open and revealing more than decency allowed. After a lot of trouble Segestes finally sat his horse, his great matted hairy chest poking out from his crumpled toga, framed under a wild ginger beard which still had the remains of dinner clinging to it. 'By thunder, this toga is a nuisance!' He turned to his son-in-law. 'Sesithacus, are you sure it doesn't make me look a fool?'

His son-in-law simpered as he mounted his horse. 'No, Segestes. You look every inch the noble Roman.'

The son-in-law was clearly a hopeless toady. I smiled. 'Safe journey home. Do you stay in the town?'

Segestes answered. 'No. You'll find us in the forests when you come to join us for a feast.' He whipped his horse into a canter and rode out of the gateway, quickly pursued by Sesithacus, and his mounted escort of warriors.

'What was all that about?' I asked Asprenas.

He shrugged and explained. 'Very few of the Cherusci have come to live in the town as yet. Most living here are dispossessed Ubians – a tribe defeated and subsumed by the Cherusci twenty years ago. The Cherusci are a proud race. If my uncle is to Romanise them, it will take time.'

'Segestes and his son-in-law seem Romanised enough.' I laughed, thinking about the ill-fitting toga.

Asprenas grinned. 'Don't be fooled by his appearance tonight. Segestes is a powerful man amongst the Cherusci. He almost became the tribal king, not your friend Julius.'

'Really? But didn't Julius become king by dint of his uncle being the previous king?'

'No – not exactly. Germanic leadership is not decided by kinship alone – although it still counts for a lot. Julius had the right blood ties, but before he won the crown he had to win over some opposing factions.'

We walked down the main military way towards the civilian settlement. 'Of which Segestes was one?'

'Exactly. He is a renowned warrior and many follow him blindly. However, he is prone to foolish flights of fancy and can be delusional when it comes to his own standing. Tonight's choice of attire is a typical example. I've never trusted him much. Far too easily bought for my liking.'

I knew the practice well. Rome would promote tribal leaders into becoming a part of the Roman aristocracy, binding them to Rome closely. Soon they would become used to the Roman banquets, stone bathhouses and the other trappings of Roman wealth. Returning to roasted game and open fires in a filthy long house rarely appealed. 'What other opposition does Julius face?'

'Another uncle of his, named Inguiomerus. He is a chieftain in the old mould. Whilst not openly anti-Rome, he believes that the Cherusci should cling to the old ways of doing things. You won't find him coming to dinner anytime soon

– not unless he can catch the main course himself and wrestle it to the ground with his bare hands,' he laughed. 'Inguiomerus is set in his ways and isn't impressed by our Roman town in the middle of their territory.'

As we left the Roman camp, I was sure I saw an ex-soldier of mine, a man from the XVIII Germanica, who had been with me at Western-Gate Pass. He ducked round a corner before I could be sure, but I thought he recognised me before turning away. Why would he not declare himself? I kept my attention on Asprenas. 'How did Julius win them over?'

'Well, as I said before, his uncle being chief before him counted for a lot, and Segestes was easily bought with Roman gold. The reason they finally chose Julius over Inguiomerus was probably down to Julius' status as a warrior – all those years fighting for Rome served him well. The German warriors in his cavalry who joined him in his overseas campaigns testified to his bravery and astuteness in battle. Good job for us they did, the whole process of pacifying the Cherusci would be a lot harder had either of the other two won the leadership. Even so, Julius treads a deadly razor-sharp line between the different factions. He needs continual success in battle to keep the men on his side. It was why Julius, together with his Cherusci cavalry, still holds a military role within the Roman army. He needs success in war to maintain the tribe's loyalty. Fortunately, he is as good an officer as they come.'

We were now in the Romanised town, and I could hear the raucous noise spilling out from several taverns in front of us. 'Speaking of officers, on my journey here I met a former friend of mine. She is married to an officer in the army. Her name is Numeria and her husband is called Otho, I think. Will I get a chance to meet him?'

Asprenas bellowed with laughter. 'Not unless you want to travel over the river Styx first!'

I was confused. 'What do you mean?'

He chuckled away. 'You refer to the "Coward's widow" – her husband is dead, and has been for over a year.'

Chapter Thirteen

Shock was my first reaction to his statement. 'What do you mean? He can't be. I only spoke to her earlier today …'

He was amused by my confusion, but otherwise unconcerned. 'I assure you he is, and good riddance too. He was a disgrace to the army, never should have served.'

Slowly, what she'd told me regarding her husband began to fall into place – *'you'll hear of him as soon as you reach the camp'*. Her husband wasn't a popular officer; his name was a byword for shame and revulsion to judge by Asprenas' reaction. I asked the legate, 'What lies to the north-east of the camp ramparts?'

'The cemetery. It's on top of a small hill. Why? Are you planning to pay your respects to him? I wouldn't bother. If I'd had my way, he'd never have been let into there – he defiles our honourable dead.' Asprenas went past the first few noisy taverns, turned a corner, and, down a quiet street, signalled that we had arrived at our destination. 'This inn is slightly more discerning than the others. You won't find any men from the lower ranks in here.'

I followed him in, my head still confused at Numeria's deception. It was so obvious now – the cemetery, not some small lookout tower commanded by an up and coming officer as I'd supposed. 'But why hadn't she just told me the truth?'

Asprenas sat at a small booth and signalled to the innkeeper to bring over some drinks. 'I imagine she was ashamed, and so she should be, her husband was a coward.'

I didn't realise I'd just spoken that last question aloud. I gave myself a mental shake. We were in a quiet tavern with low ceilings and a large fire burning at one end. A few soldiers sat at tables, and as Asprenas promised, none were below the rank of centurion. Joining them were a few civilians in the garb of the rich merchant class – brightly coloured thick woollen cloaks and richly embroidered tunics – together with a few less well-clad women, all young, and, more importantly, all pretty. I knew a brothel when I saw one. 'I thought we were going for a drink?'

Asprenas laughed. 'We are! This place serves the best wine to be found this side of the Rhenus.' A timid serving girl, with blonde hair, pretty face, and a thin frame, came over and filled two cups of wine, and then left the amphora on our table. 'You don't believe me ... try it?'

I took a sip. He was right, it was good. 'A strange place to find fine wine.'

'Not at all. This is a highly respectable establishment. Whereas the soldiers of lower rank use the common brothels under the town aqueduct, the centurions and the likes of us come here. It is quiet, and all the slaves here are well looked after – all the girls are clean. None have the pox – I can testify to that. I've slept with most of them myself.'

Sharing a bed companion with this shady nephew of the governor was hardly an enticing prospect as far as I was concerned. I looked round at the girls; they all looked to be of German origin, with blonde or red hair, large breasts, and athletic limbs. 'I'm sure they are all most grateful for your endorsement.'

He bellowed with laughter. 'You're a dry one, Cassius. Seriously, I only brought you here for a drink. It really is the best place in town.'

I took a long swallow of wine, thinking of Numeria and her dead husband. 'Tell me, what happened to Otho?' I asked Asprenas.

He sighed. 'There's not much to tell really. Otho was a tribune who joined us early last year. Straightaway you could tell he wasn't cut out for the army. He flinched when anyone raised their voice to him, was easily startled, and never held the respect of the men. Worse, he brought his awful wife along with him. They were besotted with one another, for reasons no one could understand. She was always interfering, getting him to speak up against Varus' orders. We knew it was her influence. Left to his own devices, he'd never have the spine for it.' He looked at his wine. 'That all came to an end when the fighting started.'

'Why, what happened?' Although with a sinking feeling, I already knew.

He took another pull of wine. 'Last summer we campaigned in the north against the Angrivarii. It was going well. Several of their war bands were destroyed, and we were pushing on to their heartland. I can only guess that Otho wanted to impress his wife when he returned to the summer camp. He volunteered to take a small group of scouts to reconnoitre an uncharted river we came across. Avitus was his legate, and he later told me that he thought Otho had finally found his backbone, so he agreed. Now, as I told you, Otho was never cut out for the army. He followed the river downstream for half a day, and then, on finding nothing of interest, decided to trek back to the army across country to save time. Otho being Otho, he got completely lost, night was falling, and he led his men, a group of no more than twenty legionaries, into an Angrivarii hunting party five times their size. He would have been fine if he had just stuck with his men, defended their position and waited for help. Instead, he took fright, ran off and left his men to it. Luckily an *optio*, a proper veteran named Callus, knew what to do and took command. They held firm and found a defensible position on higher ground. We came to their rescue before the casualty count got too high, although two good men lost their lives, and a further three took serious wounds. We chased off the hunting party and then discovered Otho cowering under a log.'

I drained the cup of wine and refilled it from the amphora. By the gods, is this how I'll end up? 'What did you do with him?'

'Well, unsurprisingly, the men under his command wanted to kill him on the spot. I sometimes think that would have been the kindest thing to do, then at least his dishonour wouldn't have followed him back with him: we could have made up some lie to placate his wife. But Avitus hates cowards and wanted him dealt with properly. We put him in chains and brought him back to Varus. His wife pleaded for his life, of course. By all accounts she still loved him, the gods only know why, but what could Varus do? Otho had run from battle and left his men to die? Varus had no option but to order Otho to take his own life – credit to Otho, he managed to do that without being coerced.'

I closed my eyes. 'No wonder she hates Varus.'

Asprenas turned to me. 'Who, the wife? You can say that again. She'll never admit Otho brought it on himself. She hates Varus because he ordered Otho's death, no matter that he had no choice.'

'Poor Numeria, it must have broken her heart, may Juno have mercy on her.' Not only did she lose the husband she plainly loved, she also must have felt everyone else's derision of him as another fresh wound.

Asprenas looked unimpressed. 'Sorry, I forgot you said she was a friend of yours. Fancy her, do you?' he leered. 'She's a pretty one, I'll give her that.'

I looked into the dark eyes of my companion, overshadowed by the one hairy eyebrow, and suddenly I didn't want to be around this seedy man, with his filthy sexual references. I thought of a stinging retort but reminded myself he was a legate, and Varus' nephew as well. I couldn't just walk away. 'I've known her since childhood. She grew up on the estate bordering my father's.'

He shrugged. 'Yes, I hear she is from a very respectable family.'

Something occurred to me and I blurted out. 'But wait ... what is she still doing here? If her husband died almost a year ago, surely she can return to Rome?'

Asprenas bellowed with laughter. 'You sound like Varus! He tells her that at every opportunity. He'd like nothing more to get her away from him. I tell him to pack her up in the next convoy back to Aliso and be done with it, but he is too afraid to upset her father. Apparently he is a big man in the Senate, and also a personal friend.'

Of course. If Varus was friends with my father, it stood to reason that he was also close associates with Senator Numerius. 'But why does she want to stay?'

'Who knows? Maybe just to make the governor's life more difficult. She protests each of Varus' edicts and questions his running of the province every chance she gets. Each day she comes to him with another issue to be dealt with. I don't mean to speak ill of your childhood friend, but she is a menace.' He refilled his cup, took another gulp of wine and turned his attention to some of the women who were wandering around the room.

So Numeria wouldn't leave Germany. Her stubbornness was obviously still alive and well. 'Where does she stay?'

Asprenas was obviously bored of the subject. 'How should I know? I told you, she's a menace. Somewhere in the town I guess. She isn't short of wealth.'

I dropped the subject and concentrated on finishing the wine. Soon I'd be able to leave, as it looked like one of the girls had succeeded in catching Asprenas' eye. He leered over at a particularly tall buxom German beauty, who was sitting with an old drunk on the verge of passing out. I downed the remains of the cup and was about to stand to leave when another woman caught my eye. It was the young girl Numeria introduced Marcus and I to earlier that day, the girl Julia. She wore her cowl over her head and was having a heated discussion with a barman. 'Asprenas, who's that girl over there?' I asked him.

He turned around and saw who I was talking about. 'Oh, that's the "gift taker".'

'Gift taker?' I repeated.

'Yes, she doesn't work here. She's probably just checking none of her boyfriends have slipped into here to visit one of the girls. She is very popular with some of the tribunes – some prefer a woman from Roman stock.'

'You can't mean she is a prostitute too?' I was confused. I had heard her talk; she sounded as if she was from a respectable family, and she was friends with Numeria.

'Well, yes of course. Although you'll never hear her admit it. She ran away from home to be with a tribune in the army who her family didn't approve of. The tribune died, leaving her here. The family understandably didn't want her back, so she has to survive the only way she knows how – on her back!' he laughed loudly. 'The thing is, you must never give her money. She has a small room above the saddle-maker's shop, in the street opposite. After sleeping with her, you leave a gift, something of high value, but not coinage. That's how she got her name. It helps her to convince herself that she isn't really the whore we all know her to be.'

'Unbelievable,' was all I said.

'Yes, isn't it!' he chuckled. 'She'll never go with someone from the ranks, not even a centurion. Fortunately for her, there are enough tribunes or respectable Romans in a big camp like ours just desperate for a genuine Roman lady. She calls them her boyfriends. If you're tempted, make sure you leave an expensive gift, or you'll never see her again. She doesn't come cheap.'

To judge by his knowing smile, he knew exactly how much that cost was. I suddenly felt slightly sick. I made my excuses, telling him I was exhausted, and needed to find my bed. He gave me a roguish wink, convinced that I was going to follow the young girl home. Let him think what he will about me, I thought. Tomorrow he leaves for Mogontiacum, and hopefully I'd never have the dubious pleasure of his company again.

I walked past the loud taverns, full to brimming with soldiers enjoying themselves, and took the track up to the military camp. It had been a revealing evening in more ways than one: rival chieftains vying for my friend's position; Numeria's husband dying a coward's death; and finally a young Roman girl reduced to selling her body for 'gifts'.

As I approached the gate to the camp, a centurion casually waved me through on seeing I was a tribune. I frowned at this. It was fine to be that lax in a peaceful province, but in hostile territory the guard should be checking who comes in and out of the camp. I supposed that they no longer viewed this camp as being situated in enemy territory, but even so, the men needed to keep up standards.

I walked up the military road and noticed one barracks with loud voices and laughter coming from it. I saw two centurions walk briskly over to the barrack block, stiff annoyance marking every step they took. The centurions will be putting those men on a charge, I thought. They'll be digging latrines come morning, or worse, be taking a beating from the centurions' vine-wood staffs. No matter which legion you served in, they all had their fair share of bad-tempered centurions who took pleasure from inflicting punishments. I chuckled to myself as I remembered past centurions from my own units. That reminded me. I'd seen one of my men earlier, as I walked out of the camp. An *optio* named Tetricus, I thought his name was. A good man, he might even have made centurion by now. I'd have to look him up tomorrow and find out why he'd run off without speaking to me.

A young German slave let me into Varus' large house next to the headquarters. It was completely silent within, and all the oil lamps were out. I stepped as quietly as possible on my way to my room so as not to wake anyone up – it wouldn't do to wake the governor in his own residence. I passed Marcus' room and noticed a light was still emitting from there. I opened the door a creak and peered inside. Marcus was asleep, wax tablet lying on his chest and stylus still clutched in his hand, with his oil lamp still burning by his bed on a small bedside table. I thought I'd better put it out; he'd only end up knocking it off and starting a fire otherwise. I stepped over to his bedside and looked at the wax tablet he had been composing to his father lying unsealed on top of him. I picked it up to put it on his bedside table when curiosity overtook me. Now, I know I shouldn't – it is an invasion of privacy – but most men never put anything too personal in letters as they know they will be read by someone before reaching the intended recipient, and I was technically his commanding officer and thus entitled to check his mail for any sensitive information. I still knew it was wrong – Marcus was now a friend – but the temptation proved irresistible. I opened up the three wax tablets, bound together with thongs threaded through holes bored near the rims and inscribed in Marcus' incredibly neat hand-writing.

Father, very many greetings

I hope this reaches you safe and that the camp is still in good shape and the men behaving themselves. I am sure with your guidance the men are faring well.

You will be glad to hear that I have safely arrived in Germany, and the journey has been everything I have wished for and more. However, I do have some dark tidings. We were attacked by brigands in the forest the night before we reached the military camp. You needn't worry, I am perfectly well and I acquitted myself well enough, but I am so lucky to have been put under the command of a great man like Cassius as he truly is a real hero. It was a real honour to fight by his side. When we were attacked, I foolishly engaged the men immediately. I know you warned me about keeping my head in danger, but everything happened so quickly. Cassius has more experience and he had the presence of mind to mount his horse first and chased the villains away. He saved my life. I will try and be more like him the next time I find myself in a dangerous position. Please don't worry for my welfare. With Cassius to look after me, I am sure no harm will come to me.

On arriving at the camp something happened that I am sure will change my life forever. I remember you describing how you felt when you first met my mother. I have felt exactly the same when I met a young Roman lady in the civilian camp today. Her beauty took my breath away, and I know her to have a good and pure heart. Her name is Julia and she is of a good Roman family, I am sure. How strange that the capricious gods can bring me to the girl of my dreams in Germany of all places. I promise not to do anything that will bring shame on our family, but I am sure I am already in love.

I will write again when I can tell you more. Everything is new here, and I cannot wait to get started in this new adventure. Farewell my father,
Marcus

I really shouldn't have read that. I closed the tablets, snuffed out the lamp, and went to my own room. After removing my armour and tunic and slipping into bed, I considered everything I'd just learnt.

Firstly, Marcus' impression of me is completely wrong. Not only does he wrongly think me a hero, he also thinks I saved his life, when in reality I'd tried to run and leave him to his early demise. Not only that, he thinks he is completely safe with me to look after him! It would be laughable if it also wasn't so tragic.

Secondly, he is in love with a girl who I just found out is called the 'gift taker'. Do I tell him? He is bound to find out one way or another, but it seems too cruel to shatter his illusions so quickly. Finally, he starts to show an interest in girls and then he goes too far and claims to be in love. How can he fall in love with someone just by saying hello to them? I place my arm over my face, close my eyes and decide to worry about it tomorrow. I'll put it on the list of things I need to resolve one way or another.

Chapter Fourteen

I rose early the next morning. My night had not been as late as I feared, and I'd become accustomed to awakening early. So it was with some surprise that I discovered, from a slave in Varus' home, that the governor had already left and could be found in the headquarters building, where he was to spend the day listening to plaintiffs and settling the disputes of the local inhabitants.

I supposed, as Marcus and I were to be aides to Varus, that this was something we should observe, to see if we could be of any assistance. We both ate a quick meal of millet porridge, prepared by the slaves and sweetened with honey, and then donned our armour and walked next door to the camp headquarters.

As soon as we left Varus' home we noticed the queue outside the headquarters. A whole host of local tribesmen and women were lining up to see the governor. It stretched right down the *Via Principalis*, even this early in the morning.

We walked through the main courtyard and into the main hall of the headquarters, which was flanked by two legionaries standing guard. Inside, Varus sat on a large throne and was listening to the plea of a local farmer who was having to speak through an interpreter. Marcus and I sat on a small bench to one side, where two scribes were busy taking notes on proceedings.

The interpreter, also a scribe dressed in a simple blue tunic, was a small wiry man with a long nose and a balding pate. He pointed at the farmer – a tall man with a very prominent Adam's apple – over a mournful face with a drooping moustache. 'He claims that the tribune, who visited his village, assessed the size of his herd incorrectly. They claim he owned twenty sheep and four cows, but he says ten of the sheep and one cow actually belonged to his neighbour.'

Varus leant forward and rubbed his eyes with his thumb and forefinger. 'No doubt he claims that the tax owed to us should reflect this.'

'Exactly, sir.'

Varus sighed. 'Tell him that I'm very sorry, but the tribunes were made very clear when they visited the villages to gain accurate figures on each farmer's livestock. If some of his herd was owned by his neighbour, he should have made that clear at the time.'

The interpreter explained this to the farmer who responded, in their guttural language that always made them sound angry, supplemented with many desperate hand gestures. It didn't take an expert linguist to realise that the farmer wasn't happy with this explanation. The interpreter turned back to Varus. 'He says that when the tribune came to the village, he had no idea that the herd was being counted in order to calculate tax revenues.'

Varus chuckled. 'Now there's a surprise. No doubt if he had known, he'd have hidden half his herd in the forest. It's quite simple really. Whether the sheep or cows belong to him or his neighbour, the amount of tax we extract will be the same – the value of one sheep in ten, or one cow in twenty. He can pay and then extract the coinage from his neighbour afterwards – that's if this neighbour really exists, of which I am very sceptical.'

The interpreter translated and the farmer started arguing back, this time in a raised voice.

Varus' eyes rolled up to the back of his head and he signalled to a centurion and two guards. 'That's quite enough of that. Remove the man.'

The two guards each grabbed hold of the man and ejected him quickly from the room, the man still shouting all the while. Then another plaintiff took his place; this time a very stout middle-aged women with blonde plaited hair framing a plain blunt face.

This woman was also complaining about the tax she owed the collectors, except she didn't even bother to come up with a story as to why the calculation was incorrect. Her argument was that she: 'never had to pay it before, so why should I pay it now?'

Varus looked on thoughtfully. 'Tell her that Rome needs to exact money from each province just as it does from any of its subject nations. It is the price you pay for us bringing peace to the region, new roads, and new structures that benefit the whole population – the new aqueduct for example.'

The interpreter explains this before getting a blunt response. He turned back to Varus. 'She says she doesn't want any of that stuff, so she should be able to keep her money.'

This brought laughter from the court, and even Varus smiled. 'Unfortunately, she doesn't have a choice. Please tell her to leave. Next.' The woman was led away and another took her place.

It was clear that the Germans were not taking too kindly to the new tax laws. They were finding out the hard way that Roman rule came with a price attached. I was mystified why Varus was bothering to listen to all these pleas personally. Surely he could get some lesser minion to do all this for him. Maybe he thought the governor should be seen to be dispensing justice personally. I was at a loss as to how I could possibly be of any assistance here, and by the time the tenth plaintiff came up to complain about his tax demand, I was thoroughly bored. I noticed Marcus was beginning to doze off, so I gave him a nudge and gestured that we were leaving.

We left the military headquarters, which was full of scribes, tribunes, and centurions all busily scurrying around, fulfilling the military administration for a camp approaching twenty thousand men. Marcus asked, 'Where are we going now?'

It was actually a good question. I'd been sent to Germany by the *imperator's* wife on the presumption that I could be useful, but in reality I had no idea what my duties should be. I held a military rank of senior tribune, but as I wasn't assigned to any legion, I commanded no men – well, except for Marcus – so my previous experience in the army was of little help. I needed to find some role in the military machine where I could be of use.

I looked up into the sky and judged it still shy of midday. 'Let's see if I can't put you through your paces on the training yard.' If I couldn't think a way of being useful, at least working on the training field would prevent me coming across as idle.

A smile broke across Marcus' face. 'Great! This is just like back home.'

The training yard was outside the military camp, and we walked there with the sun bursting through the clouds. 'Summer has reached us. A pleasant day to be working outside,' I commented to Marcus.

The training ground was being used by two cohorts of men who were practising with weighted wooden blades against wooden posts whilst being screamed at by supervising centurions. The routines were as common a sight as any in the army; the men learning by rote the techniques that in time might save their lives. Marcus and I stood by the side and admired the men's preparation.

'One, two and thrust!' bellowed a centurion in a loud voice as the men first struck blades against the base, then the top before thrusting at its centre.

'And again, one, two and thrust!'

Other centurions walked up and down the lines of men, cracking their vine staffs against any man they deemed guilty of not giving his all. 'Do you still work the drills in the Praetorian camp?' I asked Marcus.

'Of course. The Praetorians are more than just a guard for the *imperator* – they are an elite legion.' Marcus sounded defensive that I should question that.

I'd worked with some of the Praetorians myself and knew them to be slightly short of the elite legion Marcus thought them. Although made up of veterans, the men were stationed near Rome and therefore out of any combat zone. You could train for wars as much as you liked, but nothing focused the mind more than knowing that these techniques were worth learning if you wanted to remain alive – far greater motivation than the risk of a rap on the knuckles by a centurion's staff.

'Come on, let's get to work.' I picked up a wooden *gladius* and tossed another to Marcus.

One of the reasons I was always at odds with Numonius Vala was my insistence on training in full view of the lower ranks. He didn't think it was befitting a man of my station, but I disagreed. In my experience if the men could see you prepared to work as hard as them in the training field, you gleaned their respect, and the gods be dammed to any supposed loss of dignity to my rank.

We exercised in full armour, and before long we were clacking the wooden swords against one another. The training yard where we sparred was near the small knoll to the north-east of the encampment where I knew Numeria's husband to be buried. It reminded me of her unfortunate husband and the diminished state my childhood friend now found herself in.

'Ha! I have you again!' shouted Marcus as he cracked his wooden blade against my thigh. 'You're not at your best today.'

It was Marcus' fourth easy victory in a row and I dropped my sword and removed my helmet. 'I'm sorry, Marcus. I think I will have to leave our training until later. There is something I need to do.'

Marcus shrugged but didn't enquire of me further. He could tell I was distracted and of little use as a training companion. I left him as he started to work the drills against a wooden post, reflecting the drills practised by the legionaries in the field opposite.

I rubbed my sore shoulder – a reward from a heavy blow I received there from Marcus – and made my way into the town. I was seeking Numeria. I needed to see her again and hopefully make her see sense and persuade her to return to Rome. This extended mourning for her dead husband needed to stop – it was time to let his shade go, and leave Varus to govern the land without her interference. Numeria always was stubborn – I remembered the storming rows we'd had as children – but she could normally see sense eventually; surely she must see the folly of her remaining here?

Roman Mask

I wandered into the town and enquired into the whereabouts of the Lady Numeria's residence. It didn't take long; she was obviously well known in the town. Who could forget the disgraced officer's wife? I was directed to a modest but well-constructed house in a quiet quarter of the town which had been built in the shadow of a large silver birch, with long branches, that overhung the main courtyard of her home.

I knocked on the main door, and after a time it was opened by a middle-aged man with a bald head, simple tunic, and pleasant cheerful face. 'May I help you?'

I removed my helmet and inclined my head slightly. 'I seek an audience with the Lady Numeria.'

'I am afraid that Lady Numeria is not in attendance today. I am very sorry. Maybe you can try again in a couple of days.' He gave me an agreeable smile.

My eyes widened. 'A couple of days? Where has she gone?' This newly built town was in the middle of nowhere. She could hardly be away visiting an elderly aunt.

'The Lady Numeria does lots of work with the local tribeswomen of these parts,' he replied in a resigned tone that he clearly didn't expect me to understand, 'she will be back in a couple of days. You can come again then.'

He was right. I didn't understand. 'The local tribeswomen? You mean she is out visiting the German villages?'

'Yes, that's right.' His good-natured smile returned.

'What does she do with them?'

'She listens to their concerns, speaks to them of Roman rule, explains Rome's new tax laws and helps in any way she can.' He sounded proud but also concerned.

'But by the gods, who with? Does she have a military escort?' Even the friendliest of allied tribes was no place for a woman out alone.

'No. The Lady Numeria declines military protection – they would only alienate her from the people she is trying to help.' He sounded almost embarrassed saying this, as if he knew how stupid that sounded. 'Now, if you please, I have lots of work to be done.' He started closing the door. 'Come back in a couple of days.'

I put a firm arm against the door, preventing it closing. 'Don't you dare shut the door on me, slave.'

He stood up straight, obviously affronted, and said, 'I'm no slave. I'm a freedman!'

It made little odds to me; he was still obviously just Numeria's servant.

'My apologies. Now, can you tell me which village she is currently visiting?'

His tone changed to one more apologetic. 'I am very sorry. Numeria never tells her household where she intends to travel. It is a terrible nuisance. We never know when to expect her back.'

So if she was to die out there, after being butchered by roving wild tribesmen, nobody could even tell the Roman army where she'd gone: she would just simply disappear. 'How can you let a lady in your care behave so irresponsibly?' I demanded.

He lowered his eyes. 'I am afraid the Lady Numeria has a will of her own and cannot be swayed on this issue.'

We will see about that, I thought, but realised there was little to gain by taking it out on her freedman. 'Tell her that Tribune Aprilis came to visit and I will return in two days' time.' I forced myself to add, 'Please tell her I would be most grateful if she remained in residence until that time.' I knew there was no point in demanding anything from Numeria – that was a sure way to make her do the opposite to what you wanted.

The middle-aged man sighed. 'I surely will. It is nice to see someone from the military still has her welfare at heart.'

He slowly shut the door and I left, steaming at the stupidity of her. How many Roman women were crazy enough to roam the German countryside? It was ridiculous. Apart from the obvious dangers of rape, robbery and death from bandits, the tribes themselves probably took umbrage at an interfering Roman noblewoman playing at diplomacy. She could stir up a hornets nest in no time. Then they would kill her, and nobody would even know which village did it – absolute madness!

I trudged back into the military camp and gave myself a soak in Varus' bathhouse to settle me down. As I entered the hot water I leant my arms along the tiled side of the bath and tipped my head back, closing my eyes, and letting out a deep sigh. This was turning into a frustrating day: my two childhood friends, Julius and Numeria, were both supposed to be here but I was prevented speaking to either of them as they were gallivanting about the place trying to be heroes. Why couldn't I have normal friends?

Another lavish dinner was put on that night by Varus for his high command. His nephew Asprenas had already left for Mogontiacum so it was attended by Avitus, legate of the XVII, his lead tribune, Paullinus, the camp praefect, Ceionius, and a man I hadn't met yet, Selus, the legate of the XIX. He seemed a likeable enough man, with a trimmed beard and slightly thinning hair, he spoke with a gravely voice and was quick to compliment Varus on any particular dish he enjoyed. His lead tribune also joined us, a slender man named Grapper, so the only notable absentees were Numonius Vala, legate of the XVIII and his lead tribune. No one seemed surprised that they hadn't turned up, so Marcus and I paid it no mind.

'I saw you and your man, Marcus, training in the yard today. You both look to know your *gladius* work,' complimented Selus.

'I thank you, but in truth I wasn't at my best today. Marcus scored a few easy victories over me.'

Marcus grinned happily.

'Don't get too carried away with yourself, young man. Training in the field is one thing, fighting in combat something else entirely,' he reprimanded Marcus.

'I know that, sir. I wish to learn as much as I can from Cassius. He really is a good swordsman.' Marcus took a bite of roast chicken.

'As well you might. He has learnt to fight the hard way. I have heard of his exploits at Western-Gate Pass. You will do well to emulate him.'

Oh dear, another man who thought me a great hero. I smiled politely but said nothing. There was no point.

'I intend to take my legion out on some manoeuvres tomorrow, just simple drills and formation training. Would you two care to join me?' he asked.

'It would be an honour, sir,' snapped Marcus instantly.

I smiled at his eager response. It was nothing to get excited about. The legion would just be marching around in circles for the day. 'Unfortunately, I won't be able to join you tomorrow, but please, Marcus, you go ahead.'

Selus raised an eyebrow. 'Do you have something planned?'

I tore a small piece of bread off and ran it along my plate to soak up some of the sauce left there. I had been thinking on what I needed to do. 'If I am to be any use to Varus here, I need to get to grips with how this army is operating. I intend to spend some time in the reports office tomorrow to see how it is organised.'

'Pah, you wouldn't catch me in there. Good luck to you. Boring work if you ask me.' Selus shook his head in dismay and Marcus looked horrified by the prospect.

'Don't worry, Marcus. You enjoy the training tomorrow. I'll be with the scribes.' I wasn't exactly enthused by the task, but at least I thought I could be some use there.

And so it was that the next day I walked into the army's military headquarters. Several junior tribunes were busy at work drawing up rotas, listing men on report or compiling lists of men classified as walking wounded. I asked who was in charge, and a junior tribune named Palus, came over and saluted me. 'I am, sir. What brings you here?' He was obviously surprised that I would take an interest in the administrative running of the army. Most people of my rank shied away from anything that was considered menial.

'I am just here to observe and get a feel for what you do here,' I told him, walking around and inspecting the stacks of shelves, full to brimming with reports and filed wax tablets.

'Of course, sir,' he said. 'Would you like me to explain how it all works,' he added reluctantly. Plainly the last thing he wanted was a senior aide sticking his nose in where it wasn't wanted.

'That would be very helpful, thanks,' I said cheerfully, ignoring his reticence.

Much of what he explained was pretty standard stuff, similar to how my old legion used to be organised in Syria. Requisition orders for local livestock were filed on one wall, whilst lists of reports from the centurions made up the bulk of another. I painstakingly made sure he explained where each set of reports were kept and asked him to explain why they were kept. If this records office was anything like any of the others I knew, some reports would be kept for no reason that anyone here would know. By lunchtime I began to get a feel for the place, but something struck me as odd. Firstly, I noticed that nearly all the army's food came from local farmers. 'Don't the legions send out hunting parties of their own?' I asked Palus.

'Varus believes that by buying everything we need from the local farmers, it helps the tribes benefit from our presence,' he told me curtly.

It also made us vulnerable if they ever turned hostile towards us, I thought, but conceded that Varus' view was a valid one: once the tribes got a taste of the wealth we supplied, they would soon become dependant on it.

'But where are the military reports? All I see here are the lists of provisions, reports on the men, and the peaceful aspects of the army.'

'They go into the next room, sir.' He sounded cagey.

I looked into his eyes. 'Show me.'

He led me into the next room, which was piled high with military reports written by centurions after patrols. Straightaway I noticed two things: firstly, most of the reports were compiled by centurions from the XVIII legion, that of Numonius Vala, and secondly, most of the reports were still sealed. 'None of these have even been read,' I said aghast.

'That isn't down to us,' replied Palus defensively. 'Legate Asprenas is in charge of military intelligence. It is for his team to access all this stuff.'

That explained a lot. No doubt Asprenas couldn't be bothered with this boring intelligence work. It probably got in the way of him whoring in town. 'But Asprenas left the army yesterday, who is taking responsibility now?'

'I couldn't tell you, sir,' he answered.

'By the gods, what a way to run an army. I'll be back.' I left him and decided to find out who was taking control of the intelligence reports.

The first man I tried was Ceionius, the camp praefect. I reasoned that he would want to know who was ensuring the welfare of his camp. I was wrong. 'What, by Hades, does it have to do with me?' he told me incredulously. 'I run the camp, not the whole army. Ask the legion commanders, or better still, Varus himself.'

I didn't want to approach Varus. Any interference from me might be construed as criticism and I wasn't quite sure of my footing with him just yet. I left Ceionius in his small office in the headquarters and decided to speak to one of the legates. My first thought was to speak to Legate Selus, whom I'd spoken to the night before. He seemed a reasonable man, but then I remembered that he was out on a training exercise with Marcus. I supposed I could approach my old colleague Numonius Vala, but I was loathe to do this – his sanctimonious spirit was so tiresome. Besides, that would mean informing him that nobody had been reading any of the reports his legion were posting – I doubted that Varus would appreciate me giving Vala any more reason to have a grievance against him. That left Avitus, the stocky thick-necked legate I'd been introduced to at the dinner the other night.

I enquired to his whereabouts and was directed to first one area of the camp, and then another. Each time I arrived at his supposed location, I was told he had just left. It seemed as if Avitus was a restless man who never stood still for more than the time it took him to shout some orders at someone. It was with increasing frustration that I finally found out that he was now in a meeting with Governor Varus back at the company headquarters – which was the point I started at! I knew the prudent thing to do was to wait outside Varus' office and speak to Avitus when they were done, but by now my frustration at being directed from one end of the camp to the other made me impatient to get this over with, so I asked the guard at Varus' door to announce me at once.

Governor Varus looked up as I entered. He was standing over a table with Avitus, pouring over a sales ledger of merchant goods. 'Cassius?' He looked surprised. 'What brings you here?'

I cleared my throat. 'I was actually looking for Legate Avitus, my lord.'

Avitus turned round and furrowed his eyebrows. 'What business do you have with me?'

There was an edge of irritation to his question. I knew I should have waited till he'd finished his meeting. 'I've just been inspecting the records office next door,' I said carefully.

'What by mercury for?' he looked at me suspiciously. 'What did you find?'

'I was just acquainting myself with the military records. It seems that since Asprenas left, nobody knows who is in charge of the military intelligence.' I took a deep breath. 'I was wondering if you could tell me?'

Both Varus and Avitus looked at each other blankly. I thought so. Nobody had even given it a thought.

Varus was the first to speak. 'Well, Avitus. As you are now my senior legate, I suppose the job goes to you.'

'What! Don't be ridiculous. I have enough on my plate. Give it to Selus or Vala.'

Varus sighed. 'Selus spends most of his time on the training yard or out on manoeuvres. Can you really see him bothering with it?'

'Vala then?'

'What? And give him more reasons to criticise me? No chance.' Varus swept his arms apart crossly.

Varus' and Vala's relationship was so bad that it would be pointless Vala being given the role anyway, as the governor wouldn't listen to anything he said. 'I didn't mean to cause any disruption. There is no need to let me know now.' I started edging to the door – why did I get involved? It was nothing to do with me.

Both of them looked over at me and gave me an appraising look. Avitus spoke up. 'You're an aide to Varus. You do it.'

Varus smiled. 'Yes, what a good idea.'

Chapter Fifteen

And so it was that I became the commander of all military intelligence for the newly colonised province of Germany. I left Varus' office in a sense of complete bewilderment. I had no experience of such a role, had never worked in this field, was unused to the subtle delicacies of diplomacy and intrigue, and yet without a second thought, Varus and Avitus had promoted me into this position.

On the face of it, I should have been pleased that I'd been given a role that was primarily based in the camp and not in the field, but I unfelt uneasy taking on a position I was obviously unsuitable for. My only knowledge of the German tribes was now four years out of date, and what's more, that was when Rome was fighting the Chatti tribe to the south; I knew nothing of the Cherusci or the Angrivarii. I remembered the care taken by the legion's commanders in Syria, who worked with local experts and men with years of experience, taking military decisions with the utmost care and attention to detail. Here in Germany, where the military situation was nowhere near as stable, no one had even been bothering to do the job, and now they expected me to pick up the pieces and make informed decisions from several month's worth of unread reports. It was ridiculous, but I couldn't very well refuse the role. I had been ordered to help Varus in any capacity he wished, and besides, if I didn't do the job, it looked like no one else was going to do it at all. By Hades, why did I go and open my big mouth – why did I have to interfere? Stupid, stupid me.

The next few weeks rushed by in a blur. Marcus was delighted I'd been given such an important role, but his enthusiasm soon dimmed when he was roped into helping me read through endless lists of military records and accounts from deep-reaching patrols sent into the German interior by Numonius Vala. Reading reports of men in action reignited his desire to go into the field himself, and the endless routine of camp life was a torture to him. We still exercised in the training field each day, when I wasn't stuck in the records office, but I noticed an ever-increasing resentment of his confinement.

'This isn't what I joined the army for,' he told me whilst aiming a ruthless overhead strike at my head in the exercise yard.

I parried his blow then riposted with a deft flick of my wrists aiming at his sword arm. He backed away, but I pursued him, sensing my advantage. 'What did you join the army for?'

He struck back at me with his *gladius*. 'I came for adventure and real soldiering. I don't want to be reading about the exploits of others in the field, I want to be doing it myself, being of real use.'

I easily countered his clumsy attack. 'Oh! So you don't think you are being of real use here do you?'

He stumbled as his next strike found fresh air. 'Well am I? What have I done to be proud of?'

I tripped him as he went past me, sending him crashing to the ground. I put my foot on his back and leant my training blade against his throat. I whispered to him, 'A mistake in the field can lead to you getting yourself killed. A mistake by us, misreading some intelligence, can lead to hundreds losing their lives in an unnecessary battle or an ambush which could have been avoided. Now you tell me: which role is more important?'

He grumpily got to his feet, annoyed at my victory, it wasn't often he was beaten so easily, his frustration was affecting his swordsmanship. 'I know you're right, Cassius. It just isn't what I imagined myself doing in Germany.'

I clapped him on the shoulder and signalled that our exercises were finished for the day. We walked back to the records office where most of our days were spent.

I was sympathetic to his plight but I couldn't really help him. Most people found that army life wasn't all they had dreamt it would be. Besides, I didn't have time to fret over Marcus; I was consumed by my new role, and needed to gain as much knowledge of the local tribes as possible.

I felt a sense of unease at what I was learning. The only legate who was sending out any patrols was Vala. Selus spent his entire time training his men or putting them through manoeuvres, whilst Avitus was more concerned with using his men as builders of public works, increasing the size of the new town.

We also received reports from Julius' cavalry via messengers sent back to update the military command. It was strange seeing my old friend's neatly inscribed characters on the wax tablet, so familiar to me from our schooling. His reports were forthright and concise but gave a clear picture of the surrounding area. His cavalry worked alongside Vala's patrols when possible, but in the thick impenetrable forests in the Angrivarii heartland his cavalry were not very effective, as riding on horseback in such terrain was virtually impossible. This meant that Vala's patrols had to venture there alone.

I was baffled by Selus and Avitus' inaction but realised that this was probably due to the governor's direction. Varus was convinced that Germany was now a peaceful Roman province, and should be treated as any other. The only trouble was that it obviously wasn't at peace. Three of Vala's patrols never returned, all of whom had been sent deep into Angrivarii territory, to the dark forest of Teutoburgium. The Angrivarii were hiding something, but Varus wasn't acting on this, instead hoping that his stalled peace negotiations with them would resolve the issue. He regretted the loss of Roman life, but thought peace with the Angrivarii was still attainable.

It wasn't the only problem we faced. Relations with the Cherusci were, by all accounts, very good; they were peaceful and settled, but the Roman force was completely dependent on them. Rome's ally in the region supplied all her food, provisions, and supplies. A legion was supposed to be an independent unit, capable of surviving in any region self-sufficiently. This was the first thing I had to put right.

I managed to convince Varus that hunting parties from the legions should venture out to supply some of the legion's meat. Most was still bought in, but at least the men were using their skills to bring in some of the legion's food, gaining at least a degree of experience in hunting. It was a small victory, but at least I felt I was now doing some good.

I had less success persuading Varus to send a large expeditionary force into Teutoburg Forest. I knew they were hiding something, but Varus wouldn't budge on the issue. 'By the gods, man, you're getting worse than Vala!' he blasted at me in frustration one day. 'I told you, the peace negotiations are at a delicate point. If I send a force into their lands it will all have been for nothing. They will declare war again without hesitation.'

'But patrols in the region are being picked off. Men are being killed. None have returned from that region,' I replied exasperated.

'I expressly forbade Vala to send men there. Is it any wonder they are going missing? I told him: no more antagonising the Angrivarii. Wait until the peace negotiations are done. There is no need for us to go to war with them, and in fact, I strongly suggest that a peace accord would have been agreed by now if it was not for blasted Vala's interference.'

Avitus was in complete agreement with Varus, and Selus seemed unconcerned either way. I stewed in frustration, but had little choice but to accept Varus' wisdom on the matter. Maybe he was right? What did I know? I was only a senior tribune; Varus and Avitus were far more experienced in running a province than me. It was just hard to accept that my opinion counted for little.

Another matter of frustration for me was the absence of Numeria and Julius from the camp. I tried to visit Numeria in her town house on several occasions, but each time I turned up I was told she was away visiting the local villages. I strongly suspected she was avoiding me: no wonder, she knew I would try and convince her to return to Rome. Julius gave no indications in his reports when he intended to return to the Roman camp. It was frustrating not seeing him, but I consoled myself that at least he was out gathering some information in the region. At least one military commander, other than Vala, was bothering to do something and wasn't content just to hole up in the camp and hope for the best.

Governor Varus' lavish dinner parties went on each night, but I rarely attended. I often stayed late in the records office, reading reports by the light of a guttering oil lamp, my eyes straining from the hours of deep concentration. I sent back replies to the men in the field, telling them that their work was being appreciated and to keep on supplying as much intelligence as they could offer. At least the men now knew that the deaths of their comrades were not going unnoticed.

One evening, the endless hours pouring through reports got to me; my head ached, my backside was sore from the hard wooden benches in the office, and I needed to get out and clear my head. I thought of returning to Varus' home, and the bed that awaited me there, but decided it was too early to retire and to take a stroll instead around the camp in the early evening. It was now coming to the end of June, so the days were long, and a deep sunset lit the western sky. I stretched my back and pushed my hands down the arch of my spine. By the gods, it was good to get out of that records office. I wandered over to the far north of the huge military camp, intending to find the military hospital, where I could locate an apothecary to supply me with a herbal draught to help my tired eyes and headache. I rubbed my forehead as I went, and then out of the corner of my eye I caught the attention of the soldier Tetricus, whom I'd seen briefly on my first night in the camp. Just like last time, on seeing me, he scuttled out of sight.

'Oh no you don't. Not again,' I said aloud. He wasn't going to evade me this time. I followed the direction he had gone, slipping down between two granary blocks. I followed at a sharp pace, wondering why the soldier had run from me. I knew him as a good *optio*, a man I had fought with at Western-Gate

Pass – why should he wish to hide from me? The men at Western-Gate Pass thought me a hero, or so I thought. Could it be that they had worked out the truth? An uneasy feeling came over me as I approached a campfire built outside a barracks block, and saw Tetricus sitting there, his head bowed, in a small circle of a dozen or so men.

I knew all the men present. These were men from the first cohort of the XVIII, the same cohort that remained with me at Western-Gate Pass and had survived that terrible battle. There was stout Amandus, grizzled Gallus, the wiry Fidelis who still bore the scar along his face that he had earned standing his ground over an injured comrade. They were all men who fought with me at the pass and they all looked uneasy at my approach. Tetricus spoke first, 'So you have found us then, sir.'

I looked round at the men. All had a haunted look about them; none showed the confidence and bearing I expected of them. These were XVIII legion's first cohort, elite fighting men, and the legion's pride. 'With no help from you. Why didn't you announce yourself to me?'

They all looked around at one another with downcast eyes. Finally Tetricus answered softly, 'Why do you think, sir. Shame, of course.'

'Shame? What, by the gods, have you to be ashamed of? You are one of the finest *optio* I have ever commanded. You're all good men?'

He answered, his voice turning bitter. 'But that's just it, sir. I am no longer an *optio*, just a plain legionary now.'

I looked at his uniform in shock. He was right, the telltale insignia of an *optio* was missing; I had expected him to have made centurion by now. 'But you are still the first cohort?' I said in confusion.

Large Amandus spoke up, 'Not any more, sir. We have been moved from the first cohort. We now reside in the sixth. Any menial degrading task needing doing, you can normally rely on us to be assigned to it.' He laughed hollowly, no joy in the sound.

I sat down heavily by their fire. 'But why? What happened?'

Tetricus took up the story. He spoke in a soft husky voice full of emotion. 'Things were different after you left, sir. You were a man we could all follow. A man I would gladly lay my life down for.' I felt guilt at his words, but simply nodded to encourage him to continue. 'But when the command changed here, the army changed. Varus took over and brought that nephew of his along with him – Asprenas.' He spat out this last word, and the other men grumbled in assent. 'A right bastard officer, that one. We are all glad to see the back of that evil whoreson.'

I was shocked by his words. Criticising one of my fellow senior officers was a serious offence, not to mention the casual insults he had thrown in, but I wanted to get to the bottom of this. 'What did he do?'

'He took over command of the Eighteenth for a while. That was when the problems started.' He looked around at his companions, as if to check that they were alright with him revealing so much. They all nodded in encouragement. They trusted me, and wanted me to know their story. 'As the first cohort, all the other men in the legion looked up to us. After Western-Gate Pass we were treated like heroes. Everyone said we deserved it.' He smiled with pride. 'But when Asprenas took over he wanted to change things around. He liked his men to grovel to him. He appointed new centurions from men whose only merit seemed to be their ability to suck up to him.'

There was another growl of approval from the others. I had to be careful; was this simply the jealous bickering of men overlooked for promotion?

'We didn't like it but we accepted it, besides, most of the centurions in our own cohort were decorated men so he could hardly replace them,' he paused, 'or so we thought.'

'He replaced one of yours?' I asked, a tight knot of dread in my stomach.

'Not at first, how could he? But he was resentful of our popularity, I think. Claimed we were getting above our station, but really I think it was because none of the men in our cohort, or any other for that matter, respected him.

'Slights were aimed our way. Sometimes when we went on manoeuvres we weren't positioned in our customary position, once even being put in the second rank, near the left.'

I rubbed my chin, considering, as they were the first cohort, they should have been positioned in the first rank and to the right side of the legion: the customary strength of any army. 'Maybe Asprenas felt that section of the legion needed stiffening up? A legate hardly needs to explain his actions to his men.'

'If that were the only gripe, then we would understand, but it wasn't. Our time in the training yard was put behind others, our position in the march changed, we were often used digging latrine pits more often than leading the legion in a campaign.'

I shook my head. 'That is very sad, Tetricus. But maybe he thought your popularity with the other units had got out of hand, and you needed to be taught your place.'

A flash of anger crossed his face. 'No, sir, you're wrong. It had nothing to do with us. Asprenas wanted all the men of rank to treat him with complete subservience, but this didn't come easily to the centurions of our cohort. He claimed that they were disrespectful, but they treated him no differently to any other legate we had ever been given. And even if this was the case, why should the men of the first cohort suffer because of the wrangling of their officers? We were all veterans. We shouldn't have been treated with such dishonour.

'It all came to a head after last summer's campaign. We had been campaigning in the north, and it had gone well. We had pacified them, and it should have been a time of celebration. Instead, it was our humiliation. The old centurions, Gerius and Aurelus, came to their retirement at the close of the campaign and left the service. It was a sad day but both had served twenty years service and we waved them on their way. I was put up as a candidate to take their place alongside Junius. Do you remember him?'

I nodded my head. 'Both of you would have made excellent centurions.'

'Our senior centurion, Aquila, put us both forward to the legate, saying the exact same thing. Asprenas just laughed. He said, "I think it's time we had some new blood in your cohort. I'll make the choice myself." Both me and Junius were sent back to the camp, shamed.'

That shouldn't have happened; senior centurion's opinions were normally taken into account when it came to promoting men from the ranks; after all, they knew the men better than any other. Approval from the legate would be expected; unless either man was guilty of some indiscretion only the commander knew of. No wonder they were shamed by the refusal.

Tetricus' voice became rich with emotion as he continued. 'Aquila didn't look happy but told us we had to respect the legate's decision. Who are we to argue with a man so far above us in rank? However, without our knowledge, Aquila went back to Asprenas to try and plead our case personally, thinking he could reason with the man. As a reward, Aquila was charged with misconduct and sentenced to a flogging, and also demoted to legionary.'

'What! Aquila!' I said aghast. 'But he earned the oak leaves at Western-Gate Pass!' Alongside me, centurions Aquila and Gerius were also decorated with Rome's highest honour by Tiberius himself in front of the entire Roman army. Breaking a man like him down to the ranks was unheard of.

'Exactly, sir. Refusing me and Junius was one thing, but dishonouring Aquila was something none of us could bear. We were lined up in ranks to witness his flogging. It was here we were presented with our three new centurions, all of whom came from other units, men unknown to us, and, as we surmised, mere lackeys of Asprenas.'

There was a grumbled agreement.

'Aquila was trussed up to the punishment post, and Asprenas came to witness the punishment personally. He addressed us. "This man felt the need to question my orders. There can be no tolerance of this in my legion. Centurions continue with the punishment as we discussed."

'We all expected the new centurions to carry out the punishment, but to our astonishment, they called me and Junius forward and ordered us to administer the flogging.'

I sank my head in my hands as Tetricus spoke on. 'We both refused. Asprenas shouted at us, told us we would receive the same unless we co-operated. All this in front of the cohort. Then all the fury of Hades broke out.'

'What happened?'

'Junius spat at the legate, and threw his *gladius* at him. "If this is Roman justice, then you can have it. I'll not carry a sword for the likes of you." At his defiance, the men of our cohort cheered and then revolted. They charged Asprenas and his bodyguard, who fled, leaving us alone in the punishment yard. We freed Aquila but he was furious with us, told us we should have flogged him as ordered. He said it was unheard of for the first cohort to rebel. No thought had been given to our little rebellion, and when Asprenas returned, with his uncle Varus and several cohorts of legionaries at their command, we didn't even resist.'

Tetricus bowed his head. 'We were lucky that Varus made the decision on our punishment and not Asprenas, I guess. I'm sure if Asprenas had been given the chance he'd have decimated our ranks at least,' Tetricus referred to the old punishment of killing one man in ten, 'but his uncle Varus wanted to quieten down any talk of rebellion in his army and was lenient. Even so, Aquila was dismissed from the army and left a pauper with no retirement or station. Junius was put to death, allegedly for instigating the revolt, and I was demoted to legionary. The first cohort was demoted to the sixth, informed it was a unit of shame rather than honour, and we have been appointed to every demeaning task ever since.'

A cold anger burned in me. These were once my men: the same men who had stood by me at the pass. They were heroes, and they didn't deserve such harsh treatment. 'Asprenas has gone now,' I reminded them.

'Yes, thank the gods. Numonius Vala leads the Eighteenth legion now. He is a better man, but we're still not trusted. And who can blame him? We are the unit that rebelled, no matter that we were provoked into it. The shame of it still haunts us.'

'Varus never told me of your misfortune.' I remembered my arrival in the camp, and Varus' warm welcome. He didn't tell me that the men I'd once commanded had been humiliated by his nephew.

'Ha! I doubt the governor even knew who we were. His only concern was the Senate not finding out about our little revolt. He is a man used to collecting taxes and proclaiming laws. He's no soldier.'

I must admit, Tetricus scathing appraisal of the man was similar to the impression I was getting of him. 'So this is why you have been avoiding me?'

They all lowered their eyes again. 'We were getting used to the shame of our new station in the army. But seeing you back in the camp brought it all back. It reminded us of what we'd all lost. We were a fine unit once.'

I raised my head and looked at them all squarely. 'And you still are.' I stood up. 'I cannot guarantee you much. I've no military command here now. But I will speak to Legate Vala. You are the heroes of Western-Gate Pass, never forget that.'

I might not be able to achieve much, but hopefully I could at least stop the demeaning duties this cohort was being subjected to.

They all stood, straight backed, just like the men I remembered. 'Thank you, sir. It is good to see you again. The army hasn't been the same without you.'

All the men voiced their agreement, as I nodded my head in farewell and walked away, a lump forming in my throat. They still thought I was the same fearless commander of all those years before. They still expected me to make everything alright again.

I felt guilty that I hadn't sought them out sooner. I'd told myself that it was because I didn't want to encroach on Numonius Vala's command, but I knew the real reason: If they knew the truth about me, what would they really think of me?

Chapter Sixteen

We were just finishing our morning meal of bread and honey, as Varus' slaves came and collected the empty plates. I smiled in gratitude and remarked to Marcus, 'I need to pay a visit to Legate Vala before we start on the reports today. You can go on ahead without me. Can you start cataloguing the new ones we received from the cavalry in the east?'

Marcus looked up, surprised. 'Visiting Vala? Why?'

I looked away. 'It's a personal matter, nothing to do with our work.'

'Can I join you?' he asked hopefully.

Why was nothing ever simple with Marcus? I was taking a risk with my military career confronting Vala. Interfering in a senior officer's command wasn't something the army approved of. The last thing I wanted to do was embroil Marcus in the affair. 'What for? I told you it's a personal matter.'

Marcus wasn't put off. 'Well, most of the reports we filter through come from men of the Eighteenth. It would be nice to see the men who are out risking their lives compiling them.'

He had me there, I couldn't really argue with that. 'You can come to their headquarters building, speak to some of the tribunes there, but I need to speak to Vala alone.'

His eyes lit up. 'Of course, I won't interfere.'

We walked over to the north of the camp where the XVIII were stationed. I walked past the barracks block where I'd spoken with the men the night before, and I approached the guards outside the legion's small headquarters building.

'Tribune Cassius Aprilis requests an audience with Legate Vala,' I said on arrival, and the guard went to see whether the legate was available.

Meantime, I told Marcus, 'Now you stay here, and stay out of trouble. You can speak to who you like, but don't mention you came with me.'

He nodded his head seriously, before I was escorted by the guard who had returned telling me that the legate would see me at once.

I followed the guard into Vala's small command room. It was just as I would expect a room of Vala's to be: barely any furnishings, just a simple writing desk with a neatly piled stack of reports on it. Honestly, Vala could make the Spartans look wasteful.

He stood as I entered, brow furrowed under his steel-grey hair. 'Cassius, what brings you here?'

How to start this conversation tactfully? 'Please, do you mind if I sit?' There was only a wooden stool to sit on, but I was damned if I was going to report to him like one of his subordinates.

He nodded and sat down behind his desk. 'If you must, but I hope this doesn't take long, I'm a busy man.'

I gritted my teeth at his rudeness, but managed to keep myself calm I decided that the best course of action was simply to be honest and frank with him. 'Numonius, it is no secret that we've never been the best of friends,' – he grunted at this – 'but I know you're an honest and straightforward man. We have different opinions on how the army should be run, but both have the welfare of the men at heart.'

He narrowed his eyes, but his tone mellowed. 'Very well, what is your point?'

'I ran into some of the men from my previous command yesterday. Men who were in the first cohort when I was in the Eighteenth.'

He rolled his eyes. 'Then you know those men are now my sixth cohort.'

I steeled myself. 'They are the same men who stood by me at Western-Gate Pass. They don't deserve to be treated like this.'

Vala banged his fist on the desk. 'By the gods, man! You can't tell me how to run my legion.'

I knew this wasn't going to be easy. I tried to put on a more conciliatory tone, 'I am not trying to interfere with your command. I am just telling you that they're good men.'

Vala was still furious, standing and pacing. 'They rebelled against their legate. They shame us all!'

'They made a protest against Asprenas, not you, Vala, and they were provoked beyond measure. They never intended to revolt against the army.'

He looked down at me. 'Gods know, I didn't like Asprenas any more than they did. But you cannot let open rebellion go unpunished in any legion. They were lucky that Governor Varus was so lenient with them.'

'I agree, but why are they still working punishment shifts. Haven't they lost enough already?'

He put both arms on the table and leant over at me. 'Do you think you can tell me how to discipline my own men?'

I sat there in shock, I was expecting this to be difficult but this was ridiculous. Vala started pacing back and forwards, telling me that he was tired of being undermined by other officers, that no one could tell him how to run his legion. 'I know what the others say about me, don't think that I don't! But they can't interfere with the internal running of my legion.'

Vala was always a stickler for decorum in the army, but this was verging on paranoia. I thought the best thing for me to do was to just leave. 'Numonius, this was obviously a mistake. I apologise for disturbing you.' I stood to leave.

He spun on me. 'So, you'll report back to Varus now, will you? Tell him that my running of the XVIII is not up to scratch – that you'd be a better legate?'

The accusation was so outrageous that I didn't know how to respond. Why was he so defensive? Why would he think that I would run to Varus? Then it occurred to me. Vala wasn't just angry, he was frightened.

For the last year, Vala had been ostracised by the other members of the high command, and that isolation had obviously affected Vala more than I'd realised. He was oversensitised to any implied criticism of the running of his legion and thought that all the other officers were out to undermine him, including me.

The only way that I was going to get him to listen to me would be to take a risk. I needed to get him to trust me. 'You don't approve of Varus' running of the army, do you?'

Vala went bright red and shouted at me. 'What? How dare you question my loyalty!'

I swallowed hard. 'I share your misgivings.'

There, it was out there now, I couldn't take it back.

All the fight went out of Vala and he sat down heavily and then looked up at me. 'You've taken quite a chance telling me that. If I were to report you to Varus, you could be thrown in chains before the day is out.'

I held his gaze. 'But you won't, will you, Numonius? Because you know that I only have the welfare of the men at heart. I have no hidden agenda, unlike some of the men who surround the governor.'

He nodded in mute agreement.

I continued. 'I would never tell you how to run your legion. I'm just putting in a word for some honest and loyal men.'

He admitted, 'I have been hasty with you. My tribunes tell me that they finally have received some recognition of their work against the Angrivarii since you've taken over gathering the intelligence reports. For that alone I should have heard you out.'

I sat back on my stool. 'I want no part in running your legion, Numonius. I am just appealing for your mercy. I know they are good men.'

He closed his eyes. 'Yes, I expect you're right. I cannot reinstate them as the first cohort, but they should be treated just as any other unit from now on.'

I breathed a sigh of relief. 'They will be very grateful. They won't let you down.'

He looked up at me. 'I know they won't. None of my men ever do. It is a good legion. They make me proud. That is why it hurt so much when their deaths seemed to go unnoticed by Asprenas. It was as if none of their reports were even being taken seriously.'

Their reports weren't even being read by Asprenas, that's why. I didn't dare tell him that, but decided to get to the heart of the matter. 'What do you think of Varus?'

He shook his head as he stared at the floor. 'I think Governor Varus is a good man, but I don't think he grasps the gravity of the situation here. I don't think he understands how vulnerable we are. The German tribes outnumber us in their thousands. We need to get back on a war footing.'

I hesitated, not agreeing with him entirely. 'You cannot deny that the relationship with the Cherusci has gone well. Maybe he can do the same with the Angrivarii?'

'The Cherusci are only loyal because their king is Julius Arminius, a man unquestionably loyal to Rome. I don't trust his uncle Inguiomerus or that chieftain, Segestes, no matter that he has started dressing like a Roman. Both their loyalties are only to themselves. What if either were to supplant Julius as king?'

That didn't even bear thinking about; it wouldn't take much to turn the Cherusci back into a hostile nation. 'You think peace with the Angrivarii unlikely?'

He slapped his open palm on his desk. 'Of course I think it unlikely. I have lost three patrols in that area. Varus blames me for sending them there but there is more to it than that. We should be campaigning against them in strength, so we can *impose* a peace on them. Otherwise, any peace we obtain is illusionary.'

'Each month we waste here in this summer camp makes us look weaker. The campaigning season will soon be over, and then we will have to return to Aliso, and what will we have achieved? Nothing! That's what.'

I took a long look at Numonius Vala. It was no doubt that given the choice, he would have all-out war with the Angrivarii tribe. Sometimes, old soldiers can't accept the peace which follows a campaign, but I didn't think that was the case here: Vala was an insufferable boor, but he was no fool. 'We need to find out what the Angrivarii are up to, and whether they have mobilised any of their war host. Are you still sending patrols into their territory?'

He turned to me. 'How can I? I have already lost three patrols there. Varus has told me to send no more, and I am sick of losing my men. Why can't any of the other legions take a lead here?'

I shook my head. 'Because the other legates *believe* in Varus' policy of appeasement. I know it is hard losing men, but we need information. You don't trust the Angrivarii – then you must come up with some evidence backing up your claims.'

I felt sick that I was asking him to send men to almost certain death, but what else was there to do? An uneasy feeling stirred in my belly – I was prepared for others to risk their lives in war, but wasn't prepared to risk my own.

He let out a long sigh. 'Yes, you're right. I have known it all alone, but I was hoping Varus could be persuaded otherwise. I'll never get him to believe me without more information.'

I stood to leave and he accompanied me to the door. 'I'm glad you came to speak to me, Cassius. It's good to know that I'm not alone in my suspicions.'

As he opened the door, he saw Marcus waiting for me there. 'And is this the man I met when you arrived in the camp?' asked Vala.

He answered for himself. 'Yes, I am Marcus Scaeva, sir. Aide to Cassius, and new to Germany,'

Vala grunted. 'Is this your first campaign?'

'Yes sir, but unfortunately I spend most of my time in the records office. I wish I could see some real soldiering.'

Vala frowned. 'Well if it is action you are after, you can always join us in the Eighteenth. We can always use a man eager to face danger.'

I didn't like where this was going, so I thought I better cut it off before Marcus volunteered himself for a suicide mission. 'Marcus has plenty to do keeping me company. I am understaffed as it is. Don't take my only aide.'

Numonius Vala turned to me. 'Of course. You both do invaluable work for us. Good day to you both.'

We bid him farewell and started walking back to the camp headquarters.

Marcus was sulking. 'You don't really need me in the records office. There are plenty of scribes, and they can do anything I can.'

I knew he wouldn't let this drop. 'None of them have any military experience. They're scribes, not soldiers.'

'But that is just it. I don't have any military experience either. All I have done since arriving in Germany is stay in this camp.' His frustration was evident from his tone.

I sighed. How was I going to convince him this time? 'There will be plenty of time for you to gain military experience, don't rush to an early grave for the sake of impatience.'

He motioned to reply, but was cut off by a large commotion in the centre of the camp. Great cheers were coming from the men there and the unmistakable sound of a large host of horses. I quickly asked a passing legionary what was going on.

He looked excited to be the bringer of such news. 'It is the return of our cavalry. Julius Arminius is back in the camp, and he has brought his whole troop with him.'

Chapter Seventeen

Both Marcus and I rushed to the centre of the camp. I was brimming with expectation at seeing my old friend, and Marcus was almost as eager, after hearing so much about him.

'Did you know he was returning? I didn't see any mention of it in the reports he sent,' asked Marcus as he hurried along by my side.

I could see the mill of horses in the central parade ground, Germanic warriors garbed in Roman auxiliary uniforms, and great warhorses, each of a similar size to the tall Libyan horses Marcus and I had rode to Germany from Rome. 'No, but that's just like Julius. Always comes up with the unexpected!'

I was straining to pick out my friend from the large corps of cavalry; just as the legionary had said, Julius was back with his entire cavalry force, so the entire parade ground was full of steaming horses and sweating riders. There was a happy atmosphere amongst the men; Julius' cavalry were obviously popular with the rest of the army, which was not surprising thanks to their reputation as a top-class unit with untold victories to boast of in the field. I made out the command party, a group of large warriors with flowing scarlet cloaks and distinctive helmets with wings on their side. These must be Julius' close bodyguard, his closest warriors and trusted companions. Then I saw him, smiling as he dismounted his great white horse, looking every inch the model hero, with his closely shaved, good-looking, chiselled features and perfect even smile. His broad shoulders sat atop a classically muscular frame and as he removed his helmet, his familiar blonde thatch of hair was as striking as ever.

'Julius!' I shouted, walking through the throngs of men. He was in a discussion with Legate Avitus who had come out to welcome the cavalry back to the camp. He didn't hear me, being far too preoccupied with his conversation with the legate, slapping him on the back in familiar companionship at some joke or remark from the thick-necked general. 'Julius,' I repeated, in a loud clear voice, and this time he did turn to see who was calling him.

His eyes bulged in shock at seeing me, and he dropped his winged helmet and advanced over to me. 'By all the gods! Gaius, is that really you? What are you doing in Germany?'

I laughed at his surprise and clasped him in a tight embrace, which he returned gladly. I pulled back to look at him. 'I heard a rumour that someone I knew had got ideas above his station and become a king! This I had to see!'

Julius laughed out loud and pulled me back into a strong embrace. 'Never did I expect to see you back here in Germany. I thought your time in the legions were at an end. What made you return?'

'Once a soldier, always a soldier.' It was amazing how easy it was to return to the easy bluffing and camaraderie of years gone by. 'You don't think I can let you take all the glory in this new Roman province.'

Julius still looked bewildered to see me again. 'Well, whatever the reason, now everything is complete. I have my closest friend back by my side to witness the glory of Rome take its rightful place in my homeland. Nothing can be more sweet.'

Legate Avitus cleared his throat. 'I don't wish to interrupt a reunion between two old comrades, but we should have these men billeted properly in the camp.'

I shook myself. 'Yes of course, Avitus. I apologise for my intrusion. But please, before you are taken over by more practical matters, Julius, please meet my friend Marcus Scaeva. He has heard so much about you, I cannot let this opportunity be passed up.'

Marcus stepped forward and saluted stiffly, banging his fist against his chest. 'An honour to meet you, sir.'

Julius laughed at his formality and dragged him into an embrace. 'Any friend of Cassius is a friend of mine. I hope to get to know you well.'

Marcus looked surprised but happy at Julius' easygoing manner. It was why Julius was so popular amongst his men; he knew how to make each man under his command know their importance. Julius smiled in approval at Marcus' solid muscular frame, so similar to his own. 'You're a large lad. I bet you've been worked hard by my friend Cassius.'

'Marcus is a fine swordsmen, better than I ever was,' I admitted.

Marcus blushed at the praise but Julius looked surprised. 'Really? Better than you?' He turned to Marcus. 'Cassius was the only man in the tenth who could best me with a blade – you must be a rare talent, Marcus.'

Marcus was still blushing. 'It's an honour that you think so. I wish only to emulate you and Cassius,'

I chuckled. 'Alright, this is getting too sentimental for me.' I barked a laugh. 'Besides, you don't want to emulate this old rogue.' I slapped Julius on the shoulder. 'He'll have you up to mischief before you know it – do you remember those two baker's daughters, Julius?'

Julius laughed out loud. 'How can I forget Amata and her sister! Good times Gaius.' He shook his head, smiling, then said to me, 'But you must excuse me. Avitus is right. I will need to get the men billeted. We only intend to stay here one night, then we will return to the Cherusci village close to here.'

I felt a pang of disappointment. Did he need to leave so soon? It must have shown on my face because Julius instantly said, 'Don't worry, it's not far from here. We'll have plenty of opportunities to catch up. I intend to stay near the main Roman host for a while yet. Tonight I will be dining with Varus. Will you be joining us?'

I hadn't spent many evenings with the governor lately, being too tied up with my work, but the invitations to his dinners had never been revoked, so I gladly agreed. 'I will see you there, I have so much to speak to you about.'

Julius grinned and slapped me on the back, 'I look forward to it,' then he turned to his men, organising where they went, once again the model professional solider I remembered from Syria. I left him to it, taking Marcus with me back into Varus' home, where we readied ourselves for dinner.

After bathing, we dressed in formal togas marked with the broad purple stripe, marking both Marcus and I as members of the senatorial class. Julius was seated next to governor Varus, and he also was dressed in a toga, but unlike Segestes, the toga didn't look out of place on Julius. He was born to it, and his toga showed the thin purple stripe marking him from the equestrian class, which was the greatest honour Rome could grant a foreign prince, earned through his remarkable military career in Rome's service.

The normal guests were all in attendance: Avitus, Selus, Ceionius, and a smattering of others from Varus' high command. As usual Vala wasn't in attendance but that barely caused notice any more. I sat myself the other side of Julius, and Marcus joined me there. As ever, Varus' dinner service was impeccable; we started with some delicious baked quinces, then a course of eggs poached in wine, followed by a great ham, cooked in a red wine and fennel sauce.

Julius raised his silver goblet of wine. 'Ahh, the pleasure of a Roman table at last. After weeks in the campaign saddle, it is a relief to finally find some food of quality. Varus, you really do know how to welcome a man back,'

Governor Varus beamed. 'It's a pleasure to have you back amongst us,

Julius. You know you're always welcome in my home. As you all are.' He swept his hands round to include us all. 'We are living proof that the province of Germany will soon be as prosperous as any other in the empire.'

Julius cheered that statement. 'And soon there will be less need to spend so much time away on campaign. I'm looking forward to staying in this house over the winter.'

I remembered that Julius intended to safeguard the camp and newly constructed town in the winter, when the main army returned to Aliso; evidently that meant that Julius would be able to stay in the home of the governor.

Varus laughed. 'Just be sure to look after the place. I know your fondness for great banquets – I don't want to return to find my home has been turned into a drinking den for your warriors, or worse, a fleshpot to rival those in the town.'

All the men laughed. Julius' reputation as a man who enjoyed his wine and women was obviously not a secret from anyone here. Julius laughed as well. 'Don't worry, I'll behave myself,' he gave the governor a roguish wink, 'or at least I promise to try.'

It was quite a while before I managed to coax Julius into a conversation myself, as Julius was obviously a big favourite of the Governor. Finally, Varus' attention moved over to Avitus, reclining on the other couch next to him, and I spoke to my friend. 'So, Julius, you're still working your men just as hard. Your exploits in the field are to be commended.'

He turned to me. 'Yes, we've been securing the fens over to the east. It has gone so well that we can now return to camp earlier than I envisaged.'

I took a swig of wine. 'Oh, I know that. I have been kept abreast of your every movement since coming to Germany.'

Julius looked confused. 'How so?'

'I read all your field reports, the ones you send back by messenger. I now look after the military intelligence.'

Julius looked annoyed. 'But I thought Legate Asprenas looked after that side of things.'

I was stung by his tone; did he think I wasn't up to the task? I felt the same way, I supposed, but it hurt that my friend had little faith in me. 'Asprenas has left the army to take command at Mogontiacum. Varus appointed me to look after all the military reports.'

Julius shook his head slightly, as if to clear it, then he reassured me, 'I'm sure you'll do a fine job. The campaigns are going so well there must be little to report to the governor?'

I smiled in agreement. 'Yes, you're right. The only concerns I have are the missing patrols in the lands of the Angrivarii. What are your thoughts on them?'

Julius turned more serious. 'Vala told me of the losses of his men. It saddens me that I cannot do more to help him. Each Roman death I feel keenly.'

I lowered my voice to a whisper as I didn't want to antagonise Varus. 'Vala thinks the Angrivarii are up to something, but Varus won't hear of it.'

Julius gave a crooked smile. 'Yes, I know the concerns of Vala. He is right to be on his guard. The Angrivarii are not to be trusted like my Cherusci. However, whatever they plan, it must be limited in its ambition, as I have seen little to alert even the mildest concern in their lands to the east.'

I felt a rush of relief hearing this from Julius; spending all these hours reading reports and conspiracies was turning me paranoid. 'So you think we have little to worry about?'

Julius smiled. 'There is always something to worry about, but it is unlikely to be anything too serious.' He laughed. 'And anyway, is this really the time to be talking about such things? I haven't seen you in six years and you are talking about your work.'

I laughed. 'Of course, Julius, forgive me. You look to be faring well. Are you enjoying your new role in life?'

He grinned. 'Well, I still miss Rome at times, who doesn't? But we've made so much progress here. I'm content. Tell me, how's your family? Your parents and little Antonia?'

I didn't want to tell him how my father and I had become estranged, so I kept the conversation on my sister. 'Antonia still scolds me whenever given a chance. Her temper increases in ferocity each passing season, but otherwise she's happy.' Something occurred to me. 'Did you know she still writes to Numeria? That took me by surprise, running into her.'

Julius scowled. 'I know we were good friends with Numeria once, but that woman really goes too far these days. Do you know she visits the villages of my people?'

I put my hand on his shoulder. 'I heard. Rest assured, as soon as I speak with her I will try and persuade her to return to Rome.'

Julius grunted. 'Well, good luck with that. No one else seems to have any luck. She shouldn't mess in affairs that don't concern her.'

I chuckled. 'Come on, you know what she's like, always was stubborn.'

He laughed. 'It is good to have you back, Gaius. You must visit me in my village. Let us throw a dinner for you. Meet my closest warriors and relatives. What do you say?'

Segestes had already made me the same offer, but this time I was more than pleased to agree. A night with German barbarians didn't seem so intimidating with my friend there. 'I'd be delighted. I'm sure you'll give me a night to remember.'

We carried on drinking well into the night, Julius and I reliving old war stories or tales from our youth. We talked incessantly. It was as if the years keeping us apart had never happened. Finally Julius retired to find his bed and Marcus had to help me find my own, I'd imbibed so much wine. I collapsed on my bed, a great smile on my face. It was good to be amongst friends again.

Chapter Eighteen

Varus was shouting. 'That infernal woman!'

I groggily opened my eyes, hold my thumping head, and wondered what was going on.

The shouting was coming from Varus' open courtyard. He bellowed, 'What trouble has she brought to my door this time?'

I swung out of my bed and decided I'd better find out what all this was about. I quickly donned a tunic and laced my sandals, before cautiously making my way down the corridor. I bumped into Marcus near the entrance to the courtyard. 'What's all the shouting about?'

Marcus looked puzzled. 'I'm not sure. A slave came in and said that he was needed in the courthouse, said there was some sort of disturbance going on.'

I shook my head a little to clear it; the cloud of sleep was making it hard to think. 'Who was the woman he was shouting about?'

Marcus went a little red with embarrassment. 'The slave mentioned the name of Lady Numeria.'

My stomach clenched. 'Oh, by the gods, what trouble has she got herself into now? Come on, you better come with me.'

We swiftly crossed over from Varus' house into the camp headquarters and the large court where Varus could normally be found on any given day dispensing justice and fulfilling what he described as his 'governorly duties'. A large crowd was gathered both inside and around the doorway, made up of both Germans and Romans, all eager to find out what this latest disturbance was all about.

'Make way.' I pushed myself and Marcus through the throng, a task not made easier by the fact that I was only wearing a simple tunic and therefore nothing to signify my rank. 'Make way,' I demanded of one particularly stubborn legionary, who was intent on getting the best view possible, gripping onto the

Roman Mask

doorframe with two white-knuckled hands.

Fortunately, as Marcus and I were both large men, we managed to force our way through and into the courthouse. Varus was on his large wooden chair where he was accustomed to listening to pleas from supplicants. He was flanked by his senior legate, Avitus, and a centurion from Avitus' XVII legion. Numeria stood before him alongside a German warrior, both looking as angry as titans, whilst an excited buzz surrounded them from the watching throngs of people.

Numeria demanded of Varus, 'Where is Roman justice for this man and his sister?'

Varus held his head in his hands, and said in a tone that suggested his patience was wearing thin, 'Before we talk of justice, I need to know what the facts of this case are.'

She responded in a voice full of scorn. 'The facts are very simple, my lord Governor. Legionaries from your army raped this man's sister.'

Oh dear, this didn't sound good. No wonder Varus was in a temper.

'She was bathing in the river near her village, when three legionaries came upon her and forced themselves on her. She was brutalised by them and raped. Surely Roman law cannot permit this gross act of barbarity,'

Varus held up a hand to quieten her. 'Have the men in question been identified.'

The centurion by his side answered him. 'Three men were in the area, sir. They were returning from an errand in that village. We have the men in custody now.'

Varus let out a long sigh. 'Then all it requires is for the young girl to identify them, then we can be done with this sorry affair. Don't worry, justice will be done. Where is the girl in question?'

Numeria reluctantly admitted, 'She won't come to the military camp. I have come in her stead with her brother, who saw the men in the village just before the deed was committed.'

Varus looked up in surprise. 'How can I discipline these men when she won't even come to identify them?'

Numeria snapped in anger. 'You can hardly expect her to walk into an armed camp of soldiers, all of whom she is now terrified of. She described the men to her brother and he says it was the same three who came to the village.'

Varus sat himself straighter in his chair. 'Roman law, however, requires that she identify her assailants. I can hardly condemn the three men if she won't even identify them personally.'

'Well then, go to the village and speak to her there. We tried to persuade her to come, but she is too scared to venture near this place, and who can blame her?' Numeria looked around the throng of people, some of whom were nodding in agreement.

Varus was having none of it. 'Go to her village? Don't be ridiculous. She can come here like everyone else. You can assure her that her safety will be guaranteed. Then we will have the men flogged in front of their entire legion,'

Numeria seethed in frustration. 'We can't persuade her to come, I've told you.'

Varus opened his hands. 'Well that's hardly my fault, is it?'

'So you'll let these men off, without any punishment, after they brutally raped a young girl?'

The German warrior sensed things were not going his way and shouted out an angry stream of words in his own language. Numeria listened and translated. 'He says that after this violation, she will be soiled in the eyes of the tribe. The dishonour to her will mean no man will ever take her to wife. Her life is ruined, and those men deserve death.'

Varus said more softly, 'Look, I'm not completely unsympathetic to your situation. You will be compensated.' He whispered in the centurion's ear, who then marched over to the man and offered him a small leather pouch. Varus explained, 'In there you have thirty silver denarius – more than an ample amount to offset any financial burden this matter might impose – due to the loss of any marriage prospects for the young girl.'

Both the warrior and Numeria looked confused. 'But what of the men who perpetrated this crime, will they go unpunished?'

Varus explained. 'If she won't identify them, what can I do? The law is the law.'

The warrior looked up at Varus, shouted something that didn't sound flattering, then spat on the floor, chucking the leather purse of silver on the ground, and stormed out of the courtroom. Numeria looked up at Varus, shook her head in disgust, and followed the German warrior out.

A hushed silence hung over the room.

Varus broke it. 'Now that really wasn't necessary. Such rudeness shouldn't be tolerated. Centurion, please remove all these people from my presence. I will hear no more plaintiffs today.'

Within no time, armed soldiers had ushered the crowds of chattering people from the room. A firm stare from me deterred a particularly eager legionary from including Marcus and me in the group of people ejected from the room. I walked over to Varus, who was in conversation with Avitus. 'Do you mean to let those men off? The brother was pretty convinced they were the guilty party,' I asked him.

'Of course I don't, Cassius. What do you take me for? There is no room for rapists in my army. An incident like this can set back relations between us and the German tribes months. Avitus will deal with these men. They are from his legion after all.' He said the last bit in a heavily disapproving voice.

Avitus looked stung by the criticism, but stood straighter and said, 'The men will be flogged and then expelled from the legion. They can make their own way back to Rome, on foot, without any coin or aid from the camp.'

I shook my head in puzzlement and asked Varus, 'If you intend to discipline the men, why didn't you let the warrior and Numeria know this? Not to mention the watching Germans in the crowd?'

Varus was adamant. 'Because they have to see that Roman law is applied here. If they knew that all it took to get any Roman soldier in trouble was an uncorroborated statement, they'll all be at it.'

I wasn't convinced; it looked a roundabout way of dispensing justice to me. The Germans were angry that the men were going unpunished, when in fact they actually were, only the Germans were not to be told this? Insane.

Varus carried on bemoaning Numeria. 'Why couldn't she have come to me in person and explained the situation, rather than coming to my court with that warrior in tow, spitting on my floor and causing such a scene?'

Marcus stood up for her. 'Maybe she thought it was the best way for you to show the benefits of Roman law.'

Avitus, Varus and I, and even the centurion, all gave Marcus a withering look, as if to tell him that was possibly the most stupid statement of the morning. Marcus went bright red, averted his eyes, and stared at the floor. 'I was only saying,' he mumbled.

Varus turned away from Marcus, ignoring him. 'At least the girl in question was from the Cherusci. Julius should be able to quieten down any discontent. Thank the gods that she wasn't from the Chatti or Bructeri, or the gods forbid it, the Angrivarii – that could have led to all-out war.'

That would have pleased Numonius Vala, I thought abstractly. He was itching for a war with the Angrivarii. 'Will you tell Numeria in secret, the steps you have taken?'

Varus looked at me, fury in his eyes. 'No I will not! That woman is a menace, and I don't have to explain my actions to her. She might think she is the highest authority in this land, but she isn't. I am! Her constant interfering and questioning of my rule here is tiresome at best, and downright seditious at worst.

She needs to be reined in.'

It looked as if Varus' patience with Numeria was finally coming to an end. I needed to avert his anger, before he did something rash. 'I will speak to her, Governor. We were once close as children. Let me see if I can talk some sense into her.'

Varus looked slightly mollified that I had agreed that she was being unreasonable. 'See that you do. I have the utmost respect for her father, but she pushes me too far.'

I left the others in the courthouse and started making my way to Numeria's house. I wasn't going to be put off this time. She would have to see me, and I would make her see the folly of her position, and persuade her to return to Rome. It was high time she stopped playing at politics. Enough was enough.

I caught her up on the hill approaching her house. 'Numeria,' I called, 'Wait!'

She turned to see who followed her, recognised me, and then carried on walking.

I swallowed a mouthful of anger and jogged after her. 'Numeria, stop. This is foolishness, why won't you talk to me?'

She finally stopped and turned to me. She was wearing a loose Roman pale blue gown, with a hood that covered her head, but couldn't obscure the beauty of her sun-kissed face. 'I am sorry, Gaius. That was rude of me. I shouldn't blame you for the actions of that stupid officious pig.'

I guessed she was talking about Varus. 'You put him in a difficult situation, Numeria. He doesn't like being put on the spot like that. You're lucky he didn't throw you in chains.'

Numeria's temper was rekindled. 'Let him! At least then we could see him doing something! Instead of sitting back here in his stupid Roman town, pretending to be the master of all justice in this land.'

I frowned. 'He is the Governor, Numeria. He does have the full authority of the *imperator* in Germany.'

She narrowed her eyes. 'Then, why doesn't he use it? He lets his men run riot in the countryside, taking women at will, no matter how much it upsets the local inhabitants. He taxes the tribes to almost breaking point, and what for? Stupid Roman buildings that none of the populace want or desire. The sooner Varus is replaced by the *imperator*, the better, if you ask me.'

I had heard enough. 'But that's just it, Numeria. No one is asking you. It's not your place to question the policies of Rome's newest province. Varus was appointed by Augustus, not you. I'm sorry to hear about the death of your husband,' – at this I saw the hurt in her eyes, as if she had been dealt a great pain, however I wasn't going to be put off – 'but it is time for you to move on. Surely your husband wouldn't have wanted this – for you to waste your days tormenting the ruler of the land and playing at diplomacy in the German villages.'

The pain in her eyes disappeared, replaced by anger once more. 'Playing at diplomacy? Is that what you think I do? At least I visit the people Rome claims to rule. What do you, or Varus, or any of the high command do? Nothing. He sends no envoys, makes no concessions to any of their wants or desires. In fact he doesn't even care to listen to what they are. He just sits in his camp and lets the rest of the country fall to ruin around him.'

I felt uneasy at her criticism. Since arriving at the Roman camp, I hadn't ventured further out than the Roman town. 'But even Julius – now King of the Cherusci – says your interference in German tribal affairs is unwanted.'

She shot me a murderous look. 'Becoming king has changed Julius, Gaius. I was happy to see him here when Otho and I first arrived in Germany but that soon changed. He was cold to Otho, snubbing him in front of the other officers. He is no better than Varus and the others. Roman arrogance blinded them all from listening to my husband's ideas. Otho wanted to listen to the German people, have meetings with their tribal elders, incorporating Germans in the running of their province. All his ideas hit a blank wall of silence.'

Asprenas had mentioned Otho's habit of speaking up against Varus' orders. Was this what she was referring to? As for my friend snubbing Otho, I suspected that Julius did this as he suspected him to be a coward. Julius could be hard on men who didn't live up to his high expectations. I spoke softly, 'Are you sure that your anger with Varus is not more to do with the death of your husband, rather than his ruling Germany?'

She turned her head away, tears welling up in her eyes. Pain coursed through each of her words which she said quietly. 'Of course I am angry with Varus for the death of my husband. Otho was a good man – better than any man I ever knew – he could have done so much for Varus, if the governor had only listened to him. Instead he was expected to be a soldier. My Otho was so much more than that. Now his name is one of shame throughout the camp.'

I put my hand on her shoulder. 'I make no judgement on him, Numeria. If you loved him, then he must have been a man worth knowing. War puts men in impossible situations, it expects too much of them. Don't remember him how he died. Remember what he was when he lived – that was the real man you loved.'

Numeria was sobbing openly now, and I wrapped my arms around her as she leant her head against my chest, tears soaking through my tunic. My heart went out to her. 'This defiance of Varus must end, Numeria. You know this. It is time to go home. Let Otho rest now. I am sure I can convince Varus to give you an armed escort out of Germany. You can go back to Rome. Maybe take that young girl Julia with you.' Varus would jump at the chance. He'd provide any escort she wished provided it got rid of her. Marcus, however, would be less pleased about the prospect of the young girl Julia leaving the province, I thought, remembering his childlike infatuation on meeting her.

Numeria hung on to me. 'It would be good for Julia to leave Germany. If she could return to Rome, maybe I could convince her family to be reconciled with her.'

At last! She was coming round. 'Well, there you go. You see, returning to Rome is the answer, Numeria. Get away from this awful land.'

She pushed me away from her, and visibly pulled herself together, wiping the tears from her eyes. 'It is good to see you again, Gaius. You are a good man. However, leaving my commitments here is not as simple as you may think. Whether you like it or not, I am involved with the people of this land, and I won't desert them just because someone from my past requests it of me.' My heart sunk. By the gods, was her stubbornness returning? She continued, 'But I promise to at least think on your proposal.'

Well, that was better than nothing I supposed. It was more than anyone else had got from her. 'You do that, Numeria. I am still your friend, and I only have your best interests at stake.'

She looked up at me with soft eyes. 'I know that, Gaius. You remind me of Otho in some ways. It is a shame you never met him.'

I was more similar to Otho than I would ever dare to admit. Time to change the subject. 'I'm to visit Julius in one of the German villages, a place named *Hadufuns*.' My tongue struggled with the unfamiliar German name. 'I'll be away for a day or two. But when I return, we can speak again.'

She gave a slight smile, although her eyes remained downcast. 'I'd like that, Gaius, and I will think on what you've said, but I make no promises.'

I watched her walk up to her house, under the shadow of the large silver birch, be greeted by her freedman, and then enter her home. I hoped she would leave this place and return to Rome and civilisation. Numeria was too good to be wasted in this backwater colony, with grief for a dead husband feeding her anger and resentment. She needed to go home, maybe remarry and get on with her life. For now, I'd done all I could. At least I could tell Varus she was considering returning. That hopefully would placate him for the time being. I gave one last wistful look at the house of my childhood sweetheart and then turned and walked back to the Roman camp.

Chapter Nineteen

Marcus' tall Libyan horse whinnied nervously as we slowly walked our horses through the dark imposing trees, hoping that the barely serviceable track we were on led the correct way. A thick mist descended shortly after we left in the early evening, making our journey through the heavily forested countryside no easier than if we had left in the dark of night.

'I thought you said this village was easy to find?' complained Marcus, as he peered through the gloom, trying to decipher which way the track led.

A cold sweat was pouring down my back, but so far I'd kept my unease from showing to Marcus. 'Well, I've never been there before, have I? Julius told me the directions and said we couldn't miss it.'

Julius had said that at this time of year the light evenings made the journey easily manageable without guide or escort, but he hadn't taken into account this thick mist, which descended so quickly, and made staying on the path hazardous. What would happen to us if we were to wander off the main track? Would we ever be found? And if so, by whom?

The sound of a branch snapping went off to our left. 'What's that?' exclaimed Marcus in a hoarse whisper.

I swallowed nervously. 'Probably nothing, just some animal disturbed by our passing,' I told him, but I loosened my *gladius* from its scabbard, just in case.

'No, listen! Can't you hear singing?' insisted Marcus.

We stopped our horses and I strained to listen through the darkness, trying to ignore the sounds of nocturnal animals. He was right! A barely perceptible chant carried through the mist, very deep voices singing in unison, in an alien tongue, from a very great distance. 'That must be the village,' I exclaimed in relief.

Marcus laughed. 'Either that or a war party set on finding itself two tribunes lost in the woods.'

I returned my *gladius* to its scabbard – I must have drawn it without realising. 'I told you, we're not lost. We just don't know where we are. Besides, this is Cherusci territory. We have nothing to worry about here. It's not as if we're in the lands of the Angrivarii,' I said, more to reassure myself than to ease any fears of Marcus, who seemed to think that this short journey through the forest was a great game, and nothing to unsettle his ever optimistic outlook on life.

We followed the sound of singing further up a slight incline, until we were through the thick mist. We could just make out the light from two fires ahead. As we rose higher, the mist lessened, and we saw they were from two large flaming torches set upon a high gatehouse in an imposing stockade that engulfed the entire hillside.

'That's no village. Look at those walls – it's more of a war camp!' said Marcus, surprised at the tall wicker palisade and deep earthen ditch that surrounded the enclosure.

I looked around at the fortifications. 'Well, what did you expect? The German tribes are forever fighting one another, when they're not fighting us.' In reality, I hadn't been expecting much more than a large collection of the German long houses myself. I looked at the palisade as we approached it and saw that it had much in common with a camp of Roman design. The wooden stockade was built using traditional German building techniques – long wicker branches interwoven between sturdy wooden stakes – but the earthen pitch foundation which was surrounded by a deep ditch was textbook Roman: it looked to me as if my friend Julius had been teaching his German followers more than how to wear a Roman toga properly – even trained Roman engineers couldn't have done much better. It was all to the good, however, if Julius could train his men in Roman fighting techniques. They would have a much better chance of surviving the winter from attacks by neighbouring tribes, without the aid of the Roman army to protect her ally.

We walked our horses to the gates and stopped as two great German brutes came out to meet us. They were both bare-chested, with flowing cloaks and iron helmets. Both carried a shield and spear. One shouted something in his guttural language that sounded both unpleasant and angry, but that was no surprise, everything in their barbaric tongue sounded like that.

'We are here to visit King Julius Arminius. We're his special guests,' I replied slowly and loudly so the warrior could understand me.

Most of my words were lost on him. The slow-witted man probably didn't know any more Latin than the rest of his race, but his eyes showed recognition at the name of his king, and he pointed his spear into the interior of the camp and said, 'Arminius,' in a gruff bark.

Marcus and I proceeded into the German village, an uncomfortable feeling tingling down my spine as I walked under the stockade's great gates.

The relentless booming voices of German warriors singing had remained our constant companion into the heart of the Cherusci nation, and only now did I realise how many warriors Julius had gathered to himself here. They came out of their long houses in their hundreds, shooing away the women and children who came to gawp at the visiting Roman officers. All were well-muscled fighting men, who stared at us with flat unreadable eyes as they leant against their spears or looked up from sharpening their blades.

'Surly lot, aren't they?' muttered Marcus. 'There's more of them than I expected.'

I agreed with him wholeheartedly. This was just one German village, of which there were scores more, all surrounding our position in the centre of the valley. If the Angrivarii had anywhere near the numbers of these Cherusci, a war with them was no light matter. Maybe Varus was right to continue with his peace negotiations. 'Just be grateful these ones are on our side. If this was a camp of the Angrivarii, we'd already be dead,' was all I told him.

We reached a large long house in the centre of the village, far larger than those surrounding them. It was from here that the sound of chanting was coming from, a great roaring of voices, thrumming with an eerie regularity that set my teeth on edge. 'This must be Julius' grand hall.' I said as I dismounted.

A young boy appeared to take away our horses, and we handed him their reins.

'Should we enter? Or will someone come to greet us here?' I asked him. I didn't want to walk in unannounced and disrupt their singing class.

He said nothing, but just looked at us with grey flinty eyes, eventually nodding his head towards the great double doors of the long house.

I took that to mean we should enter, so we walked up to the doors. There was no point knocking – no one would hear me over the racket coming from inside – so I took a deep breath and pushed the doors open, and Marcus and I entered.

The hundreds of warriors inside, who sat on wooden benches behind long tables around a large central fire, stopped their chanting and turned to see who had interrupted them. The sudden silence was deafening, as at least three hundred hostile pairs of eyes turned to us. The two of us stood there, dumbstruck by the sight.

Eventually, to my great relief, Julius' voice finally broke the silence. 'My friends! You found us at last. We were beginning to wonder whether you were turning up at all tonight.'

I looked up to where the voice came from and saw that he was on a raised table on the other side of the fire, which was why I'd not noticed him as soon as I entered. 'King Arminius, it is a pleasure to see you again,' I said formally. I didn't know how prickly his tribe could be about addressing him correctly.

'Please, Gaius, call me Julius. We're all friends here,' he replied, as Marcus and I walked into the centre of the room and stood before the raised table.

At Julius's side sat Segestes, looking far more natural in bearskin and ring mail rather than the ridiculous toga I'd last seen him in. By his side sat his slender son-in-law Sesithacus, wearing his sickly sycophantic smile as usual. On the other side of Julius sat an older man I didn't know, but he was obviously a man of importance to judge by his bearing. He wore a rich textured cloak over an expensive-looking steel mail shirt. Maybe this was the uncle, Inguiomerus, who I'd heard about from Asprenas. His hair was grey and thinning now, but his face bore the same chiselled features as my friend Julius – surely a blood relation.

Julius beamed a great smile, looking resplendent and every inch the Germanic king in his rich clothing and scarlet cloak, bearing a simple golden band to mark his kingship. 'Welcome to my hall. All from Rome are welcome at my table.' He signalled to two empty seats on the raised table, where we were to join him.

Before Marcus and I had a chance to reply, we were surprised to be interrupted by the mocking laughter of a woman and a husky German accented Latin voice. 'Oh, look how we all swoon when the pretty boys from Rome appear,' said the young woman, appearing from the shadows of the room and walking boldly up to us. She was staggeringly beautiful, slender and lithe, but, unusually for a German, had raven-black hair and dark eyes that flashed fire at us. She was dressed in leathers and furs, more suitable to a warrior, but which hugged her shapely form and breasts, accentuating her femininity rather than obscuring it. Her swaying walk as she approached us, reminded me of a snake intent on her pray, as if Marcus and I were no more than two poor mice awaiting her devouring bite.

I looked up with alarm at Julius, to see if he would put this rude woman in her place, but he just hid behind an ambiguous smile whilst the women carried on her tirade against us, circling around us as she spoke, as if it never occurred to her that she was the only women in a hall full of over three hundred warriors. 'Two pretty Roman officers, no doubt from fine families, here to tell us how we should run our land. How grateful we are to them, to honour us with their presence.' Her mocking sarcasm dripped contempt, and she locked her gaze directly on mine. 'Tell me, pretty Roman. How many German warriors have fallen by your hand?'

I had lost count at Western-Gate Pass, but I could hardly tell her that. Fortunately I was saved answering when Julius finally interceded. 'Thusnelda, enough,' the Cherusci king chided, then turned to Segestes' son-in-law and said, 'Sesithacus, you should keep your wife at home. She doesn't belong here at the banquet.'

She hissed at his remark. I don't know what shocked me more: the fact that this woman was prepared to flaunt her defiance to all the tribe's leaders, or that she was married to the simpering toady Sesithacus – as well pair a hawk with a pigeon!

'Oh, don't you worry, King of the Cherusci. I mean your friends no harm.' She continued to circle us. 'I just wanted to see what Rome sees fit to send us.'

Sesithacus falteringly said, 'Please, dear. This is not right.'

She turned on her husband and said just one word, 'Quiet,' like a crack of thunder, and her submissive husband lowered his eyes in shame.

Segestes stood up. 'Thusnelda, that is enough. If Sesithacus can't bind you, don't think that I cannot!'

She stared up at Segestes, defiance marking every muscle in her body, but she said, 'Very well Father, I will relent.' She moved back into the shadows, that hypnotically swaying walk somehow mocking her supposed subservience, and sat on a small stool, eyeing Marcus and I malevolently.

'She's a scary one,' whispered Marcus to me.

You're telling me, I thought, but kept my face neutral as I looked up at the large Chieftain Segestes, who explained, 'You must forgive my daughter. I fear I was too gentle with her as a child. She can be quite wilful at times. I had hoped marriage would mellow her,' at this he shot a disapproving look at Sesithacus, whose eyes remained downcast, 'but I fear it is in her nature to defy me. Please, pay her no mind.'

A snort of contempt came from the small stool, which I tried my best to ignore.

Julius spoke up, with a laugh, as if he had found the whole incident amusing. 'Come, we needn't worry about the views of one woman. Come, Gaius, Marcus, join us at table.'

We joined him on the raised platform and we were served roasted pork from the spits on the fire and tankards of the gruesome ale the Germans drank. Marcus shuddered at the sight of the beverage, no doubt remembering his last encounter with beer, but fortunately he said nothing and contented himself by picking at his roast haunch of pork. I actually found the atmosphere more likeable than I expected – once you got used to their strange ways, the Cherusci weren't so bad. Once the food and ale were served, they lost all interest in staring at us, and contented themselves with getting hopelessly drunk on their strong beer. Segestes was as loudly outspoken as I remembered him, but was cheerful enough, in an aggressive sort of way, whilst the elder warrior, who indeed did turn out to be Arminius' uncle Inguiomerus, was more reserved but wasn't shy of making his opinion known if he thought it warranted. In between them, Julius was the perfect host, politely listening to both of them without favouring either one. It must be a real balancing act for him, I suspected, keeping favour with all the different factions of his tribe, but by the look of him, he was managing it as gracefully as everything else he ever did in his life. I was becoming more accustomed to seeing Julius as the king, no longer as my childhood friend or fellow comrade.

The discussion at the table was of the peace in the land since they'd come under Roman rule. 'We grow fat on Roman riches. Never has our tribe so prospered. Our tribal hunting grounds far outreach any in living memory, and our influence extends far into the lands of our former enemies,' boasted Segestes, holding a large half-eaten pig bone in one hand, which he pointed for emphasis.

Inguiomerus was less generous about the *Pax Romania,* and his voice was grave and severe. 'Don't be so quick to give up the old ways, Segestes. Our lands have grown, that cannot be contested, but our people have had to learn new ways. New taxes and new laws diminish us.'

I didn't like the sound of this, so I spoke up, 'How do they diminish you? You yourself agree your tribe has grown rich.'

He turned to me and narrowed his eyes. 'Aye, we have grown rich, but we must be wary we don't grow weak. Our wealth used to be derived from plundering neighbouring tribes. Once Rome has brought peace to all the lands, how will our warriors prove themselves in battle? How long before we change from a nation of warriors into a nation of farmers?'

The sooner the better I thought, but simply inclined my head and raised an eyebrow, conceding his point.

Segestes spat out his beer. 'Pah! There is still plenty of fight left in the Angrivarii. Besides we will never be a nation of anything other than warriors.'

'You think? Our lands grow, but the only way we can pay these new taxes is by cultivating the land and farming it. Hunting alone no longer serves our purpose.'

King Arminius stepped in. 'Come, uncle, is that such a bad thing?

Bringing new agricultural techniques to our lands can only benefit us.'

Inguiomerus grunted. 'Our way is the spear, not the scythe. Your father understood this.'

Julius smiled. 'As do I, uncle. I have no intention of letting our warriors grow idle, once – with our help – Rome has pacified all the Germanic tribes.'

Segestes, Inguiomerus, Marcus, and I all answered as one, 'How so?'

Julius laughed. 'Do you really think Rome's ambitions will stop at the Elbe?'

I held my tongue, but Marcus, who was easily overexcited, blurted out. 'No! We will continue, bring the lands adjacent to the Danube under our control as well.'

I sunk my head into my hands. Inguiomerus voiced what everyone present knew. 'That will bring you into direct confrontation with King Maroboduus and his Marcomanni.'

Julius smiled. 'Exactly, and we will join them in their enterprise. The Marcomanni will be brought to heel, we'll grow rich, our warriors will have their war, and everyone will be happy.'

Inguiomerus stated flatly, 'Maroboduus is not to be underestimated. His warriors are battle-hardened veterans, and he himself a proven leader.'

Marcus piped up, 'But no match for the Roman legions, and with your help, we can destroy them.'

Segestes was equally enthusiastic. 'His forces are strong, but no braver than our warriors. A war with them will be sung about for generations.'

I thought it time to remind everyone what they all seemed to have forgotten; I shook my head, and sighed. 'King Maroboduus is an ally of Rome, and a peace accord was signed between Tiberius and him three years ago.'

Julius chuckled and slapped the table with the flat of his hand. 'Come Gaius, all here know that the peace between the Marcomanni and Rome was one of convenience. Rome can never dare leave such a threat to her strength in the midst of her empire. Sooner or later, war is inevitable between the two peoples. Why not now, with the Cherusci to help Rome?'

I could see why Julius wanted to join his forces with Rome in such a war. His position as king was a precarious one, based on the military might of Rome, and he could only keep control of all the tribe's warriors through success in battle. All very well, but I could hardly advocate a war against one of Rome's allies, so I tried to downplay the prospect. 'Rome surely appreciates the Cherusci's desire to be a willing partner is such an enterprise, but truly I have heard of no such plans from *Imperator* Augustus to such a venture.' The idea of Augustus confiding any of his plans to me was laughable, but none here knew that except my friend Julius, and he would know that I must repeat Rome's official position.

Marcus punched the air in enthusiasm. 'Well, I think a war with the Marcomanni is a great idea! Big standing army or not, between us we could dice them and scatter their body parts to the four corners of the empire!'

I sunk my head back in my hands. Marcus, Marcus, Marcus, why did I bother? Using Marcus in diplomatic circles was akin to leaving a known drunk alone with your favourite amphora of wine – sooner or later temptation will get the better of him, and to the gods with the consequences.

Both Segestes and Julius clapped Marcus on the back, and even Inguiomerus smiled. All very well I thought; let's just hope none of this conversation ever reaches Maroboduus' ears, or Augustus' for that matter.

The conversation soon turned to more pressing matters, such as the hostilities between the Angrivarii and themselves, and the prospect of spending the winter without the protection of the Roman legions.

'Don't worry about the Cherusci, Cassius,' Segestes told me, 'we are more than capable of protecting ourselves, and your little Roman town.'

I shook my head. 'But isn't the plan to leave Julius there alone,' I looked over to my friend, 'with only his cavalry in the camp? How many do they number, surely not more than two thousand?'

Julius laughed. 'My trained cavalry are but the smallest tip of the Cherusci strength. I can call on thirty thousand warriors to my banner if necessary.'

'Really, so many?' I knew the Cherusci were a large tribe, but even so, thirty thousand warriors was more than I had expected.

Segestes interceded. 'Yes, and that is the immediate fighting men, the men ready for the call. If we were to gather all our fighting strength, from the farthest reaches of our lands, we could number nearly forty, nay fifty thousand.'

'How many can the Angrivarii call upon?' It was the obvious question, but took the German chieftains by surprise.

There was a long silence until Inguiomerus finally conceded, 'Their numbers are similar to our own.'

Julius looked to have had enough of this. 'Come, why are we talking of war and bloodshed. We are here to celebrate.' He lifted up his tankard and took a great swallow of beer, draining it.

The two chieftains copied him with a cheer, and even Marcus ventured a large gulp or two of the foul-tasting brew. I drank some and considered all I had heard. On the face of it, Julius should be secure; he was in control of a vast number of warriors and had secured himself an easily defensible position from the enemy Angrivarii. The only problem I could see, was how loyal were his warriors to him? Did Segestes or Inguiomerus have plans of their own?

As I considered this, I noticed the young woman, who still sat on her small stool in the corner. She smouldered as she stared malevolently at Marcus and me, and it gave me a shudder seeing such hatred in her eyes. It was a shame really; she would have been such a pretty young girl without all that anger inside her.

During the meal we were introduced to numerous Germanic warriors, one after another, and told of their great deeds, and what great services they had performed for Rome. One grizzled German warrior looked much like another after a while, but I tried my best to be gracious and to listen to each of my friend Julius' descriptions of them.

'Faramund serves in my own cavalry. Only two weeks ago he gutted a man with his great spear. He struck him so hard the spear went right through him, pinning him to the tree behind!' proclaimed Julius, and the warrior gave me a gruesome smile with a twinkle in his eye.

I smiled. 'I bet you make your mother proud?'

He nodded, seemingly oblivious to my small joke.

I sighed and asked, 'You must be a great champion amongst your people?'

Much to my confusion, both Inguiomerus and Julius guffawed with laughter. Inguiomerus explained in his thickly accented Latin, 'Faramund is a great warrior, but cannot be described as one of our champions. Such an honour can only be granted by defeating another man who also holds that title. At this time that man is Ewald. I don't think even Faramund would rate his chances against Ewald, would you Faramund?'

Faramund's Latin was much better, probably because he served in Julius' own cavalry unit, which had been fighting for Rome for years. 'I know my own worth, Inguiomerus, and I fear no man. But that doesn't make me stupid. I know I could never best Ewald in a fight, with either sword or spear.'

Marcus piped up excitedly, 'Which one is Ewald? We haven't met him yet, have we?'

Julius chuckled and asked one of his attentive attendants to fetch the Cherusci champion. 'Ewald normally eats alone. He doesn't join us in the hall unless we request his attendance. He isn't one for drinking,' he told us, with mock regret, as he swallowed a great draught of German beer. Inguiomerus gave a secret smile, whilst the toady Sesithacus blanched, but surprisingly it was Segestes who looked the most uneasy; his normal good humour evaporating at the mention of the Cherusci champion.

All the warriors we had been introduced to so far were large muscled men, so I was half expecting a veritable giant to come striding into the hall, and was quite surprised to see the lithe young man who entered through the double doors, walk up to the dais and bow down on one knee in front of Julius. 'You asked for me, my King.'

He wore only a pair of leather trousers, showing his tightly muscled upper body, which bore no sign of any excess body fat, and a closely trimmed blonde beard and shoulder-length hair, which he tied back from his head. The normal weapon of choice for a Germanic warrior was a light spear with a narrow iron head, which could be used for throwing or hand-to-hand combat, but this man had a long thin sword strapped to his back in a leather baldric, which was designed to be used double-handed if I was any judge; a very rare choice of weapon for a man brought up in the German fighting tradition. He held his piercing blue eyes in an unblinking stare; that's the look of a killer, I thought, as he stood up at a signal from his king.

The room had quietened when Ewald arrived, as a mark of respect from the noisy warriors. I expected Julius to be the first to say something, but annoyingly the young German woman rose from her stool and said, 'Ah! Brother, so good of you to join us. Have you come to be paraded in front of our Roman guests like a prize bull?'

Brother? So Ewald was the son of Segestes as well? Interesting. The German chieftain's reaction to his son wasn't one of a proud father. Also, it was strange that the two siblings colouring was so different: one with blonde hair, the other raven-black, but otherwise they moved in the same sensuously seductive manner. Ewald spoke in a soft voice, but one which held authority and assurance. 'I come when I am bid, sister. I am the king's to command.'

'Oh, so loyal Ewald, just like his favourite hound,' she sneered.

Their father took to his feet. 'Thusnelda, don't speak to your brother in such a manner. Now be quiet or you'll be asked to leave this hall.'

Ewald raised his hand and said in a soft whisper, one that brooked no argument, 'Thusnelda may speak to me as she will, Father. She is the only woman who may, and what's more, apart from my king, the only person in this hall who can address me so.'

The omission of his own father from that exclusive list screamed that all was not well within this German family, and the father's and the son's eyes locked with one another.

Thusnelda's laughter rang out. 'Oh, Ewald. Let Father be. Is it his fault that he surrounds himself with fools?' she declared, looking at her husband Sesithacus and making the obvious connection.

Sesithacus' eyes flashed anger, but he was obviously terrified of the brother, not daring to meet the other man's gaze, and only muttered, 'Thusnelda, you do your father a disservice speaking to him thus.'

Segestes growled in anger, fury getting the better of him, but Julius placated him. 'Please, Segestes, please, enough of this. Ewald is here at my behest. I only want to show our guests the finest warrior of our people. It's a credit to you that he happens to be your son. Please, Segestes, retake your seat.'

Segestes looked from his son to his king, then reluctantly, and with obvious difficulty, managed to master his temper and sat back down again. He changed the subject by demanding of one of the attendants, 'You! Refill my tankard. It is dry, and I have a thirst that must be quenched.'

The tension in the room lessened as Segestes backed down, but the warrior Ewald still carried an air of menace about him. 'Does my king require anything of me?' he asked Julius.

Thusnelda answered, 'Yes, how can we show these Roman guests how talented my brother is with that sword on his back?' She turned to me and Marcus. 'Are either of you two warriors? Or has Rome sent us men more accustomed to gentle pastimes, such as dancing, painting or poetry?'

I wasn't stupid enough to fall to fall for such obvious baiting, and I responded that, 'Poetry is no gentle pastime, in my opinion. Many of my hardest days of youth were—'

'Both Cassius and I are masters with the *gladius*! We can defeat any here!' blurted Marcus stupidly.

I turned and shouted at Marcus, 'Hold your tongue boy! Remember where you are!'

But it was too late. Thusnelda turned to Marcus in delight. 'You can defeat any man here?' She turned to her large audience of warriors. 'Did you hear that? Our young Roman friend thinks he is a better warrior than any man here.' There was a grumbling anger amongst the warriors, who clearly were not convinced of the young tribune's claim.

Marcus at least was decent enough to look shamefaced and lowered his eyes, face bright red, as I shot him a furious glare. I cleared my throat, and spoke clearly, so all assembled could hear me. 'Forgive my young friend. He has overindulged in your hospitality tonight. Too many beers can make young men say rash things.'

Marcus looked up at me in annoyance. He hadn't drunk more than a few mouthfuls of beer, but mercifully, for once, he kept quiet.

Julius said, 'It is of no matter, please forget it. Ewald, these two are my guests.'

The German champion bowed his head in acceptance but his sister wasn't so easily put off and said to Marcus, 'But you clearly claimed you both to be great warriors. Are you saying that you aren't prepared to back up this claim? Surely we could have a demonstration of your prowess, say, against my brother here ...'

Ewald turned to Thusnelda and said quietly to her, 'Leave it, my sister. He is but a boy,'

The reference to Marcus' youth was too much for him to bear. He said quietly, 'I am sorry if I caused offence by speaking out of turn. I was wrong to do so. But I am proficient with the sword, and I don't mind proving it with a small demonstration against your man if you so wish.'

Oh, by the gods, could this get any worse? Marcus was being led blindly into a trap. This 'demonstration' as the woman put it, would be no fight to 'first blood', or a fight with blunted blades, it would be a fight to the death. I knew enough of German traditions to realise that, and against this warrior, who instilled fear in even his own father, I didn't rate Marcus' chances. He was good with a *gladius*, I'd never known one better, but Ewald was obviously a cold killer, used to dealing death without a heartbeat's thought. Marcus stood no chance.

I took control. 'Marcus, you are forbidden to open your mouth any more. That is an order.' Marcus looked shocked but stood and saluted. He knew soldiers had to take orders. I continued, speaking crisply and clearly. 'Now, stand outside the hall and wait for me there. You will not partake in any armed combat demonstrations this night.'

He looked distraught to be dismissed so rudely, but saluted again, turned and marched out of the room, keeping his eyes fixed on the doors, no doubt burning in shame at leaving in such a manner, but knowing he could not ignore a direct order from me. I breathed a sigh of relief at the discipline instilled in the Roman army.

Now I needed to address my German hosts; I wasn't out of this yet. 'I am sorry for any offence my companion may have caused. I take full responsibility for his actions. He is but a hot-headed boy, who speaks before thinking.'

Julius raised an arm, in a gesture of peace. 'Think nothing of it. Ewald understands, don't you?'

Again the German champion nodded his head.

Thusnelda wasn't having any of it. 'But my king, that young man did not only insult Ewald, he claimed he was better than any warrior in this hall.' There was grumbled agreement at her words. 'He also claimed that this man here,' she pointed at me, 'was an equally good warrior, and as the tribune says himself, he takes full responsibility for the young man's actions. Either the young man must fight, or his older more experienced commander.'

She had me there. I couldn't deny it. By the gods, damn that woman. There was no getting out of it now. I relented to what she obviously planned from the start. 'Very well, I will fight your man. May I at least have a small shield to accompany my *gladius*?' The short *gladius* was a truly fantastic weapon. In a massed battle and amongst the close confines of a shield wall, it held all the advantages over longer swords, proving itself to be much more effective in such situations. However, I wasn't to fight in a massed battle. This would be single combat against a trained foe with a weapon of vastly superior reach. I would need a shield if I was to get into that reach and attack my opponent.

She smiled in triumph. 'You may arm yourself in any fashion you wish.'

Julius stood up and shouted, 'This fight will not happen. I forbid it, as King of the Cherusci. That's an end to it.'

Thusnelda turned in anger, obviously furious that her plans were being frustrated just at the point of her victory. 'But my King, he agrees! Rome cannot hold us responsible for what happens in this bout now.'

'Yes, but I can. This is my hall, and I will not have bloodshed tarnish our relationship with Rome.' He looked down at Thusnelda, meeting her glare, a determined mask framing his face. She stood her ground at first, glaring back in defiance, but soon she realised the futility of trying to change his mind: Once Julius' mind was made up, no one could change it.

She turned to her brother. 'But Ewald, it is up to you whether the challenge can go unanswered, what do you say?'

There was a long pause before he answered. The hall stood silent. Everyone, including me, seemed to hold their breath.

He looked at me and met my gaze.

'If my king wishes for this contest not to take place, then it shall not,' he said in his quiet soft voice, which still seemed to penetrate the furthest reaches of the hall.

The entire hall let out their breath at the same time. I felt dizzy at holding my breath for so long, and my heart was still beating fast as I nodded my head at him, accepting his decision, and thanking the gods secretly that I may live through this night after all.

Thusnelda let out a cry of frustration and stormed out of the hall, and neither her brother, father, nor her king tried to prevent her from leaving. I for one blessed the gods that she was finally gone. That was one German wench I wouldn't mind never seeing again in my life.

Julius addressed his warriors. 'Honour has been given. Both men accept my decision. Let no man interpret it differently.' He turned to me. 'Gaius, please join me in my own home. It is too late for you to travel back tonight. We will talk some more.' He turned to the German champion. 'Ewald, I want you to stand guard over our Roman guest's rooms tonight. No harm is to come to them. Do you understand?'

Ewald nodded his head. 'And none shall my king. None shall get past me.' It was a simple matter of fact; no idle boast.

I wasn't sure how I felt about the terrifying German guarding my room, but I wasn't going to question it now, and I followed Julius out of the hall, accepting the grudging pats on the back from the warriors as I went; obviously I had gained some respect in their eyes. I guessed that not many men had ever offered to fight the German champion and survived to tell the tale.

Chapter Twenty

'Ahhh! Wine!' Julius took a long drink from the slender drinking goblet, fashioned from the finest Greek porcelain, and closed his eyes in pleasure. 'Such a relief after all that German ale. The need to maintain appearances dictates that I cannot drink anything but beer in public, but here, alone, I can still indulge in my guilty pleasure and enjoy fine wine.'

The two of us were reclined on Roman divans, surrounded by Greek and Roman works of art, in Julius' private home, which was decorated as finely as my own house in Rome, and in a similar vein. 'Do you ever entertain any of your chieftains here?' I asked him, supping my own wine, which was a full-bodied draught and held a hint of spice from southern Italy.

Julius barked a laugh. 'And let them see me like this? They'd be up in arms in rebellion at the very sight of me!' Julius had discarded his heavy armour and furs and looked much more relaxed in a light blue tunic, and simple soft leather Roman sandals. 'This is where I come to get away from them, where I can be myself, and forget about the burden of kingship for a while.'

'Your guards see you here,' I reminded him, adjusting the soft cushion beneath my back.

He grinned. 'Yes, but they're my own men, from my own cavalry unit. They've got used to the easy pleasures of the Roman way of life, just as I have, and they don't hold the odd Roman piece of art or Italian wine against me.'

'Your champion, Ewald, he's not from your cavalry.' I shivered as I thought about the sinuous swordsman who had accompanied us from the grand hall of warriors over to Julius' home. He was now standing guard outside Marcus' room, who had insisted on going straight to bed after claiming I had humiliated him in front of everyone at dinner. I wasn't worried about Marcus' petulance. He could be like a child at times, quick to anger, but also forgave just as quickly. I was slightly put out by his ingratitude however. Marcus might not realise it, but I had risked my life offering to cross swords in his place. It was even odder to think that the man who might have killed Marcus in the hall was now guarding his room against intruders.

Julius yawned. 'No, he's not, but he's loyal enough.'

I frowned. 'But why? Surely his loyalty should be to his father.'

Julius laughed. 'Well yes, but by being the tribe's champion, he has a position of honour. It is politically expedient keeping Segestes brood happy – it helps heals rifts within the tribe. Segestes came within a whisker of becoming king himself.'

I'd heard Segestes was previously a claimant to Julius' crown. I shook my head. 'They seem a strange family. I wouldn't want any of them near me. Where's the mother in all this?'

Julius sat up on his divan. 'She died when Ewald and Thusnelda were small children. Rumour is that Segestes struck her too hard once when drunk. He's hot-headed enough for it to be the truth.'

'Thusnelda is the bold sister who hates Romans?' I thought of the malicious stares the dark woman had directed at me across the hall.

'Yes, and you're not wrong there.' He grinned offering to top up my goblet with wine. 'You might have noticed her colouring. Some say the mother was raped by a Roman legionary and she is not the daughter of Segestes at all. All the family deny this, but it might explain her implacable hatred of Roman men.'

I let him fill my goblet. 'But she's now married to Sesithacus. Surely that's not a favourable match.'

Julius raised an eyebrow. 'You're telling me? Sesithacus is a simpering fool, and Segestes knows it, but he likes someone around to massage his ego. Sometimes I think he forced Thusnelda into marriage with Sesithacus to show Ewald and his sister who the real head of the family is.' Julius laughed. 'German family politics can be more complicated than any tribal factions.'

I took another mouthful of wine. 'But why would he want to do that?'

Julius lay back down on his divan. 'Well, Ewald is devoted to his sister, and you've witnessed yourself that she doesn't exactly defer to Segestes. Maybe he thought marrying her to Sesithacus would pull her into line. It hasn't worked from what I've seen.'

I smiled. 'Yes, I've seen that myself.'

Julius chuckled. 'She's a troublemaker all right. There's never a dull moment with that family about.'

I was intrigued. 'You say Segestes almost won the crown. What stopped him? How did you come to take it from him?'

Julius stretched before explaining. 'When a king of the Cherusci dies, the tribe chieftains meet, and all claimants to the throne must declare themselves. When my uncle died, there were initially several who came forward. Members from my own family, and others like Segestes who commanded a lot of respect from the warriors he led. When I turned up with my two thousand cavalry, back from Syria, some of the chieftains said I couldn't stand. I was considered too Roman and out of touch with the tribal ways. Fortunately, as the previous king was my uncle, they couldn't prevent me from making my claim. Augustus provided me with gold to buy off most of the other claimants, until only myself, my uncle Inguiomerus, who was my father's and the former king's younger brother, and Segestes remained.'

I rubbed my chin. 'How do they decide who becomes king?'

Julius shrugged. 'It's simple really. Each chieftain votes for their chosen candidate. Each chieftain's vote is weighted by how many warriors he commands. The one who accumulates the largest number of warriors wins. The whole process takes weeks, as chieftains make bargains and shuffle amongst themselves to gain advantage from the bidding. As I was an outsider, many were distrustful of me. The warriors from my cavalry helped, by telling stories of my prowess in battle, as did the gold supplied by Rome, but both Inguiomerus and Segestes held a clear lead over me in the final days. Inguiomerus was the favourite of the older traditional chieftains who wanted a return to the old tribal ways, whilst Segestes was favoured by many of the young warriors, as he promised glory in battle and a marshalling of the Cherusci strength.'

I frowned. 'What was your position?'

Julius looked thoughtful. 'I tried to take the middle ground, saying we should honour our traditional roots, but must also use our alliance with Rome to our advantage in order to help us become the most powerful of the Germanic nations.'

I raised an eyebrow. 'An ambitious claim.' There were scores of Germanic tribes, all of which had been fighting each other for supremacy for hundreds of years. None had ever achieved a position of dominance over the others in all that time; why would Julius prove successful when all others had failed?

Julius grinned. 'I had to be bold, and gradually my arguments started gaining favour. I told them of the great opportunity the Cherusci had. Some were distrustful of me because of my perceived Roman ties, but I came to be seen as a good compromise between the other two factions.' Julius laughed. 'Although, I'll admit, Roman gold helped me convince them!

Roman Mask

'Before the final vote I gave a speech, telling the chieftains that the times had changed. Holding on to the past was no longer possible. Whether the Cherusci liked it or not, Rome was the new master of Germany, and someone who could help the Cherusci use this to their advantage was what the tribe needed now. I promised to honour our former tribal ways, which went a long way to placating Inguiomerus' supporters, but argued that using our alliance with Rome could mean us gaining unprecedented dominance over the other German tribes. That was enough to sway over many of Segestes supporters – bitter rivalry with the other tribes runs deeper than their dislike of Rome. It was a close-run thing, but I managed to win through in the end, taking the crown and becoming the leader of the Cherusci for the rest of my days, however long that may be.'

I shook my head and smiled. 'And is this how you expected your life to be? I never even knew you held ambitions to lead the Cherusci?'

Julius laughed. 'In all honesty, I never did. I wanted nothing more than to be a soldier and serve Rome in the field. But Augustus can be very persuasive, and when he asked me to take up this role, how could I refuse?'

I knew all too well how persuasive Augustus could be, or in my case, his wife. I wondered if Julius was given the same choice I was: that is to say, no choice at all. 'But are you happy as king?'

He grinned. 'Surprisingly, yes. The responsibility weighs heavily at times, and I do sometimes miss my simpler earlier life. But I think I can do some real good here. This is my destiny, Gaius, I'm sure of that now. I've never felt so alive.'

I swilled my wine around in its goblet and mused over everything he had told me. 'From what you tell me, Segestes has reason to resent you for many reasons. Can you trust him or his son?'

Julius laughed. 'No, of course not! As long as I hold onto the crown, however, they will do as I say. You saw that Ewald bent to my will in the hall, despite it displeasing his sister, whom he adores. They accept me as their king, but I tread a dangerous path, and must keep my support within the tribe – any show of weakness and they'll leap on it and pull me down. My kingship has brought the Cherusci many successes over the other tribes. Most now firmly believe in me and my vision for the Cherusci. I think I even have Ewald convinced. He's a peerless warrior, but does genuinely care about the welfare of his tribe. When he's not practising with weapons, honing his body into the ultimate warrior, he can be found listening to the debates of the other chieftains.'

I took a deep swallow of wine. 'And how good is he with that sword of his?'

Julius tone turned serious. 'Better than the finest gladiator in Rome. Faster, more deadly, than any I've ever seen. You were probably the best I ever sparred with, Gaius, but you're no match for Ewald. His speed and agility is outstanding. No warrior could ever come close to matching it.' Julius laughed. 'If only Augustus could get his hands on him, he could sell him into a gladiatorial school for more money than he ever lavished on setting me up as King of the Cherusci!'

I let out a slow breath. From what Julius had told me, he had probably saved my life by forbidding the fight from going ahead. Damn Marcus and his stupidity! 'In that case, I have you to thank that I am still here now.'

Julius laughed. 'Yes, I think you do. That sister of his would almost certainly have insisted on the contest going to the death – they normally always do. I should have realised she would have some mischief planned. I apologise for spoiling your dinner.'

I waved my hand as if it was nothing, but inwardly I shuddered. Yet another close brush with death, and owing my life to my friend Julius once more. I didn't want Julius to see how scared I was, so I tried to move the conversation away from the deadly swordsman. 'His sister has a mean spirit. I thought my sister was bad enough.'

Julius looked up. 'Antonia? How does she fare in Rome now? It would be so good to see her again.'

I smiled, thinking of her. 'Well, she's married now. To a lawyer, a man named Aulus. He's not really the sort of man I warm to, but he puts up with Antonia's scolding tongue, and I must admit he seems to treat her well.'

Julius laughed. 'If women could be lawyers, I swear Antonia would be the best of them. Aulus has a lot to live up to.'

I grinned. 'And how about your own family? What became of your younger brother, Flavus?' Julius' younger brother was seven years his junior, and had joined his brother in Rome when we were approaching manhood. I remembered him with unruly blonde hair, laughing eyes, and a cheeky mouth.

'I received a letter from Flavus only last month. He joined the Seventh legion based in Spain. He is only twenty and has already reached the rank of centurion!' Julius beamed. 'I'd have him here with me, but Flavus must make his own way in life, I guess. How can I deny him the same military education I enjoyed with the legions?'

'That's great news, Julius. I remember him fondly. I should have known any brother of yours would flourish in the legions. The Seventh Gemina is a fine legion.'

We carried on talking long into the night and reliving past experiences together in Rome and our time together in Syria. Eventually Julius brought the night to an end, telling me, 'I must be up early tomorrow. I will be taking some of my cavalry back to the north.'

I laughed. 'Ha! It's late already. Surely you can leave it a day?'

Julius rose from his divan. 'I can't neglect my military duties, Gaius. Someone has to keep an eye on the Angrivarii.'

I downed the remainder of my wine and rose also. 'On that score, I have had a result. I've persuaded Vala to start sending his patrols back into Angrivarii territory.'

Julius turned round, clearly surprised. 'But won't that infuriate Varus?'

I shrugged. 'Possibly, but it has to be done. Your men can't be expected to do everything.'

Julius put a hand on my shoulder. 'I guess you're right. I just don't want you getting yourself into to trouble with the governor. Remember you are newly returned to Germany – don't get on the wrong side of him. He comes across as convivial enough, but he has a ruthless side.'

I shook off his concern. 'Don't worry about me. You just look after our Roman patrols. We don't want any more men going missing.'

He smiled as he led me to the door. 'I'll do all I can. I know how much you care for the men.'

I nodded in agreement. 'Keep those reports coming, and take care of yourself in the field.'

Julius led me out of his quarters and pointed me in the direction of my room. He laughed. 'Now I know you're reading them, I'll take extra care in compiling them. I wouldn't want to disappoint my oldest friend.'

'Night, Julius. Sleep well, my friend.' I walked down the corridor and waved a hand at him, bidding him farewell.

I left him to find my bed, which was situated in a room alongside Marcus'. I nodded my head at the menacing Ewald as I passed him, who was still holding guard outside our rooms. He gave a small inclination of his head, but otherwise made no other sign in acknowledgement of my passing. You're a cold one, I thought. If things had turned out differently tonight, one of us would have been dead by the hands of the other. Thanks be to the gods it didn't come to that, was my final thought before getting into my bed and falling asleep.

Chapter Twenty-one

My feet kept on sticking in the cloying mud. 'By the gods! What sort of trail is this?' I asked aloud, before realising I was on my own.

Where had Marcus got to? If being stuck in this infernal swamp wasn't bad enough, I should at least expect my subordinate to be there to drag me out if necessary. I surveyed the trees; the mist was descending again, and the surrounding forest was obscured further by the fading twilight. 'Marcus!' I shouted to the trees. 'Marcus, come back here!' I demanded.

Where was he? I pulled myself out of the mud with the help of an overhanging branch, but almost lost my sandal in the process. If I get stuck in this mess once more, he'll answer for it by spending his next few weeks in the records office – no more exercise yard, no more training with the men. Just boring records. I might even get him to re-catalogue the reports we'd already processed; not that it needed doing, just because I was sick to death of this damn forest, and right now blaming Marcus for it seemed the right thing to do! Stupid boy.

I stumbled along the trail, tripping on a protruding root and tumbling to the floor. 'Ouch!' I exclaimed, holding my stubbed toe, whilst sitting on my backside. 'The whole bloody forest is out to get me,' I muttered angrily, looking around in annoyance at the surrounding ancient oak trees, with their thick boughs and intertwined branches that so effectively cut out the light from the sky. Between the trees and the mist, was it any wonder I was completely lost?

I was lost. Funny, only now did it occur to me. I appraised my situation again, scanning the trees for any sign of movement, but I couldn't see further than twenty paces, and even that only dimly. 'Marcus?' I shouted again, trying to keep the panic from my voice.

I got to my feet, and tried to pick up the pace, running along the narrow trail through the woods, leaping a rotten branch that had fallen across my path, and snagging my arm on brambles that lined the undergrowth to either side. I ignored the grazes and pushed on through the trees, intent on getting through them as fast as possible.

There! What was that? I could have sworn I saw a flash of red in the path ahead, before a fresh fold of mist floated in the wind and concealed the way ahead. 'Marcus? Is that you?' I implored.

I stopped to listen, to see if he had heard. The trees creaked in the deathly still of the forest, but other than that I heard nothing, not even the sound of the forest animals, or the hoot of an owl or bird. 'Marcus!' I shouted again.

A breath of wind went past my face and the faintest trace of sound came with it. 'Cassius' it said. That must be Marcus! At last! I ran forward and again saw the flash of red ahead before the mists once again obscured it. 'Marcus, wait. I am here! Wait for me!'

I had to be careful. I knew how the mist could confuse sounds. I had to be sure it was him: danger could still lurk in this forest. I ran along the path and again made out the silhouette of a man in front of me; was that Marcus? I was suddenly nervous, but then I saw the red of its tunic and the Roman armour over his torso.

'Marcus, thank the gods!' I exclaimed in relief, before tripping on another branch and falling sprawling into a briar patch. 'Ow! Not again! Marcus, get over here and help me out of this infernal bush!'

The man still had his back to me, and I noticed it couldn't be Marcus as he wore the armour of a centurion, not a tribune. Still, he was at least Roman. 'Excuse me, soldier, can you lend me a hand?'

The man slowly turned, revealing his face.

I felt the blood in my body turn to ice as I beheld him. 'No! It can't be!' Tears sprung to my eyes, 'You died.'

He slowly lifted his arm and pointed a finger at me.

I tried to get to my feet, to run from him, but the brambles held me fast. 'Please, Decius. It wasn't my fault. I had to let you go. I had no choice. Please, Decius.' I was babbling, half-mad with terror, tears streaming down my face, desperate to wrench my gaze from him, but unable to.

I looked into his eyes and saw only death reflecting back at me. He still held out his raised finger, and now I noticed German warriors were coming out from the surrounding trees, each with their arms held out, ready to tear me limb from limb. They were following the centurion's direction and were coming for me. 'Please, Decius, no! It wasn't my fault. Please, don't do this,' I implored in terror but knew I was wasting my breath.

The German warriors surrounded me and their bearded faces were full of hate and disgust for me. They grabbed hold of me and started to pull and shake me. I started to scream.

'Cassius, wake up!' shouted a voice.

'Decius! No! Please.' I struggled against my assailants, trying to claw the face of one bearded warrior, who was too quick and batted my approaching hands away.

I felt a slap on my face.

'Cassius, that's enough!' shouted Marcus.

I sat up in my bed and realised the German warrior in front of me was the champion Ewald, and the man shaking me was none other than Marcus. 'What happened?' I asked, taking in deep breaths. I was soaked in sweat and my heart was beating incredibly fast. 'Where am I?'

'We are in the camp of the Cherusci, of course. You were having a nightmare. Ewald came and got me when he heard you shouting in your sleep,' explained Marcus.

I shook my head in confusion. All just a dream. Just a dream.

The German warrior in the room stood up straight and folded his arms, showing his rippling biceps, under his hooded gaze: looking so similar to the German warriors I had just experienced in my dream.

I shuddered, then gulped. 'I ... I apologise.'

The German warrior said nothing, just turned his back and left the room. Thank the gods for that at least.

Marcus continued to question me. 'You were shouting a name – Decius. Who is he?'

Centurion Decius. I held my head in my hands and closed my eyes.

Marcus put his hand on my shoulder. 'Who is he?' he repeated.

'Nobody. Just a name I must have picked up in the camp in passing,' I lied. It was years since I'd last dreamt of Decius; why would he return to haunt me now?

Marcus frowned. 'It didn't sound like someone you just met in passing. You sounded terrified. I've never heard such terror.'

I gave a crocked smile. 'You wait until you face a real battle for the first time. Then you'll hear terror alright. It was just a bad dream, forget about it.' I pushed him away from me and dragged myself out of the narrow cot that had been provided for me.

Marcus tried to prise more information from me, but when I wasn't forthcoming he eventually left me to dress in peace. This latest episode was troubling. Centurion Decius, late of the XVIII legion, who perished at Western-Gate Pass, had once appeared in my dreams regularly. I remembered several occasions being shaken awake, first by Lentula or some poor unfortunate who shared my bed at that time. Later, it was my friend Spento, or my sister Antonia. Finally, when I moved to my current home in Rome, by my body servant, Patrellis. Each time they said the same. I would shout out his name repeatedly in terror and wake covered in a cold sweat and shaking. But that was four years ago. Why would these dreams return now? I still carried a certain amount of guilt regarding Decius' death, for sure, but I'd long since come to terms with my part in his demise – the man had left me no choice; I'd the rest of the men to think about.

I shook my head to clear it of these unpleasant thoughts. It wasn't that surprising that these nightmares should return. I was back in the German forests surrounded by German warriors, all of whom bore an uncanny resemblance to the ones who'd hacked poor Decius apart – was it any wonder that uncomfortable memories might be uncovered? I dressed in my armour and joined Marcus, who had gathered our horses. We left immediately, not even taking time to eat, although Julius' people made it clear we were welcome to. Julius had already left, just as he had promised to, and I had no wish to stay in this place any longer than I had to. I wanted to be back in the nice safety of the Roman camp and away from German tribal politics and uncomfortable nightmares. We rode our horses hard on the trail back, a foolhardy thing to do, as riding horses at speed along a forest trail was always treacherous – any number of tree roots or overhanging branches could unhorse us – but Marcus didn't complain, and I was so eager to get back I didn't care.

When we returned, Marcus and I went back to our work in the records offices, cataloguing the men's reports and making recommendations to Varus and his legates. Unfortunately for me, the nightmares didn't stop.

Each dream would follow a similar pattern. I would be lost in the woods, searching for a way out. Then I would encounter Decius. He would then point at me, and men would appear, surrounding me, grabbing and pulling, until I woke in terror. Sometimes the men were German warriors, at other times it was the men I'd lost at the pass. Once, a legionary who died on a routine patrol in Syria made an appearance; a man whose name I could no longer even recollect. The one constant in the dream was Centurion Decius – raising that dreaded finger, his gaze marking my death.

I grew irritable at work, the strain of working so many hours in close confinement with Marcus took its toll, and I often snapped at him for no apparent reason. Our daily sessions on the training yard proved little or no help in taking my mind off things as the lack of sleep left me slow-witted and a barely adequate opponent for Marcus who regularly left me with a new series of bruises, inflicted with his wooden *gladius*. Marcus could tell something was amiss with me, but he never asked. He heard me waking, in the room next to his, in terror each night, but knew I didn't wish to talk about it. Marcus was intelligent enough to know that some things you just don't bring up, no matter what.

Finally, after a couple of weeks, and after a particularly gruelling day in the records office, the prospect of another sleepless night was too much for me, so I bid Marcus good night and decided to go into town and get drunk. Since returning to camp, I had avoided drinking more than a cup or two of watered wine, but I was so sick of the sleepless nights, and fretting over it, I figured it couldn't do any harm. At the very least it would stop me worrying about it for a short time; that alone made it an enticing prospect.

I discarded any sign of my rank and walked into town wearing only a simple military-cut tunic – I had no wish to be recognised as a tribune – and found a table in the first drinking establishment I found; a small place, used by both off-duty soldiers and German civilians, quiet and unassuming. I ordered a goblet of wine, and drank it unwatered. I didn't raise much notice, a camp as large as the one here produced a steady stream of soldiers wanting to spend their pay on wine.

It was early evening, and I sat outside the taverna, wine in one hand, feet propped up on another stool, as I admired the sunset over the large Roman camp. I could see the small knoll over to the north of the camp, where the cemetery was located and which housed Numeria's dead husband, Otho. It reminded me that I should make time to go visit her. Ever since I'd returned from visiting Julius, I'd not bothered, being too caught up in my own problems. Maybe speaking to her of my dreams would help; maybe she would know why Decius' shade was coming back to haunt me? But then I realised telling her of my dreams would entail me explaining how Decius had died: maybe that wasn't such a good idea after all.

I stayed until the sun disappeared behind the tree-lined hills to the west, and then decided to find somewhere more lively – drinking alone had the unfortunate habit of making me morose, something I'd rather not be tonight.

The next bar I found was very different from the last. Here the customers were nearly all soldiers, of every rank, and each group of men here looked intent on making the most of their passes from the military camp. How many here really had the necessary passes from their centurions, I wondered? Surely not all – there was not a Roman camp in the empire that managed to keep all their men from absconding to a local drinking-hole from time to time. I wasn't concerned who had permission and who didn't – that was for the camp praefect, Ceionius, to worry about – I was here to enjoy myself and I got talking to a group of men from the XVII legion. They were a little hesitant at first, realising that my well-spoken Latin probably signified elevated rank, but soon relaxed when I bought them all a round of drinks. The conversation was limited and what you'd expect from soldiers in a frontier town: the weather, pay, nasty centurions, and who were the best whores to visit. I tried to find out what their opinion was of the German tribes, but they all seemed amazingly unconcerned by the army's military position. If Varus could negotiate a peace with the Angrivarii, then great, but if he didn't, it was no loss as the army was more than capable of defeating them without too much trouble.

I was getting a little drunk when my small group of companions left to find a brothel, so I bid them farewell. I wandered up a side street and entered the bar Asprenas had introduced me to that first night in the camp, almost three months ago. I found a table away from the other patrons of the bar and signalled to the barman to bring me over an amphora of wine.

I was sat in a corner seat, obscured in a dark recess of the bar, sipping my wine, observing the other patrons huddled around their tables in conversations with women of dubious character, when a girl came over to me. 'I know you, don't I?' she asked.

I looked up to see who it was, and saw that it was the young girl, Julia, who Asprenas had cruelly dubbed the 'gift taker' whore. I knew she was a friend of Numeria, so I thought I better be polite. 'Ah, Lady Julia isn't it?'

She sat down next to me, a big smile beaming across her pretty face. She was dressed in a revealing open-sleeved tunic with a plunging neckline, which was only barely concealed by a thin shawl of the lightest silk that was so sheer as to be almost transparent. 'That's right. You're the officer who came in with Numeria in the spring aren't you? You're best friends with Marcus?'

That surprised me. 'You speak to Marcus?'

She rolled her eyes. 'Of course I do! He comes and seeks me out in the town when he can get out of his duties in the camp. He brought me a posy of flowers last time I saw him. A sweet boy, but a boy just the same.'

So that was what Marcus got up to when I let him out of the records office. I'd presumed he spent his time watching the men train or was composing letters to his father – silly me. He was a young man after all, and he was quite taken with this girl. I was a little disappointed he hadn't confided in me, but supposed some things are best worked out alone – like your first love.

However, I knew this girl's reputation; does this mean that Marcus was visiting her for sex? Unlikely, she had just described him as a young boy. How to ask this subtly? 'So ... er ... what do you get up to when he visits you?' I stumbled awkwardly – very subtle Cassius; you've as much tact as a drunken horse thief.

She laughed unconcerned. 'Oh, he always wants to do such silly things. He asked me to go for a walk amongst the hills one time. Another, he offered to take me to market to buy ribbons for my hair.' She laughed merrily. 'You see, such a silly young boy. Not like my other suitors at all.'

I knew only too well what the other 'suitors' brought her, and what she gave back in return. It was a shame that Marcus hadn't discovered that himself; it would save him making such a fool of himself, and get him laid into the bargain – something, I was now almost certain, he hadn't achieved. Still, despite her describing him as a silly young boy, she must like him, or she wouldn't be so interested in talking about him so much. I thought I'd better stick up for my friend. 'He is a very valiant swordsman, probably the best in the camp.'

She rolled her eyes again. 'Oh, by the gods, not you as well! When he isn't talking nonsense about putting ribbons in my hair, he's going on about your stupid contests with the *gladius*! As if I care how many times he bests you with a blade!'

I laughed loudly. 'That's Marcus alright!' It occurred to me that she was sitting next to me without a drink. 'Here, do you want some wine, I have plenty?'

She nodded with a greedy smile, so I signalled the barman to bring over another cup. That was the good thing about drinking in a brothel – you could keep any company you liked and no one raised any notice. I poured her a cup and asked her. 'When Marcus and I first arrived, Numeria knew you. How so?'

She lowered her eyes and took a swallow full of wine. 'The Lady Numeria was very kind to me when my Festus died. She took me in and looked after me.'

Festus must be the Roman tribune she had defied her family over and followed here. 'But you don't live with her now?'

A hard edge took to her eyes. 'No, and nor will I return. Much as I love Numeria, she is not my mother, and she cannot tell me what to do. She was worse than my family in Rome.' Julia raised her head in pride. 'I do well enough alone. I have enough money to keep a roof over my head and as much food and wine as I require, plus any pretty shawl that I may choose to buy in the market. I don't need another parent.'

You may not now, I thought, whilst you are still young and pretty, but soon all the officers will bore of taking the new young Roman girl, and will be less generous with their 'gifts'. Then she'd be forced to ply her trade amongst the

Roman Mask

lower ranks, just to get by. After a couple of years on the frontier, she'd be lucky to be faring any better than poor Lentula, back in Lugdunum.

I took a sip of wine. 'And is this all you want in life?'

She turned to me, face downcast. 'Of course not, but what choice do I have? I can't return to Rome, and no officer here will marry me ...' She didn't need add the reason why; it was obvious.

I shrugged. 'You never know what life has in store for you. Don't give up yet,' I told her, thinking about my own situation four years ago when I was a broken-down drunk in Lugdunum. I would have never thought then that I could find myself back in the Roman army as a high-ranking officer. Not that I really wanted to be here, but that was another story.

She smiled, wiping away a tear from her eye. 'You're nice. I can see why Marcus loves you. He talks about you a lot.' She then added hopefully, 'Does he ever mention me?'

I looked at the young girl again; in a way she was even more of an innocent than Marcus. She must be even younger – sixteen or seventeen at most. If she had remained in Rome with her family she might have made a good match for the dashing young tribune. But instead she was a prostitute, disowned by her family, working in a frontier town, and was so far from being a prospective marriage prospect for him that she may as well wish for the moon. I thought about what Marcus had written about Julia in his letter to his father, how he had fallen for her as soon as he laid eyes on her. Would it be cruel to tell her that, knowing that once Marcus found out the truth about her, he would almost certainly shun her? 'He must be fond of you if he wishes to put ribbons in your hair,' I told her – it was pretty weak, but the best I could come up with.

Her face brightened. 'Yes, none of the other suitors want to do that! He is such a silly young boy, but he has such a pretty face.' She turned to me. 'And how about you? Do you have a woman secreted away somewhere?'

I took another gulp of wine, and my head spun. 'Well, no, I suppose I don't.' I admitted. How long was it since I'd enjoyed a woman? Too long, that was for sure.

She took another sip of wine from her cup and smiled. 'A strong handsome man like you, surely not? Who was your last love then?'

I stared beyond her and remembered my feelings for Tita: how I'd thought I was in love with her. 'I fell for a woman in Rome, but she turned out to be a big disappointment. She was a liar and a fraud, and broke my heart.'

Julia looked surprised by my admission, but not nearly as much as I was! Where had that come from? Only then did I realise how much Tita had hurt me.

The damn wine was making me morose again.

Julia looked at me sympathetically. 'I know how it hurts to be betrayed by love. I loved my Festus, I really did. But he brought me here, and then left me here alone.' A tear crept down her cheek again.

'Well, he did come off worse in the bargain. I mean, he did die,' I said lightly.

She laughed out loud. 'Yes, he did.' She giggled. 'I'm sure he didn't do that on purpose!'

The two of us carried on drinking well into the night, finishing the amphora of wine, and even ordering another. She told me of her romance with Festus and her wild decision to flee Rome with him. I told her about lost loves of my own, and the two of us became wildly drunk.

We left together and she offered to let me stay with her in her room above the saddle-maker's shop. I'm not sure what stopped me, whether it was out of loyalty to Marcus, who was taken with this girl, or just because I was so drunk I didn't see the point in joining her there. I insisted on walking back to my own bed in the Roman camp. 'It won't take me long, I know the way,' I said, then promptly stumbled over and fell face first into a puddle.

She laughed out loud and helped me up. 'Come on, you can't sleep there.' She stumbled whilst helping me as she was almost as drunk as me.

We weaved our way back to the Roman camp, giggling and falling over along the way. She felt a bit of apprehension as we approached the main gates, but I reassured her. 'Don't worry, they let anyone in this camp.'

Sure enough the centurion on guard simply waved me through when he recognised me – obviously not wanting to get involved in the inappropriate behaviour of a member of the high command.

Unbelievably, I even took her into Governors Varus' own house and up to my room which was next to Marcus'. The slaves let us in, and we stumbled up to my room, where we promptly both fell asleep on my bed. Drunk and oblivious to any problems that this might cause.

Chapter Twenty-two

I was panting, and out of breath; I'd been trying to escape from Decius, but to no avail. He stood twenty paces in front of me. He raised his finger and pointed directly at me. Men came out from the trees – my dead comrades from Western-Gate Pass – they had hatred in their eyes, and reached out their hands for me. I screamed.

I woke with a start, sitting up in bed, hands shaking and my head thumping. I groaned loudly and flopped back on my bed. 'By the gods, Decius, leave me alone.'

It was clearly late morning. Sunshine lit up my room and it was already warm from the summer's heat. I heard a sniffling sound coming from inside my room. I looked round and was startled to notice Julia there, sitting on the floor, still wearing her light tunic, holding a ribbon in her hands and softly weeping.

Oh, by Hades, I'd forgotten about her.

What had I been thinking? Bringing her back into the home of Varus! I was a guest here. I wasn't at home in Rome, living the life of a reckless philanderer anymore. Oh, by the gods, this could be trouble. I spied the water bowl in my room, and decided that I needed to splash some water on my face. I lifted the covers up, but then realised I was completely naked underneath. 'Oh!' is all I muttered.

Julia turned round, eyes red and swollen from crying, and said, 'You're awake. Your friend Marcus came looking for you.'

I rubbed my forehead and closed my eyes. 'Marcus,' I said in resignation, 'he saw you here with me?'

'Yes, I was asleep in your bed but I woke when he opened the door. He didn't say anything.' She let out a little sob. 'But he looked so angry and hurt.'

I looked under the covers at my naked self. 'Er … but we didn't do anything last night … did we?' I was pretty sure I'd remember if we had, but I had to make sure.

She shook her head. 'No, we both fell asleep.' She started crying again and bowed her head upon her folded arms which she rested on her knees. 'But he'll never believe that, will he? And can I blame him?'

I spotted my discarded tunic on the floor, reached over, and slipped it over my head. I got out of bed and in a state of panic splashed water on my face from the basin. She was right, Marcus would know of my reputation in Rome – he'd never believe that nothing happened. There was more to worry about as well. What would the governor think about me bringing a known prostitute to his home?

'We need to get you out of here without anyone else noticing.' I told her, my thumping head making it hard to think properly. 'Don't worry about Marcus. I'll speak to him later.'

She looked up at me, a sad smile on her face. 'I think it's a bit late to be sneaking me out. The household slaves let us in. They will all know about us now.'

I grabbed my head in my hands in frustration. 'How could I be so stupid? We need to get you out of here straight away.'

She bowed her head again. 'You think by getting me out of your room this will all go away? You're wrong, you know.'

Oh, by the gods, she wasn't going to be difficult about this was she? I noticed my discarded purse on the ground, picked it up, and tossed it to her. 'Look, I'm sorry. This isn't my home – this could cause me lots of trouble.'

She looked at the purse in her hands as if it was a venomous snake, and only then did I realise my mistake. She was known as the 'gift taker' for a reason.

She stood up, her face white with shock, and slowly emptied the purse on the ground, silver coins dropping out, one by one. 'You offer me coin?' she said incredulously, and I looked on speechless, not knowing what to say.

'I'm no whore!' she screamed, before running out of the room in floods of tears, tearing down the stairs in hysterics, out of the home of Varus, and down the main concourse of the military camp in full view of the twenty thousand Roman soldiers stationed there. So much for sneaking her out quietly.

I sat down on the bed heavily and again put my head in my hands. 'I'm sorry, Julia, I just didn't think,' I said to myself, closing my eyes against the awful thumping hangover. When would I learn?

What to do next? I wasn't stupid enough to think that there would be no further repercussions from this, but if I was going to deal with them, I first needed to get rid of this damn hangover. Then I could speak to Varus – a shiver went down my spine – and then Marcus.

Hangover first. I walked out of my room and headed towards Varus' private bathhouse. On the way there I passed several household slaves – none met my eye, which I took to be a very bad sign. On reaching there I jumped straight into the *Frigidarium,* ignoring the more pleasant hot waters of the *Calidarium* and the *Tepidarium.* I didn't deserve to enjoy my bath; I just needed something to clear my head. I got out, my teeth chattering with the cold, and wiped myself dry with a coarse blanket. That was better.

I dressed quickly and put on my armour. It wouldn't offer me much protection from what I faced, but it made me feel a little less vulnerable. It was time to go downstairs.

I entered the main courtyard where a slave informed me that Governor Varus wished to see me in the headquarters building, and not to keep him waiting. I wandered across the road to the headquarters and I was left waiting outside his office until well past midday, my stomach rumbling uncomfortably from lack of food and the residue of too much wine.

The time passed interminably slowly as I stood outside pondering my fate, until finally I'm admitted. As soon as I saw the governor's face, I knew I was in trouble. He wore a dour expression and his eyes held fury. He sat behind his desk, in full toga, hands resting palm down on the desk. I expected him to shout, but instead he said quite calmly. 'So, you have finally risen. I trust you slept well?'

I was completely flustered by the polite question. 'Yes … er … I mean no … erm … I'm sorry, sir.'

He thumped the desk with a fist and raised his voice. 'Being sorry isn't good enough!' he blasted, his face turning red in rage. 'How dare you bring a woman back to my home? Even Asprenas never went so far, and he was my own flesh and blood. By what right do you think you can dishonour my hospitality?'

I lowered my head. 'I'm deeply sorry for any offence I've caused. I was drunk and not thinking. I've made a grave misjudgement.'

Varus slapped the desk again. 'You were drunk. Do you think that is appropriate behaviour for a member of my high command? What sort of example do you think you're setting to the men?'

I could have tried making excuses, told him about the trouble I'd been having sleeping, or pointed out that it wasn't unheard of to see Varus himself rolling about drunk after one of his lavish dinners, but wisely I thought better of it. I'd been drunk and foolish, and I had to take what came to me. I lifted my head and stared straight ahead. 'A very bad one, sir. I am very sorry. It won't happen again.'

Varus folded his hands, calm returning to his voice. 'You're correct there. It certainly won't happen again, or at least, it won't under my roof. You can remove your things from my home, and either move into one of the barrack blocks with the men, or take up lodging in the town. That is what many of the tribunes do now, and as you have abused my hospitality, you can join them there.'

Only fair, I supposed. At least he wasn't having me flogged. 'I'll make the arrangements immediately, sir.'

He looked at me directly. 'I'm very disappointed in you, Cassius. I thought better of you than this. What your father would say to this behaviour, I don't know.'

Unfortunately my father had known me to do much worse. I cleared my throat. 'Will Marcus be permitted to stay with you? He had nothing to do with the trouble I caused last night.'

A slight smile touched his face. 'Oh, I'm aware of that. That boy is a model soldier, unlike you. But you needn't worry about his lodgings any more. He came to me this morning and asked to be released from your service so he could take up a military post. He informed me that you had more than enough scribes for your work, and he wasn't proving much use as your aide. I saw no reason to decline his request, so he has been posted to the Eighteenth legion.'

I felt a great sinking in my stomach. 'You've taken Marcus away from me,' I stuttered in shock.

Varus narrowed his eyes. 'I think you'll find that Marcus removed himself from you. I can hardly blame him. The poor boy is desperate to see some action. You can leave me now and return to your duties.'

I barely controlled my temper. I wanted to shout at the governor and call him a fool for granting Marcus' request, but I restrained myself knowing there was no point – the governor's powers were absolute in his province, and he was fully entitled to deploy any member of his command where he wished. I only had myself to blame. Varus had only granted the request to spite me. Damn the man. I gritted my teeth, and managed to mutter a curt, 'Sir,' before turning and leaving.

I needed to find Marcus immediately: explain the misunderstanding, see if I could get him to change his mind. If he asked Varus to come back to me, Varus might grant the request. I had fallen out of favour with the governor, but Marcus' standing was still high.

I walked briskly over to the headquarters building of the XVIII and requested to see Numonius Vala straight away. Now Vala was Marcus' commanding officer, protocol deemed that I should request his permission to speak to him before approaching him directly. I paced back and forth along the narrow corridor outside his office, thinking what to say whilst I waited to be seen. Mercifully, I didn't have to wait long: Numonius Vala agreeing to see me as soon as he finished issuing some order to one of his centurions.

Numonius Vala was reading a report when I walked into his office, which he put down as I entered. He looked up, surprise clearly showing on his lined face. 'What brings you here, Cassius? Have you finally got bored of Varus' company?'

I stood before his desk, hands clenched behind my back. 'In a manner of speaking, yes. I won't be staying in his home any longer.' I was damned if I was going to tell Vala why, so I got onto why I was here. 'I'm here to discuss Marcus Scaeva. I understand the governor has placed him under your command.'

Numonius smiled. 'Yes, that's right. A gift from the gods.'

That shocked me. 'What do you mean by that? How is he a gift? He's just a boy?'

Numonius shook his head. 'He is much more than that, Cassius, and you know it. He is from a well-respected family and has an impeccable service record.'

I was still confused. 'Well of course he does, but he's only just joined the army. What use is he to you?'

Numonius looked me directly in the eye. 'He wanted to volunteer for action, so I've assigned him to one of the deep-reaching patrols I am sending to spy on the Angrivarii.'

A cold dread ran down my spine, I shook my head to make sure I'd heard correctly. 'But that is crazy. He has no combat experience at all – he's too green for such a dangerous mission.'

Numonius raised a hand to calm me, noticing the shrill panic in my voice. 'Don't worry, Cassius. I'll be placing him alongside one of my most experienced centurions. I've explained to Marcus that he is only there as an observer, not as the commander of the expedition.'

This didn't make any sense. 'But then why send him at all? He'll be risking his life for nothing.'

Numonius shook his head. 'Not at all. Don't you see, Cassius, he's perfect. If I was to send one of my centurions alone with a few men, no matter what they discovered, Varus would be convinced that their reports were exaggerated or embellished with lies. The governor is too mistrustful of me to take the word of any of my men. But if I send Marcus Scaeva with them – a tribune no less, son of a well-respected commander of the *imperator's* own Praetorian Guard, a man with an unimpeachable record – then the governor will have no choice but to listen to what they say. What is more, he was assigned to me by the governor himself!' Numonius slapped his hands in triumph. 'I couldn't believe my luck when the young man presented himself with his orders marked with Varus' own seal.'

My heart sunk as I saw the logic to his plan. Marcus was perfect for this role. I wasn't going to give up so easily, however. 'But he is just a boy, Numonius. He doesn't deserve to lose his life on this mission.'

Numonius face turned serious. 'Do you think any of my men deserve to die, Cassius? Do you even know how many I've lost in that damned Teutoburg Forest? Do you think I like sending any of them on such a hazardous mission? I don't, but you yourself convinced me of the need to find out what the Angrivarii are up to. Don't go cold on me now, just because your friend will be one of them. You know how it is, Cassius. You've had to send men into the field yourself. You know you can't play favourites. They're all good men. None of them deserve an early grave.'

I bowed my head and looked at the floor in despair. I knew he was right. You could never let affection cloud your judgement when it came to issuing orders to the men. You had to choose the right men for the job, as simple as that. 'Is there no other way?' was all I could mutter.

Numonius' eyes softened a touch. 'No, I'm sorry, Cassius. I know you're fond of him, but don't worry, my men will do everything to bring him back to you.'

A wretched guilt came over me. It was I who had persuaded Numonius to resend these patrols. Only now did I realise what I was asking of these men. 'Can I at least speak to him before he goes?'

Numonius let out a large sigh. 'Of course you can. But please, don't try and dissuade him from going. He has his orders now. I'll expect him to follow them.'

I looked up at the legate. 'Don't worry, I just wish to bid him farewell. I think he is angry with me. I don't want him to leave without me settling that score at least.'

Numonius Vala pointed out the window. 'You'll find him in the third barrack block. The patrol will be leaving soon, so you don't have much time.'

I approached the barrack block where Vala directed me and found a circle of twenty men outside it making last checks to their kit, packing away essential items, checking the sharpness of their weapons, whilst the watchful eye of a steely-eyed centurion and *optio* looked on. This was obviously the patrol, and I spied Marcus, kneeling down with his back to me as he placed items in his small kit bag. I inclined my head at the centurion and signalled that I wished to talk to Marcus; he nodded his head, but a crease of worry crossed his forehead. He probably didn't want any of his men distracted as they prepared to leave, but could hardly countermand the wishes of someone from the high command.

I approached Marcus, slowly, and knelt down beside him. He was dressed in the same fashion as the other soldiers, in simple mail shirt and tunic: the patrol would travel light, not even taking shields or helmets – their best chance of survival was to stay undetected, and heavy armour would only slow them. Now I was here, I didn't know how to start, the words I'd been meaning to tell him suddenly drying up in my throat.

Marcus pushed a small blanket into his bag, gritting his teeth as he pushed it down. 'You can't stop me from going you know.'

His voice was taut and angry, as if he was barely holding onto his temper. I cleared my throat. 'Marcus, I …'

'I have orders from Governor Varus, and now my new commander, Numonius Vala. I am no longer under your command, and I will be going with this patrol. You can't stop me.' His voice rang with determination.

I rubbed my forehead. 'I know that, Marcus. I'm not here to prevent you from going.'

That seemed to surprise him, as he half turned his head towards me before turning his attention back to his bag and pulling the laces tight, sealing it. 'Then why are you here, Cassius? I don't think we have anything more to say to one another.'

It was time I lanced this boil. 'Look, Marcus. I know you're angry with me, but you must know, nothing happened between me and Julia last night. We both fell asleep.'

Marcus ground his teeth in anger, holding up his hand to halt what I was saying. 'What you did with that woman of ill-repute is none of my concern. The fact that she was in your bed at all says all I need to know about her.' He stood up and hoisted his bag on his back, testing it for weight.

I stood also, trying to explain. 'We were both drunk, Marcus. It was a mistake to bring her back, but nothing happened …'

Marcus shook his head in disbelief. 'Do you really think I care whether or not you were too drunk to have sex with her? Did you come all this way just to tell me that? She was in your bed; that is enough for me – I should probably thank you for showing me what type of girl she is. Either way, it is no concern of mine now. I have a mission to go on and your disgraceful actions are no longer any of my concern. You're not the man I thought you were, Cassius. Now, please leave me, we're about to leave.'

I bowed my head in shame. 'You're right, Marcus. I'm not the man you thought I was, but I am genuinely sorry I hurt you. So is Julia, she does care for you …' I noticed Marcus' jaw tighten in anger once more, so thought better of mentioning her again. It was time to discuss the patrol. 'Look, Marcus. Try not to leave in anger, it will eat you up and distract you from your mission. Remember all you've learnt, and listen to the centurion – I think I remember him, he's called Aeschylus isn't he?'

Marcus nodded.

'A good man, by all accounts. A cool head and a dependable nature – he'll know how to bring you all back safely.' I looked over at the centurion: a craggy-lined face sat atop a supremely fit body, with a barrel chest. He'd never been under my command, but I knew him to be well respected.

'Is there anything else?' Marcus said, trying to dismiss me, but I noticed the edge of anger had left his voice somewhat.

I took a deep breath. 'Just look after yourself, Marcus. You're a good man, and will be a great soldier – better than I ever was. Don't rush to try and prove yourself – that's how people end up dying.'

Marcus looked over to the centurion, who then looked at me, to see if he could take his men away. I nodded my head, and he barked an order for the men to form up.

I watched the patrol march out of the camp with a heavy heart, but was somewhat lightened by the fact that just before they reached the north gate, Marcus turned his head and looked back at me. He turned his head away as soon as he realised I was still watching, but at least he knew I was sorry for what I'd done. It wasn't much, but it was the only comfort I could glean from my last conversation with Marcus. His fate was in the hands of the gods now, I couldn't do anything more for him.

I walked back to Varus' home, only to find my wares had already been packed up into my saddlebags. I asked the stable boy to fetch my horse and Marcus' – his patrol left on foot, there was no room for mounted officers – and set off to find an inn in the town. I chose one near the outskirts with a large well-kept stable which could house the two horses. I sent a young slave back into the camp to let the other officers know where I could be found if I was needed, but in all honesty I didn't know whether Governor Varus even wished for my services any more. After stowing my belongings and freshening up with the small bowl of water in my room, I sat downstairs on some chairs that had been set outside on a veranda. I ordered some food – a plain stew made from lamb and beans – which I ate without really tasting it, as I stared at the surrounding forest-lined hills. Over in that direction Marcus was marching away on an incredibly dangerous mission I had helped instigate. If anything happened to him, I knew I'd never forgive myself.

'Ahh, there he is. What a nice sunny spot to be sitting,' a female voice said.

I turned my head at the new arrival and was relieved to see it was Numeria, looking radiant as ever, dressed in a Roman *stola* and headscarf. The breeze off the veranda blew away her scarf, revealing the freckles I remembered so well. I stood to greet her, wondering how she'd found me, but pleased I had someone to tell about my awful day.

She walked up to me and slapped me round the face.

My stinging cheek stung with pain. 'What in Hades …' I stumbled backwards, collapsing on the veranda chair. I was too shocked to say more.

Numeria explained. 'I came to find you in the camp, only to hear you'd skulked away to this hiding-hole. You don't think you can hide from me that easily do you?'

I shook my head to clear the ringing from it. 'I wasn't given a choice. Varus told me to leave his house.'

Numeria laughed, but not her normal pleasant ring – this laugh was full of scorn and anger. 'Ha! Finally the governor does something I approve of! What's the matter, Gaius? Did he get sick of your womanising and drinking?'

Guilt filled me. 'Something like that, yes. I take it you've spoken to Julia?'

Numeria's face was a mask of fury. 'Yes, I found an inconsolable Julia in floods of tears this morning on my doorstep. It took me a long time to pull the story from her, but I finally found out about the coin you offered her.'

Oh, by Hades, could this day get any worse? 'Numeria, listen, it was a mistake. I was confused, with a hangover, I didn't mean to …' I stumbled over my words, realising how pathetic they sounded.

She looked down at me with disgust. 'She never asks for coin from any of the men she sleeps with for a reason, Gaius. It may not mean much to you, but it is all that was holding her self-respect together as a person. You don't know how hard it is here, on the Roman frontier, to be a woman alone. She has no family, no husband or protector to look after her. She has had to survive the only way she knows. The only thing that kept her sane has been her knowledge that she has never accepted coin from any of the men. Now you have shattered that last scrap of pride she held.'

Should I tell her that I hadn't actually had sex with her? It hadn't placated Marcus any, I doubted it would make much difference with Numeria, judging by her anger. 'I'm sorry, Numeria. I didn't mean to upset her.'

Numeria still looked angry, but pleased I hadn't tried to argue my case. She wasn't finished with me yet, however; she folded her arms under her breasts. 'Your sister warned me that you had become seduced by the vices of Rome, Gaius. But then when I saw you here, I thought you'd changed. You seemed different from the other officers, thoughtful and caring, like my Otho. But I was wrong. You're just like the others. You all treat this province just like a Roman playpen: somewhere to get drunk, frequent brothels and have a jolly adventure. How did Rome ever build an empire with men such as these? You sicken me, Gaius. You all do! From now on I'd appreciate it if you stayed away from my home. Julia will be staying with me, and I don't want you upsetting her. Besides, I have no wish to see you again. Good day.'

She turned her back on me and walked purposely out of the inn, throwing a ferocious glare at a serving-boy who had the misfortune to be in her way. He stumbled backwards as quickly as he could to get out of her path, falling over in the process. Numeria marched past without a backwards glance.

The red-faced boy got to his feet and came over to enquire, 'I'm sorry, sir, I didn't realise she would be so angry when she asked for you. Can I get you anything? Some wine perhaps?'

I rubbed my still stinging face, then turned my attention to him and told him. 'No. I don't think that would be a good idea.'

Chapter Twenty-three

As it turned out, I was free to continue my work with the legions. I never was to discover whether that was because Varus couldn't be bothered to find someone else to do it, or because he knew that if he dismissed every staff officer whoever got drunk they'd be precious few of them left.

I read the reports from Julius and his cavalry and posted each report I got back from Numonius Vala's XVIII's legion, making recommendations to Governor Varus where I thought necessary. However, it wasn't long before I started to think that I should be doing more. There was still no word from Marcus' patrol – no concern yet as it wasn't due back yet – but knowing that Marcus was out there risking his life, and Numeria's criticism of staff officers who never ventured out of the camp, I realised I needed to get more information from outside the Roman enclosure. I had no soldiers to command, only a few scribes used to administration work, meaning I needed to go myself.

I rode out each day, out into the surrounding forests and fens, and visited different German settlements of the Cherusci. I won't pretend that I wasn't scared, especially on my first expedition out from the safety of the camp, but I knew I needed to do this. I received sullen looks from the German warriors, scowls from the woman and children, but by and large, I was pretty much ignored. That suited me fine: I knew very little of their language, so questioning was futile anyway. I rode through each village – large collections of long houses with thatched roofs, surrounded by stockades and earthen walls. Around each village, land had been developed for farming, but even though I was no expert, I could tell that the land was ill-suited to this use. It was either too wet, the fields not being properly drained as they would be in Italy or Gaul, or the forest was cleared badly, leaving the soil too stony and full of tree roots and stumps. This was harvest time, and in Gaul this would be a time of celebration, but here the work was mainly being done by women and old men; where most of the warriors of the tribe were I didn't know, although I remembered how many I'd seen in the main war camp of the Cherusci a few weeks ago – forty to fifty thousand warriors the Cherusci could call upon, a number I could barely visualise, but here were their mothers, wives, children, left in destitution. I imagined Julius had been gathering as many warriors to him as possible to help consolidate his position and also threaten the neighbouring Angrivarii and Chatti lands – all very well and understandable, but it left the populace struggling to gather in the crops at the most important time of year for farming. The crops I saw being collected were of poor quality and barely enough to feed the population, let alone be enough to pay the large taxes Varus was demanding in order to continue with his building works. I saw files of soldiers, mainly from Avitus' XVII legion gathering the taxes, and they weren't subtle or delicate in doing so. I remembered the scene earlier this summer, when the three Roman soldiers were accused of raping a young girl. Judging by what I witnessed of the Roman tax collectors, this was unlikely to be an isolated case. They marched into each settlement, demanded vastly exorbitant revenues – whether it looked as if the settlement could afford it or not – and then took what they liked, turning deaf ears to screaming women and children who begged them not to take so much. I saw brutish Roman soldiers leave settlements with cartloads of crops, strings of livestock and their full ledger of taxes, not realising – or not caring – that it left the village with precious little to survive the winter on. I knew how harsh the German winters could be, and if I was any judge, it was going to be a difficult one for the Cherusci.

Julius needed to be careful. I understood why he may be gathering his warriors to him – with so many rival factions clamouring for his position, he needed to show his strength – but if the general populace were to starve, it wouldn't take much to use that resentment and turn them against him. I also saw the stupidity of Governor Varus' policies. On first reaching the German province, Marcus and I were so impressed with the Roman settlement, with its aqueducts, statues, and forum: Varus' beacon of hope to the German people. Complete nonsense. Here was the true cost of his town – crippling taxes, and a populace resentful and angry.

I returned to the camp each night and made my recommendations to Varus via written report. I told him the taxes he was extracting needed to be reviewed and the methods the soldiers were using to collect them needed urgent attention. Each report was either ignored or received a curt reply, telling me not to interfere in the running of his province, and to restrict my work to the gathering of military intelligence. I was dumbfounded. How could Varus be so stupid to think that the two could be separated? A resentful populace was military intelligence that needed to be conveyed to the governor. I understood the frustrations Numonius Vala must have felt this past year. Finding his opinion was no longer finding favour with Governor Varus, there was no one else for Numonius to appeal to, so his arguments were always destined to fall on deaf ears. I wrestled with my conscience each night, in between nightmares of Centurion Decius, and wondered whether I should sit back and let the province go to wrack and ruin. I'd been ordered to stay with the Roman army for only the first year; August was coming to an end. Soon the summer would be over, and then the army would return to its winter quarters in Aliso. What did I care if the Cherusci starved and learnt to hate their Roman overlords?

But then that would mean trouble for Julius. His grip on the crown was based on co-operation with Rome. If the situation was to get any worse, it could strengthen the position of Segestes or Inguiomerus. Julius may end up being deposed – which in German terms almost certainly meant death – and all because of Varus' mismanagement of the province. I couldn't appeal to any higher authority in Germany, but that didn't leave me completely powerless. I thought about writing to my father but knew he would never interfere in another man's charge, and then I realised what I should do: I was sent here by Augustus' wife Livia. Surely she would expect me to send her a report on what I found here? It was only expected that I send her tidings on my progress in Germany. Livia may not have any official position within the empire, but she had the *princep's* ear and that was possibly more valuable than the highest connections in the Senate.

I considered what I should write. There was no point in making veiled criticisms; I only had one chance at this, so I'd better make the situation clear and the gods be damned with the consequences:

To the Illustrious Lady Livia, Consort of Augustus, Mother of Rome, greetings
I hope this letter finds you in good health. Please pass on my greetings to your husband, whose wisdom and guidance assures the future prosperity of The Republic.

Please forgive this intrusion, but I thought that I should inform you of my progress in the undertaking you charged me, this Quinquatria, which I was only to happy to undertake on your behalf.

I have found the new Roman province of Germany to be everything I remembered it to be and Governor Varus has made me most welcome. Publius Quinctilius Varus has taken great efforts in establishing a new town here, with great public buildings, all in honour of your esteemed husband. However, it is to my great regret that I must report my misgivings in this policy. This work has only been achieved on the back of crippling taxes, something the local populace is struggling to bear. Indubitably, each region must pay its share, but let us give them something they can really use, such as new trade to the region. Only then will the German tribes be in a position to pay these taxes, as currently they are not. I see anger and resentment, a seething populace brewing rebellion wherever I turn. Surely this is not an example your husband wishes to portray to the Republic's latest province and beneficiary of our great benefactor's grace? I do not wish to criticise the governor, as he has proved a most honourable host, but he ignores all my warnings and pays no heed to the military intelligence gathered by his men. I deem it necessary that your husband needs to look into his running of the province, lest Rome loses all its allies in the region.

I trust in your husband's wisdom to know the best course of action.

Ever your servant,
Gaius Cassius Aprilis

I was taking a terrible risk. If Varus was ever to discover the contents of this letter, I would not live to see the next day, but I thought it unlikely that Varus would dare break a seal addressed to the *imperator's* own wife – even so, I would despatch this letter in secret. Another worry was Livia not taking kindly to the criticism I'd levelled at Varus. After all, he was sent to Germany by her husband. But I also thought this unlikely: Livia had sent me to Germany for a reason; I certainly wasn't needed as an intermediary between Varus and Julius. Had Livia suspected all along of Varus' misrule of the province and wanted someone to confirm her suspicions? I suspected that was the case, and I was the pawn she'd chosen to fulfil this task. If any of my criticism were ever to become public, Varus could easily discredit me as the grumblings of a disgruntled officer who had been disciplined over inappropriate behaviour. My reputation was sure to suffer, but that didn't bother me overly: my damned fine reputation got me in to this fix in the first place; it was something I could live without! Either way, it would force the governor to at least look at the behaviour of his troops and review his high-taxation policy – anything to break through the wall of indifference Varus had constructed to any criticism. Varus was unwittingly brewing a sea of discontent within the German tribes. It was in his interest as much as anyone else's that he realised this.

I visited Numonius Vala's XVIII legion's offices and passed the sealed wax tablet directly to one of their official messengers just before he was set to leave for Aliso. I gave the tablet to him and disclosed that knowledge of its existence was sealed to the *imperator* and his wife only. I needn't have been so careful: if Varus wasn't even bothering to read the reports of his own officers, he was hardly likely to be monitoring their mail, but then, when your life depended on something, it was prudent to take whatever precautions you could.

I was returning to my offices when Julius returned to the camp with a small number of his cavalry scouts. I was delighted to see him, and he in turn greeted me warmly.

Julius dismounted from his white stallion. Both he and his horse were caked with dirt and mud from the road, and his horse's sides heaved with exertion. 'Gaius, old friend. Good of you to welcome me home personally!' He embraced me. 'Where is that young friend of yours – I thought he was closer than your shadow?'

'Marcus has been given other duties.' I didn't want to explain the situation with Marcus. It was still painful to think about it, and my worry for him was only increasing each day he was absent from the camp. Besides, Julius returning was the first good news I'd had in weeks, and I didn't want to spoil the occasion. 'It's great to see you, Julius. You look to have been riding hard. What brings you back to our camp?'

Despite Julius' worn appearance, he appeared to be in an excited mood. 'I have important news for Governor Varus. I must see him at once. But don't worry, you'll hear all about it soon, then we can catch up properly.' He gave me a clap on my shoulder, then signalled to a legionary that he needed an audience with the governor.

The news was clearly good, and I itched to find out what it was. However, I couldn't very well loiter outside Varus' home waiting for information, so I returned to my inn in the town and waited impatiently. Before sunset, a summons came to me, asking me to return to Varus' home for a dinner with the governor. This was a surprise. Since being asked to leave Varus' home, invitations to dinner from Varus had not been forthcoming. Julius' news must have been good if it meant Varus was prepared to forget our recent estrangement. I dressed in a newly pressed toga and made my way to the governor's home with a strange sense of guilt. I was visiting the home of a man whose reputation I'd just tried to smear to the *imperator*'s wife – this betrayal warred with my own conviction that I'd done the right thing. Varus' misrule of his province could only lead to further calamity, someone needed to know.

I was admitted in to Varus' home by one of the household slaves, a slender young adolescent boy with a thick thatch of blonde hair, who barely managed to hide a smirk when he saw it was me at the door. Understandable, I guess. The last time he'd seen me I was thrown out of the household for bringing a prostitute home. That was the sort of gossip household slaves loved. I ruffled his hair and told him to introduce me to Varus.

On admittance to Varus' dinning chamber, I noticed that the entire high command were in attendance: Julius was there and legates Selus and Avitus, together with Camp Praefect Ceionius and a few tribunes, like myself, all from the senatorial class. The biggest shock was Legate Numonius Vala reclining on a couch next to the governor; he looked uncomfortable and out of place, an appearance not helped by the fact that he was still wearing his parade armour rather than formal togas like the rest of us. If Vala had been ordered to attend, this must be big news indeed.

Governor Varus got to his feet as I was admitted. 'Welcome, Cassius. Please come in and make yourself comfortable at my table.' He held out a hand and indicated a spare couch next to Praefect Ceionius. 'Now we are all here!'

I bowed my head in response to his warm welcome, feeling even more guilty, and took my place at the table. Governor Varus clapped his hands, and the first course came out to cries and whistles of delight. It was stuffed swans' necks – an expensive dish in Rome, unheard of here; Varus was not holding back tonight. A slave came and filled my goblet with wine, but I instructed him to water it heavily: I hadn't overindulged in wine since that night with Julia, and I certainly wasn't going to start tonight.

I chatted with Ceionius next to me, but soon lost interest in his conversation. Ceionius was only really interested in gambling, and any conversation you had with him soon turned towards betting on dice, cards, or any number of small wagers he thought up. He was friendly enough, but only gamblers are interested in talking about gambling, and that was one of the few vices that never appealed to me in my time in Rome: my father's vast wealth meant winning more money was pretty meaningless. I nodded my head in agreement whenever necessary, but my attention wandered off elsewhere. I saw Julius on one side of Governor Varus, a great broad grin on his face and a full wine goblet in hand. On the other side reclined Numonius Vala, looking like he'd rather be anywhere in the empire right now than at this dinner table. He picked at the rich exotic food, almost certainly not to his taste – if Governor Varus really wanted to make him feel welcome, he should have supplied him with nothing but bread and water – and shifted uneasily, obviously out of practice from reclining when eating. I hid a smile watching him; was it any wonder he and Varus never got on? They were as different as night and day. Governor Varus ate and drank with gusto, signalling the slaves to bring on the next course as soon as the last one was finished. We ate pork, fish, and finally some exceedingly sweet honey cakes, all of which brought great applause from the guests, which delighted Varus, who preened like a stuffed peacock – the one dish even Varus couldn't conjure up this far away from Rome!

Finally Varus got to his feet, stood with a wine goblet in one hand, took a deep gulp and then addressed us all. 'Friends, it is my great pleasure to have you all here, under my roof and at my table. A finer group of men no commander could ever wish for.' He cleared his throat. 'Over this past summer many of you have wondered why we've not pursued our war with the Angrivarii more aggressively.' The governor didn't say it, but everyone present knew that he was referring to Numonius Vala, who again shifted uneasily. 'But it was my contention all along that a peace could be brokered with this tribe.' The governor looked around the table at each of us, a smile touching his lips. 'I now have news which you will all find of interest. Julius, will you continue the story,'

Julius got to his feet and explained. 'Over the last month, my cavalry, and many of my Cherusci warriors, have been patrolling the north-eastern fens, our hunting lands adjacent to the Angrivarii.' I already knew this from his reports, but most of the other people at the table were probably ignorant of where Julius' men had been stationed. 'We've seen very little activity over the past month, something very unusual for the Angrivarii, who always like to make the odd raid, or make a show of strength at our borders.' There were nods of agreement at this. Most had encountered the Angrivarii at some point since being posted to Germany. 'But this last month, nothing. Until, just a few days past, a lone rider came out from their forest of Teutoburgium and approached my war host. He asked to speak to me in person, something I granted him. He told me that the King of the Angrivarii had died from a hunting accident.' There were murmurs of surprise and shock – the Angrivarii king had ruled for over twenty years. 'And the past month they'd been selecting a new leader. The messenger told me the new King of the Angrivarii has a message for Rome: it is time to lay down the weapons of war. It is time for a peace between our nations!'

Everyone, except me, got to their feet and cheered. This was obviously wonderful news and could even mean the end of the wars in Germany altogether, but I just reclined there stunned. All I thought about was the damning letter I'd just posted. Varus may very well have brought peace to the hostile province of Germany, something no man had ever achieved, not even the great men of our age, and on the very day he learns of the success of his policies, I'd sent a letter to the *imperator*'s wife, calling him an idiot. My mind started racing, wondering whether I could get that letter back – but no, it was sent via the military despatch riders on the fastest horses the army owned, which are replaced at every way station. It was gone, I'd never catch him, and even if I did, I'd sealed the message to Augustus' wife – I doubt even I'd be able to take it back now. I finally burst out laughing. Well at least Livia knew never to trust my judgement again! This would almost certainly be the last time she thought I could prove useful in the colonies and be sent as her secret spy! I couldn't believe it. Varus had been right. Vala and I had doubted him, but he'd been right all along. At least my laughter masked my true feelings to the announcement; most of those present probably thought I was laughing in delight, not in bitter self-mockery.

Varus raised his arms for peace. 'Now, friends, please be calm.' He was smiling ear to ear now. 'Please retake your places at table. I know this is momentous news, but we must not get too ahead of ourselves. It is with great pleasure I can announce that I have already sent a peace delegation to the Angrivarii lands this very day. Let us see what this new king can offer us!'

There were widespread cheers, but Numonius Vala unsurprisingly was the first to raise a query. 'You've already sent the peace delegation? But who leads it?'

Varus sat up, smiled, and took a sip of wine. 'Unfortunately, I didn't think you would be the right choice for the delegation, Numonius.' Everyone laughed at this, as Vala had been agitating for a new offensive on the Angrivarii all summer. 'So I've sent Avitus' lead tribune, Paullinus, to head the delegation, with one century as a guard of honour.'

Numonius looked confused. 'But why so soon? My patrol is due back any day now. Surely they can shed some light on these events?' My stomach lurched as the patrol he was referring to was Marcus'.

Varus was annoyed. 'You mean the patrol you sent against my express wishes? Honestly, Vala, can't you stop bellyaching for one night. I needed to send the delegation immediately: firstly to take advantage of this unprecedented opportunity; and secondly, because if we are to get a reply before the end of the summer campaign, we have little time.'

This was true: it was the start of September. In just over a month the army would have to retire back to Aliso for their winter quarters. Numonius nodded his head reluctantly, so Varus' turned round to his assembled guests to address everyone in the room. 'Gentleman, everything we have worked for is now coming together. Let us enjoy this night and look forward to the prospect of a lasting peace in Germany.'

The other officers roared their approval and downed their goblets of wine. Several officers, including legates Avitus and Selus, gave speeches, thanking Governor Varus for his foresight and wisdom and congratulating him on his success. I knew why they were so pleased: the officers standing, those who had worked closely with Varus, were sure to be well rewarded as they basked in the reflected glory of Governor Varus' success. If the wars in Germany truly were coming to an end, these men could ask for any post in the empire they wished for, and they would be granted by a grateful Senate. For those who had opposed him, however, like Numonius Vala and I, the outlook wasn't so rosy. I saw Vala slip out of the room as soon as decorum allowed, and when the other men were distracted by a particularly ribald story from Varus, who was now showing the effects of wine and overindulgence, I quietly followed Vala, meeting him in the courtyard of Varus' home. I told him, 'You have to hand it to him, neither of us saw that one coming.'

Numonius turned to me in frustration. 'Don't you think the timing of all this is a bit suspicious? Right at the end of the campaigning season, making it impossible for us to properly corroborate it?'

I chuckled. 'Come now, Numonius. The Angrivarii didn't decide when their king was to die. We were just wrong, both of us, not just you, Vala. If the Angrivarii fall into line, the other tribes are all soon to follow. With the Chatti beaten, and both the Cherusci and Angrivarii's as allies, the largest tribes are now all pacified.' There were other large tribes, but it was the Chatti, Cherusci and Angrivarii who had proven the most difficult in the conquest of Germany. Resistance to Rome was now almost at an end.

Numonius Vala lowered his head. 'I was so sure. I was certain that Varus was wrong and the Angrivarii were preparing for a large offensive against us.'

I realised then how hard this must be for Numonius Vala. Varus would now be able to replace Numonius Vala with any man he liked. The Senate would be sure to approve the governor's every wish. Vala could expect to be returned to Rome, not quite in disgrace, but eyebrows would be raised as to why the Governor of Germany, a man whose reputation was set to soar, would wish to replace Vala just as victory was gained. Numonius would be ruined, his career in the military always tarnished by it. I couldn't expect much better – but then I didn't really care. I wanted to return to Rome and live out my days in her warm embrace, ruined reputation or not, but Vala was different; all he knew was the army, it would destroy him to lose his part in it. I put my hand on his shoulder. 'You weren't to know. Maybe the relationship between you and the governor will now improve, now he has all that he wants.'

Numonius grunted. 'Not likely. I was only invited tonight so he could boast in front of the others.'

I gave a wry smile. 'You're probably right there.' I'd learnt myself how petty the governor could be.

Julius came out of the doors to the villa. 'Cassius, there you are! Numonius as well. Come back and join us. We have plenty more wine, and everyone is in a great mood.'

I whispered to Numonius, 'It might be in your interest to do as Julius suggests. If you join in it might go better for you.'

I was wasting my breath; Numonius Vala's pride was such that he'd rather dine in Hades than try to curry favour by drinking and carousing with the other officers. He told Julius, 'I am sorry, please pass on my apologies to the governor. I have lots of reports to read through and must get back to them.'

Julius gave a half-smile. 'Of course, Vala. I'm sure the governor will completely understand.' He turned to me. 'But surely you can join us, Cassius?'

My pride barely existed any more, so I responded. 'Yes, I'll see you inside. I was just wishing Numonius goodbye.'

Julius smiled broadly. 'Ah good! I'll see you shortly. Don't take too long,' and went back inside. It was no wonder Julius was so happy. With the threat of the Angrivarii removed, he was certain to consolidate his position in the Cherusci. What was more, the prospects of his tribe were now improved – the tax levels I was certain were crushing the Cherusci would now be shared by the Angrivarii and the others tribes, lessening the burden, and what was more, it would no longer be necessary to keep all his warriors in arms. Many of the warriors could now be spared to till the fields and help running the land. My earlier concern for my childhood friend now looked naive and foolish.

I turned to Numonius. 'Are you sure you won't join us?'

He shook his head sadly. 'No, you go ahead. I never did enjoy these dinners.' He turned and walked through the main gates of the villa, looking every bit a broken man.

Chapter Twenty-four

For most in the camp, September was a happy time. News of the new peace accord with the Angrivarii was quick to spread around the campfires of the men, and as the men made their preparations to return to Aliso, there was great relief that the German tribal wars were finally at an end.

For me, however, September was a time of anxiety and worry. Marcus' patrol was ordered to return by the beginning of the month, and each day they were overdue heightened this anxiety. I tried telling myself that they were delayed due to a whole host of innocent reasons and not to immediately assume the worst. After all, September was turning out to be a wet month. Frequent rain showers came in from a northerly wind and turned the forest paths and narrow trails into slippery muddy rivulets, making even short journeys unpleasant and slow going. Marcus and the men of his patrol had marched to the centre of the Angrivarii heartland; a lot of countryside lay between us. And yet my nagging guilt at my involvement in Marcus taking this mission plagued me. I spent the days riding to the north of the camp, vainly hoping to see some sign of the returning men, but each day brought no further news.

I even offered to lead a detachment of men in search of the missing patrol, my fear of the Teutoburg Forest temporarily outweighed by my concern for Marcus and his men, but Governor Varus wouldn't hear of it. 'Don't be a fool, Cassius,' he told me. 'Do you really think I'm going to jeopardise this chance for peace just so you can hunt down your friend? That patrol should never have been sent in the first place. I'm hardly going to make the matter worse by sending another.' Varus shook his head in annoyance. 'I know you are attached to the young boy, but you are worrying over nothing. They probably just got lost in the forest and will be back soon.'

What could I say? Varus was almost certainly right. As far as the governor was concerned, the chance for peace was a far greater prize than the lives of just twenty soldiers. Marcus and his men were almost insignificant in the governor's view of the situation. Nothing, short of hard evidence to the contrary, would sway the governor from his belief that a peace could be brokered, and I had no evidence, just a nagging doubt that all was not well.

It was early one morning, after another short shower of rain, that news finally came to me of the patrol. Numonius Vala sent a legionary to my quarters in the town with a message that I should come to the camp quickly. I didn't hesitate. I threw on my military tunic and was buckling up my armour as I briskly walked into the camp and over to the XVIII's section of the military base. I'd tried questioning the legionary as to what the news was, but all he could tell me was that someone had returned at dawn and I was to come and see him.

Hope surged in me. Could it be Marcus? Had the patrol finally returned? These hopes were dashed when I walked into Numonius' headquarters and I was redirected to the XVIII's hospital where the legate was said to be in attendance. An uneasy feeling came over me as I walked into the hospital block as to what I might find there.

A man was writhing in agony, being held down by two medics, and the surgeon was speaking to Legate Vala. 'I must remove the leg soon, sir. The infection runs deep, and it may already be too late.'

Vala stood, with his arms crossed in front of him, looking down sternly at the injured patient. 'That is why I must speak to him now. If he dies, his knowledge will die with him.'

'Numonius,' I called, 'who is it?' dreading that it might be Marcus lying there, covered in mud, writhing in pain, and by the sound of it, about to undergo a very hazardous amputation of his leg.

Vala turned and told me in an urgent tone, 'Cassius. I'm glad you could come so quickly. This man is Vettius, a legionary who went out on the missing patrol. Some of my men found him wandering in a daze a short distance from the camp. He's in a bad way. He has been repeatedly asking for you by name.'

I looked at the legionary, who was being bound to the wooden table with leather straps. It was immediately apparent why the surgeon was eager to remove the man's leg. He had a jagged cut to his calf muscle, which had festered and gone bad, inducing a high fever. The wound stank of rotting flesh and oozed black pus and congealed blood. The surgeon had already laid out his surgical instruments, a variety of probes and spatulas, but it was clear that for this wound, the bone saw, which was currently being boiled in hot water by an assistant, and the cautery iron heating in a brazier were to be needed. I couldn't imagine how much pain the man was in, but judging by his appearance – face and arms covered in scratches and a thick cake of mud over his torn and bedraggled tunic – the man had travelled some distance in this state. I'd never seen the legionary before, so if he was asking for me by name, he must have a message from Marcus.

Vala and I went to the patient, and I crouched down by the man's head, which was pouring with sweat, and told him. 'My name is Cassius Aprilis, tell me what happened.'

'Cassius Aprilis, I've found you,' the man spat, before another spasm of pain wracked him and he screamed.

I tried again. 'Tell me what happened.' But the man was now writhing back and forth, pulling against the leather straps that constrained him, moaning in pain. I looked at Vala and shook my head at the likelihood of getting anything much of value out of him.

Vala turned to the surgeon. 'Can't you do something for the pain?'

The surgeon, a thin man in his forties, grey hair and long face with a hooked nose, looked doubtful. 'I have some poppy extract, but I wasn't going to administer it as he'll need to be able to fight to survive this.' He indicated towards the bone saw.

Vala shook his head. 'We'll have to take the risk. We must get sense from him.'

The surgeon shrugged and picked up a small vial, and he gently poured its contents into the man's mouth, which he held open with a firm hand. The potion worked quickly, the man noticeably calming.

'Cassius Aprilis, I must speak with you,' the injured legionary said drowsily. The poppy extract, if given in too high a quantity, can make men speak gibberish, but Legionary Vettius spoke in a soft, clear, and firm voice, his face still bathed in sweat.

I spoke into the man's ear. 'I am here, soldier. Were you sent by Marcus?'

He nodded his head. 'Yes, Marcus Scaeva told me to find you. He took command after Aeschylus died.' He gasped in pain: clearly the poppy extract didn't completely mask the man's agony.

'Aeschylus was the centurion I sent to lead the patrol,' Vala explained. 'He is a sad loss.'

'Yes, Aeschylus took a spear in the belly. Took hours to die,' added Vettius. 'I'm unlikely to fare much better. Took a spear in my calf as I ran away. I had to swim a river to escape.'

It wasn't that I wasn't interested in how he was injured or how the centurion died, but I was more interested to learn about my friend. 'Marcus still lives?' I simply asked.

The man shook his head. 'No, he's dead, they all are. They were surrounded by the tribesmen. Only I got out.'

The man started to weep, as my stomach lurched. So Marcus was dead. A cold resolve took me, and I gripped the man's hand. 'Tell me what happened.'

Vettius closed his eyes as he recounted his tale, which was interspersed with gasps of agony, as the man was wracked with spasms of pain. 'As soon as we entered the Teutoburg Forest, we could tell something was wrong. There were too many warriors, in their thousands, coming in from the surrounding areas, in great gatherings.'

'We heard the Angrivarii king died. Maybe they all mustered to elect the new king?' asked Vala.

Vettius shook his head. 'No, you don't understand. They can't all have been Angrivarii – there were too many of them, not even the full tribe could hold so many warriors. We couldn't get close to their war camp, so full was the forest with armed men. We scouted around the entire forest to try to gain estimates of their numbers, forever staying in the shadows, hiding and staying secret, as all our lives depended on it. More than eighty thousand men were gathered in that forest. At least that many, probably more.'

Vala cursed. 'Damn Varus, I told him they were up to something.'

I raised my hand for silence and asked Vettius, 'How were you discovered?'

Vettius shook his head. 'A small column of Romans came into the forest.' He gave a bitter laugh. 'Trumpets blaring, musicians playing. You'd think they were performing a victory parade through the gates of Rome herself.'

Vala declared, 'That will have been the peace delegation led by Paullinus.' And to Vettius he explained, 'They were sent by Governor Varus to negotiate a peace.'

Vettius sighed. 'Well, whoever they were, they're all dead. A war party of a thousand tribesmen descended on them and hacked them to pieces.'

I seethed in cold fury. 'They killed them all?'

Vettius shook his head. 'No. Only most of them. Two officers they took as prisoners. We tracked them, and Aeschylus came up with a plan to rescue them. We should have just let them die. They ended up that way in any case.'

Vala frowned at the man's attitude, but the man had reason. I asked, 'What was the plan?'

Vettius coughed, the movement causing him obvious pain in his ruined leg. 'Marcus and Aeschylus sneaked into the enemy camp at night, after a great feast when the tribesmen were all drunk, and freed the two officers. But they were sorely wounded, and couldn't travel quickly. We should have left them.'

'Was it Paullinus you freed?' asked Vala urgently.

Vettius snorted in anger. 'I never was to find out their names. As soon as we made it out of the camp, we tried to head back here, travelling as quickly as we could, through that damn forest.' Vettius stopped to take a breath and compose his thoughts. 'The two injured men slowed us. We had to carry them most of the way, and now the tribesmen had our trail, so they pursued us relentlessly, blowing their hunting horns, so we could hear them coming. I'm sure they only did that to increase our fear. It worked. We all ran in terror.'

I lowered my head as I imagined their terrifying flight through the forest – being hunted like wild animals. 'How did it end?'

Vettius stared up at an invisible point above him. 'Around three hundred tribesmen cornered us in a ravine. That's where Aeschylus took a spear in the belly. Marcus took command and managed to lead us all out and onto a small knoll which we could defend.' The legionary paused. 'Aeschylus died there.'

I asked hopefully, 'Could they still be there, holding out on that hill?'

Vettius shook his head. 'There were just too many tribesmen, and more were joining them all the time. Marcus knew it was hopeless, so he arranged a diversionary attack, so I could escape.'

I asked the obvious question. 'Why you?'

'Because I'm the fastest runner in the legion,' he looked down at his leg, 'or at least I was.' He started crying. 'When I got out, I saw the tribesmen descend on our tiny band of men. They were butchering them, sparing none of them, chopping them to pieces in a frenzied attack of hate. None could have survived that.'

I shuddered.

Vettius continued his account. 'Marcus told me it was important I find you, to let you know …' he stared me straight in the eye, intently. 'There weren't just Angrivarii tribesmen in the host which attacked and killed those in the Roman delegation. When he sneaked into their camp he saw there was a small number of Cherusci, led by the Germanic champion you came close to crossing swords with.'

I stood up in shock. 'By the gods!'

Legate Vala turned to me. 'Who is that?'

I turned to him. 'The German champion he is talking about is Ewald, son of Segestes.'

Vala echoed my words. 'By all the gods.'

I shook my head in disbelief. 'Both Julius and Rome are being betrayed by that snake and his son. They must have made a deal with the Angrivarii. Segestes commands at least a third of the Cherusci warriors. If they were to join with the Angrivarii they could depose Julius and turn this entire region against Rome. Two of the largest tribes in Germany would be united against us.'

Vala stood and put an arm on my shoulder. 'We must tell the governor at once.'

I stared at Vala. 'Will he believe us?'

Vala looked down at the injured legionary, with his ruined leg and mud-smeared face. 'After this, he has to.'

The surgeon enquired of the legate, 'Can we proceed now?'

He turned to the medic. 'Yes, remove his leg. Tell me if he survives. I'll be with the governor.'

'No, no, no, no, no,' stormed Governor Varus, 'I won't have it. What proof is this, the words of a half-delirious legionary? You said yourself he'd been given poppy extract?'

The governor was finding it hard to accept that all his plans for a peaceful resolution with the Angrivarii were coming to an end. Until this news, the governor was looking forward to being heralded throughout Rome as her greatest hero, now he was going to have to explain why a whole year's campaigning season had been wasted, when the Germanic tribes were as hostile as ever. Numonius Vala continually telling the governor that he had warned him wasn't helping, so I tried a more conciliatory tone. 'Governor, please, if I may, the legionary was clear in what he told us. The peace delegation have all perished. Who is to blame in all of this is immaterial. There will be no peace between us and the Angrivarii now. We must accept that.'

Varus turned on me, eyes full of fury. 'And are you happy with that? That you and Vala were proved right? Is this what you have been waiting for, waiting to see me fail?'

I was in no mood for his self-pity. 'No, Governor Varus. I'm not happy about this. I've lost a dear friend in this patrol. He died so we could receive this news, so I'm not going to allow it to be ignored.'

Varus, standing in his usual immaculate clean toga, leant heavily against a chair with one arm and raised his other hand to his face, pinching the bridge of his nose, with closed eyes, and slowly relented. 'I'm sorry about Marcus, Cassius. He was a good man. We all liked him.'

I wasn't interested in his sympathy either. 'That's as may be, but we must decide how we plan to proceed. The Angrivarii have made a declaration of war. We must respond.'

Varus nodded. 'Those foolish tribesmen. Don't they see the folly of a war with us? They cannot win by force of arms. Our legions will destroy them just as they destroy everything we confront.'

'That's why they weren't planning to contest the supremacy on the battlefield with our legions.' I'd pieced together what the Angrivarii were planning, and it all made sense now.

This got the interest of Legate Vala, whom I hadn't yet told of my thoughts. 'How do you mean, Cassius? What do the Angrivarii have to gain if they don't take the field against us?'

I sat on one of Governor Varus' reclining couches, and I now had the attention of both the governor and Numonius Vala. 'Everything. It is late September. We will be returning to Aliso in the next two weeks. This town will then be left under the control of Julius' cavalry and the warriors still loyal to him. Once we go, the Angrivarii can destroy it, and, with the help of the Cherusci loyal to Segestes, depose Julius as King of the Cherusci. By the time we are ready to return next spring, Segestes will have had time to consolidate his control of the Cherusci, and, with his Angrivarii allies, be able to secure all the lands down as far as Western-Gate Pass – and we know how difficult that barrier is to take.' I successfully defended that pass against a whole war host of the Chatti with only one cohort; its strategic importance couldn't be underestimated. 'It will set back the Roman occupation of Germany years. We will be back along the same frontiers Tiberius established. The last five years of wars will have all been for nought.'

'Curse them!' shouted Varus, thumping his fist on his desk. 'Those treacherous dogs will pay for this.' His anger was now directed at himself. 'This entire town will go, all our hard work, all we've achieved.'

A calamity on this scale would surely mean Varus being recalled to Rome and another man taking his place, but now wasn't the time to remind him of that. I needed Varus to be able to think clearly and not be overtaken by fear for his own position. 'It is not too late, Varus. We have come across their plan early, before it has come to fruition. All is not yet lost.'

Varus nodded in agreement. 'I'll see every Angrivarii and Cherusci traitor bathed in blood before I'll let them take this town. Let's see what Julius says to this revelation. He was about to be betrayed by his own tribe – you may well have saved your friend's life.'

That was at least one friend I'd saved; I'd lost the other. 'Then Julius is here? In the camp?' I'd been preoccupied with my worry over Marcus and hadn't kept a close watch on Julius' movements.

Varus nodded his head. 'Yes, I wanted him close to help advise me when the peace delegation returned. No chance of that happening now.' Varus went to the door and asked a guard to go and fetch Julius Arminius. 'Bring him to me at once. Tell him it is of the utmost importance,' he ordered briskly.

We waited impatiently, Numonius Vala, pacing back and forth, whilst Governor Varus sat behind his desk with his head in his hands, distraught that all his plans had unravelled so spectacularly. I just reclined on the couch, my mind numb with shock over the death of Marcus, a hollow emptiness filling my stomach.

I sat up when Julius entered, still in his military mail shirt, and a crease of worry lining his forehead. 'Governor, the messenger said it was urgent. What's happened?'

Varus stood and told him in a very ominous voice, 'It looks as if we have been betrayed. Betrayed by your tribe, Julius.'

Julius went as white as a sheet and stiffened, only muttering, 'Surely, there has been some mistake ...'

Varus blasted. 'There is no mistake. That great oaf Segestes has turned on me! And you as well, Julius. He was after your crown and wasn't afraid of betraying Rome to get it!'

Julius shook his head and seemed to recover himself. 'Segestes? What has he done?'

I explained. 'His son, Ewald, was seen with the Angrivarii. He must have made some deal with them. They have killed the peace delegation we sent to them, and we think they want to usurp you as King of the Cherusci.'

Julius turned to me, confusion showing in his eyes. 'But how do you know this?'

'A survivor from the patrol we sent made it back to us and told us everything. The others were all killed.' My heart sunk as I said this, but I couldn't bring myself to tell him about Marcus yet. 'Ewald is definitely a traitor, and that would imply his father is too.'

Julius looked up to the ceiling, clasping his hands behind his head. 'Segestes, a traitor? I knew I could never truly trust him, but I never suspected this. A deal with the Angrivarii, our ancient enemies, why?'

Numonius Vala took up what we had pieced together. 'Because with their help he could oust you, then unify the Cherusci and Angrivarii against us.'

Julius turned to Vala. 'You expect an attack?'

Numonius chuckled. 'Not even Segestes could be so stupid as to attack three fully armed and up-to-strength legions. No, we suspect he was waiting until we left for Aliso, then he could remove you in secrecy and firm-up his alliance with his new friends before we returned in spring.'

Julius shook his head in disbelief. 'The crafty old goat, who would have ever credited it?' He then looked to the governor. 'But if he is mustering his forces against me, I must respond.'

Varus sat down behind his desk calmly, back in control again, as he addressed Julius. 'Oh, we will definitely respond. Do you think Rome can overlook this outrage? Do you know the location of Segestes now?'

Julius nodded. 'Of course, he is in my own camp, the one Cassius visited only recently. I dined with him only last night.'

The governor smiled. 'And how many warriors does he have loyal to him there?'

Julius stopped to think. 'I have nearly five thousand in the camp, but they are my most loyal men. He only has his closest bodyguard, and a few other retainers – a few hundred at most. Most of his warriors are either in the field or at their own camps.'

'Or with the Angrivarii,' I interrupted.

Julius was now animated. 'But I will need proof. If he has tried to make a deal with the Angrivarii, it will not sit well with my uncle Inguiomerus. We need to discredit him so he cannot marshal his forces against us. You mentioned a survivor? Can I question him, and maybe take him to my camp?'

Numonius Vala shook his head. 'He is undergoing an amputation. If I am any judge, it won't save him, he is too far gone. Either way, he won't be able to travel with you.'

Julius looked at the floor, deep in thought. 'That is a shame. The other chieftains may not believe these claims.'

Governor Varus raised his hand. 'Oh, I think they will,' he then gave a sly smile, 'especially if you have a thousand armed legionaries behind you. Let's all go to your camp and confront Segestes together.'

Chapter Twenty-five

The Roman legionaries marched with grim purpose, heavy mail shirts clinking in time to the measured step of the march; each man's face etched with determination. Word had spread through the ranks about the deaths of their comrades, and these men were now angry, wanting to find those responsible. We marched with two full cohorts, both from Vala's XVIII legion, and our force was supplemented by a cohort of Julius' auxiliary cavalry, riding with the same expression of grim resolve on their faces – they knew if it came to a fight, they would be facing their own countrymen, something none of them would relish, but something their expression told they wouldn't shirk from. At the head of the column was Governor Varus, changed out of his customary toga and now fully armoured, eyes burning with fury, riding alongside Numonius Vala, Julius, and I. Varus' focus was on the forest trail, but he asked. 'Do you think he will still be there when we arrive?'

Julius shrugged. 'He has no reason to suspect we are on to him. I don't see why he wouldn't be.'

Varus snorted. 'May the gods will that you're right. If he escapes into the forest, we may never find him.'

Julius raised his hand. 'Hold on, I have an idea.' He beckoned over one of his troopers, a man I recognised from my time in their camp, and spoke to him rapidly in their own tongue. The man then rode ahead of the column and Julius explained. 'I have given him orders to go to the camp ahead of us, but not to announce our coming. Faramund is an excellent tracker. I've told him that if Segestes leaves, to track him secretly, just in case Segestes gets wind of us coming.'

Varus nodded. 'A wise precaution. I don't want that traitor getting away.'

The rest of the march was in silence, each man keeping his thoughts to himself. The prospect of this march ending in bloodshed concentrated everyone's minds.

My thoughts were of Marcus. Did he die hating me? He'd sent the messenger Vettius to me, knowing that I would realise the significance of what he'd seen, but did that mean he'd put aside his animosity to me? I'd never know now, but somehow it was still important to me – did he hate me to the end?

When we came upon the camp, Governor Varus halted the column. 'Is there another entrance to the camp?'

Julius responded, 'Yes, of course, we have another set of gates to the north.'

Varus commanded, 'Send your cavalry round to seal that entrance, I want no one getting out. You stay with me. I don't want your warriors getting the wrong idea and attacking us in ignorance.'

Julius nodded, and relayed the orders to the auxiliaries, who rode off at a fast canter to the far side of the camp. Varus then nodded to Numonius Vala who signalled the legionaries forward through the open gates of the Cherusci and past the dumbstruck sentries, who were at a loss as to what to do until Julius signalled to them that there was no reason to be alarmed.

As we marched through the camp, Germanic warriors watched us in confusion, whilst woman hurried their children inside, not knowing what this armed presence could mean. Julius' presence amongst us prevented the warriors from taking up arms, but they were still obviously wary of this many Roman soldiers entering their camp. When we reached the centre of the camp, we joined up with Julius' cavalry, who had sealed the far gates as ordered.

'Segestes!' Varus bellowed, still sitting on his horse outside the main Cherusci long house. 'Somebody bring me Segestes!'

We didn't have to wait long. The large tribesman came out of the long house, beard and hair unbound, his great barrel chest puffed out as usual, in mail and furs. 'Governor Varus, what brings you here?' he asked cagily, obviously realising that this was no ordinary social visit.

Varus got straight to the point. 'Your son has turned traitor, Segestes. We're here to ascertain whether you knew of this and are also a traitor.'

Segestes eyes popped at that. 'What? Traitor! Never!'

I spoke up. 'Your son was seen leading men who helped butcher the peace delegation we sent to the Angrivarii.'

Segestes shook his head. 'Butchering a peace delegation? Who saw him? He lies.'

'The man in question died after delivering the news, but he confirmed your son was amongst the Angrivarii who attacked them. Did you know of this?' I demanded. We'd been informed of Vettius' demise by the camp surgeon, just prior to leaving the camp. It wasn't a surprise judging by the condition we'd found him in, but it was an added spur of anger against this traitorous chieftain.

Segestes spat on the floor. 'You condemn me on the word of a dead man? Pah!' He looked up at the governor, 'I know nothing of this.'

Others were now emerging from the German long house: Julius' uncle Inguiomerus, Segestes son-in-law Sesithacus, and also his wife Thusnelda – who hissed on seeing so many Roman soldiers in the Cherusci camp.

'What brings these soldiers here?' demanded Inguiomerus, his stare frosty and malevolent.

Julius explained. 'They come with my authority, Uncle.' Julius dismounted his horse, and several of his troopers did likewise. 'Ewald has been seen with the Angrivarii. There have been many deaths. We must get to the bottom of this.'

Segestes' daughter was the next to speak, her voice full of scorn and venom. 'What insult is this? A Roman force in our own camp? Next you will agree to let them search our own homes! What do you think, Father, will you let them search yours?'

Segestes shouted at his daughter. 'Silence, woman. If this situation isn't bad enough, I don't need your bile.' He spoke to Sesithacus. 'Take your woman away and out of my sight.'

Sesithacus tried to comply, taking his wife by the arm, but she pulled it away. 'Don't touch me, worm. You've no right to touch me!'

'Enough!' shouted Julius. 'Be gone from here, your presence isn't wanted.'

Thusnelda spat on the ground, then spun on her heels, re-entering the long house after giving her husband one more hateful glance.

Julius breathed out heavily. 'Thank the gods she has gone. But let us do as she says,'

Varus turned to Julius, 'What do you mean?'

Julius shrugged. 'Let's search Segestes house. If he is innocent, he won't have anything to hide.'

Segestes didn't like the sound of this. 'Search my long house, like a common criminal? You push me too far, my king. You can't expect me to accept this humiliation.'

Inguiomerus intervened. 'What harm can it do? You said yourself you know nothing of this.'

Segestes looked startled that Inguiomerus was siding with Julius. 'Does my word count for nothing?'

Varus barked a laugh. 'About as much as your son's. Enough of this. Vala, order some men to search his long house. You!' he pointed at one of Julius' auxiliaries, 'Show my men where Segestes house is.'

A centurion and ten legionaries went to search Segestes residence whilst we waited. It wasn't long before they returned, and they carried something with them. 'We found this, my lord,' proclaimed the centurion handing Varus a rolled-up scroll.

Varus took it and unfurled it. He explained what it was. 'This is the peace proclamation I put into the hands of our envoy Paullinus myself. You can see it has been signed by my own hands.' He turned it around so everyone could see the damning evidence. 'There can be no doubt – you are a traitor, Segestes.'

It didn't take long for the giant Segestes to react. He turned to run, pushing a legionary out of his way as easily as a child throwing away a discarded toy doll, and then shoulder charged another, clearing his path so he could sprint down the main concourse towards the northern gates.

'Stop him!' bellowed Varus, face red with anger.

Julius signalled to two of his mounted auxiliaries, who quickly ran Segestes down, one of them striking the rebel chieftain's back with the blunt butt of his heavy spear, which sent the man sprawling to the ground. The two burly cavalry troopers then dismounted and dragged the still struggling Segestes back to Varus, bellowing in rage against his captors. 'Unhand me you dogs! Romanised filth, you're no Cherusci!'

The impassive troopers flung Segestes to the ground before the mounted Varus, who looked down at the large chieftain, face and unbound hair now covered in the dirt from the muddied street. 'So, Segestes, what do you have to say for yourself?' The governor asked him.

Segestes was breathing heavily, anger at his humiliating position clear in his voice. 'I'm no traitor, these charges are all lies.' He shot a glance of pure hatred at his king, my friend Julius. 'There is your traitor, Governor. Arminius has been preaching against your occupation, it is he who plans to betray you.'

This startled Varus, who turned his head to Julius and raised a questioning eyebrow.

Julius simply shrugged. 'Well, what do you expect him to say?'

Varus gave a crooked smile and nodded his head, before turning to the other German chieftain present, Julius' uncle Inguiomerus. 'Can you shed any light on either of these claims?'

Inguiomerus looked down at the dishevelled Segestes, then up to

Governor Varus, a stoic mask surrounding his flint-hard eyes. 'It is clear that Segestes has turned traitor and betrayed us to the Angrivarii. We apologise for this. He and all the other traitors will be dealt with.'

Varus bellowed a laugh. 'We will deal with Segestes ourselves. He can expect a long and painful death once I've returned him to my camp.'

Segestes sprung upwards and lunged at the governor, hands reaching to claw his face, before the two auxiliaries grabbed his arms and pinned him to the ground, and before a third came over and struck his head with a spear butt to his temple, knocking him senseless.

Inguiomerus was the first to speak. 'It should be us who deal with this traitor, not Roman law. A deal with our ancient enemies, the Angrivarii, is a betrayal of all our Cherusci values.'

Julius turned to the governor. 'He is right, my lord. We need to be the ones who clear up this treasonous nest. If you take Segestes and kill him, you will bring sympathy to his cause.'

Varus spat in anger. 'Pah! I need this man's head for what he has done.'

'And you'll have it,' promised Julius, 'but let us do it our way. He will be tried by all the tribal chieftains, all his followers rounded up, and you'll have their heads by the morning.' Julius looked over at his uncle, 'isn't that right?'

Inguiomerus nodded his head in agreement. 'It shall be done, but by our own hands.'

The governor looked torn between his desire for personal vengeance, and the diplomatic solution posed by Julius and Inguiomerus. 'This dog needs to learn the cost of crossing Rome!' Varus said between gritted teeth – he seemed to be taking Segestes' betrayal as a personal insult. 'I'll not let him escape justice.'

I realised Varus was being blinded by his anger. 'He won't escape justice, governor. What do we care how he dies? If Julius can do it for us, all the better.' I tried to reassure him, 'We needn't return to our camp – we can stay nearby and wait for it to be done.' I didn't relish the prospect of spending a night in the open, but I knew it was the only way the stubborn governor would be placated – Varus was set on returning with Segestes' head, or not at all.

Numonius Vala came to my aid. 'Cassius is right, my lord. It will look much better to the other tribes if the Cherusci rid their people of their own traitors rather than seeing us do it. It shows we value their sovereignty in internal matters.' Varus turned on Vala. 'Do you think Paullinus would have considered this an internal matter?'

Vala lowered his head. 'No, my lord. But neither do I think his shade would care who wields the knife of vengeance on his behalf.'

Finally, Varus relented. With a great sigh, he turned to Julius and said, 'Me and my men will camp outside your gates this night. I expect his head in the morning, otherwise I'll return with all three of my legions and take it myself.'

Both Julius and Inguiomerus nodded in agreement, their expressions solemn.

Varus turned his horse and we all followed, leaving the Germans to administer their own punishment to the unconscious traitor Segestes, who still lay sprawled on the ground.

We camped immediately outside the gates, which were closed to us after leaving, on a patch of level ground. Centurions kept the men in files, keeping the men alert, but there was no need. None of us would have been able to sleep this night. From behind the closed gates rose the sound of fighting, as Segestes supporters first heard of their chieftain's fate, and then were set upon by warriors loyal to Julius and Inguiomerus. Flames sprung up from behind the dark wicker walls, signifying the burning of rebel warrior's long houses, and these were accompanied by terrified screams, as the men's wives and children were burnt alive alongside their husbands. I felt sick to my stomach hearing the sound, and judging by the stricken faces of my fellow officers, I wasn't alone. Roman justice could be harsh, but we had nothing on the Germans. I prayed to the gods that I'd never find myself at the mercy of these barbaric animals. I shuddered to think that it was Julius who was instigating this purge; that it was my friend who was leading this blood-letting just the other side of the silent walls standing between Rome and her principal ally. The burden of leadership is said to change men, and if this gruesome display told me anything, it told me that Julius had changed from the civilised principled young man I'd known before. I didn't blame him, this purge of the traitors was needed, had been insisted upon by Rome, and I was in no position to judge others about the difficult decisions leadership put on men: I was a failed coward – Julius was made of sterner stuff.

A soft rain started as dawn broke, leaving a damp smell of ash in the air as the gates to the Cherusci camp were finally opened. A lone rider emerged, on a great white stallion, in full armour and winged helmet. It was Julius, and he held something in his hand. He rode slowly up to the waiting Varus, who stood with his hands on his hips, chest puffed out, stern expression on his normally placid face. Numonius Vala and I stood either side of him, and our legionaries stood behind us in strict military lines.

Julius halted his horse and threw his burden at the feet of the governor. It rolled through the mud, before turning and revealing the face of Segestes, former warrior of the Cherusci. 'There's your traitor, my lord. Rome no longer has any enemies in my camp. All his followers have been taken care of.'

Varus looked down at the decapitated head. 'You're sure there are no others?'

Julius tilted his head. 'I have only been able to take care of the ones with me here. Segestes had many warriors loyal to him. They'll be allied with the Angrivarii now, no doubt under the leadership of Ewald.'

Varus looked up at him. 'And when will they be brought to justice?'

Julius gave a crooked grin. 'I cannot take on the Angrivarii alone. After this, war between the two nations is inevitable, but with the help of Segestes' warriors, the Angrivarii now outnumber me – it is a war in which I cannot win.'

This startling admission unsettled Varus, but he ground his teeth and then spat on the ground. 'Outnumbered, you say? Cannot win? I think my three legions will have something to say about that. Tell me, how many warriors can you muster in three days?'

Julius shrugged. 'I can have at least twenty thousand warriors gathered here and ready for war. But it won't be enough to take on the Angrivarii – they will have three times that number. For me to muster my full strength it will take weeks as warriors come in from the far-lying districts.'

Varus shook his head. 'We don't have weeks. Twenty thousand will be plenty. Added to my legions that gives us more than enough strength. We will still be outnumbered, but what we have will be sufficient.'

Numonius Vala furrowed his forehead. 'How so, governor? What do you plan?'

Publius Quinctilius Varus gave a smile. 'You ought to be pleased, Vala. You have been asking me to do this all summer. We march to war with the Angrivarii and their traitorous allies!'

Chapter Twenty-six

It is said that any Roman legion is prepared to march to war within a dozen shakes of a barbarian's spear; that the legions were always alert, ready, and expectant of a good fight, and could be in the field before any barbarian hoard could rustle-up their full strength because of the legions iron discipline and rigidly efficient organisation. Stories abounded in Rome of barbarian armies being caught unawares in the early light of dawn, emerging from their primitive hovels as their warriors were still recovering from celebrating the night before, only to see the lines of men, clad in Roman steel, bearing down on their position, days, if not weeks earlier than expected.

Well, if this was true, it was not with any legion I'd ever served with, and Varus' German legions were no exception. The Roman camp was in a state of complete upheaval as their governor's unexpected orders were put into action and the army prepared to march against the Angrivarii. Everywhere, messengers were running back and forth with new orders, whilst legionaries were busy packing, cleaning and repairing items for the march. Those not busy were soon seized upon by prowling centurions and given something to do, meaning that the men made sure they looked as busy as possible: nobody wanted to be given one of the unsavoury tasks customary for slackers – the clearing of the latrines, or mucking out the cavalry stables.

There was a lot to do; for the last few weeks, the camp officers had been preparing to send everything back to the winter quarters of Aliso, escorted by the full army, ready for a relaxing few months locked up behind their camp walls before the winter snows hit. Now they were having to change these plans and prepare the men to march into the German interior with only their weapons and marching rations for a short campaign, whilst the rest of the army's equipment was sent back to Aliso under an escort of auxiliaries. Very little was being left within the army camp, as only one cohort was staying to secure the empty base; this was only a token force as the real security of the area was being guaranteed by Julius' warriors, who promised to protect the town from any Angrivarii excursions, being in the heart of the Cherusci lands. The Roman camp would only need protecting until word came of the Angrivarii being dealt with, something Varus hoped to complete within a few short weeks, a lightning raid of speed and brute force, showing the upstart Angrivarii the true power of Rome and her legions.

If the Roman camp was in a state of upheaval, it was nothing compared to the civilian town outside the camp. Most civilians were at a loss as to what their next move should be. Few wanted to take everything they owned back to Aliso with only the light protection of an auxiliary escort, after hearing of the impending war with the Angrivarii. This gave them two choices: stay in the camp and wait for the army to return, or follow the army and stay within its protection. At least a third were siding with accompanying the legions; I didn't blame them. The march through the forest would be uncomfortable and unpleasant, but at least they were guaranteed the protection that only twenty thousand armed men of the legions could provide – the knowledge that no force in the world could stand up to three full legions and survive.

Of course, Numeria wasn't one of them.

I gritted my teeth and tried to curb my impatience. 'But, Numeria, at least you'll be safe. I don't trust this situation, or the surrounding tribesmen. Five hundred men won't be able to secure the town. They won't even be able to secure their own camp. You'll be at the mercy of the German tribesmen.'

It was two days after our visit to the German camp, and the army was nearing the completion of its preparation for the march. I'd come to visit her house, to try and persuade her to accompany the army and now we argued in her home's *atrium*.

Numeria turned on me, heat radiating from her eyes. 'I've too much to do here. You said yourself you wanted me to return to Rome. Well, Julia and I have decided to do that, but first we must make arrangements for my belongings to be sent back also.'

I looked around at the functional and well-made, but hardly extravagant, furnishings of her house and asked, 'But what do you have here that can't be easily replaced in Rome at a fraction of the cost of sending it all back?'

Numeria closed her eyes and sighed impatiently. 'I wouldn't expect you to understand, Gaius, you've never made a home anywhere. Some things just can't be replaced.'

I looked around the *atrium* and tried to grasp what she meant. 'What? What here can't be replaced? I see nothing your father couldn't replace within a heartbeat of you returning home.'

Numeria snapped at me. 'This isn't about my father!'

My temper flared. 'Then what is it?'

Numeria turned her back on me. 'Everything Otho and I had together remains in this house. If I leave it all, I leave behind all I had with him.'

Oh by the gods, not Otho again. I shook my head. 'This is madness, Numeria, you must see that? The town's position isn't as safe as we all presumed. The German tribesmen, their mood has changed, their blood is up, and it is going to come to a fight soon.'

Numeria spun on her heels. 'You've no need to tell me the mood of the German tribesmen. I visit them daily. I know their frustrations with Rome, and their anger.'

I wondered when she'd make a reference to her ludicrous visits to the German villages! I put my hands on my hips and stared down at her. 'Look, I know you think you're safe here amongst the Cherusci, but even Julius didn't realise the number of traitors he had in his own tribe. You can no longer trust them. Come with the army, stay under her protection. Bring Julia too. Think of her safety as well.'

Numeria gave a twisted smile, one which held no warmth. 'Bring Julia along? Would you like to ask her yourself? I doubt very much she'll be pleased to see you again after the last night you spent together.'

I had heard enough about that particular night. I picked up a small statue of Aphrodite, and flung it at the wall, smashing it into a thousand shards. 'For the last time, nothing happened that night! I don't care what lies she has told you, I never touched her. Marcus never believed me either and now he is dead. Dead, because I got drunk once and took her back to my room. I am sorry for what I did, more sorry than you could ever know. I lost a friend because of that mistake, and I hate myself for it. Don't lecture me any more on the subject.' I sat down heavily on a small stool and bowed my head in my hands, feeling tears spring up between my closed eyelids. 'I made a mistake. I never meant to hurt anyone.'

There was silence between us; I didn't know what more I could say. I just sat there with my head in my hands, not knowing what she thought of me, and no longer caring. I'd come to her because I didn't want anyone else I cared about to come to harm, but it looked like I'd fallen so far in her eyes she no longer believed a word I said.

Eventually she laid a cool hand on my shoulder and said softly. 'I know nothing happened between you and Julia – she told me a few nights later. I should have let you know that I knew the truth, but I didn't ... I guess because I was still angry … angry that you'd taken her to your room. I'm sorry, Gaius, sorry that Marcus died. I know how much you cared for him.'

I shook my head in sorrow. 'He died hating me.'

Numeria pulled up another stool and sat next to me. She spoke to me in a soft soothing voice. 'Oh, I doubt that, Gaius. I'm sorry you blame yourself for his death, but it is often the case that those who remain living feel guilty for doing so.' She put an arm around my shoulder. 'Julia feels the same way. She hasn't left her room since she heard of Marcus's death. She cries tears of remorse and loss, but also bitterly regrets her role in his parting. But in truth, neither of you were to blame.'

Tears were still running down my face, which I cradled in my hands to obscure my weakness. 'How so? If it wasn't for him seeing us that morning, he'd have never gone on that patrol.'

Numeria shook her head slowly. 'I don't pretend to have known Marcus as well as you or Julia, but from the limited time I spent with him, even I could tell he was eager to prove himself, that he'd never be satisfied until he'd proved himself in battle in some way. It was only a question of time until he found an excuse to leave the camp and volunteer himself for some dangerous mission. You and Julia simply gave him that excuse, nothing more. He would have found a way eventually anyway.' She ran her fingers through the hair at the back of my head soothingly. 'I know it is difficult not to see yourself as the cause of his death, but really, neither you or Julia were to blame. It is all too easy for the guilt of survival to turn to self-recrimination.'

'What do you know of it?' I asked gruffly, embarrassed by my tears and admission.

Numeria turned away from me and stared the opposite wall. 'I met Otho in an empty theatre on the Quirinal Hill only four years ago in Rome, but it feels like a lifetime ago.'

I hadn't a clue what Otho had to do with the death of Marcus, but I let Numeria continue. It sounded like she had something she needed to confide.

Tears appeared on Numeria's face as she continued. 'I was visiting a friend who was taking part in the performance, and I visited her during their rehearsal. On the theatre seat sat Otho, all alone, completely transfixed by the play. I went over to speak to him, to ask him why he didn't wish to see them in the real performance later that night, rather than in a rehearsal, which was frequently interrupted by mistakes, forgotten lines, and other mishaps.' Her face brightened and a smile appeared. 'He turned his thoughtful, sensitive eyes to me, and told me that the performance was all the more real for those mistakes; it was only during the rehearsal, when the actors didn't wear the Greek masks, and they weren't surrounded by the baying patrons, that he could lose himself in the story.'

'Well, it wasn't long until I lost myself to him. Completely and utterly. I loved him, but he was only from the equestrian class, not the senatorial like me. Our marriage shouldn't have been allowed, but I begged and pleaded with my father, night after night, until he eventually relented.'

I imagined the stir their wedding would have caused amongst the gossips of Rome. Even my sister, a great friend of Numeria, had felt only pity for her marrying below her class.

Numeria bowed her head. 'I was so happy on our wedding day, and even our time together in Rome. But it was less easy for Otho. He hated the fact that everyone talked about us, and that they viewed me little better than a fallen woman now. He felt that he had ruined me, and that only by improving his standing in Rome could he improve mine. He wasn't of sufficient standing to make any inroads in politics, was never one for trade or business, so he came across the idea of joining the legions. His equestrian class was still high enough to qualify him as a tribune, and with my father's help, he could gain a posting high up the chain of command. He told me that only in the legions could his standing improve sufficiently to quieten the city's wagging tongues and become a worthy husband to me.'

I nodded my head in agreement. Otho wouldn't be the first man to rise through the social classes through his prowess in the field.

Numeria's eyes took on that faraway look again. 'I forbade him at first, telling him he was unsuited to life as a soldier – he was a slight man, Gaius, he didn't look as if he was carved out of marble like yourself – but he was thoughtful and intelligent. He told me that what he lacked in physical prowess, he could more that make up for by using his wits and his sharp mind. Eventually, I agreed, on condition that I could join him in his posting, as I couldn't bear the thought of being separated from him for three to four years. As we left Rome together, it seemed such an adventure, we were finally free of the constraints of Rome's social structure, and we would carve out a life for ourselves in the provinces of the empire. The journey to Germany was hard, but nothing that either of us couldn't bear. We had each other, and that was all that seemed to matter.

'It was when we reached Germany that things changed for the worse.'

Numeria squeezed her eyes shut, through pain at the memories, but steeled herself and continued. 'We were initially made welcome by Governor Varus and the other officers, and were delighted to settle into the new town Varus was constructing here, but once Otho started his military duties the problems started. Otho tried his best to be a good soldier but he was terrified by the dark forests and the wild tribesmen, constantly worrying that he would come under attack or ambush from the woods. I told him he was worrying too much, but each night he returned to me, he would shake and tremble from fear. I was still proud of him. I knew he was afraid, but each day he'd buckle on his armour, return to the camp and try and do his best. He came up with good ideas – plans to improve the camp's irrigation and sewerage – but all these successes were overshadowed by his apparent failing in the field. He was clumsy at best in the training field, and when he led the men out on patrol, he told me they began to sense his fear. Before long, he lost the respect of the men altogether. It started off with petty things: questioning his orders, laughing behind his back just out of hearing, but soon each day became a nightmare for my Otho.'

I nodded in understanding. The legionaries could be cruel to weak officers. It may seem harsh, but the men knew that any failings of their superior officers could lead to them losing their lives: pity had no place in the legions.

Tracks of tears ran down Numeria's face. 'Soon the other officers started to make jokes about Otho. He lost the respect of the entire high command. None of his suggestions were taken seriously, no matter how well thought out. They thought him a coward, and therefore his opinion no longer mattered.' Numeria's face hardened. 'It was so unfair! Yes, Otho was scared. But each day he faced up to those fears and led men outside the camp into the forests. Surely that proved him braver than someone who merely lacked the wit to understand the danger they were placing themselves in? I grew angry, not at Otho, but at the other officers who were making my husband's life a misery. I complained to Varus personally, without Otho's knowledge. That turned out to be a mistake. Varus merely shrugged and told me that he couldn't dictate how the other men felt about my husband. Otho was furious the night he found out about my intervention. That night was the only time Otho ever raised his voice at me, shouting at me that now everything would be worse. Once the men found out about his wife having to stick up for him, they'd never let him forget it …'

I didn't say anything. What could I say? Of course she'd done the wrong thing. It would obviously make Otho a laughing stock, but she knew that now. I just held her hand so she could continue.

'Soon after that, they left the camp for the summer's campaign against the Angrivarii. Otho barely spoke to me before he left, no matter how many times I tried to apologise. It was on that campaign that Otho's nerve finally failed him. I can never be sure, but did he only volunteer to lead those men along that river because of what I'd done? Was it the only way he felt he could rid himself of the dishonour I'd served him? After Varus ordered Otho to take his own life, I hated him, and all the other officers who looked down on my Otho, but I also hated myself. Was I the cause of my own husband's death? Did he die because he was trying to prove something to me?'

Numeria broke down in great wracking sobs of tears. I was still unsure what I could say, so I simply held her in my arms, letting her cry on my shoulder. I longed to tell Numeria that Otho wasn't alone, he wasn't the only man to feel that all-encompassing terror that leads you to run from battle or to desert comrades in need, that I also shared the same weakness, but I couldn't. For so many years I had held that secret to myself, that now I just couldn't admit to it, not even to Numeria, the one person in the world who wouldn't judge me lacking because of it. I let her cry, and then gave a small kiss on the top of her head. 'Thank you for telling me about Otho. I wish I could have met him.'

Numeria nodded her head whilst wiping her eyes. 'He was a good man.'

I stood up from my stool. 'Yes, I think you're right. In any other life, the two of you could have been happy, it was just a tragedy that you both ended up here.'

She bowed her head. 'I can't think on what could have been. It's too painful, Gaius.'

I lowered my eyes. 'Yes, I can see that. But please, Numeria, don't dismiss your own safety because of what happed to Otho. You're life is too precious to me and it should be to you too. Come with the army, you'll be safe with us.'

Numeria shook her head. 'No, I won't accompany Varus and those other fools. But you're right, Gaius, there is nothing for me here now. I will pack only the bare essentials for me and Julia and leave on the last military escort back to Aliso. We'll be safe there.'

It wasn't what I wanted but I guessed it was the best I was going to get. She should be safe enough in Aliso; that was far enough away from both Angrivarii and Cherusci land, and at least she'd have a military escort of auxiliaries to take her there. I nodded my head. 'All right, but I'll leave my two horses for you. One is mine and the other belonged to Marcus. You can pick them up from the inn I'm staying at. I want you to have a fast horse under you, at the very least.'

Numeria smiled but protested, 'I have my own horses.'

I laughed. 'Yes, I remember your show pony! Fast enough, but she'd never have the stamina of my two Libyans. Take them. If nothing else, it might put my mind at rest knowing that you're on two of the fastest horses in the region. I can pick up another mount from the military camp.'

Numeria gave a small laugh. 'All right, if you insist. But I want you to take care of yourself as well, Gaius. Don't get yourself killed trying to do something brave on this expedition of Varus'.'

I leant my hand on her shoulder. 'No chance of that, Numeria.' I kissed her again on the forehead and left her sitting there, still thinking of the dead husband she had lost to this harsh land.

I left her house and returned to the military camp relieved that I no longer needed to worry too much about Numeria. She would soon be back in the safety of Aliso and would then be able to return to Rome. Now I just needed to look after myself.

Chapter Twenty-seven

We marched out of the camp the next morning at dawn. Varus, never one to miss an opportunity for ostentatious drama, ordered the trumpeters to herald the commencement of the march with a great blast of their silver trumpets. I had to hand it to Varus – his army was a magnificent sight. I rode a large Gallic gelding alongside Governor Varus and the rest of his high command as we ascended the high hills to the north of the camp, the twenty thousand men in a long column stretching over five miles. Legates Vala, Avitus and Selus all looked resplendent in their full armour, as did the camp praefect, Ceionius, and the other lead tribunes. Ahead of us were the vanguard of the army; lightly armed auxiliaries from Spain, skilled with the bow, to act as the army's scouts. They were backed up by some heavy cavalry from Thrace – shock troops to intercept any threat to the engineers who marched behind them, whose job it was to clear the path for the rest of the army by cutting back the encroaching underbrush from the unpaved country trails along which we were marching.

Our command group was shielded by elite infantry units – the army's best – all marching in perfect order, stiff strong jaws, iron-hard eyes, framed by equally tough faces encased in steel helmets. I looked behind as we rose through the hills, and shielded my eyes from the early morning sun which bathed the hillside in a dazzling white light. Immediately behind us were the artillery, being dragged by strings of mules, before the army's pride – the eagles of the three legions, held high by the standard bearers alongside their trumpeters. They were closely followed by the legionaries, marching six abreast, with sharp-eyed centurions marching alongside, keeping the lines straight and in good order.

After the bulk of the army was the soldiers' baggage train, on mules being led by slaves, before the army's rearguard – assorted cavalry and infantry units – to protect the army's rear. Finally walked the civilians, those too afraid to stay in the town and also too wary to make the journey back to Aliso without the army's protection. They walked in an unruly mob, intermingled with livestock and beasts of burden. Even so, they couldn't detract from the remarkable sight of three full legions marching in line – a glorious sight, which even made my cynical heart swell with pride for the finest fighting men in the world.

Was I afraid? Well, it was difficult not to be concerned about what the next few days would bring, but when I saw our huge army, so disciplined and resolute, it was hard to feel any genuine fear – this force could shatter anything in its path. With any luck, this campaign would be nothing more than a week or two marching through the woodlands, burning a few undefended villages and the rounding up of a few troublemakers – surely not even the Angrivarii could be foolish enough to try and resist this remarkable show of power by Rome's governor. Maybe Varus was right, a short incisive display of force was all that was needed to beat the German tribes back into line. Never underestimate the sense of fear the prospect of facing Rome's legions in the field puts into an enemy's mind: could you really stand up to us and survive? Most came to the conclusion that they couldn't and gave up the fight before it began.

Varus noticed I was lagging behind, to take in the sight of the full army, and called over to me. 'Come on, Cassius, keep up! We don't have time to admire the view! We have a war to plan!'

The governor's spirits were remarkably high, in contrast to the dark brooding which had come over him after hearing of Segestes' treachery. Now the governor had been given the chance to strike back at those who had scuppered his carefully laid plans, and it showed by his positive outlook and return to good humour. He was dressed in full armour, in an extremely well-made breastplate which successfully hid his full belly, and gave Varus the appearance of a fit and energetic General of Rome, leading his army from the front. He was addressing his other commanders as I caught up and heeled my horse just behind him.

Varus spoke with bright eyes, full of confidence. 'Our first step is to liaise with Julius and his Cherusci. His local knowledge will be almost as much help as his army. Once we are combined, the Angrivarii will soon fall to our combined strength.'

Lucius Eggius, an excitable young senior tribune from Avitus' XVII, piped up, 'Do we need the Cherusci? Surely we can engage the Angrivarii without their aid?'

Varus smiled. 'I admire your spirit, young Lucius, but beware of overconfidence. It is Angrivarii territory we will be marching into – they will know the land much better than us. That is why Julius' help in this regard will be so useful. Besides, any victory against the Angrivarii must be seen as a victory for

Rome and the Cherusci. That is how we will cement Julius' position as king of his nation.'

Lucius Eggius turned slightly red. 'Of course, my lord, I apologise for my overeagerness.'

Varus slapped Eggius on the back. 'Nothing to apologise for. Eagerness for battle is a virtue, my boy. Just let the old wise heads like me point you in the right direction first!' Varus laughed. 'You'll be seeing action soon enough, don't you worry.'

The young man's enthusiasm for the campaign reminded me of Marcus, and it brought me back to the reason for this expedition. The Angrivarii and the treasonous Ewald had murdered my friend. I ground my teeth in anger. They deserved whatever they got for that. I'd shed no tears for what was coming to them.

It was past midday when we finally had word of Julius. The scouts reported he was leading his cavalry to our position, so Varus halted the army, and soon enough Julius led his two thousand riders – the fully Romanised fighting force – to join us. Julius rode his large white stallion with his customary straight back, his winged helmet extenuating his size and looking for all the world like a German god of war. 'Governor Varus, it is good to see you at the head of your troops. War befits you!' Julius crowed, as he brought his horse alongside Varus.

Varus laughed. 'Yes, maybe it has been too long since I took to the field. It feels good to be back in the saddle again.' Varus then looked quizzically at Julius' cavalry. 'It is good to have your men with us, but where is your full war host? I was expecting you to join us with twenty thousand warriors?'

Julius smiled. 'Don't worry, my warriors are assembled. My uncle has them gathered by the border to the Angrivarii lands. It didn't seem prudent to march them all the way to you, only to march back again. My cavalry were different. They wanted to fight by the side of your men. It is where we belong.'

Varus let out a sigh of relief that Julius had delivered his promise to assemble so many of his warriors in so short a time, relieved that their strategy was proceeding to plan. 'It is good to have you with us. Tell your men to ride in the vanguard. You can replace the Thracians and Spanish auxiliaries as you know the land better. I want you to keep an eye out for the Angrivarii. I want no surprises.'

Julius gave a grin. 'It will be an honour, my lord. Don't worry, we'll make sure nothing gets past us.'

Varus sat up straight in his saddle. 'Proceed then.' He then looked round at his command group and gave the signal for the war host to move forward again.

Julius gave me a quick smile before he led his men off. 'It looks like we'll finally be fighting side by side again, my old friend.'

I reached out and clasped his shoulder. 'There is no one else I'd prefer to have at my side.'

He smiled. 'Likewise, Gaius. I'll see you later, once we have made camp. Duty calls.'

I nodded my head in understanding, letting Julius ride off and take his position in the vanguard. I turned to Legate Vala. 'How long before we reach the Angrivarii lands.'

Vala rubbed his chin. 'We're making good time, but at least another two days' full marching. We'll see if we can pick up the pace now with Julius leading us.'

By late afternoon, the army stopped to make camp for the night. When we reached the area designated, the engineers had already done much of the preparation work, marking out flags where the earth and timber walls were to be constructed, and clearing the area of obstacles. The legionaries went to their assigned positions – the same positions that they held in the permanent camp – first erecting their leather tents from the baggage train, then setting about digging the perimeter ditch and constructing the earthen walls under the supervision of the engineers.

Julius and his cavalry, arriving first at the camp, had already dressed down their horses, and set up their horse lines. He spotted me overseeing the work and walked over to me. 'It's always an impressive sight, isn't it?'

It certainly was. Whilst some men dug the ditch, others banked up the earth into a rampart, where timber spikes, cut down from the surrounding forests, were then mounted. 'It's a sight I never tire of seeing.'

Julius grunted. 'We could have made several more miles today, if we'd forgone this of course.'

I looked at him in surprise. 'What? And leave the men unprotected? Our history is full of foolish Generals who made that mistake.'

Julius grinned. 'I know, but we're not in Angrivarii territory yet. We're still in my Cherusci lands. The army isn't in danger now.'

I let out a snort of disbelief. 'Whether it is Cherusci or Angrivarii land, I know I'll sleep more soundly knowing we have this wall around us.'

Julius laughed. 'I know, I know. I didn't seriously expect Varus to think any differently. I know that Roman army procedure is never going to change on my word. I was just making a point.'

I looked over at my friend. 'And when we get to the Angrivarii? Do you think they will put up much of a fight?'

Julius shook his head. 'I doubt it. Their gamble has failed. They wanted to take control of the area in your absence, not provoke you into an all-out fight. We'll beat them easily enough, Gaius. Don't worry about that.'

The next day's marching was uneventful enough. We passed through the high hills and onto land which was more mountainous and much more forested, which marked the borders to the Angrivarii lands. That night, after we camped, we all gathered in Varus' command tent and outlined how we should proceed into the enemy territory. We stood over a very rough map of the Angrivarii lands supplied by Julius' men, fashioned from the hide of an animal, spread out on a large table. I would have wanted a good Roman map compiled by our own engineers with their understanding of measurements and the importance of small details, but like much in this campaign, we used what we had. The previous year's summer campaign against the Angrivarii was further over to the west, so all our own field maps were of no use. Besides, I wasn't in a position to speak out, my presence wasn't strictly necessary at this meeting as I had no command of my own, but I was dammed if they were going to plan what was going on without me knowing about it. I stood at the back keeping quiet and listened to the proceedings.

Julius was the first to speak. 'I should leave now, to take command of the Cherusci army. It is over to the east, I can proceed into the Teutoburg Forest from that direction, trapping the Angrivarii.'

Varus frowned. 'But we won't know your position. Splitting our forces is a risky strategy.'

Julius shook his head. 'What choice do we have? My tribal warriors are brave, but cannot fight in the Roman fashion. We can hardly join them to your army. I can leave you some of my cavalry – they can act as your scouts and run messages between the two forces. Providing we keep in constant touch, we should be able to pin the Angrivarii in a vice.'

Varus looked up to his other commanders. 'What do you think?'

Avitus, Varus' senior legate, spoke up. 'Well, Julius has a point. We can hardly use his warriors as we do the other foreign units. They haven't been trained as auxiliaries.'

Selus interjected, 'Unless we use his warriors as a reserve force, and they're only called upon if needed. That'd work.'

Julius slammed his fist on the campaign table. 'And you think my warriors would accept such a position of dishonour? We didn't come here to cower behind the protection of Rome, we came here to fight. If I were to agree to such a thing, my kingship of the Cherusci nation would be over.'

Varus grunted. 'I understand your dilemma.'

Numonius Vala looked at the other commanders in complete bewilderment. 'Aren't we getting ahead of ourselves here? Before we decide how we need to proceed, we need more information on the Angrivarii numbers and their position. We know they have been strengthened by Cherusci rebels. We need to know their strength. Let us halt here and send some patrols to gauge this.'

Julius replied for the other men. 'Normally I would agree with your prudent and cautious plan, but I cannot stay. I must take command of my war host. We're not a standing army like yours – my warriors have gathered for battle, not a long drawn-out campaign.'

Avitus shook his head. 'We cannot fight a long drawn-out campaign either. We have supplies only for two to three weeks, but even more importantly than that, it is late in the year. If the weather turns against us we'll have no choice but to give it up until spring.'

Numonius Vala wasn't so easily put off. 'Then we should have waited until spring to launch this offensive.'

I winced at that last remark, knowing it would irritate the governor. Sure enough, Varus lost his temper and snapped, 'That's enough Vala. All summer you have been agitating for a war, and now you get your wish, you want to turn back!'

Numonius moderated his tone, and spoke quietly and patiently. 'All I'm saying it that the time to start a campaign is at the beginning of the summer, not autumn.'

Varus growled. 'Yes, well here we are, it is too late to wish for what might have been. If you were so against this expedition you should have made your position clear in the camp, not after we've marched the entire army into the fringes of hostile territory.'

Vala bowed his head, realising he had gone too far in his criticism of the governor. 'Yes, my lord. I apologise if I spoke out of turn.'

Varus stood up straighter, his decision made. 'Very well, it seems we have little choice in the matter. Julius, you may join your war host and then proceed with caution into Angrivarii territory. I want your cavalry to constantly keep us in touch with your position and to that of our enemy. Any information you learn is to be relayed back to us. In the morning we proceed north.'

I wasn't exactly surprised; if Varus was to turn back now, he'd look a complete fool. It was bad enough to be campaigning in September anyway. If he changed his mind only a few days in, he'd be a laughing stock. It was a shame though; a return to the safety of the camp, or better still Aliso, would suit me fine. The other officers and I left Varus, and as the others went off to relay the

Roman Mask

governors' orders, I went to have a last word with Julius. 'So it looks like we won't be fighting side by side after all.'

Julius grinned. 'We can't have everything, my friend,' he slapped me on the shoulder, 'but our paths may cross in the days ahead, you never know.'

'Will you be safe travelling to your army tonight?'

Julius nodded. 'Don't worry, my men are adept at tracking and riding at speed. We'll find our way easily enough.'

I took a last look at my childhood friend. 'Then I'll bid you farewell. Take care of yourself, Julius, my sister would never forgive me if anything happened to you.'

Julius chuckled. 'Oh, I'll be fine, Gaius. You know me, I always was the lucky one.'

'That's right, you were, but take care regardless. Nobody's luck can last forever.' I smiled as he mounted his large stallion and rode off into the evening dusk, hoping that this wouldn't be the last I saw of him.

The sky was a vibrant red as the dawn sun rose above the mountains and lit up the clear sky in crimson. We left the camp in the same marching order we'd become accustomed to and set a fast pace as we marched into the mountainous forested terrain to the north known as the Teutoburg.

I felt a moment's apprehension as we first entered the tall pine forests, but reassured myself by looking into the faces of our Roman legionaries, grim men of steel, whose every movement spoke of professional competence and martial expertise.

I wasn't alone in feeling a few nerves. Young Lucius rode by my side, and I noticed beads of sweat on his forehead and nervous eyes that jumped at each forest noise. It was understandable as this was probably his first campaign, so I decided to speak to him, to calm him down a little. 'Tell me, Lucius, does your family live in Rome?'

He turned in surprise at my question. 'Yes, sir ... er ... we have a residence on the Pincian Hill.' His attention shot back to the forest, as a loud snap, probably just the sound of a branch being cleared by our flanking infantry, carried to us.

I made as if not to notice. 'Oh, the Pincian. How nice. Away from the hubbub and noise of central Rome. I was often telling my father he would do well to buy a property to the north of the city. Expensive mind.'

Lucius wrenched his attention, with some difficulty, back to me. 'Yes ...

I suppose it is. Um … Cassius, can I … do you … I mean, it is nothing I'm sure …'

I gave him a reassuring smile. 'Come on, Lucius. No need to hold back with me, we're all friends here.'

He looked around to check that none of the other officers were listening. 'Well, do you think the Angrivarii know we're here yet? In their forests I mean?'

I shrugged. 'Impossible to tell. It would depend on how many men they have watching for enemies – they have a big territory. We might have slipped in without them knowing. Unlikely though.'

He looked around him. 'Why do you say that?'

I smiled. 'They are likely to have spies and informants in our camp, or if not there, almost certainly amongst our Cherusci allies.'

Lucius looked panicked. 'Then, do you think it was a mistake to bring civilians with us? Do you think we may have Angrivarii spies amongst them?'

I shook my head. 'Calm yourself, Lucius. It doesn't matter if they did get to hear of us marching their way. They have had very little time to organise themselves. We've made excellent time since leaving our camp. Trust me, it takes time for the tribes to gather their strength in one place. By then we should be on top of them.'

His eyes were wide. 'So you think we'll engage them soon?'

I shrugged again. 'More than likely.'

Lucius wiped the sweat from his forehead. 'I almost hope we do. I'd prefer to get this over with. I don't like the waiting.'

I laughed. 'Nobody does, Lucius. The moments of apprehension before a battle are always the worst part. But don't worry. Everyone feels afraid at this time. We just hide it, and then let the training take over once the fighting starts. You'll be fine, lad.'

Lucius looked relieved. 'It is so good to have you with us, Cassius. A real war hero. I feel so much better having you near.'

I felt the biggest fraud this side of the Rubicon. Here I was, giving him sage advice to help him control his fear, acting the professional old hand, when in reality it was far more likely I'd be doing the running from battle, not him. I gave him a reassuring pat on the shoulder, and he straightened in his saddle, looking much more assured. Oh, by the gods, why was I so good at living this lie?

It was early afternoon when our luck broke. Since leaving Aurorae Novus we had been blessed with good weather, clear skies and light winds, which had helped our march make good time. This afternoon, however, a strong wind picked up from the north which held a cold bite and the promise of rain. Sure enough,

Roman Mask

before too long, great black clouds came overhead and it started to come down persistently.

I rode up to Governor Varus. 'Do you think we should stop and make camp early? I don't like the look of this weather?'

Varus looked to the skies. 'I don't like it either, but we must push on. It is far too early to stop, besides I haven't heard from the Cherusci yet, and I don't know their position. As soon as we know more, we can make a decision then.'

I frowned. 'Very well, but I think this storm will only get worse.'

I wasn't wrong. The rainfall got heavier, and the forest path we were marching on became a great muddy quagmire, with rivulets of water washing away the beaten track our engineers had prepared for us. The army's march slowed as we made our way over the difficult mountainous tracks, and soon the high winds were breaking the tree tops off some of the trees, which fell into our path further inhibiting our progress.

Varus insisted we continued to push on through it, stressing the importance of hearing from our allies before we could stop, but as the afternoon wore on, the men became exhausted from the difficult conditions.

Where I'd failed earlier, Numonius Vala tried again with the governor, raising his voice so as to be heard through the pouring rain. 'My lord, we must stop. This is hopeless. The column has lost all cohesion. The unarmed and the civilians have now mixed with the main column. It will prove near impossible to form correctly if we're attacked.'

Varus turned on Vala. 'Well, you're my legate! If the column is disorganised, sort it out! We must push on. I still haven't heard from Julius. You were the one telling me that I needed more intelligence. Honestly, Vala, you try my patience too far!'

Vala saluted and rode off to try and reorganise the struggling column, which was now bogged down and getting nowhere. I could see the lunacy of our situation. Varus might not want to call off the march and make camp, but it was availing him nothing, as the army was moving forward so slowly that the amount of ground gained was virtually meaningless.

On we marched, through the rain and mud, an exhausting trek that sapped our energy and chilled us to our bones, the freezing September rains running in great streams off our heavy armour. Eventually, Varus called me over. 'I'm going to signal the engineers to start marking out an area for the men to make camp. It looks like we'll have to stop until this blows over.'

I breathed a sign of relief. At last! I nodded my head in agreement and asked him, 'What would you like me to do?'

Varus looked back at the struggling column, through the pouring rain. 'See if you can help Numonius reorganise the column. It is going to take us a while to set this camp up.' As he said this, we heard an almighty commotion as hundreds of voices started shouting towards the rear of the army. 'What, by the gods, is going on?'

It wasn't long before we found out; from above I could see thousands of spears raining down on the rear of our column. Centurions and other men took up the cry: 'We're under attack!'

Chapter Twenty-eight

If anyone noticed that the blood had drained from my face in stark terror at those words, no one said anything; probably because they were so terrified themselves. Besides, there were more pressing concerns to worry them, namely the rear of our army coming under attack by a sizeable force of screaming Germanic warriors.

In our command group, officers wheeled their mounts in confusion, whilst others shouted orders at no one in particular and some started cursing to the gods. In short, the command of the army was in complete pandemonium, completely taken by surprise by the attack. Governor Varus was no exception; he was loudly berating the absent Numonius Vala as if the attack was all his fault. 'I told Numonius to get the column in order! Damn the man! What trouble has he brought me now?'

I was terrified, but realised something needed to be done, so I took hold of Varus' mount's bridle, bringing it under control, and shouted at Varus. 'We don't have time for this, sir. The rear of the army is under attack. What are your orders?'

Varus looked me square in the eyes then, and I saw the terror in them as they rolled from side to side in panic. I repeated again, more slowly, and in as reassuring a voice as I could muster. 'The enemy has engaged us. We must deploy. What are your orders?'

Varus looked around him and managed to pull himself together somewhat. 'Of course, Cassius. We must deploy.' He hesitated. 'We are under attack. They must be repulsed.'

I was wanting something more than the blatantly obvious, and wanted to shake the governor in order to get some sense out of him. Fortunately I resisted the urge and was assisted by Legate Avitus. 'The attack is only to our rear. We can still make camp, and that will give us somewhere to fall back to.'

At least someone was talking sense.

Varus nodded his head. 'Yes, good plan. Take your Seventeenth legion up to Ceionius and build the camp. The Eighteenth and Nineteenth will repulse this attack. Tell your men to be quick about it.'

Avitus gave an ironic grin. 'Don't worry, they won't need any more incentive than that.' He indicated back at the heaving mass of Germanic warriors who were harassing the rear columns of men who had raised their shields into a defensive line.

Varus stood straighter in the saddle, coming back to himself. 'Very well, proceed.' Avitus rode off, and the rest of the commanders gathered round the governor. 'I need more information about the size of this attack. Cassius, go help out Legate Vala. We need someone who knows what he's doing there.'

That's what you get for helping a man out, I thought. You get sent to the worst part of the trouble. I let go of his horse's bridle and gave him a salute. 'Do you have any message for him?'

Varus nodded his head. 'Just tell him to get the men secured in a defensive formation. Tell him we plan to fall back to the marching camp once we have it erected. He is to sally forth against their attackers at any opportunity. I want as many of these traitorous Germans dead as possible.'

I saluted again and noticed a few of the officers nod their head to me in respect. They'd seen how I'd pulled the governor together, even if he didn't acknowledge it. I turned my horse and rode it down the column, icy terror running through me, quickly trying to think how to get out of this situation.

I halted on a small knoll which gave me a good view of the battle raging below me. The German warriors had attacked from the forested south-west, raining spears down on the Thracian cavalry and rear cohorts of legionaries. The legionaries had quickly raised and locked their shields, so damage to them was limited, but the vulnerable horses of the Thracians had fared worse, and the ground was littered with dead horses and fallen riders. The situation was bad, but not disastrous. The men had been organised by someone, probably the much-maligned Numonius Vala, and were holding their lines well. I looked around for Vala and saw him to the south, a knot of junior officers around him, issuing orders and directing where he wanted them. I spurred my horse over to him, relieved that somebody knew what they were doing.

I rode my horse directly over to his position, trying not to think about the spears which were still raining down not far from where I was. 'Legate Vala, Governor Varus has ordered me to assist you.'

Vala was pointing something out to a senior centurion but looked round as I arrived. 'Cassius, good. This is a complete mess. What are the governor's orders?'

I tried to keep my voice as calm and steady as possible, which wasn't easy, as Germanic warriors were now less than a stone's throw away. 'The engineers and the Seventeenth will be constructing a camp which we can fall back to.'

Vala looked relieved. 'Thank the gods for that. We should have stopped and done so long ago. I have no idea of the enemy's numbers, but there are a lot of them.'

I looked up at the tree line, which was lined with screaming warriors, long hair and beards caked in mud, hurling weapons at us. I shuddered inwardly and turned my attention back to Vala. 'He wants us to get the men into a secure defensive position and then sally forth as often as we can to cause damage to the enemy.'

Vala snorted in contempt. 'Ha! Easier said than done. The entire column is a mess. We can just about hold a defensive line, but each time we mount an attack against the enemy, they simply melt away. The rains have made it impossible to pursue in earnest, and we have to hold back enough men to protect the baggage train and the civilians.'

I gritted my teeth and asked the next question, dreading the answer. 'What would you like me to do?'

Vala looked around him at the enemy in the trees and his struggling cohorts, covered in mud, drenched in sheets of rain, defensive shields protecting themselves and their comrades. 'Lead the Thracian cavalry away from here. They're no use to us here, and their mounts are an easy target for enemy spears.'

I felt relief at his words. I was half expecting him to order me to lead a suicidal attack against the tree line. Taking the cavalry and running away was the sort of order I could fulfil nicely. I nodded my head sombrely. 'I'll take them to a sheltered position up on that knoll,' I pointed to the knoll I'd been standing on earlier, 'then we'll be in position to lead a counterchange if the Germans break through the lines at any point.'

Vala looked at my knoll and nodded in agreement. 'An excellent idea. It is good to have you with us, Cassius.'

I smiled. 'A pleasure,' and I rode off to the Thracian cavalry.

My first task was to gather the cavalry together; the legions were now deployed in defensive lines, making impregnable shield walls, behind which the legionaries were safely protected, but for the Thracian cavalry it was a different story. The Thracians, armoured in scale armour and armed with long cavalry swords and shields, were split up into ragged formations outside of our lines. They were fighting in small knots against marauding gangs of Angrivarii tribesmen who periodically broke out of the trees, hurling spears, whilst screaming challenges and shouting insults at the Roman auxiliaries. The field of dead horses and horsemen spoke about how effective the cavalry were being repulsing these attacks – the largely unarmoured horses were being felled by enemy spears and their riders were being hacked to pieces by the German warriors' long *sax* knives on the ground as soon as they fell. This wouldn't be as easy as I'd first thought, and my stomach twisted in knots as I rode my horse round the Roman lines, shouting at the Thracian horsemen to fall back. 'Deploy on me,' I shouted, 'Deploy on me!'

They either didn't hear me, or they were too preoccupied to listen to a tribune they were unfamiliar with. Damn it. I needed to get closer.

Every fibre of my being told me to run away – spears were being launched from the tree line, striking not a dozen paces from where I rode my horse – but there was nothing for it, there was nowhere to run to. I'd only be safe when I'd got the horseman to rally behind our lines, so I took a deep breath and steered my horse towards one knot of horseman who were busy trading blows with a large group of tribesmen armed with spears and shields.

Spears dropped either side of me, but I couldn't think about those. I needed to gather the men. and get out of there. As I got near, I saw to my relief that the tribesmen were falling back, melting into the trees. Some of the horsemen were following, thinking they were maintaining the advantage, but almost certainly being enticed to their deaths. 'Get back here, you fools!' I screamed, running my horse up to one of the Thracians and grabbing his horse's bridle. 'Pull back and deploy, all of you!'

The forty or so Thracians turned to me, their wild eyes telling me of the mixture of terror and blood-lust that had these men under its spell. I spurred my horse into their midst and demanded, 'Who is in command here?'

They all looked at one another – clearly none had realised that they were currently leaderless – and then shrugged.

I spat on the ground. 'I'm taking command. You men, follow me. We're going to gather the rest of your troop. Stick in close formation behind my lead. Any man who breaks formation will have me to answer with afterwards, do you understand?'

They looked at one another, but a few of them nodded: that was all I needed. 'Very well, you all understand.' I bellowed, 'Form ranks!' before turning my horse and riding to the next group of Thracians. To my relief, I noticed the horsemen were following me.

The next group was more straightforward. My forty horsemen came to the aid of another group of similar size. As soon as the tribesmen saw us coming to our comrades' aid, they turned and fled, and I rode my men in between our fellow cavalry and the fleeing tribesmen to prevent any possibility of pursuit. 'Fall into ranks. We are to rally the men!'

I scanned the men to see if any were going to dispute my orders, but most looked happy that someone was finally taking charge. I sized the men up and down; young fit men, helmeted and armoured in interlinking bronze scales, holding onto their weapons tightly. I'd never been sure of scale armour. It didn't offer as much protection as a good mail shirt – being vulnerable to a blow from below, which could ride up into the man the armour was supposed to protect – but it could be polished to a fine sheen, making the cavalry troop look fine on parade. Well, this wasn't the parade now, this was the real thing, and these men had better start acting like real soldiers, or none of us would make it out of here alive. 'Get into line!' I pointed to one man whose attention was on the trees. 'Get back into line. If I notice you falling out again, I'll give you to the Germans myself! Do you understand?'

He swallowed and nodded his head.

I turned my horse. 'Good, follow my lead.'

In the next group I found the cavalry's praefectus equitum, their commander. My group now numbered almost one hundred and sixty men, as stragglers had joined us as we rode around the battlefront, in pursuit of the next knot of horsemen. The praefectus wore a fully encompassing helmet with a beautifully moulded silver faceplate in the shape of a handsome youth: such a helmet might prove intimidating to the enemy, but the small eye sockets restricted the riders view, and the narrow mouth slit would prove difficult to shout orders – no wonder his cavalry *ala* were dispersed over the battlefield in a rabble.

I didn't bother giving him a salute. 'I am Cassius Aprilis, under direct orders from Legate Vala and Governor Varus. I'm taking command of your men.'

I stated it as a matter of fact, but I expected an argument – few men gave up command of their unit easily. The praefectus removed his helmet, revealing a young man's face under a thick thatch of brownish hair. Oh, by the gods. Men being led by young boys. When would the army learn? The poor boy had probably only being given the commission due to his family's connections, and now here he was, out of his depth, surrounded by enemy warriors. Madness.

He addressed me earnestly. 'I am pursuing the tribesmen into the woods. We have them on the run.'

I snorted. 'You've no one on the run. They're trying to lead you into those trees where your horseman can't manoeuvre their mounts. Any man going into those trees is a dead man, you included.'

He swallowed, looked around at the trees, unsure of what to do next. 'But … we cannot run away … can we?'

I shook my head. 'We're not running away. We're going to deploy on that knoll.' I pointed at the small hill behind me. 'Then we can ride down any Angrivarii who manage to break through our lines.'

He looked up at the knoll, and nodded. He went bright red, no doubt embarrassed that his command was being taken away from him so easily. I didn't have time to mother the young boy, but I thought it best to keep him onside; the men might find it easier to take orders from me if they saw their commander with me. 'We're going to gather up the rest of your men first. You take the lead. We're to get them to fall into ranks, then we will reform on the hill.'

He nodded in agreement and re-donned his expensive helmet – at least he should stand out on the battlefield; the men wouldn't have any difficulty in recognising their commander. We rode around the tree line gathering up the small knots of men, and before long we had all that was left of his troop following in our wake. By the time we reformed on the hill, our numbers were just under nine hundred men, well short of the thousand and twenty-four of two full *ala* – their earlier disorganisation had led to the death of a lot of their comrades, a sharp lesson for the young commander in his first battle.

I finally breathed easily, now we were safely behind our lines, and relaxed a bit. 'Tell me, what's your name?' I asked the young praefectus who was removing his ornate helmet.

'Macarius, sir.' The boy gave me his Latinised Greek name.

I tried to hold myself confidently, keeping a tight rein on my skittish mount, to stop my cowardly heart betraying my true anxiety. 'Well, Macarius, we'll need to keep the men in tight order if we're to repel any breaks in the line. I don't want the men running off to the four corners of Hades again.'

Macarius slumped in his saddle. 'I made a terrible mess of things, didn't I? When they attacked, I was so shocked. I just didn't think … I thought I had to run the barbarians off. I didn't realise I was playing into their hands.'

I nodded sagely, scanning the seething mass of muddy legionaries below, shields held high, repelling the enemies' spears which were now being flung from the safety of the tree line: the Germans had evidently given up on attacking the impenetrable shield wall directly. 'You made a mistake, Macarius. I won't lie to you, but this attack took us all by surprise. No one thought the Angrivarii were so close to our position. You at least kept your head when I pointed you in the right direction. Many wouldn't have. Learn from this and your men might have themselves a better commander for it.'

Macarius sat straighter in his saddle, pride returning. 'Thank you, sir.'

I waved away his thanks. 'We're not out of this yet. Keep the men in line, and follow my lead when the legionaries start to withdraw into the camp. We may be needed to make a sweep to cover the men as they find safety in the camp.'

Macarius' cheeks went red. 'I can't believe we're retreating.'

I spun my head to him and said sharply, 'Don't be a fool.' I moderated my tone and explained. 'We have enemy tribesmen to our rear and either flanks, there is no disgrace in falling back to strengthen our position. That's what makes us better than them. We use our heads. They fight on heart alone.'

He nodded his head in understanding, yet again embarrassed by his naivety. 'We won't let you down again, sir.'

It didn't take long for the engineers and legionaries from the XVII to construct the marching camp, but on that windswept little knoll, with the rain still pouring down in great sheets, our horses spooked and skittish from the noise of the thunder and the screaming enemy tribesmen, it felt like an eternity. Eventually the order came for the rear legions to retreat, and as expected our two *ala* of cavalry were ordered to provide a covering screen to protect the men as they slowly inched their way backwards through the muddy mass into the field camp. My cowardice briefly made me consider leaving Macarius and his Thracian cavalry then – after all, I'd fulfilled my orders and gathered them together. I could be back in the safety of the camp, behind a turf and timber palisade. But when I looked at the young commander's innocent trusting face, I realised I couldn't leave him; however unwarranted his belief in me was, he and his men now needed me to believe in themselves. Besides, he'd only muck everything up if I left him to it. I didn't save all their lives just so they could throw them away again at the first opportunity.

I was no true cavalry commander, but even I knew what was needed in this situation: speed of horse, and the sight of cold steel, to scare away any pursuit. My teeth began to chatter as we circled around to form up, but whether that was from terror or the cold, I wasn't sure. I told myself that the Germans must be running out of spears to throw. Even if some warriors carried two or three of them, they didn't have an inexhaustible supply, so as long as I kept on my horse, I should be fine. I gulped in dread and kicked my horse forward, and we cantered down the knoll and rode in a great semicircle around the backs of the retreating legionary lines. Some tribesmen broke cover from the trees and hurled spears, and a few of the braver warriors gathered in groups and tried to pursue the legionaries. However, they were not yet organised into a shield wall, and as soon as they saw the Thracian cavalry bearing down on them, they retreated back into the safety of the trees. I pulled my horse up after the long sweep along the muddy track in the midst of the Teutoburg Forest and surveyed the retreating backs of the legionaries escaping into the hastily erected camp. To my annoyance, the last few cohorts had yet to reach safety, so reluctantly I turned my horse and signalled to Macarius that we needed to do another sweep. This time it was much more dangerous. The Germans now knew our numbers and were ready for us. If they had time to erect a shield wall, we could be in trouble. I led the horseman at a full gallop, the cold wind blowing the stinging rain into my eyes, as I sent silent prayers to any god that might be listening that the Angrivarii wouldn't come streaming out of the woods in greater numbers than we could handle. Fortunately, the Angrivarii were either not yet ready or they were uninterested in making a concerted effort to bar our path. Only once did the Angrivarii come out and challenge us, but not in enough numbers to be a real threat, possibly only acting as bait for us to follow. We weren't going to fall for that this time, and Macarius and I kept the men in good order, losing no more men to the enemy spears or long knives, before we too could retreat back into the camp. I signalled Macarius to lead the men in, now the legions were all safely inside, and kept an eye on the trees as Angrivarii tribesmen finally broke their cover and started racing towards the Roman gates in great numbers. By the gods there were a lot of them. Thousands of warriors were running towards me. I turned and spurred my horse into our camp, being the last Roman to reach safety, the gates slamming shut as soon as I rode through.

Despite my fear and worry, I had managed to take a good look at our camp as I rode into it. Whilst evidence of its hasty construction was obvious, the palisade being made from stakes of unequal lengths of timber for example, the earthen banks were of sufficient height and the ramparts well enough constructed for men to man the walls. The five thousand men of the XVII must have broken all records in constructing a camp so quickly; even by Roman standards it was hard not to be impressed. We might just get out of this yet, I told myself, marvelling at the resilience of the Roman army. We'd been surprised for sure. An attack from behind, whilst deployed for the march, would have been the end for most armies, but here we were, safely behind earth and timber walls, ready to fight another day. Give it up now, Angrivarii, I thought, you'll never get the better of the legions.

The young tribune, Lucius Eggius, came up and took my horse as I dismounted, speaking loudly to drown out the German tribesmen's derisory insults from the other side of the timber gates. 'Well done, sir. That was nicely done.'

I smiled. 'It's easy when you're leading good men.' I nodded my head towards Macarius and his men.

Macarius puffed his chest out and saluted very formally to me. 'Cassius Aprilis, it has been an honour.'

I laughed. 'Just get yourself a new helmet – that one's for the parade.'

He smiled and looked at the helmet he held in his hand. 'As soon as we return to Aliso, I promise.'

I turned my attention to Lucius. 'What is the plan now? Do you know?'

Lucius Eggius reddened. 'I don't think anything has been decided yet. The senior commanders are gathered in the governor's tent.'

I wiped the sweat from my forehead. 'Then I better join them there.' I bade farewell to the two young officers and made my way over to Varus' tent in the centre of the camp.

The two sentries at Varus' tent waved me straight in when I arrived, and the arguments were in full swing as I walked through the entrance.

Varus was red-faced and angry. 'Why didn't the scouts warn us of this enemy force? How could they take us so unawares? Somebody must be held responsible for this disaster!'

Numonius Vala shook his head vigorously. 'It's no good blaming the scouts for this. In this wind and rain, an army mounted on elephants could slip through our lines. We should have stopped and made camp as soon as the storm hit!'

Governor Varus hit the temporary campaign table they were arguing around with his fist. 'Nonsense. If the men had done their job properly, we could've been prepared for this. We need to redouble the scouts, and make sure we're not taken by surprise again.'

Vala gave a snort of contempt. 'Isn't it a bit late for that? The enemy is at the gates.'

Varus ground his teeth in anger. 'That's not my fault. Where is the damn Cherusci cavalry? We need to meet up with our allies. As long as we're separated, we're vulnerable. That's why I had no choice but to push on through this storm.'

Vala met the governor's gaze. 'That doesn't mean military fundamentals should be ignored. Any army is vulnerable on the march, even a Roman one.'

'How dare you!' blasted Varus. 'I was campaigning when you were still in swaddling clothes. Don't tell me about military fundamentals.'

'Please, gentlemen.' Legate Selus raised his hand for peace. 'This bickering is getting us nowhere. We need to decide what we are to do now, not worry about what we did wrong.'

Both Varus and Vala looked at Selus and reluctantly nodded in agreement. There was still a lot of resentment between the two of them, but for the time being, at least, they were prepared to overlook it. After all, we were all in this together now, one way or another. Governor Varus took a deep breath and started again. 'Do we at least know the enemy numbers?'

Selus answered. 'It is difficult to say. Much of their host was hidden in the trees, but they have a force at least equal in size to our own, and in all probability much larger.'

I could help them here; I was the only man present to see the Angrivarii after they broke cover from the trees. I put my helmet on the table on which a map of the territory was laid. 'They number in the tens of thousands,' I told them. 'I guess their force is at least double the size of our own.'

Legate Avitus whistled. 'Forty thousand warriors? That must be nearing their full strength. They have manoeuvred their entire army between us and our line of retreat.'

I shook my head. 'We cannot know for sure this is their full force. The Roman legionary who died after bringing news of the Angrivarii in Aurorae spoke of huge numbers of warriors gathering – he estimated eighty thousand. That means there could be a sizeable force in front of us as well.'

Selus stared down at the map, a great frown over his bearded face. 'We could still punch through them, return to Aurorae to the south-west, the way we came. We'd lose a lot of men, but we'd make it. Even a force of forty thousand can't possibly stand against three full legions.'

I gave a bitter laugh. 'That's if they face us in the field. I can't see them doing that. Instead they'd harry us all the way back to the camp, draining our strength, inflicting huge casualties along the way.'

Selus nodded in agreement. 'Yes, but we'd make it. We'd live to fight another day. We could take our revenge in the spring with a fresh offensive.'

Varus wasn't so pleased about this prospect. 'I'll have no more talk about retreating to Aurorae. The situation isn't so bad that we need to talk of making a fighting retreat.'

'Isn't it?' asked Numonius Vala. 'Going to war this late in the year was always a risk. Now the weather has turned against us, we have no choice but to turn back.'

Varus stared down at the map, hoping to find some answers there. 'I don't intend to march my men through that howling mass of warriors to a humiliating retreat after our first setback.'

I knew what Varus was thinking. If he retreated now, it was impossible to view this short campaign as anything other than a complete failure. Such a defeat was unlikely to be forgiven by Augustus, who would, in all probability, then replace him as governor. I voiced what everyone else was thinking, but was too afraid to ask, 'Then you intend to push on? Further north?'

Varus looked up at me, and for the first time I saw the uncertainty there. 'Yes. We can do it. All we need to do is meet up with our Cherusci allies, then we'll have the numbers to inflict a crushing defeat on these upstart Angrivarii.'

Numonius Vala blasted in frustration, 'That's ridiculous!' and turned his back on the governor to try to control his temper.

Avitus was slightly more tactful. 'We could push on north, Governor, but where would we go? We have no idea where Julius and his Cherusci are. There may well be another hostile force in front of us, and we mustn't forget Ewald and his force of traitorous Cherusci. We have no idea where they are either. Our line of retreat is now blocked. If anything were to go wrong, we'd have no way of turning back.'

Governor Varus was saved from having to make a difficult decision when a junior tribune came through the leather tent's entrance and declared, 'Governor, sir. Riders from our Cherusci cavalry.'

Varus let out a great sigh of relief. 'At last! Thank the gods.' Then a shadow of worry crossed his face. 'But wait. How did they get past the enemy warriors?'

The tribune caught his breath, obviously excited. 'They didn't come from the south, my lord, they came from the east. They have word from our allies.'

Varus looked up to the ceiling of the tent. 'It looks as if the gods haven't deserted us just yet. Is Julius Arminius with them?'

The tribune shook his head. 'No, my lord, but their leader claims to have a message from him.'

'Bring him to me at once.'

Chapter Twenty-nine

I recognised the Cherusci messenger as soon as he entered Varus' command tent; it was the giant Faramund, the renowned tracker, and one of Julius' most loyal men. I breathed more easily knowing it was someone I knew, someone whose opinion I trusted.

Varus' earlier relief wasn't reflected in his tone to Faramund. He blasted angrily at the cavalry commander as soon as he entered the tent, 'Where in Hades have you all been? We expected word from you days ago. Where is Julius Arminius? Rome doesn't take kindly to allies who desert them at the first sight of the enemy!'

Faramund looked affronted by the governor's words and stared straight back at him, no sign of deference in his voice. 'We've deserted no one. Do not blame us for your current plight.'

Varus was taken aback by the junior officer's defiance. 'Don't take that tone with me ... by the gods man, who do you think you are?'

I intervened, trying to calm the governor by using his *prenomen*. 'Come on, Publius, let the man speak. We're all on the same side here.'

The governor looked uncertain. His emotions were running high but he knew I was right and nodded, so I turned to Faramund and asked him, 'As you can tell, our position isn't ideal. Can you tell us what you've been doing?'

Faramund nodded and smiled. 'We've been fighting Ewald and his traitorous dogs. I came to report to you a great victory!'

The spirits of everyone in the room instantly lifted and Varus laughed out loud in delight. 'You've defeated the rebel Cherusci? Tell me what happened?'

'Arminius led us to meet Inguiomerus and the main Cherusci host. He planned to head north to meet with you here. But Inguiomerus told him our scouts had discovered a large host of men to the east. Arminius guessed it must be Ewald – so we set on them.'

Numonius Vala asked, 'But why not wait until we could reinforce you?'

Faramund shrugged. 'Possibly he didn't want Ewald to get away. We didn't need you in any case. We managed to come onto their position without being spotted.' He gave a cruel twisted smile. 'We attacked at dusk, as they were trying to erect shelters for the night. His force was almost equal in size to our own, but we had the element of surprise. We came at them with flame and iron, butchering them in the near dark, defeating them utterly, the survivors breaking and fleeing into the forest in ragged bands.'

'Thank the gods,' breathed Legate Selus, and everyone nodded in agreement. 'Does Ewald still live?'

'Julius Arminius struck off his head personally, after he was captured with only his closest bodyguard surrounding him.' Faramund laughed. 'Ewald was a great warrior, but made a poor general.'

Numonius Vala turned to Governor Varus. 'This changes everything, my lord. With the Cherusci rebels destroyed, the aim of this offensive is achieved. Julius' position in the Cherusci is now assured, we can withdraw knowing that the Angrivarii are now isolated. Without any allies, we can finish them next spring!'

This point wasn't missed on Varus, who looked like a man saved, his mind whirring at his change in fortune. 'Yes, yes! Even if I retreat now, I can tell the Senate that we only withdrew when our objective had been sealed!' He punched the air in delight. 'Julius has defeated the real enemy here, the rebels in his own tribe. What is more, he has done it alone, without our aid. No one in his tribe will dare try to usurp his authority now.' He turned to Faramund. 'Please excuse my earlier harsh words, trooper. You've done well, more than well. You will be well rewarded for bringing me this momentous news! As will Julius Arminius. He shows the value of a Roman education!'

I was as relieved as anyone that Ewald was now dead. I still remembered his sinuous deadly grace and cold killer's eyes, but I needed to state the obvious before all this euphoria went to the Roman commander's head. 'This is great news indeed, but before we award ourselves a great triumph through Rome, aren't we all forgetting the forty thousand or so Angrivarii at our gates? Nobody has bothered to tell them that they've just lost this war.'

The Roman Legates all looked at one another, and Avitus even chuckled at my sarcastic note. The governor looked at me with a disapproving frown. 'Nobody has forgotten the howling mob outside our gates, Cassius.' He looked down at the map. 'Gentleman, may I have your suggestions on how best to withdraw?'

Avitus was the most forthright. 'Simple, let's wait till dawn. Hopefully the storm will have blown over by then. Then we march out and confront them. They won't be able to stand against us.'

Numonius Vala shook his head. 'We've no need to take such risks now. We can fight our way through them for sure, but it will be slow going through all those muddy trails. Do we really want to lose so many men for a battle we no longer need to fight?'

I looked at the crude map in front of us which was marked with winding mountainous trails in between a vast expense of the Teutoburg Forest. 'Why can't we join up with Julius now? Now Ewald is defeated, we can concentrate both our forces on the Angrivarii and withdraw together.'

Varus nodded and looked to Faramund. 'Yes. Where are the Cherusci now?'

Faramund shrugged. 'When I left they were pursuing the remnants of Ewald's force over to the east.'

Avitus asked Varus, 'Can't we order them back, to break off their pursuit?'

Governor Varus laughed. 'Have you ever heard of a barbarian horde being able to stop once they have the enemy on the run? We'll never get them to march north now.'

Selus gestured at the map. 'We don't have to. Why don't we go east ourselves?'

I raised an eyebrow. 'Away from Aurorae Novus?'

Selus explained. 'We don't need to return to Aurorae Novus directly. We can go east until we reach that river there.' He pointed at a winding tributary of the great river Weser. 'It can lead us all the way back, along a safe route, free from the forest and any more chances of ambush. We can even liaise with our Cherusci allies along the way, giving them any assistance they may need in running down the last of the Cherusci rebels.'

All the legates nodded their heads in agreement and Varus leant over the map, great arms either side of our projected route. 'There is a lot of forest between here and there first.' He looked up at Faramund. 'Is this route passable?'

Faramund nodded vigorously. 'That is the way we came ourselves. The trails are a bit rocky in places, but they are free of enemy and easily navigated. I took my cavalry this way. Your infantry will have no trouble. It may prove difficult for the artillery and baggage trail however.'

Varus pondered the situation. 'Hmmm ... I don't like leaving those behind.'

Selus shook his head. 'What need do we have of either now? The campaign ends here. We don't need the artillery anymore and the men can carry enough of their own rations easily enough for us to reach Aurorae Novus.'

Varus looked up. 'I won't leave our artillery in the hands of the enemy.'

Avitus laughed. 'As if they could ever use it! It takes trained engineers to operate the catapults and *ballistae*. Brainless savages wouldn't know where to start. Besides, we can burn them before we go.'

Varus looked around at everyone in the tent. 'Then we are all in agreement. We travel east, to the river?'

Everyone, including myself, nodded in agreement. There was no real choice to make really. It was the only way open to us if we didn't want to continue the campaign north, other than fighting our way through forty thousand hostile Angrivarii; something nobody relished now that Varus had his victory and could return to camp vindicated that this pointless excursion had proved worthwhile.

Varus stood up, looking relieved. 'Very well, we leave at dawn. Triple the guards on the gates, and instruct the rest of the men to take what rest they can. Tomorrow will be a long march. Faramund, how many men do you have with you?'

Faramund banged his fist on his chest in a military salute. 'One full *ala*, sir.'

Varus nodded his head. 'Good! More than enough. I want your cavalry to act as our scouts, lead the way and provide a screen around the main column, looking out for any further trouble. Your men know the area and will prove more effective than my Thracians. I want a tight shield around my legions. I want no more surprises.'

Faramund stood up straight and said in his gruff voice. 'Don't worry. We'll let nothing through – no Angrivarii whoreson will slip past our net.'

Varus smiled and then turned to the rest of us. 'Good! I will see you all at dawn. Be ready. We can't afford any delays.'

I huddled under my blanket that night, protected from the howling storm by a large leather tent which I shared with Ceionius and Lucius Eggius. All my old fears returned. I barely slept, but the few moments' peace I did gain were disturbed with dreams of Centurion Decius, who now summoned wild Angrivarii warriors out from the trees to rip me limb from limb.

Mercifully the storm blew over in the night, leaving only a steady drizzle in the grey overcast early morning. Before we departed, Varus ordered the burning of the baggage train and the entire artillery. There was no changing our minds now, as the only food remaining in the army was what we carried, and our ability to mount a military campaign was now at an end. A large number of civilians complained about losing all their possessions, and some wailed in despair at seeing all they owned go up in smoke, but most realised that Varus was making the right decision. Now they'd seen the numbers and ferocity of the Angrivarii, most were just glad to be getting out of these forested mountains with their lives and wanted nothing that would slow us down. We left by the eastern gate, and although the Angrivarii were in evidence – they'd surrounded the entire camp in the night – they were not in sufficient numbers on the eastern side to prevent us from passing. They'd obviously been expecting us to either continue our passage north or to confront them to the south, and when they saw us heading east, away from their tribal heartland, they shadowed us from a distance, occasionally daring to get closer and throwing a javelin or two at our rear guard. But in the main, they were content to hurl insults at our retreating backs, delighted to see us leave their lands, and celebrating a great victory against the mighty Roman legions. This upset several of the Roman officers and their men, who grumbled at the apparent humiliation of leaving these taunts unanswered, but it suited me just fine. Let them have their victory; let them dance all night if necessary. I knew Rome would exact its revenge in the spring. Rome would come again into the Angrivarii heartland, only this time fully prepared, at the right time of year, and most importantly, as far as I was concerned, without me.

The forest trails to the east were little more than muddy tracks, and it was slow going marching the men through the often steep passes and through mountain bottlenecks. The engineers did their best to keep the way clear, and our Cherusci scouts regularly reported back, warning of potential obstacles that might otherwise bring the progress of the military column to a halt.

Despite the relentless drizzle and overcast skies, which seemed to mirror the poor morale of the retreating Roman legions, Governor Varus was surprisingly cheerful. He spoke at length to the officers who rode at his side, of which I was one, of our great success in this campaign. I was yet to be convinced, but Varus assured us. 'It was always my intention to let Julius' Cherusci do the main fighting in this campaign – it is always best to let your allies take most of the credit in tribal wars. How better to cement their allegiance to Rome's cause?' he asked. 'That's what I will tell the Senate in my next despatch. They'll see the prudence in my plan.'

Legate Avitus wasn't quite so happy. 'We're still leaving Paullinus' death unavenged,' he complained.

Paullinus had been Avitus' lead tribune, before he'd volunteered to lead the ill-fated peace delegation to the Angrivarii, so it was no wonder that Avitus bristled at the notion that all this had somehow been part of the governor's master plan. Varus wasn't having any of it however. 'Don't worry, you'll get your vengeance, Avitus. Do you think I will forget how the Angrivarii, even now, taunt me?' We all turned to where Varus pointed, and saw in the mountains behind us a great German warrior turn his back on us and show us his bare bottom, which he slapped and wiggled around at us. Some of his companions urinated, whilst other spat insults. The sight was now becoming so commonplace, we all pretty much ignored it. Varus continued. 'We'll come back and teach these Angrivarii what it means to defy Rome, you can trust me on that one, Avitus.'

Avitus nodded his head in acceptance, but I noticed his reluctance. Varus' control over his high command is weakening I realised, it is not only Numonius Vala who is now questioning the governor's orders, but his head Legate Avitus too. The sooner we got back to Aurorae Novus, the better, I thought, for all concerned.

It was a torturous morning, as we made our slow decent down from the mountains, shivering from the cold as the relentless drizzle and chilly mountain breeze sapped our energy. The trails were too steep in places for us to ride, so we needed to dismount and lead our horses through the thick slippery mud, something that Governor Varus found particularly distasteful. 'Surely our engineers could have found an easier path than this. What are they doing leading us through this mess?'

Numonius Vala answered. 'If it were up to me, we'd stop here and send some men to scout out a proper route down the mountains. Then we'd be able to send some units to rid us of our Angrivarii shadows.'

Varus ground his teeth. 'Yes, well it's not up to you is it? We've been through this. I'm not going to waste time chasing shadows through the woods. The Angrivarii are no longer bothering us. We're not going to stop, and that's the end of it.'

The bickering between Varus and Vala had been constant throughout the morning descent, Vala being convinced that we should stop and throw off the pursuing Angrivarii. In fairness to Governor Varus, the numbers of Angrivarii we could see taunting us from a distance was gradually diminishing the further we travelled away from their lands, but we all knew they were still there, waiting in the woods, sharpening their spears and knives for any change of heart. Varus argued that stopping and sending men to confront the tribesmen was a waste of manpower, that losing men in pointless encounters was not something he'd countenance. But in truth I think Varus just wanted to get down that mountain as quickly as he could. We all did. We were all sick of the cold and the wet, the mud which made us slip and slide, the brooding overcast skies, and the sodden clothes, armour and rations.

A messenger from Faramund's scouts arrived, leading his horse. 'My lord governor, I bring news.'

Varus turned his attention away from Vala and snapped at the messenger. 'Well, what is it, man?'

The messenger responded enthusiastically. 'Faramund thinks our allies are not far. He can see their campfires in the distance, near the river. We only need to traverse this chicane and then the going is more easy. We can be with them by late afternoon.'

'Thank the gods,' muttered young Lucius Eggius; even his youthful exuberance had been dampened by the relentless drizzle throughout the miserable march.

Numonius Vala was less happy. 'Shouldn't we explore this pass first? How do we know it is our allies at the other end?'

Varus looked around at his companions before responding. 'Who else, by the gods, is it going to be? The only other hostile force has been routed by Julius and his Cherusci.'

Numonius Vala went red from his commander's impatient tone. 'I'm only saying we should remain cautious.'

Varus sighed. 'Very well,' he turned to the messenger, 'has Faramund scouted the entire length of this corridor?'

The trooper stood to attention. 'Of course, my lord,'

Varus nodded his head. 'And what did he find?'

The messenger shook his head. 'Nothing, my lord. The way is quite heavy going. All this rain has made much of it impassable, but it is still navigable along a sandy bank at least two hundred paces wide. He dispersed scouts in both directions and they all reported back signalling the region is clear.'

Varus turned back to Vala. 'Satisfied?'

Numonius Vala asked, 'Is there no other way? We will be penned between the mountains on one side and the incline to the high moor on the other?'

The trooper shook his head. 'We found no other route. It is steep and tricky, but the army will have enough room to make its way along the defile.'

As the trooper explained, the rain suddenly got heavier, drenching the already sodden men and eliciting a great groan from the ranks.

Governor Varus looked up to the skies. 'Oh, by the gods, not more rain!

A curse on this forest and its infernal weather. Get me out of this miserable demon-spawned place.' He turned back to Vala. 'Look, we're wasting time. They've scouted the pass correctly. Let us move on!'

Numonius Vala grudgingly nodded his head.

'Good, then we can be making camp by the river before nightfall. Gentlemen, a warm fire and a place to hang our soaking cloaks await. Shall we proceed?'

We all signalled our assent and descended into the forested valley, which was protected from the worst of the weather by steep sides. Only in one direction was it open, to the north-east where a narrow gap stood between the steep banks, but was filled by a swampy morass. I was relieved we needn't travel in that direction, not relishing the thought of being stuck up to my waist in stinking mud, as the rocky trail instead wound through the valley in an easterly direction, clear of scrub and trees.

Lucius Eggius spoke to me as we remounted and rode our horses along the flat narrow path which slowly descended out of the mountains. 'I'll be pleased to get back to Aurorae Novus, I don't mind admitting. I never thought I'd be pleased to see that place again, but this campaign wasn't quite what I expected.'

I looked up at the steep mountainside that rose up to our south and the equally imposing and impregnable steep banks which rose up to the high moor on the northern side and suppressed a shudder, the towering weight of the mountains looming over me making me uncomfortable. 'They never are. Although, in truth, they rarely end like this one – us retreating with our tails between our legs.'

He looked at me earnestly. 'Do you really think that's what we're doing? Should we have stayed and fought?'

I shook my head and chuckled. 'No, of course not. Keep this to yourself, but this whole expedition has been badly conceived. Armies in Germany don't normally spend their time marching in late September – the weather makes it too treacherous. We should have waited until the spring, then we could have given them a good fight.'

I omitted to tell Lucius that I intended to be far away from Germany by the spring, and therefore away from the fighting that lay in prospect in next year's campaign.

Lucius looked over at Governor Varus. 'Do you think Augustus will replace the Governor after this?'

I shook my head. 'No, he'll explain it away somehow. It'll take more than this debacle to remove that stubborn bugger. It's not so terrible a disaster. We've all made it back after all.'

In front of us, the column halted, and I asked nobody in particular, 'What's the hold up?' I looked round at Lucius Eggius and saw that all the colour had drained from his face. He didn't answer, he just pointed his finger to the top of a steep bank that rose in front of our trail, blocking our path and surmounted by a wicker stockade built along a turf palisade. There stood Julius Arminius, my closest friend and King of the Cherusci, and he was flanked to one side by Ewald, high champion of the Cherusci and son of the now deceased High Chieftain Segestes, and to the other by our scout through the mountains, Faramund. Either side of them lay German tribesmen in the thousands – no, in the tens of thousands – trapping us and bottling us up in a cage with only one exit: the way we'd come which even now was being sealed by the forty thousand Angrivarii who'd followed us down the mountain.

Chapter Thirty

Most of the twenty thousand soldiers of our army must have understood immediately what this meant: this was not how a friendly host greeted their allies. Barbarian warriors lined the bank in their thousands and now our attention had been drawn to their position. We noticed other wicker stockades – sturdy barricades built between the trees and camouflaged with mud and autumnal leaves – blocking any other route through the sheer sides of the corridor. Messengers came from the front of the column telling us that the engineers had found that the trail ended here, at this steep incline, whilst centurions all along our column shouted at the men to form up into a defensive line – not an easy task in the confining narrow path in the centre of the ravine.

I, on the other hand, was too stunned to take in what was happening.

My eyes were locked on my childhood friend who stood on top of the hill in full mail shirt and winged helmet, triumph exuding from his stance, oblivious to the rain that poured down on him, and I remembered all that had passed between us. I remembered the golden days of our youth, playing amongst the sun-soaked fields of my father's estate or the marbled colonnades of Rome: always together, always happy, closer than brothers. I remembered our times in Augustus' school, remembered when Julius leapt to my defence when a tutor struck me – for not paying attention to the poetry lesson – and us making a pact afterwards, to always defend each other, no matter what, no matter the consequences. In our childhood, when we weren't at the school, Julius had stayed with my family outside Rome. My younger sister Antonia, when she was no older than six or seven, had once had a crush on him, mooning around after him, to his delight and my annoyance. Even my father had liked him, thinking him a good influence on his sometimes wayward son, buying him his first horse, a young spirited stallion that was probably still stabled on my father's estate.

I remembered our times together in the legions of Syria – both young champions of Rome, heroes to our men, but more importantly to each other. How many times had we fought together, saved each other's lives? Every achievement we had ever strived for we secretly did to impress the other – without each other's acknowledgement, any victory seemed hollow. Was that what he was doing now? Showing off his command of this vast German host to prove to me he could? Surely it couldn't be anything more? Friendships like ours came once in a lifetime; no one could ever take the place of Julius … so why was he standing alongside a known traitor of Rome, in a position of overwhelming tactical superiority, at the head of a vast army several times the size of our own?

Varus was also confused by what was happening. He shouted up at my friend, 'Julius Arminius, what is the meaning of this? Why didn't you send word you would meet us here?'

Julius laughed. 'What? And spoil the surprise? Surely you're glad to see us?'

Governor Varus looked uncertain and stared up at the bank, lined with German warriors in their countless thousands. 'How have you gathered so many warriors? You must have every man of the Cherusci here?'

Julius shook his head. 'Oh, these are not only Cherusci you see, not at all. I have warriors from the Chatti, the Bructeri, even warriors from the Ampsiuarii and the Marsi – it's amazing how far some will travel in the aid of a good cause.'

Varus swallowed hard. 'And what is that cause?'

Julius smiled. 'To rid this forest of undesirables, of course.'

The governor asked hopefully, 'Do you mean the traitor's son you came searching for?'

I nudged my horse next to the Governor's. 'That man next to him is Ewald – the traitor's son.'

Varus stiffened and Julius laughed out loud. 'Oh, this is just perfect. Cassius Aprilis is here at the end to see me fulfil my destiny.'

I was suddenly angry at my friend's flippant tone. 'Oh, and what destiny is that, Julius? The destiny of a traitor?'

Julius turned on me. 'Traitor? Me? I've not betrayed the Cherusci and they are my only concern. But I don't have time to bandy words with you this time, Gaius.'

I spat on the ground. 'And why is that?'

He was too far away for me to see his eyes, but I was certain if I was closer I'd have seen them harden. 'Because it is time for you to die.'

Julius raised his hand and then dropped it, and thousands of light German javelins took flight in the air, and for a brief moment it was as if the entire sky had turned dark with the countless thousands of shafts sailing through it.

Then it was all confusion.

My horse let out a great squeal of pain, reared and then collapsed, throwing me clear. I landed heavily on the ground alongside another man, a junior tribune, who was screaming in pain from a badly broken leg, the bottom of his shinbone twisted at a right angle from the top half. My horse's legs were thrashing alongside me, and I looked over to see the animal had a spear lodged deep into its chest. The distress of the animal, and the screams from the tribune, competed with a cacophony of noise from the wild German tribesmen who shouted and screamed their war chants alongside the clatter of spears striking raised shields and Roman officers shouting orders to their men.

My first instinct should have been to regain my feet, but I was so confused, winded from the fall, covered in mud, bewildered by Julius' betrayal, that I lay there helpless. All around me, horses wheeled and milled in confusion, and it was only luck that prevented my death from one of those iron shod hooves as I lay there stunned.

The tribune was still screaming in pain, but someone came to his aid, and a centurion, from the commander's bodyguards, came over to help me up. 'We must get you to cover, sir.'

I looked at him, and then at my surroundings, and noticed that spears were still striking the ground, not yards from where I lay prone. I nodded to the centurion, who grabbed my arm and dragged me under the shields of legionaries who had constructed a protective shield around Varus and the high command.

Legate Avitus was shouting. 'That traitorous dog! I'll kill that man myself. A slow death. Traitorous viper!'

Governor Varus looked too stunned to speak; like myself, finding it impossible to comprehend that it was Julius Arminius who had led us to this. He simply shook his head in bewilderment.

Spears still struck the legionaries shields, in the most part falling away harmlessly, but occasionally a man would cry out in pain as a spear found a gap in the shields.

Legate Selus shouted over at Varus. 'Governor, what are your orders?'

Varus turned his head to his legate and look confused. 'My orders—'

He never got the chance to finish the sentence, as the sound of the spears striking shields stopped, to be replaced by blood-curdling war cries, as the German tribesmen descended on the Roman column in their thousands.

They came from gaps which were opened in the stockades, like a great swarm of ants, and came running down the steep side of the bank to hack and chop at the disorganised Roman ranks with spears or long knives, hacking to pieces any units that found themselves outside the main body of men.

'Form a shield wall, form a shield wall!' the cry went along the Roman ranks, as centurions desperately tried to push the men into a cohesive defensive line to repulse the German tribesmen's attack.

I looked up at the bank, swarming with enemy warriors, and felt complete terror. Not since Western-Gate Pass had I felt such terror, as the full scale of the German tribes became clear – they numbered in their thousands; the whole mountainside seemed filled with them, how could you ever estimate how many when the whole bank was teeming with so many warriors? 'By the gods, how will any of us survive this?' I asked out loud.

'By doing our jobs!' shouted a man to my left, who ran up and started issuing orders immediately. It was Numonius Vala. 'Cassius, go see to the end of the column. Get all those units back into the main body.' He turned to Varus. 'My lord, we need to pull all the units together. We are all too strung out. We need to form a defensive base.'

Varus nodded mutely, before finding his voice. 'Yes, yes, Numonius. Do what you think is best. Bring the force together.'

Then we felt a loud thunderclap, as thousands of warriors clashed their shields against our shield wall, and the Roman line almost buckled as the sheer force of thousands of Germans struck home against our precariously thin line of soldiers who desperately tried to hold back the huge tide of men against them. The Germans were hacking and slashing at our line with ferocious savagery, hatred screaming from their lips, as if pure hatred was enough alone to overwhelm our ranks. We were being assailed all along our hastily constructed line, and I felt my bowels turn to liquid.

What could I do? I'd run if there were anywhere to run to, but we were surrounded, assailed on all sides. My cowardice wasn't going to get me out of this one; finally my luck had run out, and even though and my entire being was shaken by Julius' betrayal and my own terror, I knew it was now a case of fighting for my life. The only direction I'd been given had been from Numonius Vala, so I followed my orders and went to see how the rest of the column was faring.

I ran down the column, along ranks of frightened men rushing to reinforce our line. The narrow stretch of land at the centre of the pass where our army was trapped was less than two hundred paces wide, which made it difficult for legions to deploy in their orthodox positions. Nevertheless, if the army's commanders were at a loss at how to react to the German tribesmen's attack, the same could not be said of its centurions, who with practised ease formed the men of the line into three maniples: the first rank, the *principes,* the 'best men' to take the full assault of the tribesmen, with shield and drawn *gladius*, were backed up by the second rank of *hastati,* who used their heavy javelin *pila* to great effect against the disorganised ranks of their attackers. Behind these two ranks lay the third tier, the *triarii*, all veterans equipped with thrusting spears, ready to fill any gaps in the line left by casualties. It was a classic Roman line, and if Julius thought our three legions were just going to lie down and die, these men of steel were going to show him that no Roman army ever died easily, no matter how well-orchestrated the ambush.

The Roman legionaries were making a bloody ruin of the front rank of attacking tribesmen, who were virtually unarmoured except for their wooden shields and spears. However, for each tribesman who fell, there was a multitude to take their place, and the legionaries were being hard pushed to repulse the sheer ferocity of the attack.

In my terrified state, I tried to console myself that the Roman lines were at least holding, that this unexpected attack hadn't shaken the iron discipline of the men, that the perfect organisation of the legions meant the men were ready to take on this coalition of traitorous tribes, and we weren't finished just yet.

As I ran down the centre of our column, making my way through the lighter units of slingers and archers who were deploying behind the maniples to rain their weapons down on the attackers, I saw the steely resolve of the men and felt shame that these men had been let down by their commanders, of which I was one, and led into this death trap. How could we have been so stupid? I could blame Varus, but ultimately I had been deceived by Julius too – surely I, who'd known Julius from childhood, should have seen this coming? And yet, I hadn't. Julius' betrayal was as unexpected as it was ruthless.

The screams and shouting of the men, over the clashing of arms, brought me back to my personal nightmare of Western-Gate Pass. Once again, we were trapped against a vastly superior host, only this time the scale was so much greater. This time it wasn't just one cohort of men trapped by an avalanche of attacking tribesmen, but three whole legions, twenty thousand men, caught in the eye of this ferocious storm. There would be no relief force to save us this time, as there wasn't another Roman force within a hundred miles of here.

As I approached the end of our column, I saw we weren't faring so well. Here the line was also under attack but our defence was more ragged, as civilians and cavalry were bunching up and destroying the cohesion of the disciplined Roman lines. The traditional role of the auxiliary cavalry was to form the wings of the army, to stop it from being outflanked, but in this situation, where we'd been caught on the march, the cavalry was virtually useless. We were already surrounded, and the Angrivarii, who had followed us down the mountain, were now attacking the rear guard of the army, forcing the Roman units back into a confused mass of men. Horses, civilians and Roman legionaries were all mixed together in a confused huddle, and it was only because the Angrivarii hadn't yet had time to form into a battle line of sufficient numbers that our army's rear hadn't collapsed entirely.

I saw Macarius, standing out from the other riders by his telltale helmet, and ran over to the Thracian cavalry commander. 'Macarius, what in Hades are your men doing here?'

Macarius turned to me, his face unreadable from his helmet's full faceplate. 'We need to force back these savages, sir!'

I grabbed hold of his horse's bridle. 'You can't help here, Macarius, you need to pull your men back.'

'But we can't, Cassius, the army will be cut off if I do that!' his shrill voice told me that Macarius at least understood the peril of our situation.

I shook my head. 'We're already cut off. The whole of the Angrivarii tribe is about to fall on our position here. We can only hold them if we form the legions into a defensive line.'

Macarius looked around at the battle, saw the ever-increasing numbers of Angrivarii forming and realised the truth of my words. 'But where can my men go?'

I looked around and tried to assess the situation, but there were no easy answers. 'Take your horsemen up through the centre of our lines. Dismount and lead your horses and take the civilians with you.'

Macarius shook his head. 'But that will leave my cavalry completely impotent. We can't fight behind defensive lines.'

I nodded my understanding. 'I know, Macarius, but unless you vacate this position, the whole rear of the army will collapse. We'll be hacked to pieces deployed like this.'

Macarius removed his helmet, and I saw tears in his eyes. 'I understand, Cassius. I'll lead the men out of here.'

I put my hand on his arm to thank him. I knew how hard this must be for him. I was asking him to abandon our last gateway out of this trap. Once he moved his horsemen back, we would effectively be fighting in a defensive square, surrounded on all sides with no chance of escape. It was said that Julius Caesar had once let his army be surrounded at the Battle of Ruspina so his legions could then break out and divide the enemy line, but neither of us were going to confuse

Roman Mask

Varus' incompetence with Julius' Caesar's brilliance. We were being forced into a completely defensive position, one without any chance of us dictating and maintaining tactical superiority over the enemy. Where Macarius' cavalry could normally be expected to fight on the left or right of our army, protecting our flanks, his cavalry would now be redundant in this fight; he and his men would have to watch others fight, whilst they looked on helpless. It was terrible what I was asking him to do, but I knew we had no choice. 'Thank you, Macarius.'

Macarius' Thracians pulled back and led the civilians away from the imperilled rear of the army. I saw Macarius himself dismount and take a babe from the arms of a mother, who was struggling through the thick cloying mud of the trail, and pull her away from the fighting. Around them, civilians ran in fear, faces white and eyes wild, prepared to go anywhere that was away from the howling hordes of the Angrivarii, little knowing that I'd just cut off their last chance of escape.

I shook my head, putting the civilians out of my mind, and turned my attention back to the army's rear, which was coming under renewed attack from the Angrivarii, who were now formed into large enough numbers to overwhelm the ragged Roman line. The centurions had done an adequate job sealing the rear of the trail so quickly, pulling the legionaries into three-tiered maniples at such short notice, but the legionaries were too bunched together, crushed together by the narrowness of the trail. This was hindering the legionaries' ability to fight, the front of each line being more a contest of brute strength as the two lines heaved against one another. More Angrivarii piled in to the rear of their ranks, pushing our line inexorably backwards.

I ran over and grabbed the arm of a senior centurion who was barking orders at the rear of his men, telling them to keep their formation. He spun round, spat on the ground, and shouted at me, 'Who, by the gods, are you?'

I ignored his ill temper; under the circumstances it was understandable. 'I'm Tribune Cassius Aprilis. Are you in command here?'

He looked me up and down, his old grizzled face showing nothing but scorn. 'As much as anyone is.'

There was no time for niceties. 'The line is about to collapse. We will all be dead unless we do something now. I'm taking command. Now, what is your name?'

The centurion looked surprised but answered quickly enough, '*Pilus Prior* Aurelius, sir.' He stood up straight, relieved at my no-nonsense manner; this is what soldiers of the line wanted from their commanders, a simple line of authority to obey. 'We're struggling to contain them, tribune. I'm not sure if we can hold them. Do you wish us to fall back?'

I shook my head. 'We have nowhere to fall back to, the entire column is under attack. We either hold them here, or we all die. It is that simple.'

Centurion Aurelius' eyes widened in shock. He was obviously so involved with the fight here that he hadn't realised the rest of the army was in a similar predicament. 'But my men can't hold them, sir.'

I looked over at the carnage, as wave upon wave of snarling Angrivarii were piling into the clustered ranks of the Roman soldiers. 'That is because the men are deployed too closely together, they can't use their weapons effectively. We need to widen the line … beside that rocky outcrop,' I pointed out rocks to the right side of the trail a short distance in front of the struggling legionaries, 'and pull the other men back into a reserve. The only way to stop the Angrivarii coming at us is to cut down their leading ranks.'

Aurelius swallowed hard; he knew how dangerous a manoeuvre it was I was suggesting. As the men redeployed, gaps could appear in the line which the Angrivarii could come streaming through. To his credit, he simply saluted and answered. 'I'll pull the eleventh cohort back. They can be your reserve. Once you have them formed up, be ready to plug any gaps in the line as I widen it. Some are bound to open – my men are good, but they've never seen anything like this before, sir.'

I nodded. 'None of us have, centurion. Proceed with your orders.'

The five hundred men of the XI cohort were ordered to fall back and reform behind the line, where I quickly explained their role to their senior centurion. 'We're going to widen the line, be ready to charge on my orders.'

Now we came to the most dangerous part of my plan, and I signalled to the trumpeter to blow the order for extending the line. It was a risky procedure achieved by reducing the depth of the files and bringing in men forward between them. It was both time-consuming and hazardous, but the right of the line managed to successfully anchor itself to the rocky outcrop to the right of the trail. As the line widened, the legionaries were becoming far more effective with their weapons and were using their *gladius'* to great effect against the German tribesmen, cutting them down, as their weapon arms were freed up by the increased space. But just as I thought we'd got away with it, disaster struck; two of the units, probably made up of less experienced green troops, lost cohesion as they tried to open the ranks, and the Angrivarii leapt upon this break in the line and rushed into it, killing any of the unfortunate legionaries who happened to get separated from their comrades and were left stranded in the opening. There was no time to lose; it wasn't bravery that led to my actions now, but simple desperation. I drew my *gladius* and shouted,

'Now men, follow me!' and charged into the gap followed by the five-hundred-strong reserve.

We fought in a loose formation, not the accustomed shield wall of the legions. This type of fighting wasn't from the army manual, but a last desperate throw of the dice to try and plug the gap in the line and save the rear of the army from annihilation. A great bearded monster appeared before me and thrust his spear at my gut. My *gladius* deflected the spearhead from my body, and I followed this up by head-butting the warrior in the face before turning my blade round and thrusting it into his throat. Another man took his place, and I swerved away from a clumsy attack with a long iron *sax* blade and buried my *gladius* deep into his soft belly, up to his heart. I twisted my blade as I tried to free it from his flesh, but he was a heavy-set man and collapsed on top of me, forcing me to the ground under his considerable weight. I heaved the dead man off me, but saw another warrior over me, a triumphant grin on his open mouth as he raised his spear for the killing thrust that would end my life. Before he struck, his head rocked backwards sharply as a Roman *pilum* struck him a fatal blow, burying itself in his eye and through to the brain behind. He fell away, and I leapt to my feet, not believing that I was still alive. I was breathing heavily, more from fear than exertion, but suddenly legionaries were either side of me as the line reformed and the legions pushed back the encroaching Angrivarii.

I let the men move forward without me, and I knelt down in relief as the immediate danger passed and regathered my thoughts. I felt a hand on my shoulder and looked up to see the ugly grizzled face of centurion Aurelius, who spoke to me. 'You did well, the line will hold now – look!'

I stood up and surveyed the battle line. The triple Roman line was now deployed correctly, in a paving stone formation, which left enough room in between the maniples for replacing exhausted troops and gave the three ranks enough space to fight as they had been trained in endless hours on the training yard. The effect was immediate, whole lines of Angrivarii were now falling to the trained blades of the Roman soldiers, and the less brave of the German tribesmen were inching away from the remorseless slaughter, as the rest were struck down in scores.

I resheaved my blade, which wasn't easy as my hand trembled so much; to obscure my difficulty I spoke to Aurelius in a gruff tone. 'Make sure the men don't get carried away. Keep them in good order.'

Saying such a thing to a centurion was tantamount to telling him how to wipe his own arse, but Aurelius didn't seem to care at this time. 'Don't worry, sir, we won't let you down. The line will hold. You've made sure of that. Will you be remaining in command?'

Remain in command? Was that really what I'd done? Taken command of the army's rear guard ... I'd been ordered only to report on the column's situation. I'd better get back and inform Varus. I shook my head. 'No, you'll be alright. Keep on rotating the men away from the front and keep a good reserve fresh. This doesn't look like ending anytime soon.'

Centurion Aurelius saluted, then nodded in respect, before turning back to the battle line. That man would follow me to Hades now, I thought, for all the good it would do him. I may have saved the rear from collapse, but we were now completely bottled in. Unless we found a way out of this trap, death was what awaited us all.

I quickly made my way up the column, passing the eagle of the XVII legion that was being held by the standard bearer and surrounded by veterans. As soon as the army came under attack, the eagle party would have left their position at the head of the column to be closer to their men and inspire the soldiers who fought for the glory of that standard. Their faces were grim but determined, the personification of Roman professional pride. 'We're not done yet!' their presence told, and the men cheered as they once again saw their eagle raised behind them.

All very well, I thought, but that didn't give us a way out of this mess. I looked around at our column, attacked from both front and rear, the whole hillside covered with German warriors, and prayed to all the gods that we'd be able to hold them. The German tribes were attacking in waves, coming in vast numbers to assail our ranks, and then retreating under the cover of a volley of spears from the warriors waiting behind the stockades; the fatigued warriors would then pass behind the stockades and be replaced by fresh warriors, who charged down the incline, and our line would reverberate again to the clash of arms. The only area where the attack was not coming from was the north-east, through the swamp-filled area I'd noticed as we entered the valley: could this be our way out of here? I stopped to take a look at this swamp – great pools of stagnant standing water interspersed between decaying trees, leading to the high moor which looked to be blessedly free of the forest. Marching the men through the narrow swamplands wouldn't be easy. It would prove impossible to keep any formation as the men waded and half swam through the stinking mess, but if beyond lay salvation, then why not? I imagined us making our way through there, up to the moor, but then something caught my eye through the trees – movement, fast movement, almost certainly cavalry, and as our entire force was accounted for, that meant enemy cavalry. Of course, why would Julius go to all this trouble to ambush us here, only to leave a back door for us to escape from? His cavalry were useless to him in the ambush, so he would have massed all his mounted troops here, ready to run down any Roman units that managed to emerge from the swamp. It wouldn't be difficult, the edge the Roman legions held over the barbarian was our discipline and our rigid shield walls, but taking us through that morass would make keeping any cohesion impossible. We'd be cut down as soon as we made it out of the stagnant stinking waters into the sun. This way was a trap just as much as the one we'd unwittingly walked directly into.

I shook my head in despair and continued up the column until I came on to the command group, shielded by their elite bodyguard. Once again they were arguing what was best to be done.

Varus' eyes looked sunken, and his flesh looked pallid, but his voice was still firm. 'Can we not build a defensive stockade? Like we did further up the mountains? Build a camp we can retreat into?'

Camp Praefect Ceionius answered, 'That's impossible this time. For that we need good timber from stout trees.'

Varus stared at Ceionius. 'Well? We're in the middle of a forest, how can that be a problem?'

Ceionius explained. 'Look at the trees along this trail, they are little better than scrub. The giant pines we need to build a stockade are all along the valleys' crest, which is also where the enemy is ...'

Legate Selus asked, 'Couldn't we still dig a trench and make a turf palisade?'

Avitus pointed out the obvious. 'To do this we'd still need to disengage from the German tribes long enough to dig one. Do you think they're going to helpfully call the attack off until we're ready?'

Numonius Vala shook his head. 'Building any sort of defensive structure isn't going to get us out of this. We need to go on to the offensive.'

Varus raised his hand to quieten Vala. 'We need to make sure the column is secured first, before we can talk of going on the attack. Does anyone know how the rear is faring?'

I spoke up. 'The rear is secured, although we are now completely cut off. All along the column the legions are holding off the attack, but they are under intense pressure.'

Varus cocked his head. 'Cassius, about time you joined us. Where have you been? This is no time to be going absent.'

I ground my teeth and explained. 'I was following my orders and seeing how the column was faring, and it's not good. The immediate danger is passed. The legions are not going to fold anywhere I can see along the line, but for how long can they hold off so many warriors?'

Varus shook his head in dismay. 'Do we have an idea of their numbers yet?'

Avitus answered. 'Impossible to say. Arminius claimed to have warriors from virtually all of the tribes in the region. If so, we could be outnumbered by at least four or five to one. All I know is that I have never seen so many enemy warriors in one place, and their numbers could be increasing the longer this goes on, as others find out about our unfortunate position.'

Numonius Vala slapped his fist into his hand. 'So we must attack. The longer we stay here, the weaker we get, whilst they grow in strength.'

Varus looked up at the hillside. 'I don't fancy our chances fighting up such a steep incline. Is there no other alternative?'

With sunken heart I explained what I'd seen on the way back from the rear. 'There is a flat swamp to the north-east leading to a high plain.'

Varus turned to me with hope. 'Well, that's it then!'

I shook my head. 'I wish it were so, but the ground beyond looks to be full of German cavalry. We'd be cut to pieces as we emerged from the swamp.'

Governor Varus bowed his head in despair. 'I should have known there would be no easy way out.'

Numonius Vala spoke up. 'The route to the north-east is a death trap; my scouts have already confirmed this. Let me take an attack against the centre of their line – it is our only option.'

Varus spoke softly. 'Casualties will be high making such a move.'

Vala lost his temper. 'Casualties are already high. Have you any idea how many men I've already lost since you took us into this region of Hades?'

Governor Varus looked stung. 'Are you blaming me for this? How dare you!'

Vala spat on the ground. 'I told you to scout the area properly, but you were too intent on getting back and making your excuses to the Senate!'

I thought Varus would strike Numonius Vala, but Legate Avitus got between them and said, 'This is getting us nowhere, we were all fooled by Arminius, not just the governor. Blaming each other isn't going to help. Numonius, make your attack, take whatever units you think appropriate. Governor, do you agree?'

Varus turned his back on the command group, but nodded in agreement. The governor said no more, nursing the hurt Numonius had dealt him: that this entire fiasco was all his fault. He didn't even turn his head when we all left him to prepare for the attack; Vala, Selus and Avitus talking animatedly about how it should proceed as we walked down the column behind the thin Roman lines, enemy warriors not thirty paces away.

Vala shouted over the screaming sound of the battle. 'I'll take cohorts from my own Eighteenth for the main attack, but I'll need some support from the archers and slingers.'

Avitus agreed. 'You'll have them. Anything else?'

Numonius Vala shielded his eyes as he looked up at the German tribe's position. 'We'll construct some scaling ladders to assail those stockades, but I'll also take some of Ceionius' engineers – they're not only the best at constructing stockades, they're also adept at dismantling them. Let's see if they can undermine those fortifications and pull them down from under them. I doubt Julius will expect that.'

Selus put both his hands on his hips. 'I've never known the German tribes to use fortifications like these before.'

I grunted. 'That's because they've never had a leader before to teach them how. Julius is Roman trained. He has learnt well the lessons Rome has taught him.'

Avitus and Selus both nodded their agreement, whilst Ceionius asked wistfully, 'How could we have been so blind?'

No one wanted to answer that question, least of all myself.

Vala shook his head, moving the conversation on. 'I could do with some artillery to weaken their position first, but damn Varus, he burnt it all before we left.'

Selus raised his hand. 'No good worrying about what we don't have. Let's concentrate on what we do.'

Numonius turned and looked at us. 'Yes, I agree. I shouldn't have spoken to the governor as I did. He won't forget it.'

Avitus waved away his concern. 'Don't worry about that now. Make your attack and get us out of this mess and all will be forgotten, trust me.' He smiled and clasped Vala on the shoulder. 'May the gods protect you, Vala. If the attack is successful, we'll follow with all our strength. The gods protect this enterprise.'

Chapter Thirty-one

Vala waited until the current attackers wore themselves out against the shield wall of our legions; the giant bearded warriors hurled themselves against our blades with fanatical bravery, before they started to withdraw under the cover of a volley of spears from above. So many spears. They must have been stockpiling them all summer for this. Our *pila* had run out long ago, our soldiers being forced to throw back the unfamiliar German javelins which were hard for us to use effectively from our position throwing uphill.

The Roman lines lifted their shields to protect themselves against the hail of missiles, and I cowered behind the large shields of the legionaries who were protecting the command group where all the senior commanders stood to watch our attack – except Numonius Vala, who was leading the attack personally. We'd all tried to dissuade him, but he wanted to have a good look at those stockades first hand, and that meant joining the attack himself.

I stood next to Governor Varus, face firm but deep worry lines creasing his sunken eyes. His authority was gradually being degraded, his legates making decisions without consulting him first, but he still stood straight, in his full armour and helmet, trying to show to the troops that he remained in command.

I ignored him. I was much more interested in the welfare of Numonius Vala and his attack on which so much depended. The rain finally let up, and this cheered the men readying themselves for the attack, being seen as a good omen for the impending struggle. Four cohorts would begin making the assault: the XVIII legion's crack troops, supplemented by lighter troops armed with slings and bows. They would also lead the pack mules carrying the tools for engineers to undermine the tribes' stockades. The men waited tensely as the first set of spears from the tribes banged against the raised shields, and then a trumpet sounded and the Roman lines parted allowing the four cohorts to march up the steep hillside, each in *testudo* formation. Their shields were covering every part of the men underneath as they pursued the retreating tribesmen up the hill in the archetypal tortoise formation. Missiles rained down on the raised shields but the *testudos* remained firm and though progress was slow up the muddy bank, before long they reached the top as the German tribesmen disappeared between gaps in the stockades, which were then quickly sealed.

I heard Avitus over to my right. 'Well done, Vala. You're at the top now. Let's see what you can do to those fortifications.'

Two *testudos* attacked a separate section of the stockade each: the first formation shielding scaling ladders which were held fast against the palisades, and the further rear ranks kneeling down to produce a sloping ramp of shields which led to the top of the wooden stockades. This made a slope by which the second cohort could attack up, brave men running up the sloping shields and attacking the German tribesmen who waited atop the ramparts.

The German tribes tried to counter this attack by releasing warriors from other sections of the lines to attack the *testudos* from the base, but we'd been expecting this, and units from Selus' XIX dispersed to head off these attacks.

'Is it going well?' asked Lucius Eggius nervously. The strain of the last day or so hadn't been easy on the young tribune, who had found the relentless assault terrifying and a far cry from his childhood imaginings of an ever-victorious Roman army.

I shrugged. 'So far ...'

Varus answered for me. 'Yes, don't worry, Lucius. All will be well. Our troops have already made it to the top of their fortifications. It won't be long until we have a path out of here.'

Roman legionaries certainly had made it to the top of the stockades, but were being met by a large number of warriors and were unable to clear the ramparts of the enemy. Every so often a legionary would clear the palisade, but they were soon cut down by the tribesmen. The fighting continued on the tops of their palisades for what seemed an eternity, but no headway was being made by the attacking units.

Legate Selus came over to Varus. 'There's too many of them. We need to send reinforcements. I'll send more from my Nineteenth.'

Varus ignored the fact that Selus has told him what he was about to do, rather than asking, and said, 'Very well. Do what you think is best. This attack had better be successful. We've invested too much of our strength in it already.'

Fresh units broke forward from our lines, but it was too late for one of the two attacks, who were already falling back after taking heavy losses. The stockades stood firm, adorned with jeering tribesmen, shaking their spears and shields in victory.

The reinforcements made towards the other stockade, and once again made an attack up the sloping shields of the *testudo*. They attacked in force, knowing that they must break through the German warriors if they were to have any chance of surviving. Again and again they struck against the implacable wall of German warriors who'd gathered in strength at the palisades summit. It became confused at the top, difficult to tell who was in the ascendancy, as struggling warriors fought for supremacy.

The tension for us watching was unbearable. Solid veterans, men used to wars and campaigns in far distant lands, had tears in their eyes as they witnessed the suicidal bravery of our comrades making attack after attack as they strove to usurp the tribesmen from their lofty position. Eventually a Roman trumpet blared from the top of the slope.

'What's that?' asked Lucius.

I swallowed hard. 'Vala is calling the men back.'

Varus was enraged. 'What! He can't call them back! The coward! How can he call off the attack now?'

Selus turned to the governor. 'Numonius Vala is no coward, sir. If he has called off the attack, it is for a good reason.'

Varus wasn't going to be placated so easily. 'But he can't! This attack must succeed. Send more men. Take over command from him.'

Avitus joined us. 'It is too late for that. The *testudo* has already disengaged from the wall.'

Varus' face was bright red with anger. 'That fool! I'll have his head for this!'

I looked up the slope. Something was strange. 'I don't think this is over. Look, Governor!'

The *testudo* hadn't retreated down the slope as we'd expected but stopped only a score of paces from the base of the stockade. A few Romans still ran around at the base, although what they were doing, I couldn't tell. Suddenly, the entire section of stockade collapsed, burying a poor unfortunate pack animal who'd been left at the foot of the wooden fortification. The entire army cheered as they saw one of the barricades to their freedom come crashing down in a heap of timber and sliding mud.

I clapped my hands and shouted. 'Of course! The sappers! They've successfully undermined the stockade. Vala said he'd try that. He must have known it was about to collapse and called his men back to stop them being crushed! The gods give favour to him!'

The entire Roman army was cheering and celebrating. Some men went down on their knees to give thanks, whilst other danced in circles, or threw their helmets in the air in thanks to the gods, and to Numonius Vala. Even Governor Varus laughed out loud in delight, and Tribune Lucius wept tears of joy.

Our celebrations were short-lived.

The four original cohorts, and the two from the reinforcements, abandoned their *testudo* formation and reformed into a dense *cuneus* 'pig's head' formation where the ranks were tightly formed with two leading cohorts slightly in front of the four others to either side. This was an attacking move, a formation used to break through a line of defenders – what we all expected to be waiting behind the fallen stockade.

We were wrong. Instead of lining up in a thin line on the crest of the banks, thousands of warriors streamed through the opening in the palisade and enveloped our formation like a swarm of stinging bees.

'By the gods,' exclaimed Varus, and we all looked up at what was happening in disbelief.

Their numbers were incredible. We'd underestimated how quickly Julius was able to manoeuvre his troops over to the breach in the line and turn defence into attack. Ten ... twenty thousand warriors, maybe more, streamed out of the opening in the line and fell on the six Roman cohorts who were now fighting desperately for their lives.

Avitus was shouting. 'Form up the reserve. We'll need to reinforce them quickly!'

Lucius replied, shouting in terror. 'It's too late for that! Look!'

If the six cohorts had been on level ground, they may have been able to keep their formation and return to the rest of the army without too many loses, despite being heavily outnumbered – the legions were used to being outnumbered – but they weren't on level ground. They held a precarious foothold on a very steep muddy incline, and the sheer weight of the attacking tribesmen was inexorably pushing the cohorts down the hill. The legionaries at the back desperately tried to support their comrades from behind, but it was a losing battle and the tight ranks of the legionaries soon disintegrated into a disorganised mass of men. Now the German tribesmen held all the advantages. They held the higher ground, and, being less heavily armoured, found it is easier to keep their footing on the treacherously slippery bank.

In a frighteningly short amount of time, the battle on the hill turned into a rout, and the remaining legionaries, those that hadn't already been hacked to pieces by the marauding tribesmen, turned tail and ran back to the safety of our defensive lines.

Not many made it. The most vulnerable time for any body of men, Roman or not, was when they broke. As soon as they turned to run, the tribesmen ran them down mercilessly, stabbing them in the backs with their javelins or dismembering them with their long *sax* blades. It was a sickening sight, something no man there could ever forget. Six cohorts – three thousand men – all butchered before our eyes, and us powerless to do anything to help them. To send more men out there would mean their deaths as well, we all knew it, but it was little consolation when you heard the screams of our men and their pleading for mercy. They received none from the tribesmen, who were gorging themselves in a triumphant dance of death.

A handful of our troops made it back, and that was only because the section of the line adjacent to them disobeyed their orders and launched an unplanned attack against the pursuing tribesmen, who backed off quickly, being content to find easier pickings amongst the remnants of our destroyed cohorts. Less than three hundred men out of the three thousand made it back to the lines, but the gods give favour, Numonius Vala was one of them.

He was passed through quickly to our command group, whereby he ran up and knelt to Governor Varus. He was covered in mud and blood, whether his or someone else's it was impossible to tell. His eyes looked haunted – I'd seen that look before, but not since Western-Gate Pass. It was the look of a man who'd seen more than any man should. 'I regret to inform you that our attack has failed, my lord. I take full responsibility for this disaster.'

Avitus put a hand on his shoulder. 'Don't be a fool man. No one could have done more. The attack had to be tried. We needed to breech those stockades.'

Selus added. 'And you managed to pull down one of the barricades. That is something—'

Vala bowed his head to the ground. 'But at what cost. I have lost so many men. They died in their thousands.'

We all looked to see the reaction of Governor Varus, but he looked too stunned to say anything. Eventually he looked up from the forlorn figure of Numonius Vala to the rest of his commanders. 'Check the defences of the rest of the legions. I need to retire for a while to think … please don't disturb me.'

He then turned and walked away, leaving us all speechless.

Eventually, I broke the silence and helped Vala to his feet. 'Come on, Numonius. You need to get back to your Eighteenth. They still need you.'

Vala nodded his head and got to his feet.

I whispered to him. 'Time to grieve later. Now is the time for the living.

See to your men first. Worry about the dead afterwards.'

The commanders all left to see to their units. We knew what fate awaited us now if we failed to hold back the barbarian hordes: we'd seen it with our own eyes.

Some in the army hoped that the night would bring a respite from the attacks, but those hopes were soon dashed when nightfall came. The German tribes set fire to great bales of straw and rolled them down the hill, before attacking in droves, lit up by the flames.

Despite regularly rotating the men at the front line, our troops were now exhausted by repulsing attack after attack. These terrifying night attacks sapped the will of our troops, who were struggling with fatigue as well as the fear of where the next attack was coming from. I felt the men were only managing to keep going through sheer desperation now, but time and again they managed to stand strong, with drawn *gladius* and shield, and turned back the incoming tide of warriors.

Halfway through the night, disaster struck. Some burning straw from the bales must have floated over to where our cavalry's horses were picketed. It set fire to the last remains of the horses' fodder and that panicked the horses. Stampeding horses ran everywhere, pulling men out of position and disrupting our defensive formations. The tribesmen ruthlessly exploited the gaps in our lines and made a bloody ruin of several sections of our column. We eventually managed to get the horses under control, but not before hundreds, if not thousands, had been killed by the attacking tribesmen.

It was cold and the rain returned when the sky finally turned a pale grey in the morning light, and I knew that, like a wounded animal, the strength was draining from our legions. We'd lost men beyond counting in the night attacks, and those who still remained standing were too exhausted to hold out much longer. We'd killed tribesmen in their thousands, but it didn't look like having an impact on their vast numbers, who still managed to fill the hillside with warriors looking fresh as newborn colts. I knew that time was running out for our beleaguered army.

Some of the civilians obviously thought the same, and broke out from our lines and tried to surrender to the German tribesmen. It did them no good. They were butchered before our eyes, just as the Roman soldiers had been on the hill. The German tribes had no mercy. They wanted us all dead.

With a heavy heart, I made my way to the command group, where we were going to decide what to do next. I trekked up the muddy trail from my position at the rear of the column and walked up to a raised fold of land the army commanders had taken to use to survey the battle; it gave a good overview of our position, but was far enough back from the German positions to be free of the enemy javelins which fell on the rest of the army.

Unsurprisingly, Governor Varus and Legate Vala were arguing.

Vala spoke in a harsh growl, his voice almost horse from a day and night of shouting orders. 'I don't want to lose the cavalry either, but we have no choice. We need to get the horses from underfoot. They were almost the end of us last night.'

Governor Varus looked around at the rest of us – Legates Selus, Avitus, Praefect Ceionius, Tribune Lucius Eggius and I – and almost pleaded. 'But we'll need them once we break out of this encirclement. How else will we prevent the tribesmen running us down piece by piece? We'll need them to provide cover as we escape!'

I knew what Varus was thinking. Even if we were to make it out of this valley, the legions were now in such a bad condition it was unlikely they could manage a fighting retreat through the hazardous terrain of the forest. Instead it would have to be a race to the river, or some open land where the legions could regroup and rally. For a man of Varus' age, without the aid of horses or the cavalry, it looked like a death sentence.

Vala wasn't having any of it, however. 'Once we break out of this encirclement? If we don't get the horses from underfoot, there'll be no army left to escape. They're disrupting our lines. The tribesmen have realised this, and they are going to target them each time they attack. We must act now.'

Varus snapped back. 'And how do you propose to get them from underfoot?'

Vala stood up straight, 'We have only two options. We either slaughter the horses where they stand—'

Varus scoffed. 'Waste my only cavalry by my own hand? I think not!'

Vala ground his teeth. 'Or we ask them to break out through the narrow corridor to the north-east, through the swampy terrain.'

Varus eyes popped out at this. 'But you said yourself that that path was a death trap.'

In our desperation we'd tried sending a cohort through this area. They'd virtually had to swim their way out, but the enemy cavalry had been waiting at the other end for them and had cut down the few who made it out from the swamp, the others retreating back to our lines.

Vala looked at the ground, as if what he said next was difficult. 'The horses may fair better through that terrain and make a break for it. Their chances are slim, granted, but it is time for tough decisions.'

I didn't like the sound of that. I didn't want Macarius and his men being sent to their almost certain deaths because they were in the way. I spoke up. 'We can't send them that route. They'll be killed to a man. We can't throw away so many lives. Kill the damn horses, if need be. At least then the Thracians will stand the same chances we have.'

Governor Varus dug his heels in. 'I told you. I'll not throw away my only cavalry without at least trying them against the enemy.'

I shook my head. 'But Macarius is an inexperienced commander. He has a big heart, but he is rash and untested in war. You can't expect him to lead this suicide mission.'

Legate Vala said in a sympathetic voice, 'It is sad, Cassius, but it must be done. A lot of commanders have had to grow up quickly in this battle.' Vala then made a mistake, by adding, 'If he falls, his death will be on the hands of those who sent him into this pit of Hades, not yours.'

Governor Varus wasn't slow to take the point of that last barb and blasted, 'You mean my hands, don't you? You conceited ass!' Legate Avitus had to restrain the governor, who looked as though he wanted to hit Vala.

Numonius Vala realised he may have gone too far and backtracked. 'The entire command structure needs to take responsibility. I make no accusation.'

Varus wasn't going to be placated so easily. 'Ha! For now! As soon as we get back to Rome, you will – you all will. I know it. Don't think I don't!'

This stunned us all, not least Vala. 'You're worried about what they'll say in Rome? Have a look around you, Quinctilius. Your men are dying, dying in their thousands. What chance do any of us have of seeing Rome again after your actions? I curse the day I had to take my first orders from you.'

Varus blasted back at him. 'Well, I curse the day I had to take you under my command, undermining my authority at every turn. Well, you won't have to worry about it much longer, if that is your wish. You say this Macarius is inexperienced leading his men? Well you can show him how. You can lead the cavalry out – make a break for freedom. One way or another, I'll be free of you at least.'

Legate Selus was the first to jump to Vala's defence. 'You can't do that governor. We need Numonius. He is our most experienced combat commander.'

Varus would not be turned. 'All the more reason to send him on this important mission. Who better to lead the cavalry?'

Even Legate Avitus was shaking his head in disbelief. 'But he is needed to lead the Eighteenth.'

Varus crossed his arms, determination beading his brow. 'His lead tribune, Maximinus, can take his place, that's what he's there for.'

Numonius Vala interrupted. 'He's dead.' Then he added with contempt dripping from each word, 'He died when my legion tried to break out of this hole you put us in.'

Varus momentarily looked uncertain, but knew he could not back down now. 'Replace him with who you will, but I want you leading that cavalry. You had better make your arrangements.'

Governor Varus strode off, and left the rest of his command speechless at his passing, this final vindictive act stripping any remaining vestiges of respect we might have still held for him.

There had been no more loyal a servant to the governor over the summer than his lead legate, Avitus, but it was he who spoke first. 'We could take command from him. He has brought it on himself – none will blame us.'

Legate Selus nodded in agreement.

Numonius Vala shook his head. 'No, I'm afraid not, my friends. The courage of our men is hanging by threads. If we were to start fighting each other and depose our leader now, it'll collapse entirely. However unwarranted that belief, a lot of the men still believe in him. I'll not take that away from them. Not now, not in what is their greatest time of peril. I'll lead the cavalry. My chances are slim, but so are all of ours.'

Legate Avitus nodded and clapped Vala on the shoulder, saluting his bravery, as a tear rolled down his cheek. 'Who do you wish to take command of the Eighteenth?'

Numonius Vala turned to me. 'Cassius, the men know you and trust you. Take command of my boys and get them home safely. If there is any way out of this, you'll find it for them, I know.'

I swallowed hard. 'It'll be an honour, Numonius. I'll never make half the legate you are.' I didn't know what else to say. Here it finally was, command of my own legion; for all my early life that had been the dream, and now I finally had it, I didn't want it. I'd give anything for Numonius Vala to stay in command. We didn't always see eye to eye, but I knew now that there was no better man in the entire Roman army suited to this role. 'May the gods go with you.'

He saluted each of the command in turn and then left to ready the Thracian horse for one last charge. 'I'll issue orders to all the men that if they break clear of the enemy cavalry to make all speed to the nearest Roman

Roman Mask

encampments – they will need to know the predicament the army is in and send help if at all possible.'

We all nodded in agreement, but all knew there was no help for us. The entire Roman occupation force was trapped with us. The nearest help was over a hundred miles away, but the Roman encampments and towns needed to be told so they could flee Germany as quickly as their feet could take them.

We watched the cavalry form up and ride to the north-east corridor of our small enforced enclosure. There Numonius Vala and the young Thracian cavalry officer Macarius led them into the swampy land that stretched up to the high moor to the north. The swamp waters reached up to the horses' chests, but the spry Thracian horses were surprisingly adept at fording the dark pools of brackish water, and no more than a handful of riders fell from their mounts as the two *ala* of horsemen slowly traversed the treacherous terrain. Towards the end of the corridor, Vala held up his hand to try to regroup the troop before they broke into the open. This is when we all expected the enemy cavalry to appear, as the narrow end of the pass could only admit a dozen horses at a time into the open ground, and the first to appear in the open were obviously vulnerable.

I saw with dismay, but also with a little pride, that Macarius was one of the first to break out onto the high moor, easily recognisable from his overly ornate full-faced helmet. He held there and tried to pull his cavalrymen into line as they emerged from the swamp, whilst Vala continued to urge the others through as fast as possible to strengthen the precarious bridgehead they were forming on the other side of the swamp.

Unexpectedly, Governor Varus turned up behind us, and voiced optimistically, 'He's doing well. He already has a toehold on the high moor, you see! This is no fool's errand. He'll thank me before this is over, you mark my words.'

Some of the others officers who had gathered to watch the proceedings added their agreement to his statement, excited by the cavalry's progress. Ceionius said, 'If this keeps up he may be able to secure a large enough staging post for us to lead the legions out. This could be our way home.'

I wasn't so sure. We knew the enemy cavalry were there. Why weren't they attacking? They should be able to bottle the end of the pass and deny us any exit with as little as two hundred men. Why were they holding back?

We all held our breath as the last of the Thracian cavalry left the swamp and broke into the daylight. With a great cheer from the commanders watching them, Ceionius shouted, 'They're going to do it! They're going to break out!'

It was then that the German horsemen appeared.

They rode into sight over the brow of the hill, a force of between ten and fifteen thousand, blond or red hair streaming behind colourful shields and long spears of stout wood. In the vanguard was Julius' own cavalry force, still in their Roman armour and equipment, riding down to slaughter the same men they'd fought alongside, joked, laughed, and lived with for years. It was a sickening sight.

Numonius Vala was many things, but he certainly was no coward. When he saw the approaching cavalry, he realised retreating back into the swamp was no longer an option – it would take far too long, and his men would be diced to pieces if taken from the rear – so he drew his sword and led the Thracian cavalry directly at the head of the enemy horsemen, at the Cheruscan traitors who'd turned their cloaks against Rome.

The unexpected move might have unnerved another force, led the less brave or inexperienced amongst the German tribesmen to veer off from the brunt of Vala's charge, but Julius had put his horsemen in the vanguard of his cavalry for a reason. They were both disciplined and battle hardened, and they weren't going to be put off from their kill now.

The two forces clashed with a terrific clang of sword, steel, and the screaming of men and horses alike. It reverberated along the high moor and seemed to slap us in the face for our earlier optimism. The Thracians fought manfully but were hopelessly outnumbered and soon were being enveloped by the huge mass of German horsemen. Even Governor Varus lowered his eyes in sorrow, to see the cavalry cut down before his eyes.

But then, impossibly, a small number of Thracians, who must have somehow managed to keep the momentum of their charge going, emerged from the other side of the German host. At their tip, was brave young Macarius, unmistakable in his ornate helmet, and he galloped through the German ranks to the freedom that waited at the other side!

I couldn't help myself. I ripped off my helmet and was shouting alongside everyone else watching, who were all also urging the riders on. 'Go on, boy! Run! Run!' I shouted at the top of my lungs, even though we were far too far away to be heard by the fleeing horsemen. 'You can make it! Run boy, run!'

They reached the brow of the hill, and escape looked to be within their grasp, the enemy horsemen being so intent on tearing their comrades apart. But that is what proved to be Macarius' downfall. He reigned in his horsemen on the brow, no more than a score in number, and looked back at his nine hundred comrades, still fighting alongside Numonius Vala, gradually being felled from their mounts, and his young mind couldn't accept leaving them behind.

I fell to my knees and whispered, 'No boy, don't do this, run, run …' but

I knew it was too late.

Macarius spurred his twenty riders back down the hill, into the backs of the German horsemen, taking down great sweeps of riders, who fell away, panicked by this unexpected assault. Impossibly again, Macarius made it all the way through the German host, back to his comrades, before the superior enemy host managed to regroup, and re-encircle the few remaining Thracian cavalry.

It was hard to tell when Macarius and Vala finally fell, the heaving mass of men in the centre of the melee was so congested, but fall they did, as after it was all over, two Cheruscian horsemen paraded around the battleground, spears aloft, with heads mounted on their tops. One grisly trophy wore an ornate cavalry commander's helmet, the other the helmet of a full legate of Rome.

I remained on my knees looking at the head of the young friend I'd only just got to know, when Legate Selus clapped me on the shoulder.

'They could have got away,' I said to him.

Selus sighed. 'I know, Cassius, I know.'

I turned and saw that the rest of the commanders were already walking away from our viewpoint. It was clear that there was no way out through this path for the army. The enemy had clearly only waited for our cavalry to form on the other side of the swamp so they could destroy it in one decisive strike. I repeated, 'They could have made it.'

Selus came over and put a hand on my shoulder. 'No use worrying about that now. They died heroes. Let us hope we all earn such clean deaths.' He lifted me up. 'Come on. On your feet. You don't want the men seeing you on your knees. Appearances are important. You're a legate now.'

Only then did it really strike me. I was now in charge of a legion.

Chapter Thirty-two

Technically, I still wasn't a genuine legate of Rome. That rank could only be bestowed by the Senate, and although battlefield promotions were not unheard of, my rank would remain tribune until the Senate were given the chance to ratify it, and that depended on some of us living long enough to see Rome again – something that was looking increasingly unlikely. But to the survivors of the XVIII, I was their commander, and although the men mourned the passing of Vala, they looked pleased that he had been replaced by a man they knew and had fought alongside in the past, and was not some lickspittle of the Governor's.

As soon as I rejoined them, we were thrown straight back into the action. The German tribes were buoyed by their success on the high moor and launched another huge offensive against us, both the Angrivarii to our rear, which assailed Selus' XIX, and the united tribes led by the Cherusci, who swarmed down through the gaps in the stockades; both Avitus' XVII and my legion were hard pushed to repulse their attacks.

I marched behind the ranks of my men, shouting encouragement, keeping the lines tight, and even drawing my *gladius* and taking the field myself when the fighting was particularly fierce, my normal cowardice forgotten due to what I'd witnessed on the hill. I made sure I kept the eagle party close behind the ranks of my men so they could see what they were fighting for and see that giving any ground, no matter how small was no longer an option. We either stopped them here, or we all died. It was that simple.

The fighting dragged on until the middle of the morning, when finally the German tribesmen retreated back up the hill to shelter behind their stockades. Another hail of javelins were launched from up high, which fell on shields raised by exhausted men, and killed or wounded any who were too slow to bring their shield to the fore in time.

Afterwards, I walked around my depleted legion and took stock of its remaining strength. Everywhere there were wounded. Some cried out in pain, whilst others simply sat there, staring dejected at the ground in front of them – by now, everyone realised that unless you could walk, or preferably run, escape from here was impossible. Of my XVIII, I guessed that little over two thousand men were left standing, and of those, only fifteen hundred could be expected to hold a sword. All the others were either dead or so badly wounded that their battle was over, one way or another.

The other two legions were faring slightly better, as they'd lost fewer men in the last assault on the enemy stockades, so it was for this reason that men of the XVII and XIX made up our next desperate attempt at breaking out from the enclosure. I spaced my XVIII out as evenly as I dared, filling the gaps in the line, making sure that we held the base as their attack commenced.

Avitus was leading this attack himself, with six full cohorts of the XVII, the eagle party to inspire the men, four cohorts from the XIX, and all the remaining auxiliaries, slingers and archers from Spain, who were to target the defenders behind their palisades.

Before the sun had reached its zenith, the attack was beaten back, with catastrophic losses, including the life of Legate Avitus, and the capture of the XVII's eagle.

Initially the attack looked to be progressing well. Avitus targeted the breech in the palisades made by Numonius Vala's earlier attack. The German tribesmen had tried to reinforce this area with scrub and bush from the surrounding forest, but these temporary barricades proved little obstacle for the experienced legionaries, who pulled them out of their path and streamed over them to attack the German defenders behind. At this point it was hard for me to tell what was happening from below, but I heard from others who were present in the attack that once the legions breached the outer defences, Avitus had committed his entire strength to this break in the line, his desperate troops hacking and slashing their way through mountains of German dead, only to find that Julius Arminius had made contingency plans for such a breakthrough. He held a reserve force of several thousand tribesmen commanded by the German champion Ewald. It was these fresh troops which turned the tide and threw the attacking Roman legionaries back, capturing the eagle of the XVII and killing their commander in the process. The German tribes had never been known to use sophisticated war tactics, such as holding a reserve force of uncommitted warriors – like most barbarian races, they were known to charge with all their strength until the enemy were annihilated – but this new development showed that Arminius had been teaching his German tribesmen more than how to build fancy Roman stockades.

The Spanish auxiliary soldier who was telling me this concluded, 'The German champion is terrible in battle, sir, terrible. With that long sword of his, he ploughed through the eagle's defenders like they weren't there, killing with every stroke, every movement of his body. None came close to touching him. He was death itself, striding through their ranks until the eagle was taken.'

The eagle was protected by its legion's best men, and the loss of it had an even greater demoralising effect on the survivors than the loss of their commander. It was now that many in the army were beginning to realise that they were not going to see another day.

Soon after our failed attack, the tribesmen once again attacked in huge numbers. They flooded down the steep hillsides and crashed into to our protective lines. We repulsed them again and again, but by now, many of the defenders had had enough – simple exhaustion and the lack of hope can break the will of the strongest men. Some broke ranks and ran to the tribesmen, throwing down their weapons and beseeching their mercy – they received none. The tribesmen cut them down in front of our eyes, killing every one of them. As tragic as it was, I was glad, the men needed to see that there was no way out through surrender to this foe – if Julius had been interested in a surrender, he could have sued for terms long ago. No, Julius was only interested in the complete annihilation of every one of us. Nevertheless, I wanted to make sure that no more broke ranks and tried it again, so I issued orders to the centurions that any legionary breaking the line to surrender to the enemy should be treated in the same way as an enemy tribesmen and cut down. The orders were relayed throughout the ranks and I hoped the message was clear. Even so, I knew that it was no real answer; the men needed some hope that there was an end to this. The relentless attacks were breaking down the discipline we needed to survive. I couldn't see the legions surviving another night, which meant we needed to make another try at the stockades. I went to see Governor Varus.

When I came upon the high command, Legate Selus, Praefect Ceionius, and Lucius Eggius – who despite his youth had now been given command of Avitus' XVII – were already present. Once again, they were arguing.

The governor was shaking his head. 'Another attack against those barricades is suicide. We can't afford another failed attack. Maybe if we held back in a defensive formation, we could wear these tribesmen down. Surely they must be feeling their losses. We have killed thousands.'

Selus stated matter of factly, 'Not as much as we are feeling ours. The German tribesmen are winning, and that is a great boost to any army's morale. I can't see them giving up on this now.'

Varus looked desperate. 'What about attacking the other side, against the Angrivarii, or through to the high moor? The legions may fare better against the cavalry.'

I answered for Selus. 'The legions would never get as far as facing the cavalry if we were to try that route. They would bottle us up in that swamp and take us apart piece by piece. The terrain would make it virtually impossible for us to even fight back. As for the Angrivarii, can you really see this army being able to fight its way up a mountainside protected by forty thousand tribesmen? No, of course not. We need to make it past those barricades. There is no other option.'

Varus stared up at me. 'What if I was to offer terms of surrender to Julius Arminius?'

I shook my head and gave a crooked grin. 'He would wait until we were all disarmed, chained, then he would kill every one of us. He is intent on sending a message, the gods know who to, but it is clear he needs to destroy this army in its entirety to accomplish his plans.'

Varus nodded his head slowly. 'So we are finished then.'

Selus slapped his fist into the palm of the other. 'Not yet we're not! By the gods, man, we still have some strength left, you can't give up!'

Governor Varus gave a deep sigh. 'No, no, of course not. We will carry on.'

I looked into Varus' eyes and saw a beaten man. I'd seen that same look in men at Western-Gate Pass. He had given up. I was going to suggest we make another attack, but we were interrupted by an urgent messenger for Legate Selus.

Selus angrily turned to the messenger and snapped, 'Can't it wait?'

The look on the messenger's face told us all that it couldn't.

Legate Selus took a long breath and then slowly said, 'What is it?'

Tears appeared in the messengers eyes. 'It's the eagle sir, it's lost ... the Angrivarii broke through our ranks. We pushed them back, but not before they'd taken the Nineteenth's eagle.'

Legate Selus turned round to us and saluted. 'Gentlemen, I must leave. I am sure you'll come up with the best strategy in my absence.'

Selus walked off and left us, and we all knew that we'd probably not see him again. He would try to recapture the eagle, or die in the attempt. Roman honour demanded no less.

The governor stared up at the sky and spoke aloud. 'That is two eagles lost out of three. No commander has ever lost so many and lived. I won't be the exception to this. Ceionius, will you be able to attend me?'

Ceionius lowered his head. 'Of course, my lord, if that is your wish.'

Lucius Eggius looked confused. 'But what are we going to do? What's the plan?'

I put my hand on his shoulder. 'It can wait. The Governor has something he needs to do.'

Lucius looked at me in bafflement. 'But, surely—'

I raised my finger to my lips to quieten him.

The governor and Ceionius walked away from us and found a small depression in the ground. There Varus knelt and drew his *gladius*.

Finally, young Lucius realised what was going on and said, 'But, Cassius, we can't just let him—'

I kept a firm hand on his shoulder to stop him following them. 'He's already given up, Lucius. He can't lead us any more.'

We watched in silence as Publius Quinctilius Varus, governor of the entire German province, with full imperium powers, plunged his *gladius* into his sternum and ended his life.

Chapter Thirty-three

The news wasn't a shock to the men. By now three-quarters of their fellows were either dead or dying, and you didn't need to be an expert in military tactics to see that this battle was almost done, and that the three legions were finished.

In the late afternoon the German tribesmen lifted their attack and retreated behind their stockades. Possibly the endless carnage was even beginning to affect their vast numbers and resolve, but more likely, they were just withdrawing to make their arrangement for the night attack, one which I knew we couldn't hope to repulse. I walked along the ranks of my men, past the wounded broken bodies and files of exhausted legionaries, and saw that the end was close.

Legate Selus was now dead, together with his senior tribune, and most of his legion. The legion had made a desperate attempt to reclaim its eagle which had ended in failure, and now less than eight hundred men from that once proud legion were able to wield a *gladius*. My legion was faring little better. I estimated I could muster no more than fifteen hundred, and the XVII numbered somewhere between the two. Virtually all of the auxiliaries were now dead. I had a few slingers, a handful of Spanish bowmen, but not in enough numbers to trouble the German tribes.

Of the high command, only myself, Lucius Eggius and Praefect Ceionius remained. There were a few lower ranking tribunes, but none with experience of leading large bodies of men.

I gathered all of the remaining commanders and the senior centurions together, to outline what we were going to do next. We gathered in a small shelter the men had constructed from wood and turf – all the tents had been burnt with the baggage train. It wasn't much, but it gave us some privacy from the rest of the army. I let the centurions speak first, to outline the condition of the men, but it was a similar story, whichever the legion.

Centurion Silius, a giant bull of a man with a barrel chest, and the most senior centurion remaining alive from the XVII, summed it up. 'Not only are the men exhausted, their morale has collapsed. They can't see the point in continuing the fight. Even if we repulse another hundred attacks, where will it get us? Everyone knows there is no relief force coming. Nobody even knows the plight we're in.'

Ceionius asked, 'How much longer can they hold together?'

Silius mopped his brow. 'To be honest, sir, I'm amazed we've lasted this long. I can't see how they managed to throw back that last assault. By rights it should have ended then.'

I stood and raised my hand. 'They threw back the last assault because they're Roman soldiers – that's how.' I looked around each of the men in the room, to make sure I had their attention. 'Not even Arminius can have expected us to hold out so long, against such odds, but Silius has raised a good point. Nobody knows what has happened here.'

Ceionius shook his head. 'Yes, we know that, Cassius, nobody is expecting a relief force. The nearest two legions are in Mogontiacum, two weeks march from here.'

I met his eye. 'And what is to stop the same thing happening to those two legions that has happened here?'

Ceionius looked up startled. 'Well, surely Asprenas wouldn't be fool enough—'

I finished for him. 'To make the same mistake his uncle did? I'm not so sure on that. And besides, what about the rest of the German province? What about the new Roman towns we've built? They're all full of Roman colonists, loyal citizens. All will be put to the sword if they're not warned.'

Ceionius just shrugged, but I saw this point hit home with a few of the men gathered there. Despite regulations, some would have loved ones, local wives, possibly children near the Roman bases.

Lucius Eggius, who looked as if he'd aged ten years in the last two days said, 'Alright, Cassius, you have made a good point, but what do you suggest we do about it?'

I cleared my throat. 'We'll make one last attempt on those stockades,'

Ceionius sighed. 'And what makes you so sure that we'll succeed this time when we've failed each time before?'

'Nothing. But we'll go with our entire strength, every man able to hold a blade, be they soldier or civilian. The object now is not to save the army, but to make sure a least a few of us escape to warn the rest of Roman Germany. What alternative do we have? If we wait here, we'll be overrun eventually, no matter how many more tribesmen we kill. Instead, we'll take the fight to them and make one last break for freedom.'

Lucius asked, 'What about the wounded? Or the civilians too weak, old, or young to hold a blade?'

I shook my head sorrowfully. 'Everyone who can follow, needs to be urged to do so. Everyone should be given a chance to make their own bid for freedom, but if they can't, I'm afraid they will have to be left here. I have no easy answers.'

Everyone looked at each other, thinking this through. Finally, Ceionius let out a great sigh, 'Well, like you, I don't see the point in waiting around to die. Let's go out in one final charge if we have to.' He looked around at the other commanders, who all nodded in agreement. 'But how do you suggest we do it? Just make another break for the breach in the stockade? We failed each time before.'

I shook my head. 'No, Arminius will be expecting that. We need to get him to commit his reserve force, the one he holds back on the other side of the stockade, or none of us will escape. We'll divide the troops into two battle groups. The Nineteenth doesn't have enough men to operate as a fighting force in its own right anymore, so those men will be divided between the other two legions.'

Ceionius and Lucius Eggius looked at one another and nodded. Ceionius added, 'Fair enough, then what?'

'The first battle group makes for the breach. This is to commit the defenders to this attack. Only when Arminius' reserve force is thrown against us will a signal be given, and then the second battle group breaks away from the rear of the column and attacks the other stockades. They should be lightly manned by this stage. If any of the other attacks are anything to go by, all the defenders swarm to defend the main breech.'

Ceionius looked confused. 'But how will they get past the stockades?'

I shrugged. 'They climb them, they cut their way through them, they rip them down. We will arm the leading ranks of this attack with *dolabrae*.' I'd remembered seeing some of the great picks that resembled axes, which were normally used to dig trenches by the legionaries, still with the legions. 'With over two thousand men in the second battle group, some will get through.'

Lucius saw the one obvious flaw in my plan. 'What about the men in the first battle group? They'll have no chance of escape themselves.'

I took a deep breath. 'No they won't. That is why I'll lead this first battle group myself. You and Ceionius will be leading the second.'

There was a stony silence after I said that, so I broke it by asking, 'I'd appreciate some volunteers to help me command the first group?'

Centurion Silius volunteered, as did several others, even young Lucius, but I told him he was needed for the second battle group; their path would not prove any easier, I assured him.

I stood up to dismiss the assembled officers. 'Go and prepare your men. Sort out those who can fight from those who can't. I'll be sending details of how the men will be divided up shortly. You don't have long – we attack at dusk!'

The men leapt to obey, glad that they had an objective again, although Ceionius remained behind and gave a low chuckle.

I tilted my head quizzically. 'What's so funny?'

Ceionius was sitting on a low bench in the shelter, and he lounged backwards on it. 'You know, you haven't been given any commission to take charge of this army. You were sent to be an aide to Varus. Now he's gone, by rights command should fall to either me or young Lucius Eggius.'

I looked him in the eye. 'Well? Do you want it?'

He laughed again, and raised a hand to placate me. 'No, no, don't worry, your plan is as good as any we're going to get at this stage, probably doomed to failure, but at least you have one. I have no interest in leading these men to their deaths, you're welcome to it.' He then grunted. 'Besides, if I was to take the lead, I'd be expected to lead that first battle group, not you. I'm no hero. I want to live, even if my chances of survival are small. I'd take that over yours. Who wants command if it means an early grave?'

I looked at the tired man in front of me and sighed. 'There is no shame in wanting to live, Ceionius. Up until a day ago, I would have agreed with you, but I'm not afraid anymore. For the last four years, I forgot who I was, and I'd rather die the man I am now than go back to living that lie.'

My fear had left me when I saw Macarius killed and his head raised on a spear. It was replaced by hatred. Hatred for my friend Julius Arminius who brought us to this end, for the lies he told me, the times we'd once shared, and for the betrayal he'd dealt us. I knew that leading that first group of men into the breach would be the last thing I did, but it may just give me a chance to kill Julius Arminius or destroy his carefully laid plans; that was now worth more than living.

Ceionius stared at the floor and shook his head. 'It's a shame you didn't take command sooner. Men like you are more suited to this than Varus. You might have avoided this disaster.'

I shook my head. 'Julius Arminius fooled me more than anyone. I can't castigate Varus for that. Anyway, I thought you liked Varus?'

Ceionius looked up. 'I did! When soldiering here required nothing more than dicing during the day and getting drunk with him in the evenings! I even liked his plans for the pretty little towns he was building here, and his dream for Germany. He just wasn't a soldier, never was. If he'd been given a more peaceful province, he'd have done fine. Try not to judge him too harshly.'

I gave Ceionius a careful look. 'No, it's not Varus I blame for this end, although others will. Arminius caused this. It is him I'll hold to account.'

I went back to my legion, thoughts of the upcoming attack whirling through my mind. My first thought was to keep the men ignorant of what the exact details of the plan were; after all, how could I expect the men to follow me in that first battle group when none were expected to survive? But when I saw the tired, exhausted men who'd already given so much, once again readying their arms for another attack, I realised they deserved more than that. The lies of Julius Arminius had brought them here. I wasn't going to compound that by lying to them now.

I instructed the centurions to line the men up so I could address them all, and stood up upon a raised knot of land. I told them my entire strategy. I told them of the importance of word getting out to the rest of the province, the desperate need to warn others what had happened here, and the price of failure. The men were so tired and had been through so much that none looked too bothered about what happened to the rest of Roman Germany. I couldn't say I blamed them, so I got to the point. 'The object of the first group will be to commit the reserve force behind that stockade, then those in the second will stand a chance of breaking for freedom.'

'Now, if I have to, I will divide the men up as I see fit, but I'd like volunteers to join me in that first group. I can't expect any of you to do what I'm not prepared to do myself, so I'll be leading this attack personally.'

A stony silence greeted this. Great, so much for dramatic gestures, it looked like I might be assaulting the breach alone!

A young legionary raised his hand to speak; I signalled that he should proceed. 'Do you think many will make it from that second group?'

I shrugged. 'A few, a couple of hundred at most, I guess. The Cherusci won't let them go easily. I expect them to hunt them through the forests – they'll not want word of this reaching other Roman garrisons.'

Again silence.

Finally, from the back, another raised his voice. 'We'll go with you, sir.'

It was Tetricus, and he stood beside my other comrades from Western-Gate Pass. How through all this carnage had they survived? I should have known they'd find a way. 'Thank you. How many from your cohort still survive?'

He shrugged. 'Well, only about two hundred of us left, but we're still tough fighters. We used to be the legion's first cohort.' He said the last with pride.

I smiled. 'And you shall be again.' I knew the previous first cohort had been killed virtually to a man when Numonius Vala had made his first attack, so I knew promoting the VI cohort wouldn't upset anyone.

An *optio* from another section of the crowd spoke up next. 'If they can follow you, so can we. Old Vala would have expected us to take the hard route.'

Cheers greeted this, and then another shouted. 'I don't fancy running through the woods anyway, too tired. Let the other legions do the running away.'

Laughter followed, and soon all the men present were volunteering to follow me. My heart swelled with pride, but tears stung my eyes as I knew I'd be leading them to their deaths. I signalled a messenger over to me. 'Tell Ceionius and Lucius Eggius that there is no need for the other legions to supply any men for the first battle group. The men of the Eighteenth will be leading the attack.'

Before we made our attack, I instructed two of the men to hide our eagle and submerge it under the brackish pools of the swamp. Our attack was a one-way mission, and I was damned if I was going to give our eagle to Julius easily; let him hunt through the stinking morass of peat bogs if he wanted it that much, otherwise it could stay hidden forever.

Then came the difficult task of speaking to the wounded who were unable to join us in this venture. I could have instructed one of my centurions to undertake this job, but I decided to do it myself: as it was me who was ordering them to be left behind, I should at least have the stomach to tell them to their face. I spoke to a centurion with a wound to his lower leg whom I was leaving in charge. 'Before the end, you may want to slit the throats of the more seriously wounded. It will probably be a kindness if they don't know what's happening. As for yourself, any who can wield a sword, try and use it – on yourself if you can't use it on the Cherusci. You don't want to be taken alive. I don't think the German tribes understand the concept of mercy.'

He grunted and drew his *gladius*. 'Don't worry. I still intend to take a few of them with me. I might not be able to walk, but there's still some fight left in me, don't you worry about that. Those Cherusci bastards will have a surprise if they think we're all going to give up without a fight.'

I gripped his shoulder. 'I'm sorry it's come to this.'

He gave a half-smile. 'So am I. But don't worry, we know you've no choice, besides it looks like we'll be meeting in the void sooner rather than later. I hear you'll be leading the attack on the breach?'

I chuckled. 'You're not wrong. Good luck.'

He resheathed his *gladius*, and gripped me on the shoulder. 'Same to you, sir.'

Afterwards, I went over to the head of our column and signalled to start the attack. I'd given a lot of thought to what formation to use on our assault up the hill. I thought of adopting the attacking 'pig's head' formation, but thought it would overcomplicate matters when the second group broke off to assail the other stockades. So instead we were marching in one large column, twenty men abreast, the XVIII at the front, the XVII and XIX to the rear, ready to detach itself on my signal. I wanted to give the impression that we were going to try and force the breach by simple weight of numbers – it wasn't much of a ruse, it was what we'd tried in the last attack, so Julius shouldn't see anything amiss. I was banking on Julius not realising we'd given up hope of the army being able to maintain itself as a fighting force and remain together. I knew Julius, and I knew in my position he'd still be trying to find a way to win. I remembered from childhood, from any game we played or any argument we'd have, he'd never give up, even after his chance of winning had long past. I wasn't so arrogant. I knew this battle was no longer about winning or losing; it was now about getting word out to stop this butchery being meted out to anyone else.

I was in the fourth rank from the front – many had objected to me positioning myself so close to the front, but I wanted a clear view of how the Cherusci were reacting to our attack. If I was wrong, and they saw through it and positioned their reserve force all along the stockades, I needed to know so I didn't send the men of the XVII and XIX to be slaughtered.

About halfway up, I could see the German warriors shouting and signalling frantically to one another; they looked surprised that we were still able to mount such a large attack – they'd probably thought this battle nearly done. It felt good that we could still surprise them. German warriors swarmed from other areas along the stockade, just as I'd hoped, to mass at the breach, where our attack was aimed. But there was still no sign of the reserve force. I needed to wait until I'd seen them before making my signal.

About twenty paces from the breach, I ordered us to break and charge, which we all did, running with as much energy as we could muster, crashing over the branches and scrub the Cherusci had put up as a feeble barrier, and into the ranks of German warriors at the mouth of the opening in the stockades. If the Cherusci hadn't been so overconfident, they may have made a better job of repairing the break in their palisade, but as it was, we smashed through into the midst of their warriors, our heavier armour giving us an unstoppable momentum as we crashed through their hastily erected shield wall. Now was the crucial point in the plan I knew Julius would only commit his reserve force if he thought the hill's defenders couldn't repulse this attack on their own, so my Eighteenth would need to fight like demons to take the top of the hill.

They didn't let me down.

The men fought with a desperation only the soon to die know. My men seemed impervious to wounds or the fall of a comrades; they just surged forward regardless, attacking with cold fury and pure hate at this traitorous foe. Soon the tribesmen were falling backwards, away from this terrible onslaught, and I was hacking down at a fallen defender's raised shield with my own *gladius*, when I heard German war horns, signalling the reserve force coming to their aid.

I let the attack continue without me, sheaving my *gladius*, as I prepared to wait until the right moment; if I signalled too soon, Julius might be able to pull his men back, so I needed to make sure the timing was perfect. I saw Ewald and, wonders of wonders, Julius himself – clearly visible with his winged helm – leading his large force of warriors into the fray against my resurgent XVIII. That was good, Julius being in the attack personally meant he would find it more difficult to adapt to changing circumstances. He probably hoped that this was going to be the battle's climax and wanted to be a part of it – trust his vanity to get in the way of reason. I waited until his entire line – several thousand warriors – were clashing with the vanguard of my legion, before I asked the trumpeter next to me to make the prearranged blast. Julius would know all our trumpeter signals, so I'd arranged with the other battle group that the signal to break and assault the other stockades would be the signal for 'retreat and withdraw'. This was to fool Julius into thinking he was succeeding in repulsing the attack, and to deter suspicion from onlookers when the rear of our column broke off from the attack. I didn't want the German tribesmen to realise their stockades were coming under attack until the last moment.

The cohorts to the rear of our column broke off and attacked the stockades either side of our attack at the breach; there were nearly four hundred paces of stockades, so there was plenty to choose from. Lucius Eggius attacked to one side, Ceionius the other, and they used a variety of techniques to assault the barricades. Some stockades we assaulted with the sloping *testudo* formation, used by Vala earlier in the battle, some climbed directly up the wicker stockades with *gladius* in hand, whilst others attacked the stockades with *dolabrae,* the giant pickaxes that smashed through the wicker walls of the palisade. The plan looked to be working, but there was no guarantee that any of them would be able to get past the defenders of the stockades. However, we were committed now so I needed to keep Julius' focus on our attack as long as possible, then, by the time he realised he'd been duped, hopefully some of the men will have broken out of the enclave.

The best way to keep Julius' attention was to keep him fighting, and if I was going to die here, I wanted to at least give myself a chance of killing Julius before I went. I drew my *gladius* and ran to the front of my column, urging the men forward into the attack. We'd done our part of the battle plan, now it was just time to fight!

Near the front of the column, my tiny force was surrounded on three sides by the huge numbers of German tribesmen, who were desperately trying to break through the resolute Roman shield wall. I knew it couldn't last; not only were my men hopelessly outnumbered, they were exhausted from two days of almost constant fighting, and eventually the Germans would break us down. I wanted to delay that as long as possible, so I shouted at my men to continue to hold, to give everything, to keep the line tight. They didn't disappoint me; they hacked and slashed, and bled the Germans; more and more Cherusci warriors were cut down by the deadly *gladius* wielded by my hardened men of the XVIII, only to be replaced by more warriors, bearded faces full of hate and anger. Eventually, after what seemed an eternity of carnage, our line started to buckle. I did my best to strengthen the line where gaps appeared, using a small reserve force I was holding back for this purpose, but I knew the end was close; we'd be cut apart once we lost our formation. I looked up at the heaving mass of German tribesmen and tried to make out Julius. There he was, winged helmet marking him out. He was shouting orders at the rear ranks of warriors, directing them away from the battle to the other stockades. Finally, I guessed, he'd realised that the other stockades were under attack, and he was sending men running to strengthen those defences.

But whilst Julius had grown up ordering disciplined Roman armies, he was finding out the hard way it wasn't so simple with a disorganised rabble like the Cherusci warriors. German tribesmen were breaking off from the back of the army, but not in any organised fashion. Where a Roman army would neatly peel off the rearward ranks, they were leaving in large groups, without any thought where it might leave them vulnerable. I laughed as I saw Julius screaming in rage at the uncomprehending warriors around him. He was right to be angry; although they still had plenty of warriors, too many had left from one section of his line, leaving it exposed and vulnerable. Now was our chance! I told my centurion in charge of the small reserve force to follow me. We were going to attack. We surged through our own shield wall, and the legionaries moved aside as we rushed through their ranks and straight into the weakened section of the German line. I slashed the throat open of one large warrior barring my path, before sticking my *gladius* into the soft stomach of the warrior to his side. My men surged behind me, cutting down warriors to either side, as my small attack penetrated deep into the German host. I cut, parried, thrust, and fought in a frenzy, the hours of practice with Marcus keeping my sword arm strong and deadly. The tribesmen fell back in confusion, away from our unexpected attack, and we broke through their ranks. No battle plan was formed in my head now. It was instinct that was ruling my actions, as I fought to reach Julius, to ram my *gladius* down his throat. I was close, so close. I could feel he was near.

The centurion behind shouted, 'Sir, the way is open, we can escape!'

I cut the brow above the head of the man in front of me, and he fell back holding his face, then I looked to see where the centurion was pointing. He was right. The German ranks had parted to the left of our attack and left a gap. 'This is our chance, run!'

I shoulder charged the next man, knocking him off his feet, and my men followed me towards the escape route as we surged forward. My heart leapt with elation. We were so close. The dark forest under the canopy of looming trees was less than a dozen paces away.

But then the sinuous form of Ewald barred our path. He ran in leading a group of large warriors, probably Julius' bodyguard. These were no normal warriors, but experts with blade and spear, and they tore into my small troop of men, Ewald cutting down men in a deadly graceful dance that swept men out of his path as easily as a scythe through wheat. Our attack finally foundered, but more legionaries joined us; the other units from my broken Eighteenth must have followed my attack out, and they were all pushing towards the opening in the line. I looked around me, to see how the battle was faring, but it was so hard to see through the massed ranks of German warriors. But what I did see made my heart leap for joy; a few, not many, no more than a handful of my Eighteenth, had broken through the German warriors to the thick forest on the other side and were sprinting to freedom. It wasn't much of a victory, but it was all we had, and I stumbled after them, seeking the sanctuary of the trees, only to slip on the mud a handful of paces from freedom. I tried to regain my footing quickly, but it was too late. A large warrior loomed over me, and I saw no more …

Chapter Thirty-four

My head was killing me, and my mouth was so dry and parched, it hurt to swallow. I opened my eyes and tried to sit up, but something was preventing me. My head spun and I felt the urge to vomit; I fought it back down, and tried to gather my bearings.

'You awake then?' someone to my left said. 'You're going to regret waking up. Would've been a kindness if you'd never opened your eyes again. Soon you might not have them.'

I tried to hold my head, which was throbbing in agony, but I couldn't, and I realised my hands were tied securely behind my back. I looked up to see who was talking to me, and saw that it was a legionary, also tied, but sitting up, mud and blood smeared over his face, with a look of complete dejection. I was in a line of Roman soldiers, all tied. Some looked terrified; others looked so completely broken that they no longer cared what befell them.

Someone whispered over to us, 'Quiet, don't make so much noise, you'll bring her over again.'

The legionary chuckled. 'She's not about to forget we're here. She's going to get us one time or another.'

I shook my head and awkwardly managed to sit up, my head still spinning and with another urge to vomit. 'Who are you talking about, and where are we?'

He chuckled again. 'In the most desolate region of Hades, that's where we are, and she's the worst demon you're ever likely to see in the short time remaining in your life.'

He looked over at me, assessing the top of my head. 'Looks like you were hit on the head with a shield boss. Didn't anyone ever tell you to keep your helmet on?'

My lips were so sore and chapped it hurt to talk. 'I must have mislaid it somehow, how careless of me.' I looked at the man's insignia. He was from the XVII, Avitus' old legion. 'How did the attacks go on the stockades? Did any make it pass them? Did many escape?'

He shrugged. 'Maybe a handful, no more than that, lucky buggers. I wasn't so lucky. Fell off the stockade when I was trying to climb up it. Must have knocked myself out, as I woke up here.'

I was excited. 'So you saw some make it out?'

He shrugged again. 'What difference does it make? It won't help us any. Look up at the trees, and you can see how we're all going to end up.'

I looked up to see where he was indicating, and my heart froze.

A Roman legionary was nailed to the tree looming above us. His genitals had been mutilated and his eyes put out. Blood lay congealed around his mouth, so I guessed his tongue had been cut out as well. In horror, I realised when his head moved that the man was still alive.

'By the gods,' I said.

The legionary spat on the ground in front of him. 'The lady's the worst. The others will just nail you to a tree and leave you to die. She cuts your bollocks off and will pluck your eyes out. You don't want to attract the attention of that mean bitch.'

He nodded over in the direction of another line of soldiers, all similarly tied to ourselves, and at its head, Ewald's sister, Thusnelda, was supervising another solider being pinned to a tree. His tongue had been cut out, so he didn't make much noise, and I could only guess at the pain he was in. My blood ran cold at the thought of the same happening to me; I'd thought I'd found my courage again on the battlefield, but this was different. This horror defied all reason.

My legionary explained, 'They're doing it to honour their gods, we think. She has priests around her that mutter all sorts of curses and gibberish as they hoist them up there. Our turn will be soon.'

I didn't know much about the German gods, other than Tiuw was their god of war, and Frigga their goddess of fertility. I remember someone once telling me they were a bloodthirsty lot but I never expected anything like this. I looked on in stupefied silence, not believing what I was seeing, as the next man was taken from the line. He screamed and struggled, but was easily overpowered by four large warriors who pinned him to the ground. Thusnelda then cut off his genitals, as his screams turned into a panicked screech that cut me to the bone. Next to go were the eyes, and then finally his tongue, whereby the screams finally ended. I threw up on the ground in front of me.

The legionary chuckled. 'I was almost sick the first time I saw it. I've seen over thirty now, I'm long past feeling it.'

From the other direction, we heard screaming. 'No, it's not my turn yet. We haven't started this line yet!'

I turned and my heart sunk again. It was Tetricus, the former *optio* of the XVIII, and he was being manhandled by four large Cherusci warriors, as two of the German priests, old haggard men with mud in their hair that made it stand up in grotesque spikes, chanted away in their barbaric tongue.

Tetricus was struggling for all his worth, but the men held him in an iron grip.

'These ones will just take his tongue out, he's lucky,' informed my unfazed legionary.

Tetricus was shouting, 'No, no, it's not our turn yet. Someone tell them. It's not our turn!'

He spotted me in the line. 'Sir, Cassius, please! Help me, sir, help me! Tell them it's not my turn.'

He still thought me the hero tribune, the man who'd got him through Western-Gate Pass and could make everything alright again. But here I was, completely helpless, hands tied behind my back, looking on with gritted teeth, as Tetricus pleaded with me. I looked at his frightened rolling eyes, in impotent frustration, panic mixed with hatred of these filthy barbarians.

I couldn't stand this any longer.

It wasn't bravery that made me surge to my feet, but anger, hatred, and desperation. My hands were still tied, so I couldn't do more than lurch upwards, but somehow I was going to fight back. I ran towards the shocked priests, and launched a flying head-butt at one that crashed into his face, splitting his nose asunder.

The watching Roman soldiers cheered, and a few jumped to their feet, but the four warriors quickly overpowered me, pinning me to the ground, whilst other German tribesmen ran over and kicked and shoved the others back into line. One of my captors whispered in my ear, in very bad Latin, 'You can take his place for that, dog.'

They dragged me to my feet, where I saw Tetricus weeping on his knees, one priest lying prone on the ground, blood pouring from his ruined nose as the other attended him.

A women's voice rang out in harsh tones, the words indecipherable, but clearly an order. My Latin-speaking guard chuckled evilly, 'You've done it now. You shouldn't have brought her over.'

They presented me to the daughter of Segestes, her beautiful face twisted in glee as soon as she recognised me. 'Oh, it's the pretty Roman!' She laughed out loud, an ugly sound full of malice and spite. 'Oh won't my husband be pleased he lived.'

Her husband? Wasn't that Sesithacus? What did he have to do with anything?

She gripped my face around my chin, her long nails digging painfully into my skin. 'It'd be a pleasure taking out this one's tongue and eyes,'

I still stared at her in defiance, but inside my stomach was twisting in knots, terrified by what she was going to do. I forced myself not to show my fear. 'Do your worst, bitch,' I spat.

She laughed in cruel pleasure. 'Oh, how I'd love to take your pretty eyes and your defiant tongue, Roman. But I think my lord husband will be angry with me if I were to spoil such a prize.'

The Latin-speaking guard grunted in displeasure.

She smiled coldly. 'Don't worry. This one's fate won't be any easier.'

She then started issuing orders in the language of the Cherusci, which I was unable to understand, and I was transferred into the care of the warriors who'd accompanied Thusnelda.

Her final orders were issued to the Latin-speaking guard, spoken in my language so I could be in no doubt as to what was to transpire. 'Continue with the sacrifice of the one he tried to save, but be sure to mutilate him first. Take his manhood, eyes, but leave his tongue. I want the gods to hear his suffering.'

Tetricus started weeping as he overheard, and begged, 'No, please, don't, don't do that!'

She laughed and started walking away as my captors dragged me behind her.

The other legionary who'd spoken to me simply nodded as I was taken past. 'I'll see you soon in the void.'

Before we'd walked a dozen paces, Tetricus was screaming in agony, his suffering a harsh rebuke to my futile resistance. I felt sick, confused, and bitter, as I was led through the forest. I saw wounded Roman captives being nailed to trees or tortured in horrific ways. Hundreds were dying this way. The poor unfortunates that hadn't been granted a clean death in the battle; they were now finding out that there are some fates worse than death. Tetricus' screams accompanied every step through the forest, sending the Roman captives awaiting their fate into moans of despair.

I walked past Roman civilians undergoing the same fate as the soldiers, whilst some unfortunate women who'd trusted their safety to the Roman army were now being noisily raped before a crowd of cheering and laughing warriors, eager to take their turn before the women joined their men by being sacrificed to the Cherusci gods. These people had no mercy for the Romans, be they male or female, solider or civilian. All were to die to their gods in as gruesome a manner as could be devised.

Thusnelda raised an eyebrow as she saw the disgust on my face as one women's throat was slit before my eyes. 'Her head will look well on a pole, don't you think? We will make trophies to mark the fate of all who defy the Cherusci.'

I shook my head in anger. 'Defy you! We were your allies!'

She chuckled. 'Oh, pretty Roman, surely you realise now that that was never the case.'

The warriors holding me dragged me along, my head spinning in revulsion, until we came upon a makeshift campsite, milling with warriors, exultant at their victory.

'Oh look, Roman, my brother is at work!' She crowed in delight as we approached the campsite. A large circle of warriors surrounded three Roman captives who'd been stripped naked, but were all armed with a *gladius*. In the centre of the circle was Ewald, a slight sweat covering his unclothed well-muscled upper torso, armed with his long sword.

The three Romans were terrified, but, presumably realising they'd no choice, attacked together hoping to overwhelm the fearsome Cherusci warrior. Ewald swayed from their attacks and scythed them down with his long sword, taking mere heartbeats to despatch three trained and battle-hardened legionaries. They were left dying on the ground.

She looked at me, her eyes twinkling. 'You see how fast my brother is, Roman? None can stand before him, none. Maybe we'll give you to Ewald to send you to our gods.'

I didn't bother answering, knowing it would only please her. As I was dragged through the cheering warriors I took a sidelong glance at the German champion who looked up from cleaning his blade. He eyed me coldly, as a snake would a mouse, his dark eyes giving no clue as to his thoughts, as if killing three men meant less than the bother of having to clean his blade afterwards. Despite the horrors I'd witnessed, I still gave a slight shudder as I met those cold eyes.

My attention was soon taken away from Ewald, as the warriors in front of me parted, revealing Julius Arminius sitting on a throne made from captured Roman spears and shields, and crested by three golden eagles – those of the XVII, XVIII, and XIX legions; my hiding of the Eighteenth's standard had presumably been as ineffective as anything else we'd tried against this foe. He looked relaxed and calm, and turned a beaming smile on Thusnelda as she presented me to my former boyhood friend. 'My lord King, I bring you a gift!'

The warriors holding me threw me at Julius' feet, my face landing in the mud as my bound hands made breaking my fall impossible. I spat out the mud that filled my mouth, and desperately tried to wriggle to my knees.

He laughed. 'Oh, Gaius! Does nothing kill you, my friend! I could have sworn that you'd find your end in the battle, but no, here you are, surviving against all the odds!'

I raised my head and turned my gaze to the man I once loved more than any other, my eyes burning with hatred. But one question overwhelmed any other. 'Why Julius? Why did you do this?'

He cocked his head. 'Why, Gaius? Because I believe in the destiny of my people. Isn't that right, my dear?'

Thusnelda draped herself on Julius, running her hands over his broad chest, and kissed him on the forehead. Oh, so it was like that was it? I looked at Julius in disbelief. How could he desire this monster? Granted she was beautiful, but she was so full of spite and malice, I'd rather take a crocodile to my bed ... horrible woman. But how was this possible? I'd seen Julius' men bring down her father with my own eyes? Maybe Thusnelda and her brother didn't know of the death of Segestes. Could I somehow sow some seeds of division? I addressed Julius' woman. 'I saw Julius present Varus your father's head. Did you take him to bed with the blood of your own father on his hands?'

She turned to me and narrowed her eyes, but then unexpectedly laughed. 'As a matter of fact, I think I did.'

She stood and walked over to a cage standing behind the makeshift throne, where I'd presumed a caged animal of some sort lay trapped. She took a spear off a warrior standing nearby and poked the occupant with it. A muffled squeal answered, and I saw it was a dishevelled man robed in rags and grime that cowered within the cage. His beard and hair was unkempt, and his eyes and tongue had been removed, so it was difficult to recognise him at first, but when she poked him with a spear a second time, I saw his face clearly. 'Sesithacus,' I said out loud.

Thusnelda's husband reacted to his name and ran to the bars of his cage and started shaking them. Thusnelda struck him with the point of the spear, driving him backwards. 'Down worm! You know you're not allowed to do that. Do you wish me to punish you again?'

Sesithacus cowered to the back of his cage and curled up into a ball, shaking his head and rocking back and forth. I dreaded to think of the agonies his wife had been inflicting on him.

I looked at Julius. 'A nice lover you have there. Do you think she'll treat you any better when she has you in a cage?'

Julius cocked his head as he looked at me. 'Oh, that'll never happen, and besides, she isn't my just my lover, she's now my wife.'

I looked at him in disbelief. 'You married the daughter of the man you executed?'

Julius' eyes widened. 'Oh, Segestes isn't dead. He's far too important for that. He's in captivity in my long house, guarded by some of my finest men.'

I blurted incredulously, 'But I saw his severed head!'

Julius smiled. 'No, you saw the head of a member of my bodyguard who had the misfortune to bare an uncanny resemblance to Segestes, and once you hack somebody's head off, it really is so difficult to tell. It was Thusnelda's idea.'

I shook my head dumbfounded. 'But why would she want you to take her own father into captivity?'

He smiled. 'That was the price of Ewald's and Thusnelda's compliance in this venture. They've both hated their father ever since he'd beaten them as children and murdered their mother in a drunken fit. It was why Ewald became so good with that sword of his. Once he did, the beatings stopped – for both of them.'

I turned my head back around to look at the Cherusci champion, Ewald. Could he really have hated his father so much that he'd countenance betraying him? What sort of family was this?

Thusnelda came back to Julius and put her hand around his neck and explained. 'The beatings may have stopped, but he still found ways to belittle me. Marrying me to that fool, Sesithacus. To think that I had to endure that weak worm's paws on me.' She spat, 'My father deserves a painful death. I only wish I could give him one.'

Julius told me, 'Some of Segestes' most loyal men fought valiantly to free him, those I needed to kill. You heard that whilst you and Varus waited outside my camp. Most of his warriors, however, were more pragmatic. They saw I was the stronger leader, and, providing I spared his life, were content to follow me. Knowing Ewald followed me helped persuade them. Everyone respects a warrior of his calibre.' He turned and stroked his new wife. 'Don't worry, my dear. You have plenty more to practise your skills on. Why don't you return to your work? Let me speak to Gaius alone.'

She froze. 'I want to be the one to take out his eyes and tongue.'

His face hardened. 'I decide who does that task, not you. Now be gone.'

She took her arm away from his shoulder and stalked off, hissing, but I saw a twinkle of pleasure in her eyes just before she left. She liked the fact that

Julius could master her, I realised. Is this the attraction for you, Julius? Knowing you can dominate the one woman no one else ever could? Have you really become so twisted that even in matters of the heart, you can only think in terms of domination and conquest? What a vain man you've become, I thought.

He turned to Ewald. 'Continue the contests, surely you can find some who can give you a little more of a test.'

His warriors cheered as three more legionaries were brought forward and made to attack the champion with *gladius*. These three lasted longer, but whether that was because of their skill, or because Ewald was drawing out the contest, I didn't know. He danced in between the three Romans, deflecting their blades and reposting with blinding speed, as the surrounding Cherusci warriors cheered on any new cut or sight of blood.

Julius only half watched the contest. 'You nearly spoilt my plans when you offered to fight him in my hall. I didn't expect that.'

I grunted. 'How so?'

He explained. 'Thusnelda and I came up with the plan to entice your man Marcus into a fight with Ewald. Marcus' reputation with the blade was known throughout the Roman camp, and Ewald killing him was to galvanise my warriors into believing that we could defeat Rome. I certainly didn't expect you to take his place though. You always did have more guts than brain. I should've let him kill you.'

Julius still thought me brave, how ludicrous. 'Then why didn't you?'

He shrugged. 'Perhaps out of past loyalty for what we once shared.'

I shook my head in disgust. 'Don't you dare talk of loyalty – you don't know the meaning of the word. You've betrayed everything you once stood for.'

His face turned to anger. 'Betrayed? Me? No, no, Gaius, that is where you're wrong. I haven't betrayed my people. My people are the Cherusci, not Rome.' He stood up from his throne and paced back and forth. 'You're right. A few years ago I wanted nothing more than to be a loyal servant of Rome, serve her as a soldier, and win her praise. But how did they repay me? They sent me here, against my will, to be their puppet on the throne of my dead uncle.'

I ground my teeth. 'So you did all this out of revenge? To get back at Augustus for sending you here?'

He looked at me in surprise. 'No, Gaius, that's not it. When I came here I found, much to my surprise, that I loved my people. I loved their wild nobility, their bravery, their passion. All my life, I'd been running from them, trying to be what I wasn't, trying to be a good Roman, but when I returned here I realised that this was where I'd always belonged. Only Rome had taken that away from me –

blinded me with her wealth and power. Here I began to see clearly again. Can you really blame me for loving my own people?'

I snorted in contempt. 'You've led your people to ruin. You may have won here, but Rome will return in greater numbers.'

He turned on me and smiled. 'Oh really, you think Augustus can muster up another twenty thousand men, do you? And where will they come from? There are only two more legions to the north of Germany, and only two in Gaul – you forget, I know all of the troop positions. I was part of the Roman high command here. Soon I'll unite all the tribes behind me. After this victory, all will flock to my banner. The Cherusci will take their place at the head of the German nations and we will assemble an army so large the very ground will tremble at its passing.'

I shook my head. 'Untrained barbarians against legions? We all know how that ends.'

He turned sharply at that. 'My untrained barbarians didn't do too badly against your legions this time, did they? How many of you escaped? Two hundred, maybe three? All of those are being tracked down in the forest by Faramund and thousands of my warriors. None will escape, we'll kill them all. Soon I'll be making a peace accord with Maroboduus and his Marcomanni, Rome already fears him, and once his strength is combined with mine, we'll crush whatever resistance Rome can put in our path.'

A treaty with the Marcomanni? My blood ran cold at the thought. He was right. Maroboduus held over seventy thousand seasoned warriors, a standing army of great strength; could the very foundations of Rome herself be about to be shattered? It seemed impossible, but only a few days ago I thought destroying a Roman army the size of ours was impossible, and Julius had managed it. However, I wasn't about to show Julius my fears. 'You'll never get away with this.'

He turned to me and smiled. 'Oh, I think I already have, friend Gaius. You helped me do it.'

I looked up sharply at that. 'Me! How?'

He sat back down on his throne. 'When I first heard you were put in charge of gathering intelligence, I was worried, I'll admit it. I know you've got a brain under that arrogant persona of yours, and you certainly couldn't do a worse job than that lazy idiot Asprenas. I'd been working on this for a long time, and I was worried that my old friend returning might upset all my plans. But then I realised your affection for me would be your undoing and that I could use it to my advantage. It was you who told me that Vala was sending patrols back into the Teutoburg Forest. After that, with my connections, it was easy to find out which part of the forest they would be scouting, and I could send Ewald and some of my warriors to take them down. I'd have never known without you.'

By the gods, I didn't think I could feel any more guilty about the death of Marcus, but now I could; I'd betrayed that patrol by informing Julius. Why hadn't I seen that? Was that what the shade of Centurion Decius had been trying to tell me? What a fool I'd been.

I looked up at Julius, arrogantly lounging on his throne in front of me, and my anger spurred me to my feet, hoping in some way to wipe that awful grin off his face. But after my success with the priests, the guards were ready for me, and one knocked me on the head with the butt of his spear before I'd even made it to my feet, sending me sprawling to the feet of Julius once more.

He chuckled. 'Temper, temper, Gaius. That is no way to behave in front of a king. Now, much as I've enjoyed talking to you, it's time we moved on.' He looked up at the guards and told them, 'Take him away and nail him to a tree.'

Chapter Thirty-five

I was dragged away from Julius and his jeering warriors, and escorted by four of the great burly men back into the forest. There wasn't any fight left in me and I didn't struggle – not that it would have done me any good, the tight grip on either arm by two of the warriors was as tight as an iron vice. No jabbering priest escorted us, and Julius' woman didn't re-emerge for which I was at least slightly grateful – not that the prospect of being nailed to a tree by any of my guardians thrilled me, but at least she wouldn't be there to chop my cock off first.

They were heavy-handed as they dragged me through the forest trail, administering a painful blow to the back of my head when I lost my footing and tripped on an exposed tree root. How well any of my guards spoke Latin, I couldn't tell, as they only conversed in their native tongue, at one point stopping to argue which direction to take me. Two of them seemed content to take me back to the area I'd come from, where Tetricus had met his end, but the other two wanted to take me to the west of the encampment. Which tree I was nailed to didn't concern me overly, but in any event the largest of the four warriors got his way. After some pushing and shoving, I was taken west, to an eerily quiet grove of oak trees with wide trunks, thick interwoven branches, and a dark canopy of leaves which blanketed out the sunlight and gave a musty smell which brought to mind the age of these ancient trees.

I raised my head and saw immediately why I had been brought to this grove of trees. Nailed to one of the trees was Ceionius and to another was Lucius Eggius. Both were unmoving and appeared to be long dead, whilst other trees contained senior centurions and junior tribunes. This appeared to be some sort of senior officer's club, an exclusive grove for the destroyed army's command. Possibly Julius was still so ingrained with the hierarchy of the Roman army that the thought of the senior offices being despatched alongside the lower ranks rankled with him. I tried to summon some pity for my young friend Lucius and Ceionius but couldn't as fear was now taking over my entire body. I started to tremble from head to toe as the realisation of what lay in store for me finally hit home. I looked from side to side in panic to try and find a way out, and though I knew it to be futile I started to struggle wildly. I was slapped hard around the face to quieten me, and forced to my knees. Another guard grabbed my hair from behind and forced my head upwards to stare into the face of the large leader of the group of guards, who drew a long *sax* blade and chuckled as he grabbed my chin and aimed his blade at my right eye.

I tried to shake my head, and squirmed. 'Please, by the gods, no.' But his grip was implacable as he very slowly and deliberately took his time.

I was staring directly at him as his grip around my chin suddenly slackened, and his expression changed from malicious cruelty to one of confusion. Then I noticed the red line along his neck just before his head neatly rolled off his shoulders, leaving a bleeding stump.

Then all was chaos and confusion.

The warriors holding me released their grip, and I was once again sent head first into the dirt as they screamed and bellowed, drawing their weapons and charging at an unknown assailant. I could hear the sound of blades clashing, but I just tried to regain my feet, and lurched upwards to get away from this demon-spawned grove. My hands were still bound behind my back, so I overbalanced and once again was sent sprawling. Come on Gaius, I told myself, up, up, up, got to go, got to run. I stumbled upwards again and managed a lurching run for a few steps, as I tried desperately to run for freedom.

Just as I thought I might make it, as I approached the last of the oaks, I heard someone behind me. He grabbed me and forced me to the floor with a hand over my mouth, which stopped me screaming in frustration and misery. I'd almost got away. I was so close, and now they had me again.

I was turned onto my back and stared directly into the face of Marcus Scaeva, before passing out in shock.

Even after reviving me, it took Marcus a while to calm me, pinning me down as I continued to struggle in a panic at seeing Marcus return from the void, his face covered in mud and streaked with blood.

'Shush ... Cassius, calm yourself ... we need to be away from here, and soon,' said Marcus, his head scanning the trees to his left and right.

I managed to compose myself enough to mutter, 'What about the guards?'

He shrugged. 'Don't worry about them, they're dead.'

I was incredulous. 'You killed them all?'

He turned to me, and his eyes showed a determination I'd never seen before as he hefted his *gladius*. 'I've become quite adept with this, Cassius. I don't think you'll get the better of me by throwing dirt in my eyes anymore.'

A tingle went down my spine. Was this the same naive innocent young man I brought to the forest only a few months before? He had a steely edge to him now, which was both reassuring and terrifying at the same time. The boy Marcus was gone, replaced by this cold killer with grey eyes that were now as hard as flint.

I tried to clear my thoughts. 'But you were said to be dead, your position overrun. I heard the tale myself.'

He shook his head. 'No time for that now, we need to be out of here. I think the other warriors were too distracted by what was going on in their camp, but sooner or later they'll notice their companions aren't returning.'

I nodded in agreement as he helped me to my feet and cut the bonds holding my hands, passing me some water to drink from a flask he carried which I drank greedily. I was full of questions, but my natural survival instincts told me that we needed to be as far away from here as possible, and the questions could wait.

Before we left the grove, Marcus stopped and turned to me. 'We better hide the dead guards. They'll find them eventually, but it might buy us some time.'

I nodded and helped him move the four bodies under a thick bush of brambles, and I noted that apart from the one he'd kill by decapitation, the other three had all been killed by a textbook single thrust of the *gladius*; Marcus wasn't boasting when he said he'd become adept with that weapon.

I took one of the guard's long *sax* blades for myself; it was a clumsy weapon made from poor iron with a dull blade, but I figured it was better than nothing. Marcus shook his head. 'You'll need a proper weapon, not one of those meat cleavers. Fortunately this forest is full of spare Roman blades.' He reached up to a tree not twenty paces from the bramble bush and removed a sheaved *gladius* from a cadaver's belt. With horror I saw that the corpse in question was that of Varus. His body must have been retrieved by Julius' cronies and hoisted up here with the other dead commanders. I should have burnt the body, I thought to myself, as Marcus passed the weapon into my trembling hands. 'This is no time to worry about the dead,' he said, 'only vengeance will quieten their shades.'

He turned and disappeared down a dark trail, and I looked down blankly at the weapon in my hands before sheaving it in the empty scabbard on my belt and following after him. I was disquieted by his cold manner, so alien to the youth I'd once known. Marcus led the way, stepping lightly through the underbrush, moving as silently as a forest nymph, as I blundered behind him, exhaustion making me clumsy as an ox.

We headed west, away from the main camp of Julius' Cherusci, periodically diving into cover as groups of warriors came across our path. Marcus was expert at scouting the path ahead, seemingly knowing instinctively when enemy tribesmen were about to cross our path, long before I'd heard or sensed anything. We'd hide under the cover of bushes or wild scrub as the tribesmen passed. They were often joking and full of high spirits at their great victory; my heart beat wildly, too scared to breathe, until Marcus calmly signalled that it was now safe to continue.

Eventually we came to a small hidden depression near a large fallen oak tree, which had cleverly been concealed with branches and leaves, and Marcus told me. 'We'll be safe here for the moment, I've hidden here for the past two days, although we must remain quiet. The tribesmen are complacent now, full of their victory, but we need to remain on our guard.'

I nodded in agreement and squeezed myself through a gap in the branches and we both huddled inside. I was grateful for a thick Roman cloak Marcus passed me, which he had stored in his hideaway.

My intention was to stay alert, to watch out for any sound of passing Cherusci tribesmen, but the warmth of the cloak, together with my utter exhaustion, meant my eyes soon started closing, and in no time, I was asleep, finally getting a respite from the horror, fear, and anxiety of the past few terrible days.

It wasn't until the next morning that I awoke with a start, worried that falling asleep had left me vulnerable to capture once again. Marcus again quietened me, with firm reassuring hands and soft-whispered words. 'Carefully, Cassius, there is no need to worry, I've seen no sign of pursuit near us, and we've had a quiet night.'

I nodded to show I understood.

He handed me a flask of water and some cured beef, which I devoured ravenously, realising how hungry I was.

He smiled, and said softly, 'We can talk a little if you like, but keep your voice low. Sounds can travel.'

I swallowed some water down my sore and parched throat. 'Are you sure it's safe?' I whispered.

He nodded. 'I've not heard a soul all night.'

I was full of questions, but the most striking one was, 'How is it you're alive? A legionary named Vettius told me you'd all been killed.'

Marcus' face momentarily lit up. 'So Vettius made it? He survived too?'

I shook my head. 'I'm afraid he died of his wounds, but he made it back to camp and told us the story. He said you'd been overrun.'

Marcus looked downcast on hearing of the death of the legionary. 'I suppose it would have made no difference if he'd lived, he'd only have survived long enough to die here.' He looked me in the eye, and once again I was unsettled by how much my young friend had changed. 'He was right. We were overrun, and every single one of my comrades were cut down before my eyes, but me they spared, me they kept ... they thought I could be of use to them.'

Marcus told me the whole story, in a faltering tone at first, his demeanour returning to the awkward youth I remembered, before strengthening as he told me all that had befallen him. He recounted the tale I'd heard from Vettius; the rescue of Paullinus and the death of centurion Aeschylus when they were trapped on the hill and surrounded.

His forehead creased in a frown. 'I knew I had to get word to you, that it was Ewald who I saw in the Angrivarii camp. I knew it was significant, even if I wasn't sure why. So I despatched Vettius with a message for you. I knew you'd know what it meant.'

I shook my head. 'I got the message, but missed the sheer scale of the treachery. I went to Varus, and we went to the Cherusci camp and accused his father, but we were wrong.'

Marcus looked surprised. 'Segestes wasn't involved?'

I gave a short bitter laugh. 'No, and he even told us who the traitor was: Julius Arminius. Ewald and his sister wanted their father deposed. Julius gave them the means to achieve this. It was their price to join him in his treachery. We fell into his hands and ultimately led our entire army to be slaughtered, all by his design.'

Marcus looked at me strangely. 'Your friend Julius was responsible for all this, and not Ewald?'

Was Marcus wondering whether I was complicit in my friend's treachery? I nodded. 'It is Julius who is the viper. Ewald is merely a pawn in his game. Julius fooled Varus and all three of his legates, but most of all he fooled me. I knew him better than anyone. I, of all people, should have realised what he was capable of. But I didn't ... and now all these deaths ... If you think I deserve to die by your hand, I will not try and evade the blade. The loss of this army was as much my fault as that of Varus.'

He shook his head. 'We can all be taken in by someone. Who could ever envisage this?'

Who indeed? The destruction of three entire Roman legions; the greatest defeat in Rome's long history; Twenty thousand dead. Oh, by the gods, how can this have happened?

I couldn't dwell on that now. 'But how did you escape? Were you involved in the battle here?'

Marcus stared at the floor for a bit, and he struggled to get the next words out. 'My time with the Cherusci was hard ... they didn't treat me kindly and wanted to extract as much information out of me as they could.'

He meant they tortured him. Now I'd seen their cruelty first hand, I knew how hard this must have been. 'Anything you told them under duress is understandable, Marcus. Everyone breaks in the end. Ask any of the army's questioners. The fact that you're still alive is all you need to worry about.'

He ground his teeth. 'They whipped me, burnt me, cut me ... but I couldn't tell them much. I really didn't know that much, but they wouldn't listen. Each day, more questions, more pain, again and again. I wished for death, but they were careful not to get near that point. Instead it was just pain, questions, pain, day after day.'

His arms and legs had a thick covering of mud and grime, which partially concealed them, but now I knew to look, I could see they were covered in burns and scars. Who knew what was hidden under his clothing? I shuddered. 'How did it end?'

He shrugged. 'I guess they thought they'd finally got all they could from me and never bothered to take me from my cell again for more questions. My cell was in one of the wooden long houses of their settlements, but fortunately for me the roof leaked, so I could drink some water which occasionally trickled through the crack in the wall after it rained.' He gave a shadow of a smile. 'Luckily for me, it rains a lot here.'

I let my breath out. 'How did you get away?'

He shrugged. 'Most of the warriors left, I guess, to gather here, leaving only old men and boys in the settlement. They probably thought me dead, so covered in sores and burns was I. When one young fool came in to check on me, he didn't even close the cell door when he gave me a shake to check. It was the last mistake he made. I broke his neck with my bare hands. Then I crept out of the settlement, killing two more men in the process.'

I wasn't sure which was more horrible, hearing what my friend had undergone, or the casual way he now described killing.

He continued. 'I first tried to make my way back to the Roman camp, to tell you all what I knew, but when I came out of the forest, I came across the tracks of a huge host so regular and regimented that it could only be that of a

Roman army. I followed your tracks and they led me back here, but by the time I'd got here, you were all surrounded, and I knew the army was doomed. I watched helplessly from the clifftops above as you made your last desperate attempt to break free from the encirclement. I wished there was more I could have done, but there was nothing.'

So Marcus had seen my last desperate throw of the dice – the charge we made that finally finished us. Did he realise it was his old friend who led them at that point? I asked him, 'Did you see how many broke out?'

He inclined his head and shrugged again. 'A few, more than a hundred, but not many more. They ran towards the river. Let's hope they make it.'

A thought occurred to me. 'Why didn't you follow them? Why were you there to save me from the four guards when they were about to nail me to a tree?'

He chuckled. 'I had no idea you were still alive, Cassius. My plan was to sneak into the Cherusci camp and kill Ewald, but as I got close, I saw you there and couldn't leave you. It was simply the will of the gods, or else blind chance.'

I swallowed hard at this, remembering how close that blade had been to my eye before Marcus had chopped the tribesman's head off from behind.

Marcus looked at me intently. 'But now you're safe, I plan to continue my mission and kill Ewald, and as your friend Julius is also culpable, kill him as well.'

I couldn't help myself; the sheer lunacy of the plan made me laugh. 'Don't be ridiculous, Marcus. Both are surrounded by thousands of warriors. Even if you could best either with the blade – still open to debate in Ewald's case – it makes no difference. You'll never get near either of them. What do you plan to do, hack your way through an army that has just destroyed three legions?'

'Don't laugh at me, Cassius.' The cold way he said this brought me up short. 'I know it won't be easy, but if I can come upon them in the night, or when they're off their guard, I believe I can do it. I'll sneak into their camp, kill them whilst they sleep. I'm not interested in how they die, just as long as they do.'

I made sure my face was serious as I answered him, but shook my head. 'It won't work, Marcus. Julius is no fool. He knows the importance of posting proper sentries and guarding his back. He has been Roman trained, remember, and he will be on his guard constantly – not from you, but from rival factions within the German tribes. Nobody, not even you, can get near him now.'

He shrugged. 'Then I will die trying. What does it matter? One more dead Roman in a forest of thousands?'

I sighed. 'Marcus, you can't throw your life away like that. I know you've been through a lot, but giving your life away now will achieve nothing.'

His face hardened, and his stubbornness took over. 'I'll not run away.'

I shook my head. 'This isn't about running away, Marcus. We still have a mission to complete.'

Now it was Marcus' turn to laugh. 'A mission! The entire army has been destroyed! What mission!'

I grabbed hold of his arm, and said, 'Exactly, the entire Roman occupational army of Germany has been destroyed and nobody knows about it! Do you think Julius plans to stop here? He has united the German tribes, something nobody has ever done before, not in their thousands of years of history. There are two legions at Mogontiacum, but their commander is Varus' nephew, Asprenas, and we know how much time he bothers to spend gathering intelligence. What's to stop Julius repeating what he achieved here? They'll be thinking that Varus has this entire region under control, but Varus is dead, together with all his men.'

Marcus looked worried; he knew I was right, but he didn't want to give up on his suicidal plan just yet. 'Others escaped. I saw them – they were running down to the river. Only one needs to get word to them.'

I gripped more tightly on his arm. 'And what if no one makes it? Julius told me his warriors were hunting down all those who broke out, and was confident that he'd kill them all. We don't know whether this is true, but we have to presume that it is. We are the only two Romans left alive who are to the west of the German host. All the others have fled east to the river. We can track back a different route, past our camp at Aurorae Novus, and warn the cohort Varus left there, not to mention the civilians still there.'

Marcus looked upwards, not meeting my eye, trying to find a way round my argument. 'You could go alone ... Once I killed Julius, the tribes may disunite again.'

I shook my head. 'And maybe they won't. Maybe some other leader, someone like his uncle Inguiomerus will just take over, and that's even if you are successful, something we both know is impossible. Our chances of getting word to Rome are doubled if we go together. It is your duty to warn them.'

Marcus' head slumped, knowing that I was giving him no choice. I wanted to remove the burden from him, so he wouldn't blame himself for running away, so I told him, 'And besides, Marcus, you are forgetting one thing. I still outrank you. I am ordering you to assist me in getting word to Aurorae Novus. Let's take only what we need and leave immediately.'

He looked at me sharply, but then nodded in agreement. 'I'll never be free of your damn orders, will I?'

I smiled. 'Not if I can help it. Now, what do we need for the journey?'

It didn't take us long to get ourselves ready. One of the unfortunate benefits of the army's destruction was that there were ample supplies to hand, as long as one wasn't squeamish about looting from the dead. I discarded my heavy tribune's breastplate, and we donned simple Roman mail shirts – we wanted to travel quickly, and there was no one left alive to be impressed by a tribune's flashy armour. We also took enough dried beef and grain to sustain us through the journey, and left as soon as we were set – something I was pleased about. I wanted to be as far from this valley of the dead as possible. Besides, I didn't want Marcus changing his mind and thinking up a new harebrained scheme.

We needed to be careful as we climbed up the steep incline the Angrivarii had so successfully blocked off during the battle. There were still plenty of warriors around, but we managed to evade them without too much trouble, only once having to resort to violence when we came across an Angrivarii warrior sitting alongside a narrow incline of rocks. Whilst I desperately tried to think up a way to traverse the narrow pass and find a way around, Marcus slipped up behind the warrior and slit his throat.

He signalled me to follow, after throwing the body off the side of the mountain, and told me, 'We don't have time to make diversions. You said yourself – lives depend on us.'

I just nodded and followed behind him, too wary of him to argue.

Chapter Thirty-six

We followed the path the army of Varus had taken back up the mountains and away from the point where she met her eventual doom. At first, avoiding Germanic warriors was difficult, having to duck out of sight and treading carefully through the undergrowth. But gradually, as we progressed up the mountain, sightings of the enemy became rarer, and we could travel more swiftly. We passed the camp where we'd retreated after the first attack, before our fateful march down the mountain. It had been completely burnt to the ground; the Angrivarii hadn't left any part of it still standing, as if they wanted to destroy any reminder that Rome had ever penetrated so far into their lands. Of the wounded that Varus had left there, there was no sign, but I was pretty sure they'd not fared any better than those captured by the Cherusci and were now nailed to various trees with their eyes plucked out.

We crossed the point where the army was first ambushed, and where I'd taken command of Macarius' cavalry. Was it really only a few days ago? It felt like a lifetime. As we came to the edge of the Teutoburg Forest, and the trees began to thin, my hopes started to rise that we might actually survive this terrible ordeal and reach the relative safety of Aurorae Novus. Those hopes were soon dashed as soon as we left the forest and entered the high hills that overshadowed our former home. Clearly visible were several columns of smoke; we knew what they signified immediately – Aurorae Novus was aflame.

Marcus' wanted to sprint ahead to get there as quickly as possible, but I knew such an action was pointless, even if I hadn't been too exhausted to comply. 'We are at least two days march from the camp, no matter how fast we travel, by the time we get there, it will all be over, if it isn't already.'

Marcus still looked agitated. 'But, the civilians … some might still be alive … we must …'

I realised then what scared him, and reassured him. 'Don't worry,

Marcus. Julia isn't there. I arranged for her to leave with Numeria before I left. They will both be safe in Vetera, the other side of the Rhenus, by now.'

Thank the gods I had insisted she leave Aurorae Novus, although equally I also remembered my preference for her to follow the army; thankfully she'd ignored that particular bit of advice – the thought of Numeria or Julia being subjected to the sort of treatment I'd witnessed in the forest didn't even bear thinking about. 'They'll both be fine, Marcus,' I told him.

He nodded and agreed, but didn't say anything more. The issue of Julia was still obviously a barrier between us, so I let the subject drop. Amazing really, we'd both seen men die in their thousands in the last few days, seen more suffering and death that any man should see in a lifetime, plus my own life had been saved by Marcus, and yet an argument over a young girl still stood between us. How strange the human heart was.

For two days we maintained a steady pace across the hills, sleeping huddled up in our cloaks for only the darkest turns of the moon, and setting out again at the first break of dawn, until we came to the hill which overlooked Aurorae Novus. There was nothing left.

The Roman camp had been completely burnt to the ground, and even the large stone buildings demolished. It was the same story for the Roman town that surrounded it. Every home had been set afire, and the great stone public works, those that Varus had been so proud of, demolished. The great aqueduct was now a pile of rubble, alongside the bathhouse, and the statue of Augustus had his head taken off and lay discarded on the ground. The scale of the destruction was shocking.

Marcus shook his head. 'Why would they do that? Why not keep the town for themselves? Why demolish what has taken so much effort to construct?'

I knew the answer now. 'Because they hate us, Marcus. They hate Rome and everything she represents. They don't want to live in stone towns and benefit from the fruits of civilisation. They prefer to hoard their hatred and destroy any reminder of it. We'll never tame them. Civilisation to them is as abhorrent as living in chains. If only we'd seen it sooner.'

He spat on the ground. 'What do you think became of the people left here?'

I hung my head. 'You don't need me to answer that, Marcus. You know what has happened to them. They won't have left any alive.'

He pulled himself straighter. 'Then there is no need for us to remain here. Let's be gone, we still have a long way to go until we reach Aliso. Hopefully we can get to that camp before the same happens there.'

I nodded in agreement and followed Marcus. I remembered our meeting with the Roman commander, Caedicius, in the spring. He'd only had a cohort of men from the XIX with him then, but at least Aliso was connected to the larger fort of Vetera by a good Roman road. Providing they got sufficient warning, the camp could either be reinforced, or, at the very least, abandoned so the inhabitants might survive.

We left Aurorae Novus behind us and broke out of the foothills and back into woodland again, picking up the trail for Aliso. By now, we were both exhausted; even Marcus' boundless energy was finding the punishing trek through the wilds of Germany hard going, so on the fourth day after leaving the ruins of the Roman town behind, we decided to rest by a small river.

We removed our mail shirts and stripped off, waded into the cold but welcome relief of the water, the gentle current blissfully refreshing after our punishing journey. I sunk my head under the water and felt so pleased to finally wash off the blood, mud, sweat and grime from the battle and arduous journey. I surfaced and turned round to tell Marcus what a relief it was to feel clean again, when the words stuck in my throat. Marcus had his back to me, up to his waist in water, washing the mud and dirt from his body, but once the mud cleared I could see the extent of the wounds the tribesmen had inflicted on him whilst in captivity. 'By the gods,' I muttered, horrified by the amount of livid scars and burns on his back; virtually his entire back was crisscrossed in whip marks, and marks from the branding iron. 'What did they do to you?'

Marcus turned his head, saw what I was looking at and just shrugged. 'The Cherusci aren't afraid to be rough with their prisoners.'

I swallowed hard. 'Oh Marcus, I'm so sorry you had to go through that.'

He shook his head. 'Don't be. It's made me stronger, that's all that matters now.'

I was incredulous. 'But Marcus, you must still be in so much pain, surely there must be—' I never got to finish my sentence, we both turned at the sound of laughter and armoured men coming down the sandy river bank . There were six large Cherusci warriors, all bearded and ugly, laughing at finding their prey in a hopelessly vulnerable position.

Marcus reacted first and shouted, 'Cassius, a weapon! Now!'

Without thinking, I turned and grabbed our two sheaved *gladius* that were on a rock beside me and threw one to Marcus who, in the blink of an eye, drew it from its scabbard and ran out of the water at the men.

They looked surprised we wanted to make a fight of it, but one reacted quickly enough to throw a spear at Marcus, who incredibly grabbed it directly from the air, turned it around and used it to deflect another spear coming his way. I followed his lead and charged out of the water, just as Marcus threw his spear back, taking one warrior directly in the chest. Another warrior threw a spear at me, but I dove under it, rolling to regain my footing along the sandy bank and thrusting my *gladius* directly into the belly of the warrior before he managed to draw his *sax* blade. Another took his place, aiming a wicked overhand blow with his *sax*, which I just managed to raise my blade in time to deflect. He had the advantage of a shield which he used to physically knock me backwards, but I kept my feet and made a series of attacks towards his body. He may have had the advantage of a shield, but was no match for my speed, and his ripostes with his ungainly *sax* blade were clumsy. I swayed out of the way of one and slammed my *gladius* through his heart, and he keeled backwards.

I looked around expecting to find another warrior bearing down on me, but instead saw that Marcus had killed two more and was chasing the last surviving tribesmen back into the woods. He would have caught him too, but once the warrior reached the cover of the trees, his sandaled feet fared much better on the forest floor than Marcus' bare feet, and Marcus had to break off the pursuit when he punctured his foot on a forest thorn. 'Ouch! Ahh! By Hades!' he shouted.

'Let him go, Marcus, you'll never catch him now.' I scanned the trees for more warriors, but none appeared.

Marcus limped back to the sandy clearing, cursing, 'He'll bring others,'

I shook my head. 'That can't be helped now. It must have been a scouting party. Let's get dressed and be out of here.'

Marcus looked around at the five dead warriors and chuckled. 'I bet they couldn't believe their luck finding us both naked swimming in the river. Didn't do them much good though, did it?

I shook my head in disbelief. 'We are lucky to be alive. I've never seen someone catch a spear from the air before, Marcus. That's quite a trick.'

He turned to me and told me honestly, 'I've never tried it before – I just did it instinctively. If I'd thought about it, I'd have probably missed it.'

I grinned. 'Well, I'm glad you didn't. Even so, it was a close-run thing. If they'd formed a shield wall as they should have done, we'd both be dead.'

He grabbed his tunic and slipped it over his head. 'I suppose they thought we were little threat – two naked men in a river.'

I donned my mail shirt and knelt down to do up my sandals. 'We were lucky, that's all.'

Marcus rubbed his sore foot before putting on his sandals. 'Luck be damned. We survived by our skill at arms, the both of us. Six to two, who but us could overcome such odds?'

I shook my head again as I helped him to his feet. 'There is always someone faster and quicker than yourself, Marcus, never forget that. Now, let's make as much distance from here as possible. It's a shame they didn't have any horses. I'd give anything for a good horse now.'

Marcus and I jogged along the trail, wary of the pursuit that we knew would follow. After a mile or two, I realised we needed to lose the mail shirts; we weren't going to get out of this by fighting now, just speed of foot, so we discarded them.

We ran the whole of that day; only our supreme fitness keeping us going after the exhausting last few days. We knew they were pursuing us, and though we'd seen no sign of them, we somehow knew they weren't far behind. Eventually, after the sun dipped below the horizon, when we really could run no further, we collapsed by a natural shelter in the lee of small hill and fell straight asleep. Neither of us even had the energy to post a watch, just hoping that our pursuers had also stopped for the night.

We woke early the next morning, both of us aching in every limb and every muscle, and after filling our canteens from a nearby stream, ate the last of our cured beef. We mentally prepared for another day's hard journey along the trail back to Aliso.

I rubbed my sore legs and massaged my calves before we set out. 'I don't know if I can face another day's running. I never thought I could run so far …'

Marcus frowned. 'Trust me, when they are right behind you, blowing their hunting horns, you'll find some extra energy from somewhere. I remember our flight after rescuing Paullinus.'

'They have cavalry. It's not going to take them long to run us down on horseback.' I was pessimistic about our chances of escaping; we had no choice but to head for Aliso, but any fool would know which direction we were heading.

Marcus slapped me on the back. 'All the more reason for us to get going. Let's not wait until they're on top of us.'

We jogged throughout the morning, running in silence to conserve energy. My body was now wracked with pain, and I was struggling to keep up with the younger, fitter, Marcus. By lunchtime, I'd had enough. I collapsed by the side of the trail and told Marcus I needed to rest.

Marcus looked blown too, as he bent over and passed me a canteen of water. 'Alright, let's rest, but we can't stay here long. We won't be as lucky if they catch us up again next time. They'll be ready for us, and with greater numbers.'

I drank deeply from the canteen, gulping down the water. 'You should go on without me, Marcus. Alone, you stand a chance.'

He sat down heavily beside me. 'You know I won't do that, Cassius, so get it out of your head.' He rested his head in his hands, and shut his eyes in exhaustion.

I was too tired to argue and I knew he was right; he'd never leave me.

After our laboured breathing slowly calmed and we'd captured our breath, Marcus whispered, 'Can you hear something?'

I sat up and tried to listen. Was this the sound of our pursuit? There was nothing except the normal sounds of the forest, wind through the trees, birds chattering, but then … yes, the wind changed and I heard what he was talking about, a high-pitched screeching. 'Is it the Cherusci?'

Marcus shook his head. 'It's coming from ahead of us, not behind.'

We both got up and slowly made our way towards the noise, *gladius* drawn, wary of trouble. We turned a bend in the trail and found the source of the disturbance: an overloaded cart with a broken wheel, two large Libyan horses still hitched to its yoke, and two very angry young women screaming at the tops of their lungs at one another. It was Numeria and Julia.

Julia shouted, 'Well, you said you knew how to harness the horses, not me!'

Numeria screamed back. 'This has nothing to do with the harness. All you had to do was point the horses in the right direction!'

Julia flapped her hands in anger. 'Well if it was so easy, why did we spend all yesterday morning stuck in that bog? You were steering the horses then, not me!'

Marcus and I looked at one another blankly, before we turned back to the women and I said in my loudest parade ground voice in order to get their attention, 'Two grand ladies of Rome, squabbling like children, riding through the countryside without a care in the world, arrogantly making enough noise to shout their location to any who might care. How very Roman.'

They broke off their argument immediately and turned to us. After a moment's shock, Julia shrieked, 'Marcus!' and clapped her hands.

Numeria was cooler, but even she looked relieved to see us. 'Oh, thank the gods, someone who knows what they're doing.'

I was less happy. 'What, by all the gods are you doing here? You were meant to have left almost two weeks ago. You should be safe in Vetera by now.'

Numeria folded her arms under her breasts. 'Don't take that tone with me, Gaius. We left as soon as we could. It just took us a long time to pack all our belongings. Then, we have had a nightmare journey. Trying to navigate this cart over this beaten trail has proved impossible. I wish I'd never listened to you in the first place and remained in Aurorae Novus!'

I shook my head in disbelief. 'You were never meant to bring any possessions. I gave you those two Libyan warhorses to ride, not be used as cart horses! It's a miracle you got this far. You knew there was no road to Aliso. What were you thinking?'

Julia pointed at Numeria and said sharply. 'She said we could make it if we were careful. It wasn't my fault the stupid cart broke. The horses wouldn't go in a straight line—'

Numeria snapped back at her. 'Well, Valerius said we could navigate a cart over the trail. I'll be having sharp words with him when we get back to Aurorae Novus.'

Marcus and I looked at one another. We both knew that telling them wouldn't be easy. There was no point putting it off, however, so I said, 'Numeria, I'm very sorry but I'm afraid you won't be returning to Aurorae Novus. Not now or ever. If Valerius is the name of your freedman, and he remained in the town, he'll already be dead.'

Both women looked at me in shock. Numeria gasped. 'No! Governor Varus assured us the town would be protected.'

I shook my head, and tears welled in my eyes. 'Varus is dead too. They all are – everyone. Marcus and I are all that's left.'

Chapter Thirty-seven

It took a while for us to explain everything that had befallen the army, and a while longer for the two of them to come to terms with the fact that everyone was really dead; it seemed too incredible that they were all gone. The tragic loss of one life is enough to stun the senses, but for so many to have fallen together was almost more than the mind could comprehend. We sat them down by the stricken cart, and Julia soon started weeping and clung to Marcus tightly. He was unsure how to react around her, but knew that he couldn't turn her away at such a time. So he simply put his arms around her and let her cry herself out in great wracking sobs.

Numeria's reaction was more complex. Firstly she was angry that Varus had mismanaged the situation so catastrophically. She banged her fist on the cart with tears streaming down her eyes. 'This would never have happened if he'd listened. I told him the tribes were angry.'

She broke down and fell to her knees crying, realising that there was no longer any point in blaming Varus; he'd paid with his life, along with all the others who'd never listened to her advice. Grief for the loss of all the people she'd lived with, everyone she knew in Germany, all now dead. The life she and Otho once shared was now completely gone.

Finally, after a lot of tears, Numeria asked, 'What does this mean for us?' There was a hint of fear in her voice.

Julia looked up at Marcus. 'Surely the tribes have had their fill of death?' The frightened way she said that told us that even she didn't believe it.

I shook my head. 'We have no time to lose. We need to make it to Aliso and warn them of all that has transpired. They'll be as oblivious as you two.' I turned to Marcus. 'Unhitch their horses. We'll have to ride double, but at least we won't need to run any more. Hopefully the horses are as full of stamina as we were promised. They'll need to be. Aliso is at least two or three days away.'

Julia asked. 'What about the cart and our things?'

I grunted. 'We leave it. We'll take nothing with us other than whatever food we can stuff in the saddlebags. The horses will be overburdened riding double anyway, so no exceptions. We encountered some tribesmen only yesterday, and one got away. Warriors will soon be on our tail in their thousands. Let's not be caught by them.'

Both women went as white as sheets and nodded without argument.

The two Libyan geldings looked to be in good health. They pranced as soon as Marcus released them from the yoke of the cart and saddled them with the two saddles Numeria had fortunately brought along in the back of the cart.

I mounted mine and pulled Numeria up behind me, and we started off at a brisk clip, Marcus and Julia following behind. On the first day we made steady progress, but despite my eagerness to reach Aliso, I was careful to stop and walk the horses regularly, in order to give them respite from our weight. I knew we'd be lost without them.

Despite our perilous predicament, it was good to have Numeria so close to me, to feel her arms around my waist and her breathing next to me. I tried to concentrate only on practical matters, discussed only what was needed, trying to be the professional soldier for once, but the closeness of her was difficult to ignore. I told myself it was only due to the emotional journey of the last few days, but I wasn't convincing even myself.

When it neared dusk, Marcus' mount missed a step in the gloom, and stumbled on a slippery part of the trail. No harm was done, but I knew we needed to stop for the night. If one of our mounts were to break a leg, we'd all be lost. 'We'll camp a good way off the trail. Even if they continue to pursue via torchlight, they'll never be able to track us. We should be safe enough.'

I wasn't completely sure of that, but I wanted to come across as certain. It wouldn't profit anyone to spend the night terrified of capture. We hobbled the horses and settled down for a light meal, made from our dwindling supplies of grain. Afterwards, Marcus and Julia separated themselves from Numeria and I and found somewhere to bed down for the night. We couldn't risk a fire, but fortunately the night was mild, with no rain in the air, so one area of the forest was as good as anywhere else. They obviously wanted to be far away from us so they had some privacy. Marcus had his arm around her as he led her away. It looked as if the journey had done much to heal old wounds.

Numeria smiled as the two young adults walked out of hearing. 'I think Marcus is good for Julia. She needs someone like him in her life.'

I smiled. 'He's still in love with her, you know.'

She chuckled. 'Any fool can see that, Gaius. They still have a lot of talking to do. It will be difficult for him to come to terms with the life she led at Aurorae Novus, but I think he will in time.'

I frowned. 'I just hope he can forgive her, for that night ...'

Numeria laid her hand on my arm. 'Honestly, do you really think any of that matters now, after all that's happened?'

I shrugged. 'I remember you were pretty angry at the time.'

She gave a light laugh. 'Oh dear, Gaius, I was quite hard on you, wasn't I?'

It was good to hear her laugh. 'I'm pretty sure I deserved it.'

She shook her head. 'No, not really, Gaius. If truth be known, I think the only reason I was so angry was that I was a little jealous. I'd never have admitted it, but hearing about you two brought up some uncomfortable feelings. That's why I was so angry. I felt I was betraying Otho by having feelings for anyone but him, and I took that out on you. It's me that should be sorry.'

I sighed. 'You really did love Otho, didn't you?'

She nodded. 'Yes, but it is so hard to keep the memories of him without the pain of loss. That's why I felt I was betraying him. You're everything he ever wanted to be, Gaius. You're brave and strong, and everyone in the army respects you – the perfect soldier in every way.'

I looked up at the stars, poking through the branches of the trees above. 'Oh, Numeria, is that what you really think? You really think I'm the perfect soldier?'

She looked surprised by my reaction. 'Everyone knows you are.'

I laughed. 'It's all a lie, Numeria. Do you know why I got so drunk that night with Julia?'

She frowned in confusion. 'I just thought it was you acting irresponsibly ... I didn't really think about it. You're hardly the only soldier in the camp who liked a drink.'

I shook my head. 'I was drinking heavily because of a recurring dream. One which involved a man named Decius.'

She tilted her head. 'Who was he?'

I let out a deep breath. 'Centurion Decius was under my command at Western-Gate Pass when we were cut off by the Chatti the last time I was in Germany.'

She shrugged. 'I've heard the story, the whole of Rome has. You kept them at bay until relief came ...'

I shook my head. 'Yes, but the whole of Rome doesn't know the full story, nobody does. Not everyone under my command thought we should wait until we were relieved. Centurion Decius was one of them. He claimed I didn't know enough about the German tribes. He was a veteran of eighteen years campaigning, so his opinion carried a lot of weight with the men. He kept on arguing for us to try to break out, make a run for it. Even after I overruled him, he wouldn't let up. He tried to convince the other centurions, the rest of the men, undermining my authority.'

Numeria eye's narrowed in sympathy. 'It must have been very difficult, but you needed to do what you thought was right.'

I looked at her. 'But that's just it, Numeria. I didn't know I was right, not really. The lives of over five hundred men were in my hands, but I wasn't sure if the reason I was staying put was nothing more than the fear of failure. Decius was very convincing. He almost convinced me.'

She looked puzzled. 'But you did stand your ground. I know that much is true.'

I looked down at the ground and admitted something I'd never told anyone. 'A break came in the fighting. The Chatti partially retreated, leaving us a way out down via the river, but I knew it was a trap. It was too obvious, too contrived. Why leave the one area unguarded that offered us the greatest chance of our escape?' I held up my hand when she looked to interrupt. 'I also saw my opportunity to rid myself of Centurion Decius. I told him to lead a breakaway group, see if he could get help. He was only too eager to comply – it was what he wanted all along after all. I hand-picked his men for him, choosing all those who'd been supporting him the most vocally. I knew I needed to get rid of all those who didn't believe we were doing the right thing by holding our ground. They were breaking the morale of the entire cohort, and I couldn't have anyone else undermining my authority.'

Numeria said nothing; she just let me continue in my own time.

'Centurion Decius took a band of thirty men down to the river under cover of darkness. Sure enough, not long afterwards, we heard signs of fighting, and I knew the trap had been sprung. At first I thought I'd done the right thing. All the men left under my command realised escape was no longer an option, and I'd been right to order us to stay. My authority was now unquestioned, as I could have given no better demonstration of what fate awaited us if we failed.'

'But then the Chatti came back, and threw the heads of our fallen comrades over the stockades to taunt us with their deaths. Only then did I realise how much I'd betrayed those men. I'd used their lives to prove that I was right … no man should have that power over the life of others.'

I choked back tears, struggling with the memory.

Numeria put her hand on my shoulder. 'I can't tell you that you did the right thing, Gaius, only you know the right or wrong of that. But the rest of those men survived because of you, Gaius. They lived because you were strong enough to hold them together.'

I shrugged. 'Much good it did them. Most who survived have been killed along with Varus now.'

She shook her head. 'Even if they are all dead, and none of them have escaped Julius and his Cherusci, that still gave them another five years of life. Time for some to father children, others to fall in love or prosper in any other fashion you care to name. Don't begrudge the gift you gave those men. It was precious, and they all knew it.'

I couldn't meet her eye. 'But what about the betrayal of Decius and the men I sent to their deaths?'

She lifted my head, forcing me to look her in the eye. 'It was awful was happened to Decius, but you said yourself, it was what he wanted – he wanted to try and break out. You gave them that chance. Don't spend your life blaming yourself for his mistake. I won't have it, Gaius. You're too good a man to waste your life in regret.'

I wrenched my gaze away from her. 'But that's not all, Numeria. I left the army under false pretences soon after Western-Gate Pass. I could no longer do it, no longer hold my nerve. My will had been broken. I spent the next five years living off a reputation I didn't deserve.'

She put a finger to my mouth. 'And yet you still returned here and fought alongside Varus, fighting to the bitter end in a losing cause. Did you fail then?'

I shook my head. 'I did all I could. We were defeated before we marched into that valley. Julius had us completely trapped, nothing could have saved us.'

She pulled me over to her and cradled my head near her breast as I started to sob quietly. It was such a relief to finally have told someone the truth about my life. For so long I had hidden behind a lie and it was as if a great burden had been taken from my shoulders. 'So you don't hate me?' I asked her.

She lifted my head and gently said, 'I could never hate you, Gaius. Even when I tried, I never could.' And she kissed me.

I kissed her back, gingerly at first, and then my passion took over and I took her in my arms as five years of anxiety and a lifetime of pent-up desire for this woman burst through. I felt the contours of her strong, supple body, writhing with desire next to mine, and ran my hand down the back of her *stola*, feeling the bare skin under the homespun cotton. She kissed me more fervently, and I slipped my hand into her robe and released a breast which I suckled to her groans of pleasure. Within moments, I parted her stola, revealing her beautiful sun-kissed naked body, and pulled my tunic over my head as she grasped my naked torso, kissing my chest before moving her hands down to my bare buttocks. I felt the wetness between her legs, and as I pulled them apart and entered her, she gasped in shock and pleasure. We moved in rhythm with one another, uncaring about anything else in the world at that time but this one moment of release.

Afterwards, long afterwards, as I lay in her arms and we dozed in complete relaxation, it occurred to me that I'd never felt such contentment and security. Thousands of warriors were on our tail, I'd undergone the most terrifying experience, seen untold death and suffering, but now I was with Numeria, I felt complete again, back to the man I was before Western-Gate Pass. I didn't know what the future held, but I was no longer afraid. I was ready for whatever life had in store.

I drifted off into a deep dreamless sleep, safe in the knowledge, that, together, Numeria and I would see this through.

I was awoken by a very surly Marcus, who gave me a nudge with a foot and told me, 'We need to be on our way, dawn has broken. We don't have time to lie abed.'

I woke up groggily and looked around, realising in embarrassment that Numeria and I were barely covered by my large cloak that I'd used to cover us last night. 'Of course, Marcus. We'll be ready very soon.'

It was obvious what must have transpired last night. Numeria and I were both naked under the cloak, and I gently nudged her awake. Marcus walked off stiffly, whether out of moral criticism at our actions, or simply because he thought the timing could be better – I wasn't sure. But if Marcus was disapproving, Julia was anything but. She stood behind Marcus and grinned over at us, beaming from ear to ear. She asked Numeria as she woke, 'Morning, Numeria, will you wish to bathe before we set out this morning? You were always instructing me that proper polite Roman ladies washed each morning. Shall I attend you by the stream?'

Numeria muttered under her breath, 'Oh, by the gods, I'm never going to hear the end of this ...'

I stifled a laugh, and Numeria answered in as casual tone as she could muster, 'That is alright, Julia, thank you for your offer, but I'm sure you can be of more use helping Marcus with the horses.'

Julia's eyes twinkled. 'Nonsense, what do I know of horses? Here, let me grab your *stola* for you, you'll catch a cold otherwise, being as exposed as you are ... oh dear, the *stola* is ripped. How can that have happened? Still never mind, it'll serve, I guess. It will still cover up *most* of you.'

Numeria sat up in annoyance and grabbed the *stola*. 'Thank you, Julia, I'll be fine now.'

I spied my tunic, tossed casually a few paces away, and reached over to slip it over my head. I thought I should probably say something to Julia to put an end to the teasing, but a fearsome glare from Numeria – when I cleared my throat to speak – soon told me I better keep quiet. Instead I went to find Marcus.

As I walked away, I heard Julia telling Numeria, 'There you go, you look much more respectable now. No one could tell you've just spent the night in the open ... so lucky you had something to keep you warm at night.' She giggled as she followed Numeria down to the stream, who was trying her best to shoo her away.

I found Marcus with the horses. He was running his hands down their flanks and told me, 'They're holding up extremely well. You'd never tell they'd spent a day being ridden double.'

I patted the closest horse's thick neck, relieved that Marcus didn't want to discuss the night before. 'Yes, good stock these Libyans. The Cherusci won't have anything to match them, not even Julius' own cavalry.'

He ran a hand over the horse's rump, and then lifted a saddle onto its back. 'I hope you're right. Our lives depend on them now. We have a lot more to lose now.' He signalled over to the two women, who were washing by the stream.

I nodded. 'We'll be alright, Marcus, we have to be.' I gave myself a mental shake, and put away any thoughts of the consequences of capture. 'Let's try and make as much ground this morning as we can.'

Numeria and Julia joined us, and true to our word, we made good ground, soon leaving our impromptu campsite far behind. It felt good to have Numeria's arms snugly wrapped around my waist as we rode along the trail for Aliso. We stopped at lunchtime, and ate sparingly, before leading the horses for a time, mindful that we needed to care for them.

Soon afterwards, we heard the first war horn.

Wasting no time, we mounted up and rode the horses as fast as we dared along the trail. We had to be careful, as it was strewn with overgrown brush that could easily obscure a fallen log that could lead to a horse breaking its leg.

We heard more horns blaring, and when I pulled my mount up to look back along the horizon, I could see far in the distance the trail full of mounted warriors.

Numeria whispered in my ear tensely. 'Why have they sent so many to capture us? It makes no sense.'

I shook my head. 'They're not here to capture us. That's the vanguard of their entire army. They're coming for war.'

I pulled my horse round and took off after Marcus, apprehension creeping down my spine. We continued to ride the horses hard, forced to become more reckless to keep the distance between us and the advancing host. The war horns stopped, but each time I looked back, the enemy horses had gained on us, their mounts being less encumbered. We ran the horses throughout the afternoon, and I blessed the gods when I finally spied the great silver mountain in the distance, the mountain that I knew overlooked the camp of Aliso.

Marcus drew his horse alongside mine as we pulled up. 'The horses can't take us so far, we'll end up running them to death.'

I knew he was right; both horses were blowing. Even the Libyans' legendary stamina had its limits. 'We have no choice, Marcus. We have to ride them hard.'

Numeria said, 'If that is their army coming, then they're not interested in us, we could hide in the forest somewhere, let them pass, and then go round them.'

I shook my head. 'No, we have to reach Aliso first. The camp there knows nothing of what's happened. Julius' cavalry will appear to them to be regular Roman auxiliaries. If they approach the camp alone, they need only ask for the gates to be opened and they will be – that's why the war horns have stopped, they don't want to alert the Roman camp.' I couldn't be sure, but now I thought about it that was probably how they'd taken Aurorae Novus so quickly.

Marcus swore and spat on the ground when he realised I was right. 'Let's be going then. We'll either make it or we won't. It's in the hands of the gods now.'

I nodded and he spurred his horse forward, which once again gamely broke into a canter, followed by Numeria and me. It was approaching dusk, and the silver mountain was looming above, when the first of the enemy outriders spied us and set off in pursuit. We were so close now. It seemed too cruel to fail right at the end, so I spurred my horse faster. 'Please boy, almost there, just one last effort,' I whispered in his ear, beseeching to every god I could name that he didn't let me down now.

I looked behind me and could see it was indeed Julius' cavalry who were now close behind. As we broke out of the trees, I saw the camp of Aliso in front of us, still mercifully untouched and manned by Roman sentries standing along her tall palisades.

Both our mounts were fully lathered and running full pelt for safety, as we screamed at the sentries, 'Open the gates! Open the gates!'

What it must have looked like to the watching Roman sentries, I wasn't sure, seeing two mounts being chased down by a troop of Roman auxiliaries, but thankfully they opened the gates and our horses flew through, and I quickly drew my mount up and shouted at the nearest *optio*. *'Shut those gates now!'*

He looked stunned, but the urgency and authority in my voice made him obey quickly enough and he signalled to shut the gates before the first of the enemy outriders could pass through. I sighed in relief as I saw the two great gates bang shut, and the locking bar placed down sealing them.

'Thank the gods,' I said, as Numeria and I slipped off our mount. I put my head to my horse's forehead. 'No finer steed has every run in the Circus Maximus than you. We owe you our lives.' The horse was trembling, and breathing far too heavily, completely blown by the last run.

The *optio* came up behind me, sternly demanding, 'Who in all the gods are you? And why have I just shut out a troop of our own cavalry?'

I turned to him. 'They're not our cavalry. They would have killed us all. I'll explain everything, but first find a groom to look after our two horses, and double the guard on the walls. I need to speak to your commander, Caedicius.'

I wasn't wearing any symbol of my rank, only being dressed in my military tunic, which was now little more than rags, but either the command in my voice or the mention of his commander's name convinced him that I was telling the truth, and he started issuing orders to men around him.

Numeria hung onto my waist in exhaustion as Marcus and Julia came over to us. Marcus grinned. 'We made it, Cassius, we made it!'

I shook my head sadly. 'Don't get overexcited, Marcus. We're not out of this yet.'

Chapter Thirty-eight

'All dead? Every one of them?' Caedicius was having difficulty believing all we'd told him. He paced up and down in his large headquarters building, shaking his head in disbelief. 'We were expecting them any day. We've cleared out each of the barracks blocks, made them ready to house the men. I can't believe they've all gone.'

Marcus said softly. 'A few survivors may have escaped to the east.' Caedicius whipped his head round at this, but Marcus was to disappoint him, 'but they will number only in the scores, not the hundreds, and will be no help to you even if they evade the Cherusci tribesmen hunting them.'

I put my hand on Marcus' shoulder to quieten him. 'I'm afraid all three legions are gone, Caedicius. You and your five hundred men are all that remains of the entire army of the German interior.'

Caedicius looked upwards. 'Varus, the old fool, taken in by a traitor.'

I frowned. 'Arminius fooled more than Varus. I'm afraid we were all taken in.'

Caedicius looked at us. 'I even liked Arminius, thought he was a good soldier and a good influence on the governor.'

I shook my head. 'We all did. We were all wrong. We don't have time to discuss what has passed, though. We need to plan what to do next. Right now your cohort is all that stands between the Rhenus and an enemy host of unimaginable size. All the civilians have now been brought inside the camp, is that right?'

He nodded. The Cherusci horsemen had backed off to the shelter of the tree line after the gates were closed on them, but I knew they'd be back as soon as the main body of Julius' host caught up with them.

I rubbed my eyes with the balls of my thumbs. I was still tired, but now wasn't the time for rest. 'That's good, although this camp won't protect them for long unless we find a way to get them to safety.'

Caedicius frowned. 'So you want us to abandon Aliso. Give it up without even a fight?'

I swallowed hard. 'No.'

Marcus turned to me in surprise. 'You don't? I thought you said that was what we were here to do?'

I shook my head. 'Initially, yes I did, but I've thought it through. Why has Julius Arminius brought his entire army here? Just to destroy this one outpost? Why bother?'

Marcus looked at me blankly, but I could tell by the way the colour drained from Caedicius face that he began to understand. 'He doesn't intend to stop at the Rhenus.'

I nodded. 'The bridge at Vetera has a large fort, but it is barely manned these days, it's not much more than a supply depot. If he takes the crossing there, then he is into the interior of Gaul. He told me he plans to make a treaty with Rome's greatest rival, King Maroboduus of the Marcomanni. How better to seal the deal than gifting him Gaul?'

Marcus looked aghast. 'Two huge barbarian armies running loose through the Roman world!'

I grunted. 'It's worse than that, Marcus. They may be able to conquer the entire region, take this uprising to the very gates of Italy. The very fabric of the western half of the empire is at stake.'

Caedicius interjected. 'But surely the legions of Gaul can stop him?'

I shrugged. 'Which legions, Caedicius? There are only two legions based in Lugdunum, the rest are as far away as Cisalpine Gaul. Remember, he has just destroyed three legions here. If he joins up with Maroboduus, who knows what his strength in the field will be?'

Marcus raised a finger. 'There are the two legions at Mogontiacum!'

I hadn't forgotten about the two legions based on the fringe of Germany, on Gaul's northern border, but we couldn't rely on their help. 'Even now they may be under attack. Remember, Arminius has been planning this uprising for a long time. The men at Mogontiacum are likely to be as unsuspecting as Varus was. We know how useless their commander Asprenas is at gathering intelligence from our work in the records office. This uprising may have spread to that area of Germany too, and even now they are in a similar plight to us. We can't take the risk.'

Caedicius stopped pacing and sat down at the campaign table next to us. 'Alright, you don't need to stress the danger of the situation to me any more. If Rome loses Gaul, she may collapse altogether, such is the importance of Gaul to Rome now. We now know the dangers. How do we stop him?'

I stood and put my palms on the table, looking at the map displayed on the campaign table. 'Our best chance is still to stop him at the Rhenus.'

Marcus frowned. 'So you wish to fall back to Vetera after all?'

I shook my head. 'No, we can't take the risk of being caught on the road between here and there and being cut to pieces before we reach it. No, we must hold here. Arminius can't afford to leave a fortress at his back in hostile hands. It'd be tactical suicide, and we know he's no fool, so he'll have to destroy us before he moves onto the Rhenus.'

Both nodded in agreement.

I pointed out the distances on the map. 'We'll need to send messengers to the legions at Mogontiacum and Lugdunum, tell them what has transpired here, and get them to reinforce Vetera with all their strength. Once the river crossing is secured, we can abandon Aliso and withdraw. They'll never be able to take Vetera once it's reinforced.'

Caedicius folded his arms and leant forward examining the map. 'Agreed. But how do we withdraw once we're under siege?'

I laughed. 'We'll have to work that out when the time comes. Tell the messengers that they must send a signal arrow into the sky once Vetera is safely secured. Then we'll know our job is done and it's time to escape.'

Marcus held his chin in his hand. 'The legions at Mogontiacum are closer, but that'll still mean we have to hold out for five days at least – a tough ask for only one cohort.'

I shrugged. 'And if those legions don't come to our aid, it'll be ten days at least for the ones from Lugdunum. But what else can we do? We must try. Our walls are strong and high, and unlike in the Teutoburg, we know he's coming this time.'

Caedicius sighed. 'I suppose you want to take command of the fort now?'

I shook my head. 'No. The men know you. We can't risk the morale of the men by me taking over now. Besides, neither Marcus nor I know anything about defending a fortress. You'll remain in command and marshal the camp's defences. Marcus and I will remain at your disposal.'

Caedicius looked relieved. 'Thank you, Cassius. My men and I won't let you down.' He stood up and saluted. 'Thank the gods you're with us, Cassius. A braver soul never fought for the Republic than you.'

Even I laughed at that one.

We watched from the ramparts as Julius' vast army surrounded the camp, strings of warriors ransacking the small town outside whilst others hurled insults at us from their positions at the tree line. I cursed how quickly Julius had managed to advance his entire army. I'd hoped to try and evacuate the civilians, and more importantly Numeria and Julia, by cover of darkness, so they could slip away and make their way to Vetera. Now the main body of the enemy host was here, the risk of discovery was too great. We daren't send them out unprotected and we could hardly spare any men to act as a military escort. If the entire camp garrison and civilians had left as soon as I'd told Caedicius the circumstances we might have made it, but now that chance was gone. Would I have insisted on us making a fight of it if I'd known Numeria would be stuck here too? Would I have jeopardised the safety of the whole of Roman Gaul for one woman? Probably, so it was for the best that the decision was made for me, and I no longer had the chance to back out. Numeria and I would see this out together, or die together now; it was as simple as that.

'They're a rude lot, aren't they?' observed Marcus, who stood beside me, both of us once again in full burnished armour, scanning the enemy host as they took up their positions.

I clenched my hands tightly, the knuckles going white behind my back, as I tried to remain calm at the sight of the huge army of tribesmen. 'Insulting the enemy is very important for the German tribes, part of the ritual of battle, a bit like a gladiator calling out a challenge before they match blades.'

He grunted. 'Damn rude if you ask me.'

I smiled, despite my nerves. 'Well, watch this. Caedicius has a surprise for them.'

We turned to watch Caedicius issue his orders to his engineers and let loose a long line of *ballistae*, which shot up into the air and landed in the great Cherusci host, killing scores and causing pandemonium; the rest retreated back into the tree line.

I watched the carnage in satisfaction. 'Stupid fools. They thought because they were out of bowshot range they were safe, but *ballistae* are another matter all together. Julius should have known better than to let his men get so close.'

Marcus nodded. 'That should pin them back.'

My eyes popped open in terror. 'I don't think so, look!'

Angered by the volley of *ballistae* bolts, the German tribesmen lost all discipline and broke free of the trees and ran at us in a vast unorganised charge, looking like a great tide of water rushing towards the camp. 'So many of them,' I whispered.

The engineers continued to fire the *ballistae*, and even let off the great *trebuchets*, which hurled giant rocks, crushing several men at a time. But it was a drop in the ocean in comparison to the enemy's huge numbers, and they kept coming forward, screaming in hatred and defiance. When they were thirty paces from the walls, the legionaries hurled their *pilums* at them, and the front row collapsed in a heap, but the host kept coming until they broke against the foot of our barricades. Here they were halted by our thick wooden and turf palisade, and they died in their scores as the defenders hurled Roman javelins down upon them – we weren't short of supplies, the camp was fitted out for hosting the full army of twenty thousand men. We wouldn't be running out of the *pilums* any time soon.

Marcus grabbed my arm in excitement. 'They've no idea how to scale the ramparts at all. They haven't even brought scaling ladders!'

It was true. The great mass of men simply milled about at the foot of the fortifications in confusion as the Roman defenders heaped death upon them. Some threw their light javelins at us, so the legionaries needed to keep their shields high to deflect any that made it over the palisade. It was as if the enemy had come without any plan for assaulting our fortress, being completely unprepared for this type of warfare. Some warriors tried hacking the base of the timbers with axes or *sax* blades, but I knew that was a waste of time, whilst others tried to climb the ramparts along the backs of their comrades; these were cut down easily by the disciplined legionaries.

I looked down at them, screaming and shouting in pain as they milled in confusion under our walls, but couldn't feel any pity for them; these were the same men who'd butchered all our comrades in the Teutoburg Forest, and my heart was hardened to their suffering. 'They are nothing but a rabble after all. Julius will need to keep their tempers in check if he ever wants to dig us out from our hole. Blind fools.'

Eventually, the tribesmen broke off their attack and withdrew, to the accompaniment of *ballistae* killing countless more as they fell back to the safety of the trees.

Caedicius looked over at us and said loudly so all his men could hear. 'A promising start, wouldn't you say?'

The legionaries gave a nervous laugh as their tension was released. The men had been shaken by the sheer ferocity of the attack, but as it became clear how light our casualties were – no more than a handful wounded by the thrown weapons – their confidence increased and the men began to believe that this wasn't such a hopeless cause after all.

The tribesmen hadn't fared so well. Great heaps of broken and dying men lay at the foot of our walls, crying and writhing in agony from countless wounds inflicted by the implacable legionaries standing above them. Their host might be large, but no force could ignore loses like that. Julius now knew he was in for a fight. We weren't going to fold easily.

Over the next few days, we didn't have it so easy. There were no further attacks that day, but they came back in the night, this time with scaling ladders which they'd hewn from the woods, and ropes fashioned from strong vines. We set flaming beacons above the walls to see by, and repelled each attack, inflicting heavy casualties, but this time we started taking losses ourselves, and whilst the enemy could afford high losses, we certainly could not. Marcus and I joined the men on the wall with drawn *gladius*, hewing the tribesmen as they tried to scramble over our walls, desperately cutting away their vines, or forcing their scaling ladders from the wall. Eventually, the attack petered out, and we slumped by the stockades, too tired to celebrate, but relieved that they'd been forced back again – only to have them attack again at dawn.

The next few days were tough on the defenders and no easier for Marcus and me. We daren't venture far from our walls, knowing that it would only take one attack to make it through our defences and we were all dead. We got what rest we could between each attack, dozing by the stockades, but were forced back into action as the tribesmen came at us again and again.

I desperately wanted to spend some time with Numeria, to grab some respite from this endless fighting on the walls, but knew I could not desert the other men. I contented myself by watching her from my vantage on the walls. Caedicius' small contingent of men had no camp surgeon, so Numeria and Julia had joined several of the other civilian women in caring for our wounded, setting up an impromptu hospital in one of the empty barrack blocks near where Marcus and I were stationed. I soon saw her ordering others around, noting with satisfaction that she'd managed to first take charge of the small hospital, and then being amused when I noticed that her role then became unofficial spokesperson of the small civilian population, who took direction from the hospital's new fearsome matriarch.

The camp was bursting with supplies to feed and provision Varus' entire army over the winter, so we weren't hungry, and young boys brought us water, food, and fresh *pilums* to hurl at the enemy. All the men needed to concentrate on was repelling the enemy from the walls.

Caedicius turned out to be every bit as good a camp commander as I expected. He made sure each section of the camp was well protected, getting runners to constantly keep him informed of which area was coming under the most ferocious assault, so he could direct his forces accordingly. He also directed the fire of his unit of engineers; their use of the *ballistae* and *trebuchets* was becoming increasingly useful.

Even so, by the fifth day, every one of us was exhausted, fatigue making the effort of repelling each attack that much harder, and we all started looking in hope for the signal arrow in the direction of Vetera that would signify that the bridge had been secured by the legions from Mogontiacum.

No signal arrow came.

Some argued that we could have missed it, that surely the legions had made it that far by now, but Caedicius and I knew that wasn't the case; with so many men looking out for our salvation, we knew we'd have seen it. So we carried on – what else could we do?

Each day we repulsed the attacks that were, thankfully, coming more sporadically. A lot of the tribesmen were content to remain on the fringes of the battle, preferring to get drunk and celebrate their victory at the Teutoburg rather than hurl themselves at our walls. We noticed they were becoming less frenzied, less desperate, as their losses finally taught them caution, and they attacked our walls now with respect, though still with dogged determination. The night attacks ceased after two more unsuccessful attacks proved particularly costly to the enemy, so we could at least sleep at nights, even though we still dared not stray from our positions.

Nevertheless, their attacks during the day never ceased entirely, each day enough warriors would summon the courage for a new attack, and the exhaustion of our men was becoming increasingly worrying. How much longer can these men be expected to continue under this duress? Did Julius realise that he couldn't starve us out, but might be just as successful by wearing us out?

By the tenth day, we were all desperate.

The morale of the men had slumped. I began to hear murmurs from the men of being abandoned, and any chance of escape had now gone. Caedicius, Marcus and I did our best to deny any such misgivings, but we were hardly sure ourselves; how could it be taking so long? We had no choice but to keep going, but if fighting such terrible odds was bad enough before, at least we thought we were doing it for a purpose; if our messengers warnings had been ignored, did that mean this was all for nothing?

The next day, we came close to disaster. The east wall was almost lost, only saved by Caedicius' quick thinking, reinforcing it with a squad from the south wall. But even so our casualties were high. Neither Marcus or I discussed it, but we knew the end was close.

On the twelfth night, as I lay slumped next to Marcus by our position on the west wall, Numeria came to join me. Marcus nudged me awake as she approached, and I tiredly stumbled to my feet, surprised by her appearance. 'My lady, what are you doing here? It's the middle of the night. Surely you need to get some rest?'

She smiled sadly. Her gown was covered with bloodstains from the men she'd been treating, her hair tangled, and the dark bags under her eyes showed the strain of tiredness. She was still the most beautiful sight I'd ever seen. 'So formal, Gaius. Since when have you addressed me as, my lady?'

I took her arm, and led her away from Marcus, who smiled and then turned his attention back to scanning the dark forests that surrounded the camp. I laughed quietly. 'Since you became the camp's doctor. I hear you've been treating our wounded.'

She shook her head as we walked along the stone battlements, stepping past the exhausted men who lay slumped along the walkway. 'I wish I was a real doctor, or we had one here. All we can do for the men is bandage their wounds, and give them kind words. It is precious little, but our knowledge is too limited to do more.'

I held her hand tightly. 'Every man here is grateful for all you do for them, Numeria. Marcus and I have heard the tales of the healing hands of you and your women. Half the men in this camp are in love with you already.'

She smiled mischievously. 'Only half, Gaius? I must be losing my touch.'

One legionary roused as we were passing, and reached up his hand to us. 'The gods favour you sir, and you, m'lady.'

I clasped his hand in reassurance as we passed. 'Get some rest, Legionary. It'll be another big day tomorrow.'

He smiled and sank back. 'Thank you, sir. I won't let you down.'

I said, 'I know you won't, soldier. You're a man of the Nineteenth.'

We left him grinning, and Numeria stroked my bare arm. 'You seem to be quite a hero to the men yourself. Are the other half in love with you?'

I chuckled at her jest. It was true that both Marcus and I were now very popular amongst the men. We'd fought in different areas each day, wherever the fighting was the fiercest, and now had a strong reputation within the ranks. 'The men respect my record, that's all.'

She stopped and looked out over the walls to the dark forested land beyond. 'I think you know it is more than that, Gaius. All the men talk of you and Marcus when they come to us. It lifts me to know that they share my love for you.'

I looked out at the great dark expanse. All was quiet along the tree line. The German tribes were all asleep and barely anything stirred. 'Numeria, this is difficult to say,' my voice began to break, 'but things are getting desperate, if it comes to it …'

Numeria turned and laid a finger on my mouth. 'Hush, Gaius. The women and I have discussed this. If the worst happens we have some root from the Britannic yew tree that one of my women swears by. None will take us alive.'

I nodded, blinking back tears. I wasn't surprised that something from that bleak mist-shrouded isle would prove deadly. It was said that the island to the north of Gaul, across the narrow sea, was enchanted, and ruled by wild druids who used sorcerous ways over a barbaric people, beyond the help of civilisation. Could they be any worse than the German tribes? I doubted it, noting the dark silhouettes of the heads of some unfortunate Roman legionaries who'd been dragged from the walls during the fighting, and now were adorned on poles outside the camp. 'It is good that you're prepared,' was all I managed to say to that.

She put a cool hand to the back of my head and stroked the back of my neck. 'Come, Gaius, let's not talk of such things, I've barely spoken a dozen words to you since we've arrived in this camp. Surely we have more fitting subjects to discuss?'

I nodded, wanting to tell her the true depth of my feelings for her, when something caught my eye.

Numeria said, 'What is it, Gaius? You look like you've seen a shade of the dead?'

I looked around the walls to see if anyone else had spotted it. They had, the sentries were talking in excited tones. 'Not our deaths, Numeria, the sum of all our hopes! That's the signal arrow. Vetera has been reinforced! Look!'

Numeria looked to where I was pointing, at a small bright spark in the distance, and clapped her hands in delight, 'What do we do, Gaius?'

I grabbed her hand. 'Come, we need to speak to Caedicius at once!'

Chapter Thirty-nine

It was a small select group that met in Caedicius headquarters to discuss what we were to do next; Marcus and I were there, Caedicius and the two most senior surviving centurions, a barrel-chested bull of a man named Lucilius and an old veteran with the unusual name of Fenestela were also present. But on my insistence, Numeria also joined the discussion to speak for the civilian population who had just as much to lose in this as the surviving military.

Caedicius sat at the table and rubbed his forehead before starting. 'Now the signal has been seen, we've fulfilled our obligations to Rome. We need only escape with our lives now.'

Fenestela grunted. 'Easier said than done. There are still a lot of big hairy barbarians who are going to be pretty angry now they realise the bridge is closed to them.'

I shook my head. 'They might not know yet. I doubt they are as good as passing messages as the Roman army. They could still be oblivious.'

Marcus queried, 'Might not one of the tribesmen have seen the arrow too?'

I shrugged. 'What if they have? They won't know what it signifies.'

Lucilius swept his hand across the table. 'So we should leave at once. We haven't had a night attack in days. Let's slip out before anyone notices. The tribesmen will still be in their blankets, and providing we're quiet, we stand a good chance of slipping past the sentries. I can have the men ready to go almost immediately.'

Numeria smiled, but clearly objected. 'Your soldiers may be ready to march, but the civilians certainly are not. There are women and children, some old and frail. These last will need to be put on horses and led out carefully so as not to make any noise.'

Fenestela snorted in contempt. 'We can't worry about old crones! If they can't march and keep up, they'll need to be left behind. This isn't a day outing. All our lives are at stake.'

Numeria inclined her head. 'The ones in question don't look much older than you. Do you suggest that you should be left behind too?'

Fenestela barked a laugh. 'Pah! I can march as far as anyone, you just try me. I might not look as pretty as I once was, but by Juno, there's still life in me yet.'

Caedicius calmed them both with a placating gesture. 'Everyone has the right to make a break for it, but if any can't keep up, they're on their own, I'm afraid we can't make exceptions.'

Numeria nodded. 'That is all I am asking. Just give me some time to make arrangements for the journey. We'll all keep up.'

I agreed. 'You'll have all the time you need. We shouldn't move out tonight in any case.'

Everyone turned their heads to me, and Marcus asked, 'Why, by the gods, not? If we remain another day, we have to repulse them from the walls once more. It was a close-run thing earlier. Do you think we can risk it?'

I shrugged and then explained. 'We'll have to. We can't leave tonight, even if we do manage to slip past their guards in the dark, as we don't have long until dawn. It is over twenty miles to Vetera. Arminius' cavalry will catch us along the road.'

Lucilius wasn't so sure. 'It'll be hard explaining to the men they need to fight another day. I say we leave at once and have it done with one way or another. If they hear us, at least we can give a good account of ourselves and go down fighting.'

Marcus slapped the table in approval, but Caedicius overruled them both. 'I agree with Cassius. Let's wait until they're feasting tomorrow night. They'll all be getting drunk, just like they do every night, and that'll be the best time to slip past them. They're not organised like a proper army. They've no discipline. I doubt they've even bothered to set sentries around our entire periphery. I'll send out scouts tonight to find the weakest areas to exploit and lead everyone through tomorrow night. Then we'll have enough time to get to Vetera without anyone noticing.'

Fenestela said, 'If you plan to slip past them, you'll need to leave some men here to man the walls. They'll notice soon enough if the palisades are bare.'

I grunted. 'We could set up decoys, place the stuffed manikins the archers use for practice and put armour on them.'

Fenestela laughed. 'The tribesmen are undisciplined, not stupid. Do you really think that'll fool anyone?'

Caedicius agreed. 'Fenestela is right. We'll have to ask for volunteers. We'll leave them some fast horses so they can try and make a break for it in the morning. By then the main body of men and civilians should be close enough to Vetera for it not to matter.'

Numeria was incredulous. 'Who'd ever volunteer for that suicide mission?'

Lucilius turned to her and said softly, 'You'll be surprised how many will take up the offer, my lady. Some of the men will have families amongst the civilians. They will do what they can to increase the chances of them getting away. Others will volunteer simply to help their comrades, figuring they have less to live for than their brothers in arms. We'll get enough volunteers, I promise you.'

Numeria bowed her head. 'Yes, I'm sorry. I shouldn't have spoken out of turn.'

Fenestela reached out and took her hand in his old knurled fist. 'Don't worry, lady, we'll get you home alright.' He then gave me and Marcus a wink. 'We can't have these flash tribunes taking all the credit.'

The next day we were attacked at midday as usual. It was difficult for me, as I felt responsible for every life lost, as if each death was personally my responsibility because I'd made the suggestion to remain the extra day. Nevertheless, the men once again threw back the attacking barbarian hoard. When night began to fall, I knew I'd made the right decision because a great storm blew down from the north, sheets of rain and wind that would make the journey to Vetera uncomfortable but would mask our departure more effectively than any diversion. The men were lined up for departure, together with the great convoy of civilians that Numeria had organised into small groups to allow for them to make as swift an exit from the camp as possible. The old, infirm or wounded were all mounted on horses, which were being led by civilians hand-picked by Numeria herself. She didn't plan on leaving anyone behind.

'The gods favour us, Cassius. Slipping past the tribesmen shouldn't prove difficult in this,' said Caedicius cheerfully, but also loudly, so I could hear him over the storm.

I was helping Numeria with the saddle to the horse she was going to lead out. Its hooves were bandaged in rags to mask any noise they made, but in reality, the howling gale which was making talking so difficult made them redundant. I shouted back, 'I can't believe our luck. Do you know the route we wish to take?'

He nodded. 'Yes, the sentries marked out areas free of tribesmen. Hopefully they won't know we're gone until the morning, when Marcus has said he'll defend the camp.'

My heart stopped. 'Marcus? What do you mean? Why Marcus?'

Caedicius looked confused. 'I thought you knew. He volunteered to lead the men who are staying behind.'

I turned sharply to Numeria and demanded, 'Did you know about this?'

She looked alarmed. 'Of course not. I've had my hands full organising the civilians.' She looked around, until her gaze settled on Julia, who was helping a pregnant woman onto a placid-looking mare. 'Poor Julia. She'll be devastated if Marcus doesn't make it back.'

'Marcus will make it back to Vetera. I'll make sure of it,' I said fiercely.

Caedicius looked at me quizzically. 'How do you mean?'

I took a deep breath. 'I mean, I plan to stay with Marcus and help get him out.'

Numeria was aghast, pleading, 'Oh, Gaius, you can't! Please don't do this. We need you, Gaius, you can't possibly …'

I grabbed her hand and looked into her eyes. 'I have to, Numeria, don't you see? If not for Marcus, I'd be nailed to a tree in the Teutoburg with my eyes plucked out. He brought me out. I'd be dead if not for him.'

Caedicius left us alone, realising that this was a personal decision he shouldn't interfere in, but Numeria didn't share his reticence. 'No, Gaius, please, you can't leave me alone now. I lost Otho to this war. I can't lose you too, not after all this …'

I squeezed her hand, and blinked back the tears that threatened to overwhelm me. 'I have to do this, Numeria. I can't let go of my courage again. I lost it once, only to find it again in the horror of the Teutoburg. I'll not live without it again.'

She shook her head, tears running down her face. 'I don't care about courage and bravery and all that foolishness, it means nothing to me.'

I leant my head against hers. 'I know, Numeria. That's why I love you.' I stopped and paused to let this sink in, before continuing. 'But it matters to me. I can't go back to the man I became in Rome, full of self-loathing and cowardice. If Marcus didn't make it back, I'd never know if I could have made a difference and brought him out. I must go to him.'

Numeria held onto me, sobbing. 'Please do your best to come back to me. Don't throw your life away, Gaius. I love you too much to lose you.'

I took a deep breath and pulled away from her. If I didn't leave her now,

I'd never be able to. 'Don't worry, Numeria. I'll see you in Vetera, and tell Julia not to worry either. I'll be bringing Marcus with me.'

Numeria pulled herself straighter, wiping away the tears from her eyes. 'You make sure you do, Gaius Cassius Aprilis, Tribune of Rome.'

I smiled in gratitude and saluted her.

Caedicius raised his arm to signal that the convoy was ready, and they opened the north gate just enough to let them file through. He led the three hundred surviving soldiers and four hundred and fifty civilians out into the storm. I mounted the north wall and watched them go into the night, praying that they made it into the tree line without being spotted. The rain and wind buffeted me, almost blowing me from the stockade, so fierce was the storm, but I thanked the gods for it, knowing that the tribesmen would be taking shelter from it and it was this little convoy's best chance of finding safety. I watched the convoy pass out of sight and disappear into the dark, and thanked the gods once again that I heard or saw no sign of the alarm being raised from Julius' Cherusci. I waited there a long time, just to make sure that they'd made it into the trees and safely away, until, relieved, I went to find Marcus.

I found him on the west wall, the one that overlooked the main German tribesmen's camp. He had a few Roman legionaries with him and the old gnarled centurion Fenestela, who laughed drily when he saw me. 'Did that lady of yours shame you into staying too? I swear it was her words which made me stay for this fool's errand. Why should anyone wish to stay, she asked? Why not you, old Fenestela, I asked myself and couldn't find an answer.'

I put my hand on his shoulder. 'We're not dead yet. I plan for us all to get out alive from this somehow.'

He chuckled. 'You just haven't worked out the "somehow" yet?'

I grinned. 'Exactly.'

Marcus was astonished to see me. 'Cassius, what are you doing here? You should be with Caedicius and the others.' His eyes then narrowed in suspicion. 'You can't stop me from staying here you know. I won't leave until the morning, not until I know the convoy is safe.'

I smiled at my friend. 'I wouldn't dream of trying to stop you staying, Marcus. Now, what is your plan?'

He took me into a small tower built into the walls and out of the storm, and told me that he had been left thirty men, not many, but enough to give the impression that the walls were still being manned. He organised them into small squads, and set them walking along each section of the wall. If the tribesmen were to wonder why there were so few, that could easily be explained by the awful weather.

He ran his hand through his soaking wet hair. 'As long as they see people moving about on the walkways, I can't see them suspecting anything.'

I nodded in agreement. 'And what about the morning? What's your plan then?'

Marcus stumbled in confusion. 'Well, I haven't got one. I didn't think it mattered. By then the convoy will be safe in Vetera, or as near to it as not to matter anymore. I thought we'd just hold the walls for as long as we can, then make a run for it. We have a few fast horses up near the north gate. We'll ride them out if any of us make it that far.'

I shook my head, glad now that I'd stayed. 'We can't possibly hold the perimeter with only thirty men, so why bother? You said yourself that the convoy will be safe by then, so why throw our lives away?'

Marcus stumbled to answer that. 'Well, what else can we do?'

I explained my idea. 'Let's keep up the pretence for as long as we can. Keep the men marching along the walls throughout the night and into the morning, but as soon as they look to notice something is amiss, or start to form to attack let's fire some of the barracks buildings and then leave.'

Marcus frowned. 'Give up the camp without a fight?'

I nodded. 'Exactly, we have nothing to gain by holding it. We'll set fire to enough of the building to create some smoke and confusion, but leave enough intact so that the tribesmen are more concerned with looting the camp than finding us. We then take the horses and ride north as fast as we can, before turning west and making our way to Vetera.'

Marcus grumbled. 'That doesn't sound very honourable, fleeing before the enemy.'

I looked him in the eye and told him seriously. 'Come on, Marcus, this is no time to be worrying about honour. These thirty men's lives are at stake. They have put their trust in you by volunteering to remain here with you. The least you can do is to try and get them out alive.'

Marcus smiled, and his whole face lit up. 'I'll never be free of your sensible orders, will I?'

I laughed. 'Not if I can help it. Now, let's tell Fenestela and the men the plan.'

The storm raged on as we kept up the pretence throughout the night and long into the morning. Marching along the walkways, back and forth, varying the number of men in each group to try and give the impression of greater numbers. Eventually the wind died down and the rain began to slacken, before finally stopping, and the tribesmen came out in greater number to observe, no doubt beginning to realise something was wrong. Normally by this stage of the day virtually the full complement of defenders would be visible on the walls, and there was only so much thirty men could do to keep up the deception.

I wasn't concerned. We'd given the convoy of civilians long enough to make the twenty miles to Vetera, so when the Cherusci looked to be gathering for an attack, I ordered the men back from the walls and set about firing selective buildings and barracks blocks.

As soon as the tribesmen saw the smoke, we heard a great roar outside the camp and knew that they were coming, in their thousands, scaling the undefended walls like ants crawling over a corpse.

I kept the men in good order, slowly retreating through the camp, setting flaming torches to the preprepared stockpiles of pitch and timber, making sure only to fire one building in four. As I expected, the attacking tribesmen, instead of securing the camp immediately as a Roman force would, set to looting the undamaged building, hunting out troves of personal belongings, weapons, and valuables. There was plenty for them to choose from; the camp was full of winter supplies and Caedicius had fled with only the bare essentials for the trip. I wasn't concerned about denying the enemy any of it, relying on the barbarians' greed to allow us the chance to escape.

We worked our way to the north gate, where our strings of horses were kept, hoping that Julius hadn't had the foresight to send another force around to seal off our escape route. As we neared the gate, I ran over to Fenestela. 'Good work, centurion. We have a free run to the woods now. I hope your men can ride as well as you can set fires.'

Fenestela gave a crooked grin as he wiped the soot and smoke from his eyes. 'I doubt that, sir. We're more used to marching than getting on the back of a horse. I'm sure some of the men would be happier making a run for it.'

I clapped him on the shoulder. 'The men can do what they like once they reach the tree line. It'll be best for the men to split up, head north for a while, and only start breaking west when they're far from the camp and any pursuing Cherusci.'

He nodded. 'It's going to be a rare run for safety, sir – twenty miles through the forests – but I'm glad to be given the chance for it. Now it's come to it, I don't fancy dying overly much after all.'

I laughed. 'You're not alone there. Now, where's Marcus?'

Fenestela looked confused. 'He said you and him had prepared a surprise for the Cherusci. He was heading over to the south gate when I left him. Don't you know what he's talking about?'

My heart sunk. 'That infernal boy, can't he ever ...' I shook my head. 'Never mind, I'll get Marcus out. Lead the men out and run hard for the trees, then split up before continuing north.'

Fenestela looked concerned. 'Let me come with you, sir, or at least send a few of the boys with you.'

I shook my head. 'No, none of you can help now. You're only duty is to escape now. Take the men home, Fenestela, but leave the two tall tan Libyan horses. Marcus and I will need those later.'

Fenestela looked reassured that I had a plan to escape, but in reality, it was only a ruse. I had no idea what Marcus was planning, or where he was. I just knew I had to get him out soon or we'd both be ending our lives here. I ran through the smoke-filled camp, discarding my helmet and bronze breastplate that would mark me as a Roman from a distance. I soon saw tribesmen running through each intact barrack block, greed making them unobservant to their surroundings, but still forcing me to lurk in the shadows. I stopped to think – what was Marcus planning? Knowing Marcus, he'd want to be doing something heroic – what could it be? Even he couldn't be planning to defend the camp single-handed. What was near the south gate? Suddenly it came to me! And I cursed him for a fool, whilst admiring his nerve.

I ran to the walls and along their base, making my way to the area near the south gate where I suspected Marcus to be waiting. During the siege, Caedicius had improvised and mounted a few *ballistae* on the walls there in order to stop the German encampment encroaching on the camp's southern edge. No tribesmen barred my path. The walls held nothing of interest for the Cherusci and so were left unmanned. I jumped onto the ladder that led up to the walkway and found Marcus there, lining up a *ballistae*, now pointing into the camp rather than out, which he'd loaded and was ready to shoot.

'You stupid, irresponsible, young idiot. What by all in Hades do you think you're doing here? Do you actually want to die?' I asked him as I clambered up the last few rungs of the ladder.

He chuckled when he turned and saw me join him on the platform. 'No more than you obviously. How did you know where I was?'

I sighed. 'It takes a fool to know what a fool plans, I guess. Come on Marcus. Let's get out of here. What good can we do here?'

He shook his head. 'I just need one shot, one chance to kill him. Then I'll

Roman Mask

go.'

I look up to the sky above in despair. 'Kill who? The whole camp is overrun.'

His eyes narrowed and his hands clenched more tightly on the *ballistae* in determination. 'Your friend Julius Arminius. The viper that killed my twenty thousand comrades and whose death has been earned a thousand-fold by that treachery.'

My eyes opened widely in surprise. 'Julius is here? In the camp?'

Marcus nodded. 'I saw his winged helmet as he came over the wall surrounded by his bodyguards. He's here alright. I just need one clean shot at him, then this'll all be worth it.'

If it had been anyone else, I'd have overruled him and ordered him to follow me out of the camp, but for once Marcus was right. Julius did deserve to die, and my hatred temporarily outweighed my terror. Marcus' plan wasn't very sophisticated, but it might work. One clean shot at their tribal leader and this whole alliance of the tribes might just fall apart. It had to be worth a shot. I looked over at the empty second *ballistae* next to Marcus. 'Two shots are better than one. How do I load this thing?'

Marcus smiled. 'You place the bolt in the top end, then wind back the winch holding the string. It takes a while. These machines are normally manned by three trained engineers.'

I picked up a bolt. 'I'll manage. Keep an eye out for Julius. I don't want to miss our chance.'

It took me a long time to wind the winch back. These weren't weapons you could shoot rapidly at the best of times, and without anyone to help pull the string back it was a painfully slow process, but nevertheless, I managed it. The two of us took aim on the camp below us, asking just one last favour of the gods – that we weren't discovered until given the opportunity to kill my one-time friend.

A fog of smoke drifted over the camp, stinging our eyes, and making it difficult to concentrate on the camp below, which was full of looting warriors. Many of them were increasing the number of fires by setting alight the remaining buildings once they were cleared of anything of value. Soon this camp would be nothing but a burnt-out husk.

Then I saw him.

The fog of smoke temporarily cleared, and Julius was walking along the main avenue of the camp, laughing and joking with the warrior who walked alongside him, the tracker Faramund who'd led us into the trap in the Teutoburg Forest. My stomach knotted to see Julius enjoying the destruction that surrounded him, and I gritted my teeth in anger as I lined up my *ballistae*.

Marcus shot first, but his aim was off, and he cursed as the *ballistae* bolt sailed clearly over both the warrior's heads. They halted and looked around in confusion, possibly feeling the passing of the bolt overhead, but unsure what it was. I didn't panic, I knew shooting downhill was difficult from when I'd shot a small bow as a child hunting small mammals in the woods near my father's estate – ironically enough, with Julius more often than not. I adjusted accordingly, and aimed slightly lower than normal, lining up Julius' legs rather than his head or torso.

It would have hit him full in the face, I'm pretty sure of that, if he hadn't turned slightly in the last heartbeat to speak to his tracker. The bolt instead seared off one of the wings of his helmet, and buried itself in the throat of the Cherusci tracker.

I cursed loudly, as Julius looked around in shock and saw me on the wall standing behind the *ballistae*. He staggered back a few steps, either in stunned surprise at seeing me still alive, or due to the close call he'd just had with death.

Marcus picked up another bolt, but I turned on him. 'Don't be a fool, we don't have time to load another. We had our shot. It's time to go!'

Marcus looked up at me and reluctantly agreed, throwing the bolt down in disgust at our missed opportunity. I grabbed him by the arm, pulling him to his feet, and we ran along the walkway, heading for the north of the camp.

I knew it wouldn't be long before Julius recovered himself and set warriors on our tail, so we sprinted as fast as we could manage, leaping down the ladder at the other end of the camp several rungs at a time. I blessed the gods that Fenestela had left our two Libyan horses near the north gate as promised. We vaulted into the saddles and spurred the horses through the gates into the open grassland that opened up before us. We headed directly for the trees, head down, galloping for all we were worth. A wild elation rose up in me as I realised we were going to make it.

Then I heard Marcus cry out in pain alongside me. I turned back to see what had happened, and then pulled my horse up. I saw that Marcus had one of the light Cherusci throwing spears sticking out of his shoulder, in the gap at the top of his breastplate. He slumped on his saddle, his horse veering wildly off to the right as it sensed its rider's sudden lack of control. I rode over and grabbed the panicked horses' bridle, and pulled his horse to a stop. Marcus grunted as I pulled the spear from his shoulder, realising in dismay, as it gushed blood, just how far it had penetrated. I looked back at the camp and saw that the other spears thrown by warriors from the camp walls were falling well short, meaning that Marcus had been felled by a final desperate blow as the luck of Janus finally deserted us. I saw warriors were now emerging from the camp and I couldn't delay any longer. 'Can you hold onto your saddle until we make the trees?' I shouted in desperation to Marcus.

He nodded silently, but remained slumped on the saddle, hands gripping tightly to the horse's reins, but the strength seemingly all but gone from his body. I didn't have time to worry about that now. If I didn't get him out of here now, we were both dead, so I rode both our horses into the trees and tried to lose the pursuing warriors in the forest. Before long, I realised riding was all but impossible with the overhanging branches, so I dismounted and led both Marcus' horse and my own, picking a way through the forest trails as best I could.

I checked on Marcus, who still remained in his saddle grimly holding on, seemingly by sheer willpower alone. I noticed that his face was worryingly pale and his lips were turning blue, both bad signs. But I knew I dare not stop to check his wound, as pursuit was too close behind. I stumbled across a streambed, which I followed for a time as it allowed me to increase my pace. I still did not dare ride, and I figured the stream would make tracking me harder than through the forest floor – suddenly pleased I'd at least killed Julius' chief tracker. We followed the stream for at least a mile, when I decided it was time to start breaking west. I led the horses away on foot, into a clearing where I finally stopped and let Marcus all but fall from his horse. I propped him up by a tree and removed his breastplate as he gasped weakly in pain.

It was an ugly wound, a ragged tear that had entered behind and beneath his collar bone, and not exited until it reached the top of his pectoral muscle. I knew his lung may well be punctured and he'd lost a worryingly large amount of blood. I cut off a section of his cloak with my *gladius* as I tried my best to bind the wound, and at least managed to partially staunch the blood. 'There you go, Marcus. We'll soon have you fit and well. Numeria and Julia couldn't have wrapped it better themselves.'

Marcus smiled, but croaked, 'It's no good, Cassius, you'll have to leave me.'

I shook my head. 'The sun will rise in the west before that day comes, Marcus. Come on, on your feet.'

He was too weak to get to his feet alone, but I managed to pull him upwards and manhandled him back into his saddle. He slumped upon it, but at least managed to hold on. I led the horses away, but turned at a noise behind me, and I then realised that Faramund wasn't the only warrior of the Cherusci who could track two horses through a streambed. Ewald came into sight, his long blade already drawn, walking with his customary deadly serpentine grace.

Chapter Forty

I expected to be instantly surrounded by Cherusci warriors, following their champion, ready to either drag us back to Julius or to kill us where we stood. But I couldn't make out any others in the vicinity, nothing but the sound of the forest, the wind rushing through the treetops.

I looked around nervously, still scanning the trees to see if I was mistaken. 'You came alone?' I asked incredulously.

He didn't answer my question, just unclipped his cloak which he let fall to the ground and lifted his long sword in a challenge, saying in his broken Latin, 'Let us see what's the best Rome can offer.'

I swallowed hard, realising that that meant me; Marcus was unable to even stand, and I was the one who'd offered to match blades with him in the hall of the Cherusci. I should have realised that a man like this would never let a challenge like that go unanswered. I unslung the small round shield I kept on my saddle and drew my *gladius*, and walked round to the front of the horses where Ewald awaited, his long sword grasped in a double-handed grip, pointing at the ground, bare chest breathing evenly, fierce eyes boring into mine.

Marcus weakly croaked to me as I passed him, 'You can do this, Cassius … just don't think … just … just let your *gladius* take him.'

I'd had better pep talks before a sword bout, having no idea what Marcus was talking about, but I reassured him with a nod as I passed him: his life was dependant on this contest just as much as mine. I tried to control my terror as I walked out to confront a man of nightmares, having only myself to rely on now – there'd be no one to save me this time.

I cursed the fact that I'd discarded my breastplate and helmet, but, looking at the lean muscular frame of Ewald, surmised that it was probably for the best that I wore nothing to slow me down. I'd seen how fast this warrior was, and would need to rely on my small shield to offer me my only protection. We circled one another around the clearing, watching each other as wary as circling wild animals in the Circus Maximus.

Then he struck a series of blows that came at me in a speed that took the breath away. My shield only narrowly took the first blow, then my *gladius* parried the next two, as I retreated rapidly only just deflecting the fourth with my shield again.

He circled before coming at me again. This time I was ready, but even so his speed nearly breached my defence each time; only my quick wrists and reactions preventing his long blade disembowelling me from an underhand slice that slipped under my shield.

Now at least the fear was gone, replaced by iron-hard focus; I knew that one slip would cost me my life. I managed to counter a few of his attacks with ones of my own, but his defence was every bit as good as his attacks, and he deflected them easily before forcing me backwards with a rapid succession of blows. I retreated, parrying each blow with either blade or shield, but increasingly aware that I was completely overmatched. This was a swordsman without peer; his footwork and the strength and accuracy of each stroke showed no sign of weakness, nothing I could exploit, no way through that icy calm and ruthless application of breathtaking skill.

He gave me a shallow cut on the shoulder, then the hip, as he began to find my measure. Nothing too serious, but enough to weaken me slightly and increase his advantage, forcing me into an ever more defensive posture. I tried every trick I knew to distract him, pretending to notice something behind him, taunting him with insults, even faking a slip then throwing dirt in his eyes – something that nearly cost me my life, as he simply moved his head out of the way of the dirt and then aimed a vicious overhand blow that nearly took my head off. I managed to regain my feet but was becoming more panicked, as I knew this man was going to kill me.

I backed away further and looked around for a way to escape, but saw Marcus still lying prone and impotent on his horse, still trusting me to find a way out of this, and a calm came over me. I knew I couldn't run, couldn't leave him, so if I was to die, then so be it; suddenly the words Marcus had said to me made sense – defeating a man of Ewald's speed could never done by outthinking him, outwitting him, his technique was too sure, too perfect. If I was going to beat him, I needed to trust my instincts alone, and throw all caution away. As Ewald closed in for the kill, I spun into an attack, aiming blow after blow at my attacker. He parried each one, but the ferocity of my attack shocked him, and he stepped backwards for the first time in the contest.

We started matching blades at an increasing tempo, my body and sword arm led by instinct alone, channelled by years of training with this weapon. I became completely attuned to my *gladius* as I struck with an absence of thought or emotion, parrying or striking at blinding speed, my blade an extension of my own will. Never before had my body been so in engaged in a contest, my entire self being a reflection of this dance of death, advancing forward, spinning to avoid his blade, swaying away from a thrust or slice, leaping forward to attack once again.

Back and forward we went in this song of ringing iron and blade, until finally I threw the edge of my shield into the swordsman's face, breaking his nose before following it up by a thrust of my *gladius* directly into his stomach.

He grunted and slowly fell to his knees, before looking up and saying just one word: 'How?'

I reversed my grip and sliced it across his throat, nearly decapitating him. I stood over him, breathing heavily, still expecting the lifeless body to rise, so I could continue this dance once more.

It took a while until I came back to myself, as I slowly recovered my wind and stared down at the corpse of my vanquished foe, not believing what had happened. My body stung, from several shallow cuts, and my hands now trembled slightly, but otherwise I was unharmed. I went over to check on Marcus. He was still slumped on his horse, which was agitating from the smell of the blood and pulling on its hobbled reins. I stroked the horse's mane, calming it, and saw that Marcus was now only semi-conscious. He half-opened his eyes and whispered to me, 'I saw you, Cassius, you were magnificent …'

I was dismayed by how weak Marcus looked. 'Don't worry about that now, Marcus. I need to get you back to Vetera as quickly as I can. If you don't mind, I'm going to have to bind you to that horse.'

He gave a slight nod, his eyes closing in exhaustion. 'Do what you think best.'

I cut the leather bindings from Ewald's scabbard that was tied to his back and used those to bind Marcus to his horse. I then covered him in Ewald's discarded cloak, trying to make him as comfortable as possible. I didn't like moving him in such a fashion when he was so sorely injured, but knew I'd no choice; I either got him back to Vetera quickly or he'd die.

I led our horses west until I hit the road. I scanned it in either direction first before taking ours onto it and riding as quickly as I dare chance Marcus' fragile health. Twice I needed to take us off the road as enemy horseman rode past; fortunately they were careless of their surroundings, sure that they were now in complete control of their forests. The twenty miles to Vetera seemed to take an eternity, as I constantly needed to check Marcus' condition wasn't getting any worse; my greatest fear was that I'd make it to Vetera only to find I had a corpse bound to the horse. He remained in a semi-conscious stupor, which wasn't good, but at least he wasn't any worse. It was dusk when, with relief, I finally saw the bridge at Vetera. My relief didn't last long; I was dismayed to see a camp of a few hundred Cherusci tribesmen sealing the approach to the bridge.

I hid Marcus and our horses in the trees and crept nearer to spy on the camp, noting that it was made up of cavalry. I saw how unorganised the camp was – groups of warriors with no semblance of order. My first thought was to somehow signal the Roman camp on the other side of the river so that they could lead a sortie out and clear this rabble from their gates. But then I figured that my signal might just as easily give my position away to the Cherusci. I decided the best course was one of simplicity; with no sentries, as long as I covered myself in a Cherusci cloak and kept myself well-hooded, I should be able to pass through it unhindered in the dark – or so I hoped.

The cloak was easy to procure. I simply waited until one of the warriors left the camp to relieve themselves, then slipped up behind him and slit his throat with my *gladius*. I returned to Marcus, made sure he was well-covered in Ewald's cloak, and then waited until it was approaching full dark. The tribesmen were now starting to drink by their fires, as I slowly rode us through the camp. It was nerve-wracking knowing that at any moment we could be discovered, but all the warriors' attention was focused on the Roman camp on the other side of the bridge; none seemed to be giving even a glance in the direction of the forest, so it wasn't until we were almost on the bridge itself that someone finally barked out a challenge, and I was forced to spur our mounts into a gallop. We flew onto the broad Roman bridge across the river.

Two warriors barred our path, but after coming this far I wasn't going to stop now. I ran our mounts directly at them, and they fell away to the side rather than be trampled by the two great galloping geldings.

A few warriors were quicker to react than the others and threw javelins at our retreating backs, but it's hard to hit a moving target in the dark, and we passed through unharmed, reaching the gates of Vetera where I was relieved to see Roman sentries waiting for us. They'd obviously been alerted by the disturbance on the bridge.

I rode up to them, throwing off my Cherusci cloak, declaring, 'I'm Cassius Aprilis, the last Roman this side of the Rhenus.'

A centurion grabbed my horse's bridle. 'Oh, we know who you are, sir. I knew you'd make it out somehow.'

It was Fenestela, large grin on his gnarled and ugly face. 'These are the boys from Lugdunum. We have two full legions here. You're safe now.'

I shook my head in confusion. 'What happened to Asprenas' legions from Mogontiacum?'

Fenestela spat in disgust. 'Pah! He holed himself up in his camp and refused to believe the messengers' we sent him – said he needed clarification. You were right about him, Cassius. He's rotten, that one.'

I put Asprenas out of my mind. I wasn't surprised by his incompetence – he was the nephew of Varus after all – and I had more pressing concerns. 'Fenestela, you need to take care of Marcus, he's taken a deep wound in the shoulder.'

The old centurion instructed the legionaries with him to cut Marcus from his horse and prepared to take him away to the camp surgeon, where Fenestela promised he'd get the best of care.

I dismounted and checked on my friend. 'How is he?' I was worried that that last gallop over the bridge would have opened his wounds.

Fenestela looked at the wound to his shoulder as the legionaries removed the temporary binding I placed there. He shrugged. 'Difficult to tell. It's bad, but I've seen worse. At least it doesn't look infected. It will be for the gods to decide if he makes it.'

The legionaries took him away on a stretcher, and I went to follow, but Fenestela stopped me. 'You've done all you can for him now, sir. Let the surgeon do the rest. You can't help him anymore.'

I nodded, realising that the last thing the surgeon would want is some concerned comrade interfering with his work. Fenestela was right. It was for the gods now to decide whether he'd live, not me.

Fenestela looked me up and down. 'Are you injured yourself, sir.'

I shook my head. 'Only a few shallow cuts. Nothing I can't care for myself.'

Fenestela laughed. 'Care for yourself? I think there is a particular woman who might have something to say about that. She's been driving herself mad with worry for you, although don't tell her I told you that. You better go see her first.'

Epilogue

I waited in a large marble room in the palace of Augustus, bright spring sunlight streaming through the large open veranda, revealing a stunning view of the city which brought back wistful memories of when Julius and I had been schooled in this very palace in our youth. I felt a surge of anger rise as I recollected Julius and our time together. I closed my eyes and let it pass; this was no time to lose myself in memories of our lost youth.

I stood up and walked over to the veranda, ostensibly in order to take in the view, but also to conceal my nerves, which were playing on me sitting on the *princeps'* overly ornate furniture, as I waited for an audience with his wife. As I walked out onto the open balcony, the Circus Maximus spread out underneath, slowly filling up with people, ready for the chariot racing which was to start later in the afternoon. I slowly paced back and forth, holding my hands behind my back.

We had wintered in Vetera, as Marcus slowly recovered from his wounds, thanks in no small part to the care administered by Julia. They'd grown extremely close over the winter months as she nursed him back to full health. Marcus' one-time juvenile infatuation had turned into a genuine love for the girl. She then travelled back to Rome with Marcus, Numeria and I as soon as the passes had opened again in early spring. Julia was staying with Numeria and her father for the time being, but Numeria was hopeful that she'd be able to broker a reconciliation with Julia's family. There was no longer anyone left alive who knew of the life Julia had led on the frontier so any scandal attached to her had died in the Teutoburg along with Varus. How strange that something so terrible could transform the life of someone for the better in such a way, but the gods did have a strange sense of humour sometimes. After that, who knew, maybe the marriage Marcus and Julia craved would be possible after all? They were both from good families, and the match might prove favourable to both parties.

I was having less luck convincing Numeria to reinstate the betrothal that we had abandoned in our youth. Her feelings for me were not in doubt, but she felt it would appear unseemly to Otho's family if she were to remarry so soon after his death, and that I'd need to remain patient. I agreed, but only begrudgingly.

I'd hoped to slip back into life in Rome quietly without any fuss, but despite my best efforts to remain inconspicuous, the Roman gossip was soon alive to the fact that Cassius Aprilis was back, and what was more, he'd survived the great disaster that had befallen the German legions. The whole of Rome was still stunned by the news of the terrible defeat, shocked to the core that a Roman army of that size could be annihilated and that the entire province was now lost. The invulnerability of Rome, so long taken for granted by its populace, had for the first time in living memory been questioned, and that terrified them. So it wasn't long before people came calling on me to find out what I knew. Most enquirers I could simply dismiss or ignore, but when a summons from Augustus' wife came for me, I knew I had no choice but to attend, and so I now waited in trepidation to speak with her.

As I paced back and forth, I heard bellowing from the floors above and looked up nervously. I'd heard the rumours that Augustus had taken to shouting out in anger and despair at the shade of Varus, asking for his legions back. It seemed that Rome's *imperator* was taking the loss of his army no better than the rest of the city. 'Varus! Give me back my legions!' I heard shouted again, and I swallowed hard, hoping that his anger didn't stretch to the few remaining survivors, of whom I was pretty sure only myself and Marcus were presently in Rome. I'd met others – men who slowly drifted into Vetera over the winter months – no more than a bare two score in total, even some from my XVIII who had made it to the river after our last desperate attack; but in the main they were broken men, shadows of the strong soldiers who'd marched with Varus into the forest. Everything they'd known was now gone: their way of life, their friends, their legions … everything.

A Praetorian Guard came through to the room I'd been waiting in and informed me that, 'The Lady Livia will see you now, if you'd like to follow me.'

I was led to another area of the palace, which at least took me away from the mad ranting of Augustus, and I found his wife sat demurely on a stool in a small room overlooking a garden with a fountain and spring flowers.

'Cassius, so good of you to join me. Please take a seat,' Livia told me, not moving from her stool to greet me.

I thought better of reclining on the ornate divan in the room, and instead chose a small stool like the Lady Livia was sitting on herself, drawing myself up next to her. 'The pleasure is all mine, my lady, you know I'm always honoured to meet you.'

She gave me a cold smile which never quite met her eyes. 'Such a pleasant and polite young man you've become.'

I nodded my head at the compliment.

'Has it really been a year since I sent you on that assignment? How the time flies, it seems like only yesterday.' Her eyes hardened. 'We can't pretend that it was in any shape or form a success, can we? A disaster on this scale is unprecedented in our history – three lost eagles!'

I started to stammer my objections; surely she couldn't be blaming me for the disaster in the Teutoburg!

She held up a hand. 'Relax, Cassius, I know it wasn't your fault. I have your letter here.'

She showed me the letter I'd sent her, all those months ago criticising Varus, a small binding of wax tablets. 'At first I was surprised at the tone of your letter, thinking you might be exaggerating the dire consequences of Governor Varus' actions, but as events have unfolded, it appears you were correct. I only wish we'd had more time to act on your warnings, but alas … it is too late now.'

If she expected sympathy from me, she wasn't going to get it. I'd been in that damned forest, not her; I just sat there mutely and let her continue.

She ironed out a small wrinkle on her dress with one hand, then looked up at me again. 'My husband has taken the loss of the legions very badly, so I'm afraid it wouldn't do to offer you command of any of the Praetorian Guards cohorts. It just wouldn't look right – a constant reminder of that great failure.'

I nodded, masking a smile. I'd forgotten about my supposed reward for doing Livia's bidding. She was welcome to it; I didn't want it now anyway.

Livia sighed loudly. 'That young man Julius Arminius has a lot to answer for. He has won a rare victory over us, with three legions destroyed. Our strength is severely weakened. It is a perilous time for the Republic.'

I wiped away the sweat which was beading on my brow. 'And what about Maroboduus and his Marcomanni? Has he joined Arminius?'

She shook her head. 'Maroboduus has stayed loyal to Rome, no doubt much to the displeasure of Arminius. If Caedicius hadn't stopped Arminius before he reached the Rhenus, it might have been a different story, but as it is, Maroboduus is astute enough not to turn against Rome.'

I breathed a deep sigh of relief; an alliance of Rome's two greatest enemies had been averted. It was no wonder that the name of Caedicius was now the toast of Rome. In need of a hero, they'd celebrated Caedicius – the commander of Aliso who'd defied Arminius and saved Roman Gaul in the process. I didn't begrudge Caedicius his fame; I'd had years of it and wanted no more of it.

Livia looked towards the fountain, with its gentle bubbling water. 'Arminius will find that Rome doesn't forget defeats easily. Even now, every young able Roman wants to avenge our defeat – my own grandson wishes to lead an army against this traitor. Rome hasn't finished with Arminius yet.'

She looked me directly in the eye. 'You've proved to be quite adept at reading a situation. That cannot be ignored. It wasn't your fault we didn't have time to act on your warnings. I should have sent you sooner. Nevertheless, I think I may have more uses for you in the future.'

My blood ran cold.

She gave me one of her cold smiles again. 'But don't worry about that now, I'm sure you wish to enjoy some time in Rome?'

I nodded gratefully. 'I've missed the city very much,' I told her only half truthfully; I certainly hadn't missed being manipulated by her and her husband.

She looked up to the Praetorian Guard. 'You may escort Cassius Aprilis out. I'll know where to find him if I need him again.'

The End

Historical note

The historical significance from the loss of Rome's three legions in the Teutoburg forest cannot be overstated. Rome was just ascending to the peak of its power and would hold Europe, and most of the known Ancient World, in its grip for a further four hundred years. At the time Germany was on the brink of becoming another colonised state – or so Rome believed. The actions of Arminius not only shattered Rome's ambition but also separated Northern Europe's development from the other Roman dependent states of Western and Eastern Europe. To illustrate this, I could ask the hypothetical question of whether the history of modern Germany would be different if her language, customs, and ancient infrastructure had been derived from the Roman & Latin model, as France and Spain's were?

I won't try and answer that question, because I am certainly not qualified, however many historians have, with tragic results. The far-right ideologies of Nazism used Arminius' victory in the Teutoburg as a propaganda tool in the 1930's and this is possibly why the subject has been (understandably) avoided in more recent enlightened times. However, I don't think we should hide away from the events of the Teutoburg as it is clear that the effects were far reaching and profound, and I believe Hitler only managed to use the subject as a propaganda tool due to a general ignorance of the real events.

So how did it happen? How did Rome at the height of her power manage to lose its hold on Germany in such a spectacular way? Most ancient historians put the blame squarely on one person: Publius Quinctilius Varus. Is this fair? Certainly his policies of high taxation and trying to force the German tribes into a Roman way of life didn't help, but he was hardly the only Roman Governor to be guilty of that. Did he underestimate the strength of the German tribes? Was he naïve enough to believe that the Roman legions under his command were incapable of defeat? Almost certainly yes to both, but that still does not tell the entire story, as Arminius was only able to defeat the Roman army through betrayal and deceit and it was possibly only Varus' failure to see through the traitorous Arminius that he should be held to account for. After all, he was warned by the Chieftain Segestes shortly before the battle – although most accounts put this encounter in the Roman camp rather than the German village, depicted in my novel. For such a warning to have been ignored, it can only be because he trusted Arminius completely, and he cannot have been alone. The entire Roman high-command must have been taken in, to leave themselves so open to his treachery. That's why I wanted to personalise this betrayal in my novel, and created the boyhood friend of Arminius to tell the story. However, most of the other characters and events were taken from genuine historical accounts or sources on the period, and given a little artistic-licence moulded into my story.

Could the defeat have been even worse? As terrible as it was for Rome to lose three legions and the province of Germany to Arminius' betrayal, the loss of Gaul would have torn the Roman Empire apart. So did Caedicius' defiance at Aliso help save the Roman Empire? Marobodius of the Marcomanni was very definitely a real threat to Rome, and if Arminius had managed to form an alliance with him, anything could have been possible. But beyond this, there is no evidence to suggest that Arminius had designs over the River Rhine, and it is only speculation that he could have taken his rebellion further.

Rome, of course, was not finished with Arminius. There was the small matter of the three Eagles he took at the Teutoburg to be reclaimed, not to mention her lost pride and the need to reassert her authority in the world. But that is a story for another day....

Acknowledgements

Thanks to both my father, Alan Brooke, and sister, Heloise Brooke, who were both so helpful in both the writing and editing of this book. Also, a thank you to Fergus, the sadly departed family dog, who kept me company whilst I wrote this novel (and prevented many writer's tantrums).

About the Author

Thomas Brooke was born and raised in South West London, and works as a senior I.T. manager in the fashion industry.

Roman Mask is his second novel, although the first is not available for sale.

You can find out more about his writing at:
www.thomasmdbrooke.com